Middy And Ensign

By

George Manville Fenn

Middy And Ensign
by George Manville Fenn

Copyright © 2023

All Rights reserved.

ISBN: 978-93-59954-83-7
Published by

DOUBLE 9 BOOKS
2/13-B, Ansari Road
Daryaganj, New Delhi – 110002
info@double9books.com
www.double9books.com
Tel. 011-40042856

ABOUT THE AUTHOR

George Manville Fenn was a very productive author of novels, a writer, an editor, and an educator from England. He was born on January 3, 1831, in Pimlico, London. He mostly learned on his own; he taught himself Italian, French, and German. During the years 1851–1854, he went to Battersea Training College for Teachers and then became the head of a state school in Alford, Lincolnshire. In the early 1850s, Fenn started to write short stories and pieces for newspapers and magazines. The Old Forest Ranger, his first book, came out in 1856. Afterward, he wrote more than 100 books, many of them for teenagers and young adults. He was one of the most famous writers of his time, and his books were well-liked and read by many people. He also worked as a reporter and writer for Fenn. Among the newspapers and magazines, he worked for was The Boy's Own Paper, which he ran from 1866 to 1874. He worked hard to make children's books better and was a strong supporter of education and reading. The Englishman Fenn passed away on August 26, 1909, in Isleworth.

CONTENTS

Chapter One
On Board The "Startler"

The close of a hot day on board Her Majesty's ship "Startler," whose engines kept up a regular pulsation as the screw-propeller churned the water astern into golden and orange foam. The dappled sky and the rippled sea were a blaze of colour; crimson, scarlet, burnished copper, orange chrome, dead, and flashing gold,—all were there, on cloud edge and wave slope, mingled with purples, and greens, and blues, as the sun slowly descended to his rest.

There had been a general disposition all day long to lie under awnings, and pant "like tired dogs," so Bob Roberts the midshipman said; but now officers and men, in the lightest of garments, were eagerly looking for the cool evening breeze, and leaning over the bulwarks, gazing at the wondrous sunset sky and gorgeous sea.

The deck of the clean, smart-looking vessel had a very picturesque aspect, dotted as it was with groups of officers and men; for in addition to the crew, the "Startler" carried four companies of Her Majesty's somethingth foot, the escort of the British Resident and his suite, bound for Campong Allee, the chief town of Rajah Hamet, on the Parang River, west coast of the Malay peninsula.

The Resident was to be the help and adviser of the Mohammedan potentate, who had sought the protection of the British Government; and to fix him in his position, and save him from the assaults of the various inimical petty rajahs around, the corvette was to lie for some months in the river, and the residency was to be turned into a fort, garrisoned by the troops under Major Sandars.

Bob Roberts, a fair, good-looking, curly-headed lad of sixteen, was standing with his back leaned against the bulwarks, his cap thrust back, and his hands deep in his pockets, staring defiantly across the deck at a lad of about a year or so older, who, as he stood very stiff and upright by the cabin ladder, returned the stare with interest.

The latter had just buckled on his sword, and, in spite of the heat, buttoned up his undress coatee to the chin, ready for the short spell of drill which he knew would take place before the officers dined; and after giving the finishing-touch to his gloves, he rather ostentatiously raised his sword, then hanging to the full length of its slings, and hooked it on to his belt.

"What a jolly shame it is that we should only carry a beggarly little dirk," said Bob Roberts to himself, as he tried to look sneeringly at the young ensign before him; for the latter came across the deck with rather a swaggering stride, and stood before the midshipman.

"Well, young Jack tar," he said, with a touch of contempt in his tone.

"Well, young Pipeclay," retorted the middy. "I say, how tightly you've laced your stays to-day. Mind where you go, or you'll get some pitch on your lovely uniform. My word, how handsome you look!"

"I tell you what it is, Master Bob, or Robert Roberts," said the young ensign, flushing, "if I did not feel that I was stooping by so doing, I should tell you that you were an impudent puppy of a boy, and give you a good caning."

"No, no! please pray don't do that, Mr Ensign Long, or Tom Long, or Long Tom, or whatever you call yourself," retorted the middy, assuming an aspect of mock terror. "You frighten me into fits almost; and if you did try to cane me you'd split that coatee of yours all up the back, or break your staylace, or do yourself some mischief, and—"

Just then there was the sound of a bugle, followed by the tramp of feet; and the young officer, scowling fiercely, turned half-right, and as he did so let his sword down, so that the end of the scabbard might clatter against the white deck as he marched off to where the men were assembling, while the middy burst into a hearty laugh.

"You two gents is allus a quarrelling," growled a wonderfully copper-faced old sailor, giving his lower jaw a twist. "You puts me in mind of the gamecocks as the Malay niggers we're going amongst keeps, to strut up and shake out their hackles afore they has a set-to."

"Well, he is so cocky, Dick," said the middy, "and struts about, and—"

"That's what I say, sir," said the old sailor, leaning his arms on the bulwark, "just like a gamecock."

"And assumes such an air of superiority," continued the middy.

"Just like you do, sir, to'rds us common sailors," said the man, chuckling.

"Don't you tell lies, Dick," said the lad sharply. "I always treat the sailors as an officer and a gentleman should."

"So you do, sir, so you do! and it was only my gammon. But you do wish you was a swaddy now, and wore a red coat instead of a blue."

"No I don't, Dick," said the lad colouring; "but I do think we naval officers ought to wear swords, the same as those boy-soldiers."

"So you ought, sir;" said the sailor, winking to himself; "but never you mind about that, sir. If so be as it comes to a brush with the niggers, I'll grind you up a cutlash, with a hedge so sharp as you might shave yourself with it. Perhaps you'd like me to do it now, sir, if your razor is feeling a bit dull?"

"Now, look here, old Dick Dunnage," said the middy; "that's cheek; and I won't have cheek from you, so I tell you."

"Cheek, sir," said the old sailor, with assumed innocence. "I didn't mean to shave only your cheek, sir, but your chin as well."

"Now that'll do, Dick. I'm not ashamed of having no beard, and I'm not ashamed of being a boy, so now then."

"Course you ain't, sir. There, I didn't mean nothing disrespectful. It was only my fun. This here 'bacca as you give me, sir, baint the best I ever had. Lor! how hot them poor fellows do look, buttoned and belted up as they is," he continued, as the soldiers fell into line. "It's a deal better to be a sailor, Master Bob."

"Ever so much, Dick," said the middy. "How long is it since you were out here, Dick?"

"How long, sir?" and the sailor thoughtfully, as he sprinkled the sea with a little tobacco juice; "six year."

"And have you been more than once, Dick?"

"Four times altogether, sir. Let's see: I was at Singapore, and at Penang, and Malacky, and up the country at a place they called Bang, or Clang, or something or another."

"And what sort of a country is it, Dick?" said the boy eagerly.

"Wonderful country; all palm-trees and jungles, and full of rivers and creeks, where the long row-boats, as they call prahus, runs up."

"Those are the pirates' boats, Dick?"

"That's right, sir; and precious awkward things they are to catch, Lord love you! I've been after 'em in cutter and pinnace, firing our bow gun among them, and the men pulling like mad to get up alongside; but they generally dodged in and out of some of these mangrove creeks till they give us the slip, and we had to pull back."

"Shouldn't I like to be in chase of one of the scoundrelly prahus!" cried the lad, with his eyes flashing.

"That you would, sir, I'll lay," said the old sailor; "and wouldn't you lay into 'em with that very sharp-edged cutlash I touches up for you!"

"Now look here, Dick, you're chaffing," said the lad; "now just drop it."

"All right, sir," said the man, with a laugh twinkling at the corner of his lips.

"It is a very fine country though, isn't it, Dick?"

"Wonderful, sir. There's gold, and tin, and copper, and precious stones."

"Did you ever find any, Dick?"

"Well no, sir; but I've known them as has found gold in the rivers. The Chinees gets most on it."

"There now you're chaffing again, Dick," cried the lad. "Chinese indeed! Why we're not going to China."

"'Course we aint, sir, but the Chinees swarm in the place we're going to. I ant chaffing now; this here's all true—as true as that the chaps all wears a dagger sort of a thing with a crooked handle, and calls it a crease."

"Yes, I know they all wear the kris," said the lad.

"Yes, sir, and a plaid kilt, just like a Scotchman."

"What?"

"A plaid kilt, like a Scotchman, sir, and they calls it a say rong; and the big swell princes has it made of silk, and the common folks of cotton."

"Is this gammon, Dick?"

"Not a bit on it, sir. They wears that crease stuck in it; and they carries spears—limbings they calls 'em—and they can throw 'em a wonderful way."

"They poison the kris, don't they, Dick?"

"No, sir, I don't think they do," said the sailor. "I asked one man out there if they didn't; and he pulls his'n out of its sheath, and it was all dingy like, and as sharp as a razor, and he says in his barbarous lingo, as a man put into English for me, as his knife would kill a man without poison."

"What sort of wild beasts are there, Dick?"

"Tigers, sir."

"Honour bright, Dick?"

"Honour bright, sir; lots on 'em. They feeds 'em on Chinees."

"Feed them on Chinese, Dick?"

"Well sir, the tigers help theirselves to the coolies when they're at work."

"Anything else, Dick?"

"Lor, bless you! yes, sir; there's elephants."

"Are you sure?"

"Sure, sir. I've seen 'em, heaps o' times; and rhinosseress, and hippypotimies, and foreign birds, and snakes."

"Are there snakes, Dick?"

"Are there snakes! He says, are there snakes?" said Dick, apostrophising the sea. "Why the last time as ever I was there, they caught a boa-constrictor as was—"

"Don't make him too long, Dick," said the boy laughing.

"I won't make him too long," said the sailor solemnly. "Let's see, sir; this here ship's 'bout hundred and fifty foot long."

"Yes, Dick, but the boa-constrictor was longer than that," said the lad, laughing.

"I won't go to deceive you, Mister Roberts," said Dick, "no more than I did when I was learning you how to knot and splice. That there boa-constrictor was quite a hundred foot long."

"Get out!"

"Well, say fifty, sir."

"No, nor yet fifty, Dick."

"Well, sir, not to zaggerate about such things, if that there sarpent as I see with my own eyes—"

"Why you couldn't see it with anybody else's, Dick."

"No, sir, but I might have seen it wi' a spy glass. This there sarpent as I see it lying down stretched out straight was a good twenty-five foot."

"Perhaps that may have been, Dick," said Bob Roberts, thoughtfully.

"Yes, sir, it were all that; and when it was alive it must have been fifty foot at least."

"Why, Dick?"

"Cause they stretches out so, sir, just like worms in the garden at home do."

"Gammon, Dick. Serpents don't stretch."

"Don't stretch, sir! Just you wait till you get a thirty-footer twissen and twining round you, and see if they don't stretch."

"All right, Dick; and when he does, you come and pinch his tail, and make him open his mouth; and when he does that you pop in a bit of your nasty tobacco, and he'll leave off, and go like a shot."

The old sailor chuckled, and said something about Mister Bob Roberts being a nice boy, while the party in question walked aft to see the company of soldiers on deck put through half-an-hour's drill, making a point of staring hard and derisively at the young ensign, who saw the lad's looks, grew angry, from growing angry became confused, and incurred the captain's anger by giving the wrong order to the men, some of whom went right, knowing what he ought to have said, while others went wrong, and got the company hopelessly confused.

The result was that Ensign Long, of her Majesty's somethingth foot, was severely snubbed, just as Mr Linton the resident, and his daughter Rachel Linton, were looking on.

"I wouldn't have cared if they had not been there," said Ensign Long to himself; "but if I don't serve that little wretch of a middy out for this, my name is not Long."

Chapter Two
Introduces more Friends; with a few Words on the River Parang

The men were dismissed, and gladly got rid of coatee, rifle, and belt, to have a lounge in the cool of the evening; the dinner was ready in the captain's cabin, where lights already appeared; and, soon after, the tropic night came on, as if with a bound. The sky was of a purple black, studded with its myriads of stars, which were reflected with dazzling lustre from the smooth surface of the sea. But not only were the bright star shapes there to give splendour to the wave, for as far down as eye could reach through the clear water it was peopled with tiny phosphorescent atoms, moving slowly here and there, and lighting up the depths of the sea with a wonderful effulgence that was glorious to behold.

Under the vessel's prow the divided waters flowed to right and left like liquid gold, while, where the propeller revolved beneath the stern, the sea was one lambent blaze of fire ever flashing right away, covered with starry spots that glistened, and rose, and fell, on the heaving wave.

As the evening crept on, the various lights of the ship shone out clear and bright, notably that from the binnacle, which was like a halo round the face of the sailor at the wheel. There was a faint glow from the skylights too, and a lantern was hung here and there about the quarter-deck, where soon after the officers assembled to chat and smoke, while their men in turn enjoyed their ease.

The ship rushed swiftly on its way, having passed Penang the previous day; and it was expected that on the next they would be at the mouth of the river, a native city upon which was to be the home of all for many months, perhaps for years.

The officers were discussing the character of the rajah, some being of opinion that he was a bloodthirsty tyrant and upholder of slavery, whom the British Government were making a great mistake in protecting, while others declared that according to their experience the Malays were not the cruel treacherous race they had been considered, but that they were noble, proud, and thorough gentlemen by nature, and that if they were properly treated the life of an Englishman amongst them was perfectly safe.

"Well, gentlemen," said a little fat man, who seemed to do nothing but perspire and mop his forehead, "they say the proof of the pudding is in the eating. I know one thing, however, Parang is a glorious country for botanical specimens."

"Just the thing for you, doctor," said Mr Linton, the resident.

"But it won't be just the thing for you, gentlemen," said the little man, "for as sure as my name's Bolter, if you don't strictly follow out my orders some of you will be losing the number of your mess."

"Come, that sounds well," said a quiet-looking man in white jacket and trousers; "we are going to Parang to help to put down slavery, and we are to be put into a state of slavery by the doctor here."

"He'll deal gently with you sometimes," said the grey-haired major in command of the troops. "Never turn a deaf ear to his discourses on plants, then you will be indulged."

"What a nice revenge I could have on you, major!" said the doctor, laughing, and rubbing his hands. "Ha, ha, ha! and I could double your dose."

"Yes," laughed the major; "and after all it is the doctor who really commands these expeditions."

"Ah, well," said the little gentleman, "I'll do the best I can for all of you. But don't be rash, my dear boys. You must avoid night dews, and too much fruit, and over-exertion."

"There, there, doctor," said the major, laughing; "you needn't trouble yourself about the last. I'll undertake to say that none of my fellows will over-exert themselves."

"Unless, sir, they are called upon to fight," said a rather important voice.

"Oh, I beg your pardon, I'm sure, Mr Long," said the major seriously. "Of course we shall not study trouble then."

The officers smiled, and looked from one to the other, greatly to Mr Tom Long's annoyance. In fact he felt so much aggrieved at the way in which his remark had been received, that he proceeded to light a very large cigar before rising to seek another part of the deck.

"If you smoke that big strong cigar you'll be ill, Mr Long," said the doctor quietly.

"I'd cut it in half, Long," said Captain Smithers, "and give the other half to young Roberts."

"I know what I can smoke, sir," replied the youth haughtily. "Perhaps you will take one."

"I! No, thanks. They are too strong for me." And with what was meant for a very haughty, injured look, Ensign Long strode slowly away.

"Thank you, doctor," said Major Sandars. "It's just as well to snub that young gentleman sometimes. He's a fine young fellow, and will make a splendid officer; but really there are times when I get wondering whether we have changed places, and he is in command."

"Oh, all boys go through that stage," said the resident quietly. "He has just arrived at the hair-brushing, make-yourself-look-nice age, and feels at least eight-and-twenty."

"When he is only eighteen," said Captain Smithers.

"He is only seventeen, I believe," said the major, "and the youngest ensign in the service. By the way, Linton, I believe Long has formed a desperate attachment for your daughter."

"Yes, I had noticed it," said the resident drily; "and as Ensign Long is seventeen, and my daughter twenty-three, it will be a most suitable match. But he has a rival, I see."

Captain Smithers started slightly as the major exclaimed,—

"Who may that be?"

"Our dashing young friend, Mr Bob Roberts."

There was a bit of a scuffle here as the whole party burst into a roar of laughter.

"Oh, I beg your pardon, Roberts," said the resident. "I did not know you were there."

Bob Roberts felt red hot with shame and annoyance, as he made a rush and retreated from the group by whom his presence had been unperceived.

"I hope, Linton," said Captain Horton, in command of the "Startler," "that my youngster there has not been behaving impertinently to Miss Linton."

"Not at all," said the resident quietly; "both Mr Long and Mr Roberts have been full of respectful admiration for the young lady, who has sufficient common sense to behave to the silly young gentlemen as they deserve. It is all connected with the hair-brushing stage, and will, I have no doubt, help to make them both grow into fine manly young fellows by-and-by."

"Why, I can see through the mill-stone now," said the doctor, laughing.

"What mill-stone, doctor?"

"Why, I have been puzzling myself as to why it was those two boys were always squabbling together. I see now; they're as jealous as can be. I say, Mr Linton, you ought not to bring such a bone of contention on board as that daughter of yours, and her cousin."

"Seriously, my dear doctor," said the resident, "I do sometimes feel that I am to blame for bringing those two motherless girls out into the jungle; but Rachel declared that she would not be separated from me; and Miss Sinclair, my sister's child, seems more like one of my own, and shared her cousin's feelings."

"They are two ladies, Linton," said the major, "for whom we feel the deepest respect; and, speaking selfishly, I am only too glad that my wife has a couple of such charming companions."

"Yes," said Captain Horton; "and if I had known what I know now, I should have let Mrs Horton have her wish, and accompany me."

"Well, gentlemen," said the resident, rather sadly, "I don't know, but I have a sort of presentiment that it would have been better if we had been without ladies, or soldiers' wives, if you come to that; for I cannot conceal from myself that we are bound upon a very risky expedition, one out of which I hope we shall all come safely."

"Oh, we shall be safe enough," said the major.

"Do you think there is really any danger, Mr Linton?" said Captain Smithers, rather hoarsely.

"Why, you are not afraid, are you, Smithers? Come, you must not show the white feather!"

"I am not afraid for myself, Major Sandars," said the young captain, quietly; "and I hope I shall never show the white feather; but when there are women and children in an expedition—"

"Oh, come, come," said the resident, gaily; "I am afraid I have been croaking. There may be danger; but when we are surrounded by such brave men as the officers and crew of the 'Startler,' and her Majesty's somethingth foot, I see, after all, nothing whatever to fear."

"Fear? no!" said Captain Horton. "Why, we could blow the whole place to Cape Horn with my guns; and the Malays would never face Sandars' boys, with their bayonets."

"Did you notice that sentry, Smithers?" asked the little doctor, in a low voice, of his companion, as the conversation now became less general.

"Sentry? which one?"

"This one," said the doctor. "Don't speak aloud, or he'll hear you."

"Private Gray? No, I did not notice anything. What do you mean?"

"The light of that lantern shines full on his face, and he made a movement that drew my attention when we were talking of there being danger."

"Indeed?" said the captain.

"Yes; he was evidently listening to the conversation, and I saw him start so that he nearly dropped his piece; his face was quite convulsed, and he turned of a sickly pallor. The light was so strong upon him that I could see his lips whiten."

"Or was it fancy, doctor?"

"Fancy? No, my lad, that was no fancy; and I hope we have not many more like him in the regiment."

"Well, for my part," said Captain Smithers, quietly, "I have often wished that my company was composed of Adam Grays."

"Adam, eh? To be sure; I remember the fellow now. Well, he's a poor descendant of the first Adam, for if that fellow is not an arrant coward my name isn't Bolter."

"Really, doctor, I think you do the man an injustice. He is a very superior, well educated fellow; and it has often puzzled me how he became a private soldier."

"Scamp!" said the doctor, shortly. "Some runaway or another. The ranks of the army are made a receptacle for blackguards!"

"Hang it, doctor!" cried the young captain, warmly, "I cannot sit here and listen to such heresy. I confess that we do get some scoundrels into the army; but as a rule our privates are a thoroughly trustworthy set of fellows, ready to go through fire and water for their officers; and I only wish the country would make better provision for them when their best days are past."

"Ah, that's right enough," said the doctor; "they are all what you say, and they do deserve better treatment of their country. I mean, ha, ha, ha! to make teetotallers of them this trip. I'm not going to have the men poisoned with that red hot country arrack, I can tell them."

"It is terrible stuff, I believe."

"Terrible? It's liquid poison, sir! and I don't know that I sha'n't try and set up a private brewery of my own, so as to supply the poor fellows with a decent glass of beer."

"Poor fellows! eh, doctor? Why, you said just now they were a set of scoundrels."

"Well, well, well; I didn't mean all. But look at that fellow Sim—there's a pretty rascal for you! He's always on the sick-list, and it's nearly always sham."

"I'm afraid he is a bit of a black sheep," said Captain Smithers.

"Inky black, Smithers, inky black. I shall poison that fellow some day. But I say, my dear boy, the brewery."

"What about it?"

"What about it? Why, it would be splendid. I mean to say it is a grand idea. I'll get the major to let me do it."

"My dear doctor," said Captain Smithers, laughing, "I'm afraid if you did brew some beer, and supply it to the men, fancy would go such a long way that they would find medicinal qualities in it, and refuse to drink a drop."

"Then they would be a set of confoundedly ungrateful scoundrels," said the doctor, angrily, "for I should only use malt and hops."

"And never serve it as you did the coffee that day, doctor?"

"Well, well, I suppose I must take the credit of that. I did doctor it a little; but it was only with an astringent corrective, to keep the poor boys from suffering from too much fruit."

"Poor boys! eh, doctor? Come, come, you don't think my brave lads are a set of scoundrels then?"

"I said before, not all—not all," replied the doctor.

"Ah, doctor," said Captain Smithers, "like a good many more of us, you say more than you mean sometimes, and I know you have the welfare of the men at heart."

"Not I, my lad, not I. It's all pure selfishness; I don't care a pin about the rascals. All I want is to keep them quite well, so that they may not have to come bothering me, when I want my time to go botanising; that's all."

"And so we have fewer men on the sick-list than any regiment out here?"

"Tut! tut! Nonsense!"

Just then the ladies came up from the principal cabin, and began to walk slowly up and down the quarter-deck, evidently enjoying the delicious coolness of the night air, and the beauty of the sea and sky.

Captain Smithers sat watching them intently for a time, and then, as he happened to turn his head, he caught sight of the sentry, Adam Gray, and it struck him that he, too, was attentively watching the group of ladies. So convinced did the young officer become of this, that he could not refrain from watching him.

Once or twice he thought it was only fancy, but at last he felt sure; and a strange angry sensation sprang up in his breast as he saw the sentry's countenance change when the ladies passed him.

"An insolent scoundrel!" he muttered. "How dare he?"

Then, as the ladies took their seats at some distance, he began thinking over what the doctor had said, and wondering whether this man, in whom he had heretofore taken a great deal of interest, was such a coward; and in spite of his angry feelings, he could only come to the conclusion that the doctor was wrong.

But at the same time what he had heard and seen that evening had not been without its effect, and he found himself irritable and vexed against this man, while his previous good feelings seemed to be completely swept away.

At last he rose impatiently, and strolled towards where the ladies were sitting, and joined in the conversation that was going on round a bucket of water that the doctor had just had dipped from over the side, and which he had displayed, full of brilliantly shining points of light, some of which emitted flashes as he stirred the water with his hands, or dipped glasses full of it, to hold up for the fair passengers to see.

"All peculiar forms of jelly-fish," he said aloud, as if he were delivering a lecture, "and all possessing the power of emitting that beautiful phosphorescent light. There you see, ladies, if I had a spoon I could skim it off the top of this bucket of water, just like so much golden cream, and pour it into a glass. Very wonderful, is it not?"

"Look, look, doctor!" said one of the ladies, pointing to the sea, where a series of vivid flashes rapidly followed one another.

"Yes, my dear, I see," he replied; "that was some fish darting through the water, and disturbing the medusae. If you watch you can see the same thing going on all round."

So glorious was the aspect of the sea that the conversation gradually ceased, and all on the quarter-deck watched the ever-widening lines of golden water that parted at the stem of the corvette and gradually died away, or were mingled with the glistening foam churned up by the propeller.

For the sea seemed to be one blaze of soft lambent light, that flashed angrily wherever it was disturbed by the steamer, or the startled fish, that dashed away on every side as they swiftly ran on towards the land of swamp and jungle, of nipah and betel palm, where the rivers were bordered by mangroves, the home of the crocodile; a land where the night's conversation had roused up thoughts of its being perhaps the burial-place of many a one of the brave hearts throbbing within the timbers of that stout ship—hearts that were to play active parts in the adventurous scenes to come.

Chapter Three
Doctor Bolter cures one Patient, and is left with another

"Is that Parang, that dim light out yonder, captain?" said the major, pointing to what looked like a cloud touching the water.

"Oh, no," was the reply. "That is part of Sumatra. Our destination lies off the other bow, due east from where we are lying now."

It was a glorious morning, and the sun at that early hour had not yet attained to its greater power. The ladies were on deck, enjoying the morning air; the soldiers were having morning parade, and looked clean and smart in their white clothes and puggarees. The sailors were giving the last touches to brass rails and cabin windows, and were coiling ropes into neat rings; and altogether the deck of the "Startler," with its burnished guns, presented a bright and animated spectacle, every one seeming to have some business on hand.

There was a little bit bustle about the steerage ladder, where four sailors were hauling a sick man up on deck; and as soon as they had him lying in the sunshine upon a mattress, the doctor bustled up—Bob Roberts, seeing Ensign Long at hand, going up and looking on, after the two youths had exchanged a short distant nod.

"Well, Sim," said the doctor, briskly, "how are you this morning?"

"Very—very bad, sir," replied the invalid, a big bony-faced man, who looked very yellow.

"Put out your tongue," said the doctor.

Private Sim put out such an enormously long tongue that Bob Roberts gave his trousers a hitch, and made believe to haul it forth by the yard, very much to the ensign's disgust.

"That'll do," said the doctor, feeling the patient's pulse, and then dropping the hand, "Now what am I to prescribe for you, Sim, eh? You feel a terrible sense of sinking, don't you?"

"Yes, sir; terrible."

"As if you needed strengthening food?"

"Yes, sir."

"And some kind of stimulating drink—say wine?"

"Yes, sir," said the patient, rolling his eyes. "I feel as if a little wine would do me good."

"Has the buzzing sensation left your head?"

"Very nearly, sir."

"And you don't feel so much pressure on your chest?"

"Well, sir, not just now."

"Less pain too, under your left shoulder?"

The major walked up just now.

"Yes, sir; it's not quite so painful."

"But you slept well?"

"Pretty well, sir, for me; I should think I had quite an hour's sleep last night."

"A whole hour, eh?"

"Yes, sir."

"Well, doctor," said the major, "what do you think of your patient? I hope you are better, Sim?"

"Thanky kindly, sir," said Private Sim, screwing up a terrible face.

"I was thinking which I ought to prescribe," said the doctor, very seriously. "Sim's is a peculiar case. There's pressure on the brain, and also congestion of the vascular system of the spinal column."

"Indeed!" said the major.

"Yes, sir," replied the doctor, pursing up his lips, "and I'm hesitating between two courses."

"Try 'em both, doctor," said Bob Roberts, laughing with his eyes.

"Right, youngster," said the doctor, clapping him on the shoulder, "I will. We'll have the moist application first, and the warm dry application after."

Private Sim screwed up his face a little tighter.

"If I might make so bold, sir," he said in a whining voice, "I think what you've given me's done me ever so much good, and all I want now is rest."

"Rest, my man!" said the doctor. "Nonsense man! You want the most brisk and active treatment. Yours is a sluggish system, but we'll soon put you right. Here, my lads," he continued to the sailors, "bring a stout rope, and lash it round his chest. We'll give him four dips overboard for the head pressure, and then four dozen on the back to increase the circulation."

"Oh, doctor!" groaned the man, looking round for sympathy; but only to see everyone within hearing on the grin.

"Don't you be afraid, Sim; I'll soon put you right," said the doctor kindly. "I'll make a man of you."

"I don't think I could bear it, doctor. I mean I do really feel better, sir."

"Let's see if you can stand, Sim," said the doctor.

The man rose groaning, and held on by one of the sailors, who, at a word from the doctor, slipped away, and left the invalid standing.

"You are better, decidedly, Sim. You couldn't have done that two days ago."

"No, sir."

"There, now walk across the deck."

"If I'm able to walk, sir, shall I have to be dipped?"

"Walk away, and go below to your mess, you idle, shamming scoundrel," cried the doctor.

Private Sim opened his lips to speak, but the look he received was too much for him, and he slowly walked off, trying hard to appear ill-used, till he reached the companion ladder, down which he shuffled to the intense delight of the men.

There was no land in sight, but the sea was glorious in the brilliant sunshine—so clear and blue that the darting fish could be seen far below; and before long, Bob Roberts had borrowed a fishing-line from Dick, the old sailor, baited the hooks, and was trailing it behind the vessel, in the hope of catching enough fish for a dinner for his mess.

At first his sport was not very good; but after a time he captured a large glistening fish, evidently, from its silvery skin, belonging to the mackerel family; and this so excited Ensign Long, who had been looking on rather contemptuously, that he borrowed a line of the boatswain, and was also soon at work fishing.

The lads had such good sport that the officers looked on quite amused, and the ladies under the awning asked from time to time to be shown the glistening captives that had been taken.

Soon after the doctor joined the party, to discourse learnedly about the various fishes, which he classified as he pointed out their peculiarities, assuring his fair hearers that far more beautiful specimens might yet be taken.

Rachel Linton, a fair, very intelligent looking girl, was much interested in the doctor's descriptions, as was also her cousin, Mary Sinclair, a dark, handsome, but delicate, brunette, of nineteen, full of questions, which the doctor took great delight in answering.

Bob Roberts and the young ensign vied one with the other in hurrying up with their fish, as they were successful, Ensign Long looking hopelessly disgusted as he saw the middy catch and carry three fish in succession beneath the awning, while he could not get a bite.

Soon, however, his turn came, and with a look of triumph he bore a long silvery fish with bars of azure blue across its scaly armour, to where the ladies were seated, Bob Roberts biting his lips as he heard the exclamations of pleasure uttered by each of the cousins in turn.

"Never mind," he muttered, "I shall have a startler directly, see if I don't," and he fished away, changing his bait, or replacing it as it was lost in consequence of the rapid motion of the steamer through the water; but all in vain; not a single fish came to his side, while on the other side Ensign Long was having tremendous luck.

Wearied out with trying, the lad sat at last holding his line in one hand, but paying no heed to it, for his eyes were directed beneath the awning, where all looked dim as compared with the sun-glare outside; and here from time to time he saw Long enter with some new prize, which the doctor took, and held up to the ladies, the more brilliantly coloured being consigned to one or the other of a couple of buckets of water, which one of the soldiers in undress uniform, whom the middy recognised as the sentry of the previous night, kept replenishing with fresh water dipped from the sea.

"He isn't a bad-looking chap," said the young midshipman, as he sat on the bulwarks in a very insecure position. "I wish I was filling the buckets and holding up the fish for the ladies to see."

He glanced once at his trailing line, and saw the bait flash in the water, then he glanced back at the party beneath the awning.

"How black Captain Smithers looks," he said. "That soldier must have splashed him, or something, for he looks as if he was going to have him tried by court-martial. Here I think I shall drop it. Hang it all! if that fellow Long hasn't caught another. What did she say?" he cried, drawing in his breath with a hiss. "'You are ever so much more fortunate than Mr Roberts.' Oh, I'd give something to have her say that to me, and—murder! I've got him this time—"

He made a convulsive grasp at a rope, and just saved himself from falling overboard, for a vigorous snatch made by a large fish at his bait had been quite sufficient to disturb his equilibrium, his activity alone saving him from a terrible ducking, if not from being drowned.

He recovered himself though, and thought no more of his escape in the excitement of finding that he had hooked a heavyish fish, and which took a good deal of playing; for just as it seemed exhausted, there was a fierce, furious snatch at the line, and the captive appeared to have grown heavier.

"He's almost too heavy to lift out, Dick," he cried to the old sailor who came up.

"Ease him then, sir, and take it easy," said Dick; "tire him quite out, and then haul in quickly."

Bob Roberts obeyed, and to his intense delight, gradually hauled his fish to the surface, where he could not make out what it was by its shape, only that it was a blaze of blue, and gold, and silver, flashing in the sun.

"Hi, doctor! I've got such a beauty!" he shouted, dragging at the stout line, till with a rush he hoisted his fish on to the deck.

"Well, that's a rum 'un, sir," cried the sailor. "Why it's a young sea sarpent."

"What have you got?" said the doctor eagerly, as the lad hurried excitedly beneath the awning with his prize.

"I don't know, doctor," said the lad. "But look, Miss Linton—Miss Sinclair, isn't it curious?"

The lad's cheeks flushed, and his eyes sparkled with delight, as he held up by the line what seemed to be a good-sized fish, of five or six pounds' weight, with a very long brilliantly-coloured eel twined tightly round and round it, in a perfect spiral, several feet in length.

"Why, you've caught a fish, boy," said the doctor, examining the prize through his glasses, "and it has been seized and constricted by a sea snake. Dear me! bliss my soul! that's very curious. Look here, Captain Smithers, and ladies. Gray, a fresh bucket of water. Most singular thing!"

"I thought he got precious heavy all at once, doctor," said the lad, looking from one to the other. "That chap darted at him then."

"Ye–es, I suppose so," said the doctor. "Lovely colouring, to be sure! See how tightly it has constricted the fish, ladies. Just like a piece of woodbine round a stick, only the coils are more close."

"It is very beautiful," said Miss Linton, approaching more closely, so that she could feast her eyes on the vivid colouring of the water-snake, which was about five feet in length, but whose coils seemed to grow more close as the fish ceased to flap as it was held up by the middy.

"I'm glad you like it, Miss Linton," he said, darting a triumphant glance at where Ensign Long was now fishing in vain. "He didn't catch two at once," the boy muttered to himself.

"I wouldn't go too close, Miss Linton," said the doctor, "for some of these sea snakes are reputed to be poisonous. Lovely thing, isn't it, Smithers?"

"Very," said the young captain drily; "but pray take care, Miss Linton."

"I am not afraid," said the lady, looking up at him with a quiet air of confidence, just as Private Gray bore in a fresh bucket of limpid sea water, and set it down at her feet.

"Now then," said the doctor; "hold still, Roberts."

"All right, sir; but it's jolly heavy," said the boy.

"Then give the line a shake, and the snake will fall into the bucket. Or stop; I will."

But he was too late, for the lad had already given the line a quick shake, with the result that the snake uncoiled like lightning, and darted at the nearest object, that object being Miss Linton's arm, round which it coiled with the rapidity of the thong of a whip round a stick.

The resident's daughter was brave and strong minded, but as she felt the contact of the creature's cold scales upon her bare arm she could not forbear from shrieking aloud; but even as she uttered the cry, the young soldier, Gray, had caught the snake round the neck, causing it to loosen its hold, but only to coil round his own bare arm, round which it twisted, and twice seized the wrist with its little mouth.

"The snake has bitten me," said the young man, hoarsely, as he dashed its head rapidly against one of the chairs, and then cast it, broken but writhing, upon the white deck.

All this took but a few moments, and then Private Gray stood, gazing with a strange wild longing look at Miss Linton, as the doctor exclaimed, —

"Quick, Roberts, to my cabin; the ammonia. Ladies, go away, please, quickly."

He caught the young soldier, and forced him back in one of the chairs as he spoke, for already a ghastly pallor was overspreading his countenance.

"Is it—is it poisonous, doctor?" whispered Miss Linton, as she darted a horrified look at Gray.

"Deadly! my dear young lady," he replied hastily. "The poor fellow has saved your life. And only last night," he thought, "I said he was a coward."

Chapter Four
Doctor Bolter rubs his Hands, and
Captain Smithers looks Green

As soon as Bob Roberts returned with the ammonia, and realised what was wrong, he pulled out his pocket-knife, placed his foot on the reptile's neck, as it still writhed feebly, and cut off its head.

He had hardly completed his task though, before he was summoned by the doctor to assist him. Here, however, he was forestalled by Miss Linton, who, ignoring the request to go, had in the most business-like way helped to lower the fainting man upon the deck, and supported his head while the stimulant was administered.

"Pray go away, Miss Linton," exclaimed Doctor Bolter then; "this is only a task for a trained nurse."

"I am a trained nurse," said Rachel Linton, quietly; and drawing a cushion from a chair, she placed it on the deck, lowered the injured man's head upon it, and then, seeing the doctor's intention, held the patient's arm while he freely used a lancet about the tiny marks made by the serpent's teeth, and rubbed in the ammonia.

Captain Smithers meanwhile had not spoken, but stood watching Miss Linton, with a strange look upon his countenance, shuddering, though, once or twice, as he saw the ghastly face of the injured man, and his fixed half-closed eyes.

"What can I do next, doctor?" said Miss Linton, in a quiet, eager voice.

"Nothing at present, my dear young lady," he said, looking at her admiringly. "Why, what a brave-hearted girl you are!"

"Brave?" she said. "What, to do this for one who saved me perhaps from death? But tell me, doctor, will he live?"

"I don't know; I hope so; it is impossible to say. It is such a rare thing for a man to be bitten by one of these creatures. I never had such a case before, and I ought to have known better; but I did not know it was a dangerous species of snake."

He held the soldier's pulse as he spoke, and then frowned, and mixing more ammonia and water, raised the poor fellow's head, and poured the liquid between his half-clenched teeth.

"Try and swallow it, Gray, my good fellow."

The young man opened his eyes as if awakened from sleep, stared about till they rested on Miss Linton, when they closed again, and he drank the stimulant with difficulty.

"Stand back, please. Captain Smithers, keep every one away, and let us have all the air we can."

Thus appealed to, the young officer motioned back those who pressed forward, the news of the accident having spread through the ship, and all who dared ascending to the quarter-deck.

"How provoking!" exclaimed Major Sandars. "One of my best men too, doctor. Really, Bolter, I must put a stop to your natural history researches."

"Confound it all, major!" cried the little doctor, angrily; "it was an accident. That young dog caught the snake, and—no—no! it's all right, Roberts. It was my fault; I ought to have foreseen what would happen."

Ensign Long had begun to congratulate himself on the fact that Bob Roberts was about to have a good wigging, but found out that he was wrong, and felt annoyed to see how important a part the lad played in the proceedings to fight back the effects of the deadly poison.

"Take my coat off, Roberts," said the doctor. "Gently, boy, gently. That's right. Now the ammonia; good. Raise his head a little. Poor fellow, we mustn't let him slip through our fingers. That's it, Miss Linton. Miss Sinclair, will you get a big fan, and give him all the air you can?"

He was obeyed to the letter; while Captain Horton and the resident stood near, ready to help in any way they could, for the news had caused the deepest concern through out the ship.

"Yah!" cried Private Sim, with an ugly snarl; "there's yer nasty favouritism. See how they're all a-cuddling and messing that there Gray up, orficers and women and all. Might ha' died afore they'd ha' done anything for me."

"Why, you caulking, miching lubber," growled old Dick, "you had ten times as much trouble 'stowed on you as you deserved. Tell you what, my lads," he continued, addressing a crowd of soldiers and sailors who had been discussing the event forward, "it's this here sorter thing as makes me saddersfied to be a common sailor. Yer orficers may row and bully yer sometimes for not being smart enough; but I never knowed a orficer yet as wasn't ready to run the same risks as the men; and when you're down, Lor' bless my 'art, nothin's too good for you. 'Member the skipper coming and bringing us horindges, Joe Tomson, when we had the feckshus fever?"

"Ay, ay, mate," growled a big sun-tanned sailor.

"Right you are, mate," said a big sergeant. "It's just so with us. I've knowed our officers run out under fire to bring in wounded men, and get shot down theirselves. You remember Captain Smithers doing that, out in China, Billy Mustard?"

"That I do," said a fair red-faced private, with a merry look in his eyes. "He brought me in on his back. I'm waiting to see him down some day, and carry him in."

"To be sure," growled old Dick. "Orficers is orficers, and there 'aint one aboard this ship as wouldn't jump overboard to save any man, even if it was such a grumbling warmint as old Sim here."

Private Sim snarled, and showed a set of yellow teeth, as he held out the palm of his left hand to give it a severe punch with his right fist; after which ebullition he seemed to feel much better, and went and leaned over the side.

"I hope Private Gray will get better," said Billy Mustard, who was a great favourite with the men from the fact that he was famous as a fiddler, and could rattle off anything from "Money Musk" up to "The Triumph;" and as to hornpipes, the somethingth said there wasn't a man in the service who could touch him. Billy Mustard had won the hearts of the sailors, too, during the voyage, from the way in which he sang "The Death of Nelson," with many another naval ditty, to which the whole forecastle could rattle out a hearty chorus. "I hope Private Gray will get better," said Billy.

"Ah, we all hope that," said Sergeant Lund. "Not that Adam Gray's a friend of mine. He's too much of a gentleman; and when he's going through his drill, it always seems as if one was putting a young officer through his facings. Not that I wish him any harm; but if he's a gentleman he ought to have got his commission, and kept out of the ranks."

"Well, sergeant," said Billy Mustard, "I don't see that it matters much what a man is, so long as he's ready for dooty, and I will say as Gray never sticks himself up, but does his dooty like a man."

"Yah! he'll turn out no good," snarled Private Sim, looking round.

"Well, for my part," said old Dick, "if I was to go in for being cunnle of a regiment, I should like that there regiment to be all private Simses, and then I'd have all the officers doctors."

"And a big hospital for barracks," said the sergeant, laughing. "And rations of physic served out every day," cried Billy Mustard.

There was a hearty laugh at this; but it was checked directly, as the men recalled that one of their number was lying in grievous peril; while Private Sim glanced round, uttered a snarl like that of a hyena, then turned back and gave his left hand another punch.

"Laugh at me, will yer?" he growled, "when I'm so jolly ill. Just let me get hold o' that there fiddle o' yours, Master Billy Mustard, and I'll smash it, see if I don't."

He seemed to feel better after this threat, and stood leaning over the bulwarks, and spitting down into the sea, while one of the sailors went aft to learn some tidings concerning Adam Gray.

Meanwhile, the centre of an anxious knot of observers, the young soldier lay breathing very feebly in spite of the stimulants frequently administered; and Bob Roberts, as he knelt close by on the deck, watched with a strange feeling of heart-sickness coming over him. He could not conceal from himself the fact that he had been the cause of all the suffering; and full of self-reproach, he knelt there, considering whether he should ever forget that scene, with the pale face of the fine young fellow lying before him.

Gray seemed to be in no great pain, but to be suffering more from a strange delirium caused by the working of the tiny drops of poison injected in his veins. He muttered a few words occasionally, and started convulsively from time to time; but when spoken to, he calmed down, and lay, apparently, waiting for his end.

"Don't know; can't say," was all that could be got from the doctor, as the hours crept on—hours when the heat of the sun was terrible; but no one left the injured man's side.

The specimens in the buckets were forgotten, and died; the cause of the misfortune grew dry and shrivelled, where it had twined and wriggled itself, half a dozen yards away, the dangerous head being thrown overboard by Bob Roberts, and swallowed by a fish before it had descended many feet.

Both the resident and the captain had tried to persuade the ladies to leave the sick man's side; but they had declined to go, and Doctor Bolter had nodded approval.

"Thank you, my dears, thank you," he said. "It's very kind of you; and I'm glad enough, I can tell you, to find that you've both got something in you besides fine young ladyism."

"I wish we could do more," said Rachel Linton, quietly.

"So do I, my dear," said the little doctor; "and I wish I could do more, but I have done all I can. Nature must do the rest."

The long, hot day passed on, and evening was approaching before the doctor took anything more than a glass of wine and water and a biscuit; and at last, when every one had judged by poor Gray's aspect that all now was over, and Major Sandars came up and thanked him for his patient endeavours to save the poor fellow's life, the doctor felt his patient's pulse once more, raised the closed eyelids and gazed at the pupils, and then rose up, dropped into a cane lounging chair, and began softly rubbing his knees.

"Now, ladies," he said firmly, "go below and dine. I order it. Sandars—Horton—if you have any good feeling left in you, you'll send relays of Jacks and privates to rub my poor knees. I say," he said, looking round with a smile, "that was a close shave, wasn't it?"

"Close shave?" said the major, as the ladies drew back, apparently hurt at the doctor's levity; and poor Bob Roberts, kneeling at the injured man's feet, lowered his head so that those near should not see the unmanly tears gathering in his eyes, though he was somewhat comforted on seeing that Ensign Long was almost as much moved.

"Yes," said the doctor; "you might have got all the nobs of the profession, and I don't believe they could have done better."

"No," said Captain Horton rather coldly. "You have worked hard, Doctor Bolter."

"Hard? I should think I have. I tell you what it is, sir, you would not have felt more pleased than I do if you had been made an admiral."

"But the man is dying fast, Bolter," said Major Sandars.

"Dying, sir? why he has been dying fast all day."

"Then is not this rather unseemly before ladies?" said Captain Horton.

"Unseemly? Before ladies?" said the doctor in a puzzled way. "Why, can't you see for yourselves? Ha, ha, ha!" he said, laughing softly. "Don't you see the remedies have beaten the poison. There's a delightful sleep he has dropped into."

"Sleep?" exclaimed Miss Linton.

"To be sure, my dear. Look what a lovely perspiration is coming out on his forehead. There, come away, and let him sleep. He'll be nearly well by to-morrow morning."

Bob Roberts leaped up from the deck, as if sent by a sling, made a dash at Ensign Long, swung him round, indulged in a kind of war dance indicative of triumph; then looked extremely ashamed of himself, and dashed off into the gun-room to spread the news that the doctor had saved Gray's life.

"That's not a bad sort of boy," said the doctor, looking after Bob; and then, as Ensign Long raised his chin in the air, and looked very dignified, "tell you what Sandars, if I were you I'd get Captain Horton to make a swop. Let's give him Tom Long in exchange for the middy. What do you say?"

Tom Long marched off, looking very much disgusted; and Sergeant Lund having been summoned to bring a file to watch by the sick man, the much relieved party went down to dinner.

Chapter Five
Up the Parang River

That evening the anchor was dropped off the mouth of the Parang river; and as the night closed in all eyes were directed to the thickly-wooded country on each side of the stream, whose banks were hidden by the dense growth of mangrove trees, which, now that the tide was up, seemed to be growing right out of the water, which those on board could see through their glasses to be smoothly flowing amidst the stems.

Further inland tall columnar nipah palms could be seen fringing the tidal way, and apparently growing amidst the mangroves, with the water washing their roots.

Dense green vegetation, and a broad flowing muddy river — that was all that greeted the eyes of the eager lookers-on, till darkness set in. Not a trace of town or village, not even a fisherman's hut or a boat. All was vegetation and the flowing river.

Once Bob Roberts thought he saw a boat coming down the stream, and in the distance it very strangely resembled some little craft with upright mast and dark sail; but as it came nearer it proved to be a patch of root-matted vegetable soil, washed from the bank, and having in the centre a small nipah palm, which slowly passed from might, to be cast ashore upon some mud bank, and again take root.

But as the darkness fell, the distant glitter as of tiny sparks amidst the trees took the attention of all. They were too distant to see the phenomenon to perfection; but the faint sparkle was very beautiful as the myriads of fire-flies, by which it was caused, flitted and changed from place to place, which was now dark, now scintillating in a most peculiar manner.

The captain had decided not to attempt the passage of the river till morning, all on board being very ignorant of its entrance, though, judging from the configuration of the coast, the most they had to dread was being grounded for a time on some bank of mud or sand. This part of the coast was so sheltered that there was no surf; and when the anchor was let go, the corvette swung round easily, to lie almost without motion on the calm still waters of the river's mouth.

But though no sign of human habitation had been visible, as the night wore on those on board became fully aware of the fact that the jungle had plenty of denizens, for from time to time strange roarings were heard, and then splashings in the water, as of wild creatures bathing. Once or twice too, as Bob Roberts and Ensign Long, companions for the time being, if not friends, leaned over the bulwarks, they fancied they could hear some great beast swimming towards them.

"What can it be?" said Bob in an awe-stricken whisper, as the strange snorting and splashing grew nearer.

"'Nosserus," said Dick the sailor, who generally contrived to be pretty close to the youths, and depended upon them largely for his supplies of tobacco. "It's one on 'em having a wallow, like a big pig, somewhere in the shallows."

"That's a tiger, isn't it!" said Tom Long, as a hoarse roar came over the smooth surface of the water.

"Shouldn't wonder, young gentlemen, if it were; but I'll say good night, for 'taint my watch, and I think a turn in won't be bad preparation for a hard day to-morrow."

Everyone expected a busy day upon the morrow; but it was long before the two youths could tear themselves away from the side of the vessel, for there was something so mysterious and weird in the look of the black water, in which the stars just glimmered; while right before them all looked dark and strange, save where there was the distant twinkling of the fire-flies, ever changing in position.

"Hark!" whispered Long; "there's a splash again. That can't be close to the shore."

"No, that's not a hundred yards from the ship. I say, Long," whispered Bob with a shudder, "I shouldn't much like to swim ashore. I'll be bound to say that was a crocodile."

"I shouldn't wonder," was the reply; and they still stood trying to make out the cause of the strange splashing noises, till, utterly tired out, they sought their cots, and were soon fast asleep.

The getting up of the anchor roused the two lads soon after daybreak, by which time steam was up; and with the faint morning mists slowly rising like silver gauze above the dense belts of trees, the steamer began slowly to move ahead.

The tide was flowing, and the mangroves were deep in the water, though not so deep but that their curious network of roots could be seen, like a rugged scaffold planted in the mud to support each stem; while as they slowly went on, the dense beds of vegetation, in place of being a mile off on either side, grew to be a half a mile, and soon after but a hundred yards, as the steamer seemed to be going straight into a broad bank ahead.

As they approached, though, a broad opening became visible, where the course of the stream swung round to the right; and after passing a point, the river rapidly contracted to about a hundred yards in width, and soon after was narrower, but still a smoothly flowing stream by the eternal mangroves. At last some signs of life began to appear, in the shape of an occasional crocodile, which glided off a muddy bank amidst the mangrove roots, into the water. Here and there, too, the long snout of one of these hideous reptiles could be seen, prone on the surface of the water, just above which appeared the eyes, with their prominences, as the reptile turned its head slowly from side to side, in search of some floating object that might prove to be good for food.

The sight of these beasts was too much for the officers, who were soon armed with rifles, making shots at the muddy-hued creatures, apparently with no other effect than for the long horny head to slowly sink beneath the water.

Captain Smithers proved himself to be the best shot, for after splashing the water with a bullet close to the head of one of the saurians, his attention was drawn to another, between the steamer and the shore, apparently quite unconscious that the vessel could injure it in the least.

Judging from the size of the head, this was apparently the largest crocodile that had been seen; and taking long and careful aim, Captain Smithers at last fired, when the monster lashed the water furiously for a few moments with its tail.

"He's hit, and badly," said Doctor Bolter. "It's a big one, too. What a splendid specimen it would make!"

As he spoke, his words as to the size of the creature were verified, for the crocodile suddenly shot itself half out of the water, showing its head, shoulders, and a good deal of its horny back, before turning over and diving down, displaying its hind legs and tail before it disappeared.

"That was eighteen feet long if it was an inch," said the doctor, excitedly; "but he has gone to the bottom."

"Yes," said Captain Smithers, quietly reloading, "we shall not see it again. How is your patient, Bolter?"

"Oh, pretty well all right again, thanks. It was a lucky escape for the poor fellow."

"Very!" said Captain Smithers, thoughtfully. "What bird is that, doctor?"

"A white eagle," was the reply, as the doctor followed with his glasses the flight of a magnificent bird that rose from a stunted tree, flew across the river, and away over the mangroves on the other side.

Soon after, as the steamer still made its way onward in mid-stream, the river being very deep, as shown by the man busy in the chains with the lead, a flame of blue suddenly seemed to dart from a mangrove root, and then another and another, as some of the gorgeously-coloured kingfishers of the peninsula shot off along the surface up the stream.

On still, and on, with every one on board eagerly on the look-out for novelties, but all growing somewhat tired of the unbroken succession of dull green mangroves. At last, however, after many hours of slow and cautious progress, the mangroves gave place to tall and beautiful palms, showing evidently that the steamer was now beyond the reach of the tide; and this was farther proved by the fact that the stream was now dead against them, running pretty swiftly, but, in place of being muddy, delightfully clear.

Faces that had looked long and solemn as the supposition had grown stronger that the country was nothing better than a mangrove swamp, became more cheery of aspect, especially when, through an opening in the dense clumps of palms with their feathery tops, the blue line of a distant range of hills could be seen.

Then came, as they rounded a point, the first trace of human habitation, in the shape of a Malay village, which in the distance bore a marvellous resemblance, in its steep gabled roofs thatched with palm-leaves, to some collection of cottages in far-distant England. But soon it was seen that every cottage was raised upon posts, that the walls were of woven reed or split bamboo, and that the trees that shaded them were cocoa-nut and areca palms.

Onward still, but more slowly and cautiously, lest the steamer should take the ground. Now and then scattered patches of cultivation were seen, in the shape of paddy fields; clusters of fruit-trees stood here and there; native boats were drawn right up on the mud, or secured to posts; and now and then buffaloes could be seen, standing knee-deep in the water, with dark-skinned children running to and fro, terribly excited at the sight of the strange ship.

Onward still, hour after hour, past village after village, wonderfully same in appearance, and the river still kept broad and deep enough for the navigation of the steamer, till night came on, and she was anchored in mid-stream, with the wild jungle coming close down to the water's edge on either side.

At early morn the journey was continued till a broad reach of the river was ascended, at the far end of which was a good-sized island, in which was a palm-thatched building of some consequence, while, only separated from it by a narrow arm of the river, stood the largest collection of houses they had seen, with what was evidently a mosque by the river side. There was an abundance of boats too, and what strongly resembled a stockade; but what most took up the attention of all on board were a couple of long, low, well-made vessels, each displaying a curious figure-head bearing a faint resemblance to some fabulous monster; and in these armed boats both the soldiers and sailors of the little expedition were quite right in believing that they saw nothing more nor less than the much-talked-of vessels of the kris-bearing pirates of Malaya, the well-known, much-dreaded prahus.

Chapter Six
How Tom Long tried the Durian

A little bustle on deck, the rattling of chains, the splash of an anchor, and Her Majesty's ship "Startler"—well manned, and armed with guns that could send shot and shell crashing through the town on the river's right bank—swinging to her moorings; for she had reached her destination—the campong, or village, of Sultan Hamet, the native Malay potentate, who was under British protection, and who sought our aid to rule his land beneficially, after our manners and customs, and who now professed the most ardent friendship for those who were ready to do their duty; though the trust they felt in the Malays was not untempered by suspicion—in some cases, perhaps, with fear.

It was a very busy time for all, and after the "Startler" had been made what Dick the sailor called snug—that is to say, firmly anchored head to stream, for they were now far above the reach of the tide—a strong party of the blue-jackets were landed upon the pleasantly umbrageous island, along with the soldiers; for this island was to be the site of the residency, and it proved to have four good-sized buildings amidst the trees, which had been roughly prepared by Sultan Hamet's orders.

Doctor Bolter was almost the first man to land, and for a long time he was fussily perspiring about, as he abused the sanitary arrangements of the place to every man he met, pausing last of all to stand mopping his face in front of Bob Roberts and Tom Long.

"Pretty sort of a wilderness to bring us to, young gentlemen!" he exclaimed. "I don't know what to start at next. The place will be a very hot-bed of fever, and we shall all be swept away."

"What do you say to this for a neat spot, doctor?" said Bob Roberts.

"Neat spot? what for?"

"Burying ground."

"Burying ground? What do you mean, sir?"

"To bury us all decently, doctor," said Bob, grinning. "And I say, doctor, who's to bury the last man?"

"If you were under my charge, Master Bob Roberts," said the doctor, panting with the heat, "I should reduce that vital force of yours a little, sir."

"Thanky, doctor. But I say, doctor, which is to be the resident's house?"

"That, sir; and those three buildings are to be turned into barracks, and fort, and officers' quarters; and how I am to get them all into a sanitary state, I don't know."

But the doctor did manage it somehow in the following days, when, in spite of the heat, every one worked with a will; the resident's house was improved, and boats were constantly going to and from the "Startler," whose hold was something like a conjuring trick, as it constantly turned out household necessaries and furniture. Handy workmen amidst the soldiers and Jacks were busy, fitting, hammering, and nailing; so that in a very short time the resident's house began to grow ship-shape.

At the same time the officers' quarters were being prepared, and the barracks as well; while plans were made to strengthen the fort, dig ditch, form glacis, and generally make the place tenable against a possible enemy.

Plenty of Malays were enlisted to help; but beyond bringing wood, and acting as carriers, they did not prove to be very valuable workers. But all the same, the preparations went on, various chiefs coming across in their boats from time to time, watching with no little wonder the changes that were being effected, talking together a good deal about the stands of arms in the little barracks, and the nine-pounder field-pieces that were brought ashore from the "Startler's" hold.

The inexhaustible bottle was nothing to that ship, for no sooner did the adjutant make out a list of requisitions, and send in, than the hold began to disgorge, and boat-loads of stores came ashore; till, in a marvellously short time, the white tents, saving one or two large ones, disappeared from where they had been first set up amongst the trees, and with a celerity that perfectly astounded the Malay visitors, the island assumed an aspect that seemed to say the English visitors meant to stay.

Meanwhile, the country people grew less shy, and boats came with fruit and rice for sale, one of the first being visited by Bob Roberts—Tom Long, who had evidently meant to be there before him, coming directly after.

The ladies had landed and taken possession of their new abode, where several of the soldiers were busy forming a garden; and it had struck both the admirers of Miss Linton that an offering or two of fruit and flowers would be very acceptable, after the long confinement on ship board.

The sampan, or native boat, that the two lads had come to visit, was fastened to a rough bamboo landing-stage, that had been one of the first things fitted up at the island; and, to their great delight, they could see that the boat was stored with various vegetable productions, some of which were sufficiently attractive to make the lads' mouths water, to the forgetting of the main object of their visit.

"Hallo, soldier!" said Bob Roberts, as he saw Tom Long come up, looking very aggressive.

"Hallo, sailor boy!" said Tom Long, superciliously; and then they stood looking at each other, quite unconsciously like a couple of Malay game cocks in bamboo cages, on the afterpart of the sampan. These two pugnacious birds were evincing a strong desire for a regular duel; but as the bamboo bars of their cages prevented a near approach, they stood there ruffling their plumes, and staring hard in each other's faces.

"Seems a strange thing that a man can't come down to buy a little fruit and some flowers, without your watching him," said Bob, at last.

"I wasn't watching you, boy," said Tom Long, superciliously. "There, spend your penny, my man, and go about your business."

"Look here, my stuck-up red herring," cried Bob, setting his teeth hard, "Captain Horton said that the naval officers were to set an example of gentlemanly behaviour before the natives, or I'll be blowed, Mr Tom Long, if I wouldn't punch your head."

"Blowed—punch head," sneered Tom Long; "that's gentlemanly, certainly."

"Look here," said Bob, who was stung to the quick by the truth of this remark; "do you want to fight, Mr Tom Long?"

"Mr T. Long presents his compliments to the middy boy of the 'Startler,' and begs to inform him that when her Majesty's officers fight, it is with some one worthy of their steel."

"Ha, ha! Haw, haw! Ho, ho, ho!" laughed Bob, cutting a caper expressive of his great amusement. "Her Majesty's officers—some one worthy of their steel. Ha, ha, ha, ha! I say, Tom Long, how happy and contented her Majesty must feel, knowing as she does that the gallant officer, Ensign Long, is always ready to draw his sword in her defence. Here, you stop! I got here first."

"Sahib wants my beautiful fruit," said one of the dark-faced men in the sampan, towards which Tom Long had stepped.

"Hallo!" said Bob, going up. "You are not a Malay?"

"No, sahib: I Kling, from Madras. Sell fruit—flowers. This Malaya man."

He pointed to a flat-nosed, high-cheek-boned man with him, who was dressed in the inevitable plaid sarong of bright colours, and wore a natty little plaited-grass cap upon his head.

Bob turned, and saw that this man carried a kris stuck in the folds of his sarong, which had slipped from the hilt, and he was now busy with a little brass box and a leaf. This leaf of one of the pepper plants he was smearing with a little creamy-looking mixed lime from the brass box, on which he placed a fragment of betel-nut, rolled it in the leaf, thrust it into his mouth, which it seemed to distort, and then began to expectorate a nasty red juice, with which he stained the pure water.

"Hope you feel better now," said Bob, who, in his interest in the Malay's proceedings, had forgotten all about the squabble with Tom Long. "Ugh! the dirty brute! Chewing tobacco's bad enough; but as for that—I'd just like to get the armourer's tongs and fetch that out of your mouth, and then swab it clean."

"No speak English; Malaya man," said the Kling laughing. "Chew betel, very good, sahib. Like try?"

"Try! No," said Bob, with a gesture of disgust. "Here, I say; we'll buy some fruit directly: let's have a look at your kris."

The Kling, who seemed to have quite adopted the customs of the people amongst whom he was, hesitated for a moment, looking suspiciously at the two lads, and then took the weapon he wore from his waist, and held it out.

Bob took it, and Tom Long closed up, being as much interested as the midshipman.

"I say, Tom Long," the latter said, with a laugh, "which of us two will get the first taste of that brown insect's sting?"

"You, Bob," said Tom Long, coolly. "It would let out a little of your confounded impudence."

"Thanky," said Bob, as he proceeded to examine the weapon with the greatest interest, from its wooden sheath, with a clumsy widened portion by the hilt, to the hilt itself, which, to European eyes, strongly resembled the awkwardly formed hook of an umbrella or walking-stick, and seemed a clumsy handle by which to wield the kris.

"Pull it out," said Tom Long, eagerly; and Bob drew it, to show a dull ragged-looking two-edged blade, and of a wavy form. It was about fifteen inches long, and beginning about three inches wide, rapidly narrowed down to less than one inch, and finished in a sharp point.

"It's a miserable-looking little tool," said Bob.

"Good as a middy's dirk," said Tom Long, laughing.

"I don't know so much about that," said Bob, making a stab at nothing with the kris. "I say, old chap, this is poisoned, isn't it?"

"No, sahib," said the Kling, displaying his white teeth.

"But the Malay krises are poisoned," said Bob. "Is his?"

He nodded in the direction of the Malay, who was trying to understand what was said.

"No, sahib, no poison. What for poison kris?"

"Make it kill people, of course," said Bob, returning the rusty looking weapon to its scabbard.

"Kris kill people all same, no poison," said the Kling, taking back his dagger. "'Tick kris through man, no want no poison, sahib."

"He's about right there, middy," said Tom Long. "Here, let's look at some fruit."

This brought Bob Roberts back to the object of his mission; and realising at once that Tom Long's object was a present, he, by what he considered to be a lucky inspiration, turned his attention to the flowers that were in the boat.

For the Malays are a flower-loving people, and there is nothing the dark beauties of this race like better than decking their jetty-black hair with white and yellow sweet-scented blossoms.

Bob was not long in securing a large bunch of arums, all soft and white, with the great yellow seed vessel within. To this he added a great bunch of delicately tinted lotus, and then sat down on the edge of the boat to see what Long would purchase.

Tom Long was hard to please; now he would decide on a bunch of delicious golden plantains, and then set them aside in favour of some custard apples. Then he wondered whether the ladies would not prefer some mangoes; but recollecting that they had had plenty of mangoes, and the delicious mangosteen in India, he decided upon some limes and a couple of cocoanuts, when the Kling exclaimed, "Why not sahib buy durian?"

"What the dickens is durian?" said Tom.

"Durian best nice fruit that grow, sahib."

"Oh, is it?" said Tom. "Then let's have a look."

The Kling said something to the Malay, who stooped down, and solemnly produced what looked like a great spiney nut, about as large as a boy's head.

"That durian, sahib," said the Kling, smiling.

"Oh, that's durian, is it?" said Tom, taking the great fruit in his hands, and turning it over and over.

"Nice-looking offering for a lady," said Bob Roberts, laughing. Tom Long looked up sharply, and was about to speak; but he said nothing, only kept turning the great fruit over and over.

"Taste nice, most nice all fruit, sahib," said the Kling.

"Here, let's try one," said Bob, laying down his flowers; and the Kling signed to his companion to give him another, which the Malay did with solemn importance, not a smile appearing on his face, nor a look suggestive of his being anxious to sell the fruit in the boat.

The Kling took the great wooden fruit, laid it on the thwart of the boat, and reaching a heavy knife from the side, he inserted it at the head of a faint line, one of five to be seen running down the wooden shell of the fruit, and following this mark, he was able to open the curious production, and divide it into portions like an orange. In each of these quarters, or fifths, were two or three great seeds, as large as chestnuts, and these were set in a quantity of thick buttery cream or custard.

"Well, all I can say is that it's precious rum-looking stuff," said Bob. "Which do you eat, the kernels, or this custardy stuff?"

"No eat seeds, sahib; eat other part," said the Kling.

"Come along, soldier," said Bob; "I'll eat one bit, if you will?"

Tom Long looked too much disgusted to speak, but in a half-offended manner he picked up another quarter of the durian, and examined it attentively.

"Phew!" ejaculated Bob, looking round. "What a horrible smell. There must be something floating down the river."

They both glanced at the flowing silvery waters of the river, but nothing was in sight.

"It's getting worse," said Tom Long. "Why, it's perfectly dreadful!"

"It's this precious fruit," exclaimed Bob suddenly; and raising his portion to his nose, "Murder!" he cried; "how horrid!" and he pitched his piece overboard.

"Why, it's a bad one," said Tom Long, sharply: and he followed the middy's suit.

The Kling raised his hands in dismay; but leaning over the side, he secured the two pieces of durian before they were out of reach, and turned to his customers.

"Good durian—buteful durian," he exclaimed. "Alway smell so fashion."

"What!" cried Bob, "do you mean to tell me that stuff's fit to eat?"

The Kling took up the fruit; and smelt it with his eyes half-closed, and then drawing in a long breath, he sighed gently, as if with regret that he might not indulge in such delicacies.

"Bess durian," he said, in an exaggerated ecstatic manner. "Quite bess ripe."

Bob stooped down and retook a portion of the strange fruit, smelt it cautiously, and then, taking out a knife, prepared to taste it.

"You are never going to eat any of that disgusting thing, are you, sailor?" cried Tom Long.

"I'm going to try it, soldier," said Bob coolly. "Come and have a taste, lad."

In the most matter-of-fact way, though quite out of bravado on account of Tom Long's disgusted looks, Bob took a long sniff at the durian.

"Well, it is a little high," he said, quietly. "Not unlike bad brick-kiln burning, with a dash of turpentine."

"Carrion, you mean," said Tom Long.

"No, not carrion," said Bob, picking out a good-sized fragment of the fruit upon his knife; "it's what the captain calls *sui generis*."

"All burra sahib like durian," said the Kling, showing his white teeth.

"Then the burra sahibs have got precious bad taste," said Tom Long, just as Bob put the first piece of the fruit into his mouth, rolled his eyes, and looked as if he were about to eject it into the stream, but did not; gave it a twist round, tasted it; looked less serious; began to masticate; and swallowing the piece, proceeded to take a little more.

"There, it won't do, Bob Roberts," said Tom Long; "say it's horrible, like a man. You can't deceive me. What does it taste like?"

"Don't know yet," said Bob trying the second piece.

"What a jackass you are to torture yourself like that, to try and take me in, middy!"

Bob helped himself to a little more.

"Well, what does it taste like?"

"Custard," said Bob, working away hard, and speaking between every dig of his knife; "candles, cream cheese, onion sauce, tipsy cake, bad butter, almonds, sherry and bitters, banana, old shoes, turpentine, honey, peach and beeswax. Here, I say; give us a bit more, old cock."

Tom Long was astounded, for after finishing the first piece of the evil-smelling dainty, Bob had begun the second, and was toiling at it with a patient industry that showed thorough appreciation of the most peculiar fruit in the world.

"Tipsy cake, bad butter, old shoes, peach and beeswax," and the other incongruities, rang in Long's ear; and to prove that he was not deceiving him, there was Bob eating away as if his soul were in the endeavour to prove how much he could dispose of at one go.

It was too much for Tom Long; his curiosity was roused to the highest point, and as the Kling was smilingly watching Bob, Tom signed to the Malay to give him a piece.

The solemn-looking Asiatic picked up another fruit, and while Tom looked impatiently on, it was opened, and a piece handed to him, which he took, and with Bob's example before his eyes took a greedy bite—uttered a cry of disgust—and flung the piece in hand at the giver.

The Malayan character has been aptly described as volcanic. The pent-up fire of his nature slumbers long sometimes beneath his calm, imperturbable, dignified exterior; but the fire lies smouldering within, and upon occasions it bursts out, carrying destruction before it.

In this case Tom Long's folly—worse, his insult to the master of the sampan—roused the fiery Malay on the instant to fury, as he realised the fact that the youth he looked upon as an infidel and an intruder had dared to offer to him, a son of the faithful, such an offence; then with a cry of rage, he sprang at the ensign, bore him backwards to the bottom of the boat; and as the midshipman started up, it was to see the Malay's deadly, flame-shaped kris waving in the air.

Chapter Seven
How Dick related the Visit

With a cry of horror Bob Roberts leaped forward, and caught the Malay's wrist in time to avert the blow, the Kling starting forward the next instant, and helping to hold the infuriate Asiatic; while Tom Long struggled up and leaped ashore, where a knot of soldiers and sailors were gathering.

"Don't say anything, Tom," cried Bob. "Here you—tell him he did not mean to offend him," he continued to the Kling, who repeated the words; and the Malay, who had been ready to turn on the midshipman, seemed to calm down and sheathed his kris; while the Kling spoke to him again with the result that the offended man sat himself down in the boat, gazing vindictively at the young ensign ashore.

"Here, no more durian to-day, thank you," said Bob, handing the Kling a dollar. "And look here, you sir; don't let that fellow get whipping out his kris on any of our men, or he'll be hung to the yard-arm as sure as he's alive."

"He much angry, sahib," said the Kling, whose swarthy visage had turned of a dirty clay colour. "Soldier sahib hurt him much."

"Yes, but if we hadn't stopped him he'd have hurt my friend much more."

As he spoke Bob nodded shortly to the Kling, and leaped ashore. "Sahib not take his flowers," said the latter, and dipping them in the river, and giving them a shake, he left the boat and handed the beautiful blossoms to the young sailor, who directly after joined Tom Long, who looked, in spite of his sunburnt visage, rather "white about the gills," to use Bob's expression.

"That fellow ought to be shot. I shall report this case," cried the ensign angrily.

"I don't think I should," said Bob quietly. "You see you did upset the poor fellow, and they are an awfully touchy lot."

"It was all your fault for playing me that confounded trick," cried Tom Long, passionately.

"Trick? I played no trick," said Bob, indignant to a degree at the accusation.

"You did," cried Tom Long, "humbugging me into eating that filthy fruit."

"Why, it was delicious," cried Bob. "I should have gone on and finished mine if you hadn't made that upset."

"I don't care; it was a nasty practical joke," cried Tom Long, "and—I beg your pardon, Roberts," he said, suddenly changing his tone, and holding out his hand. "I believe you saved my life."

"Oh, nonsense!" said Bob. "He only meant to prick you with his kris."

"Heaven defend me from all such pricks!" said Tom Long, devoutly, as he held the middy's hand in his. "I say, Bob Roberts, I wish you and I could agree better."

"So do I," said Bob, giving the hand he held a hearty shake; "But we never shall. I always feel as if I wanted to quarrel with you, as soon as we meet."

"So do I," said Tom Long. "You are such an aggravating little beggar."

"It is my nature to," said Bob, laughing. "But you won't say anything about this affair, shall you? It will be a lesson how to deal with the natives."

"If you think I had better not, I won't," said Tom Long, thoughtfully. Then, with a shudder, "I say, I felt just as if I was going to have that horrid kris in me. I shall never forget this, Bob Roberts."

"Oh, stuff and nonsense! Here, I say, have one of these bunches of flowers, old fellow."

"No, no; I don't want them," said the ensign, colouring up.

"Yes, yes; take one. Quick, here are the ladies. I'm going to give my lotuses to Miss Sinclair," he said quietly. And as Tom Long's fingers closed upon the arums, the ladies, who were walking with the resident came close up.

"Ah, Mr Long," said the latter, "what a lovely bunch of arums!"

"Yes sir," said Tom, looking very red in the face; "they're for the mess table."

"Your lotuses are lovely, Mr Midshipman Roberts," said Miss Linton, smilingly greeting the frank-faced lad.

"Aren't they, Miss Linton?" said Bob. "I'm just going to send them aboard to the first luff; he's rather poorly."

They parted; and it was quite true, for after looking rather shame-facedly the one at the other, the ensign bore off his arums to the mess-room, and the lotuses were sent on board the "Startler" by the very next boat.

There was nothing more said respecting the adventure with the Malay boatman; but the two youths, who were a good deal puzzled in their own minds as to whether they were friends or enemies, exchanged glances a day or two later, when stringent orders were issued respecting the behaviour of the Englishmen to the natives. The men of both services were warned to be very careful, especially as it was the custom for the Malays to carry the deadly kris. The character of the people too was enlarged upon, their pride and self-esteem; and strict orders were given, to be followed by severe punishment if disobeyed, that the people and their belongings were to be treated with the greatest respect.

Every one was as busy as could be, for there was an immense amount of labour necessary to get the place into a state satisfactory to the various officers. Great preparations were being made too for the first meeting with Sultan Hamet, though it was a matter of doubt whether he would come to the residency in state, or expect the English to call upon him in his palm-thatched palace.

"He's a rum sort of a chap," Dick the sailor said, freely giving his opinion. "Sultan, indeed! What call have they to say he's a sultan? Why, Sergeant Lund, Billy Mustard, and that sick chap Sim, who went ashore with despatches, come back last night, and they say it's no more a palace as he lives in than a pig-sty. It's for all the world like a big bamboo barn, thatched with leaves."

"What's that?" said Bob Roberts, coming up, with the young ensign, to where two or three of the sailors were, under the trees, talking to a group of soldiers.

"I was a telling of 'em about what Sergeant Lund told me, sir," said Dick, pulling his forelock, "that this here sultan as we've come here to protect lives in a place as is just like a big bamboo barn standing on stilts. And Lor' ha' mercy, they say it was a sight: with leaves, and cabbage stumps, and potato parings chucked about under the place!"

"Now come, Dick," cried the middy; "no yarns, please."

"Well sir, of course I don't mean real English cabbage stumps and potato parings, same as we has at home, but what answers for 'em here, and coky-nut huxes and shells, and banana rinds, and a nasty bad smelling kind o' fruit as they calls doorings."

Bob gave the ensign a comical look.

"Why Billy Mustard says—and this here's a fack—as the smell o' them doorings."

"Durians, Dick."

"All right, sir," said the old sailor; "that don't make 'em smell a bit better—the smell o' them things knocked him slap off his feet."

The men laughed, and old Dick went on—

"Everything about the place was as ontidy as a bilge hole; and when our ambassadors—"

"Our what?" said Bob.

"Well, them as carried the despatches, sir—got close up, they was told to wait because the sultan was asleep. When seeing as a reg'lar party of the Malays, every man with his bit of a toasting fork by his side, come round to stare at 'em, Sergeant Lund he says to himself, 'Lor'! what a pity it is as I haven't got Private Tomkins, or Private Binns, or two or three more nice smart, handsome chaps o' that kind with me, instead of such a scuffy couple o' fellows as Sim and Mustard.'"

Here, of course, there was a roar of laughter, for Privates Tomkins and Binns were amongst the listeners.

"Come away," said Tom Long, frowning. "I don't like mixing with our men."

"No, no: stop," cried Bob. "They won't think any the less of us; we're off duty now."

Tom Long wanted to hear what was said, so he remained.

"And one of our nice hansum young orficers," continued Dick, in the most solemn way, "and a middy and some smart Jacks."

"And Dick Dunnage," said one of the soldiers.

"Well, he did mention me, but I was too modest to say so."

Here there was another laugh.

"'How so be,'" continued Dick, "he sez; 'must make the best o' what material we got,' so he pulls his men together, squares their yards, and coils down all their ropes tidy, tightens the breechings o' their guns, and lets the poor benighted savages of niggers have their fill o' staring at real

British sodgers. Then they turned civil, and brought 'em out drinks, and fruit, and pipes; and they was very comfortable, till some one come out and said as the sultan was awake, and wanted his cocks, so the chap as went as interpreter told them; and then there was a bustle, and some three or four chaps went and fetched some fighting-cocks, and took 'em inside the barn—I mean the palace; and our fellows was kept waiting till the sergeant hears a reg'lar cock-a-doodle-doo, just for all the world as if he was at home, and he know'd by that as one of the birds had won. Just about a minute after some one come and beckoned him, and he goes up the steps into the palace, as had bamboo floors, and carpets lying about; and there was the sultan up at one end, sitting on carpet, and all his wives and people about him."

"How many wives had he got, Dick?" said the midshipman.

"About a dozen, sir. But I'll just tell you how many he'd have had if my missus had been one on 'em."

"How many, Dick?"

"Just one, sir; she'd clear out all the others in a brace o' shakes. She wouldn't stand none o' that nonsense. Why, bless yer 'art, there was one had got a golden pestle and mortar—"

"Gently, Dick! gently!" said the midshipman.

"It's a fack, sir, and as sure as I stand here; and she was a bruising up betel-nuts for him to chew, and another was mixing up lime, and another spreading leaves, whilst—there, I dursn't hardly tell you this here, because you won't believe it."

"Let it off gently, Dick," said the middy, "and we'll try and bear it."

"Well, sir, hang me if one of his wives—the oldest and ugliest of 'em—wasn't sitting there holden a golden spittoon ready for him to use whenever he wanted."

There was another roar of laughter, and Dick exclaimed,—

"There, you ask Sergeant Lund if every word a'most I've said ain't quite true,"—which, with the exception of Dick's embellishment about the handsome sailors and soldiers, proved to be the case.

Chapter Eight
Tom Long's Wound

Doctor Bolter had been very proud of the cure he had effected in the case of Adam Gray, whom, from that day forward, he looked upon in quite a different light, obtaining his services as often as possible in carrying out what he called his measures for preserving the camp in health, and he was constantly sending Gray on missions to the major. But the doctor and his plans were set aside one morning, when there was an order for a general parade; and it was evident that there was something important on the way, for a good deal of bustle was visible on the deck of the steamer.

The news soon leaked out that the resident and officers were to make a state visit, full of ceremony, to the sultan; and in consequence there was a general turn out, in full review order, with the band. The sailors landed, and were drawn up on the shore, looking smart in their white, easy-fitting dress; and the steamer's cutters were soon after busy, landing the greater portion of the troops with their officers, in full uniform; while quite a crowd of Malays assembled on the beach, staring, some in wonderment, some manifestly in dislike, at the strangers.

The grand muster took place beneath the shade of some large trees, as far as was possible, for the heat was intense. Every one was in his best; and Ensign Long marched by Bob Roberts with a very bright sword beneath his arm, and putting on a pair of white kid gloves.

The middy tried to take matters coolly; but the thoroughly consequential air of his companion roused his ire, and he longed to do something to upset him.

That was, however, impossible, for the arrangements were complete; and the march inland, about a couple of miles, commenced with the Malays now drawing off into the woods, till—what looked rather ominous—the little force was left entirely alone.

The officers commented upon the fact, and felt a little suspicious, but their doubts were set aside by the appearance of a little party, of evidently some importance, for two, who seemed to be chiefs, were mounted upon small elephants, and these, by the voice of one of the party—a handsome, dark youth, in brilliant silk sarong and baju—announced themselves as coming from the sultan to act as guides.

This changed the state of affairs, and the idea that there might be treachery afoot was completely dismissed from the minds of all, save when, now and then, the gleam of a spear head was seen amidst the trees in the jungle; and Major Sandars pointed out how easily they might be led into an ambush.

Captain Horton was by his side, and that officer agreed that it would be easy; but, at the same time, gave it as his opinion that the best policy they could affect was an appearance of full confidence in the Malay potentate, while they kept strictly on their guard.

Farther back in the line of troops Private Gray was marching along, feeling anything but easy in his mind; for as he glanced now and then to his left, he kept making out the gleam of steel, or the white garments of some Malay amidst the trees; and at last, just as Captain Smithers was abreast, he pointed out to him the fact.

The captain felt disposed to resent it as a breach of discipline; but the young man's manner was so earnest, that he nodded, and watchfully turned his head in the same direction.

"What do you think then, Gray?" said the captain. "They are only people taking an interest in what is, to them, a great sight."

"I'm suspicious, sir, by nature," said Gray, "and I can't help feeling that we are living on the edge of a volcano."

"Do you always make use of such fine language, Gray?" said Captain Smithers with a sneer.

"I beg your pardon, sir," was the reply; "I was trying to speak respectfully to my officer," replied Gray.

Captain Smithers frowned, and felt annoyed with himself for his meanness.

"Yes, yes, of course, Gray," he said, hastily; "but there is nothing to fear."

"Nothing to fear!" thought Private Gray; "and we are trusting ourselves entirely to these people, who are known to be treacherous; and the ladies and the women of the regiment are all on that island, protected by only a weak force!"

Strangely enough, Captain Smithers had very similar thoughts to these as they rambled on, in tolerable coolness now, for they were beneath the trees.

They both thought afterwards that their fears were needless; and following the guides, they soon after were formed up in front of the sultan's house and those of his principal men, all of which, though certainly somewhat better than the sergeant's account to Dick Dunnage, would have led any one to expect, were of an extremely simple and lowly character.

Here the officers waited for their audience of the great man, Mr Linton being particularly anxious to make arrangements for carrying out the political business upon which he was engaged; but after waiting half an hour, one of the principal chiefs came out to announce that the sultan was too unwell to receive them.

The English officers flushed up, and looked upon the message as an insult, and for the moment there seemed a disposition to resent it; but the wise counsels of Mr Linton prevailed, and the order was given to march back.

Just then the young chief who had acted as interpreter before, and who spoke very good English, approached the place where Bob Roberts and the ensign were standing.

"I am very sorry," he said; "I meant to ask you to refreshments. Will you take cigars?"

They had only time to thank the young chief for his courtesy and take their places, as the march back was commenced — this time without guides, for none came forward, which was looked upon as so ominous a sign that extra care was taken, the men marching with loaded arms.

The precautions were not unnecessary; for they had hardly effected half their march, when there was the loud beating of a gong heard upon their right, followed by the same deafening din on the left.

The men were steadied in the ranks, and every one was on the alert; but still there came nothing more to cause alarm till they had arrived within half a mile of their landing-place, when, as they were passing through a more open portion of the track, there was a shout, and a shower of limbings came whizzing past them. Again a shout, this time on their left, and another shower of the keenly-pointed spears whizzed by.

There was a short, sharp command or two as the soldiers faced outwards, and every other man fired, sending a ringing volley crashing through the forest.

There was another din, made by the beating of gongs, and a few more spears were thrown, one of which struck Ensign Long; and these were replied to by another sharp volley, which crashed through the trees, making the twigs and leaves rattle as they pattered down. Then there was a dead silence, as the troops waited for fresh orders.

Bob Roberts, who was close by the ensign, turned pale as ashes as he saw the ensign stagger back, to stand literally pinned to a tree, in which the blade of the limbing had buried itself. All feeling of jealousy had passed away, and, catching Long by the hand, he gazed earnestly in his face.

"Are you much hurt, old fellow?" he cried hoarsely, as he realised the fact that the keen spear had passed diagonally through the youth's breast before it buried itself in the soft endogenous tree.

"I don't know yet," said Tom Long quietly; "but the brutes have ruined my best tunic."

"Hang your tunic!" cried Bob, excitedly. "Here, fetch the doctor. No; help here to get Mr Long to the residency. Bring up a dhooly."

"I suppose I shall feel it when they draw out the spear," said Tom Long calmly.

"Do you feel faint?" cried the middy. "Here, who has a little rack?"

"Here's some water, sir, in my canteen," said Sergeant Lund. "Forward!" rang out from behind just then; and then the voice of Captain Smithers made itself heard, —

"Who's that down?"

"Ensign Long, sir," some one said.

"Poor lad! poor lad!" cried the captain. "Ah, Long, my dear boy, how is it with you? Good heavens! Quick, my lads; bring up a dhooly."

"Hadn't we better get the spear out, sir?" said Bob Roberts, anxiously.

"Yes, out of the tree, of course," said the captain; "but mind—steady! Here, let me. I won't hurt you more than I can help," he continued, as he drew the spear out of the palm, and then hesitated as to how they were to manage to carry the injured man, with the lengthy shaft passing through his chest.

Tom Long solved the question himself by taking hold of the spear handle with both hands and giving it a tug, while every one present gazed at him with horror, expecting to see the terrible stains that must follow.

Bob Roberts dragged out his handkerchief and rapidly doubled it, ready to form a pad to staunch the bleeding—rushing forward to clap it to the wound, as the ensign tore the spear from his breast.

"Open his tunic first," cried Captain Smithers; and he bore Tom Long back on to the ground, tearing open his scarlet uniform, while the injured object of his attentions began to work his left arm about.

"I say, gently," he said. "I don't think I'm much hurt."

"You don't feel it yet," cried Bob Roberts.

"Look out there!" cried a voice in authority somewhere behind; and then a couple of men ran up with a light hospital litter for wounded or sick men.

"It went—it went—" said Tom Long, slowly.

"Why, confound you, Long," said Captain Smithers; "you've not been scratched."

"No; I do not think I am," said the ensign, getting up, feeling himself carefully about the chest. "It went through my tunic and under my left arm."

"Why, you've got about six inches of padding in your coat," said Bob Roberts, whose hands were busy about the young man's breast.

"Yes," said Tom Long; "more or less."

"Forward!" shouted Captain Smithers; and the march was resumed, with Tom Long looking very woeful about the two holes that had been made in his scarlet tunic, and gradually growing terribly annoyed, as he saw Bob Roberts pretending to stifle his laughter; while the men, in spite of the danger on either side, tittered and grinned as they kept catching sight of the young officer's scarlet cloth wounds.

Major Sandars was equally anxious with the resident to get back to the island, for a feeling of dread had risen up that the residency might have been attacked during their absence. In fact, it seemed now that they had been out-generalled; and if their fort, and provisions, and stores should be in the hands of the Malays, their position would be perilous in the extreme.

As Bob Roberts went on, he found the men eagerly discussing the matter, not from a feeling of fear, but of love of excitement; and, among others, Private Sim was saying in a low voice, that if he had only been well and strong, nothing would have pleased him better than fighting his way back through the jungle, "anywheres—to the world's end if they liked."

Meanwhile, though it was evident that there was a large body of Malays on their right, the answer they had got to their first attack had kept them off, and the long line of troops and blue-jackets went on unmolested by their enemies. Every precaution was taken; and in some of the denser portions of the jungle they regularly felt their way with advance guards and flankers, who, poor fellows, had a most tough job to force their way through the tangled creepers and undergrowth.

At length, however, the river was reached, and it was evident, to the great delight and relief of all, that the island was safe, and the steamer lay in its old position, unmolested by prahu or attack from the shore.

Every man breathed more freely on seeing this; and the boats coming off, the whole party were rapidly transferred to steamer and to isle, where a council was called, and the situation discussed.

It was a peculiar position for the little force which had been sent up the country to help and protect Sultan Hamet, who, in return,—had refused to see Her Majesty's representative, and allowed them to be attacked by his people on their way back.

The question to decide was, whether, after such an insult as they had received, the little force ought not to at once retire from their position, though the bolder spirits were in favour of holding it at all costs, and trying to read the sultan such a lesson as should scare his people from venturing to molest the English any more.

The council was interrupted by an embassy of a couple of chiefs from the sultan himself, who solved the difficulty by announcing that the attack was not made by their ruler's people, but by a certain rajah, whose campong, or village, was a few miles up the river. This chief was a respecter of no one, but levied black mail of all who passed down the stream. Every boat laden with slabs of tin or bags of rice had to pay toll for permission to pass on in peace; and if resistance was offered, he had guns mounted upon his stockade, and a couple of well-armed prahus, whose crews liked nothing better than confiscating any boat whose owner endeavoured to resist the rajah's demands.

Any doubts as to the truth of this story were set aside by the sultan's earnest request that the English officers should at once proceed up the river and severely punish this rajah, who was a thorn in Hamet's side.

With the promise that the matter should have proper consideration, the two chiefs took their departure; and the rest of the evening was spent in examining different Malays from the village, all of whom told the same story, that it was Rajah Gantang who had made the attack, and that he was a perfect scourge to the people round.

The next day further investigations were made; and had any doubt remained, it was chased away by the appearance of two long war prahus, pulled by a large number of rowers, and crammed with Malays.

These vessels were allowed to float gently down with the stream, stern foremost, when, as much out of bravado as anything, several shots were fired from the small brass swivel guns on board, the little balls rattling through the steep roof of the men's quarters; while before a gun could be brought to bear, the oars rapidly plashed the water, and the two prahus were swept back round a wooded point up stream, well out of sight.

This was sufficient for the officers in command, who issued such orders as placed all the men in a state of the most intense excitement, for it was evident that there was to be an expedition up the river to punish the audacious chief, who was probably in profound ignorance of the strength of the power he had braved.

Chapter Nine
A Night Attack, and a Misfortune

It seems a curious thing to a man of peace that a man of war should be in a state of high delight at the prospect of an engagement wherein he may lose his life; but the fact is, that when two or three hundred men are bound to attack some enemy, each single individual knows full well that somebody will be wounded, perhaps killed, but believes that it will not be himself.

So it was then that on board the "Startler" there was no little excitement. The grindstone was in full use to sharpen cutlasses, and in addition there was a great demand made on the armourer for files to give to the lethal weapons a keener edge, one which was tried over and over again, as various messmates consulted together as to the probability of taking off a Malay's head at a blow.

"What you've got to do, my lads," said old Dick, "is to keep 'em off. You as has rifles and bagnets always show 'em the pynte; and you as fights with your cutlashes, keep 'em well away off your sword arm; then you'll be all right."

Capital advice if it could be acted upon, and a way of avoiding all kris wounds, but useless against the Malays' other dangerous weapon, the limbing or lance.

All the preparations were made over-night, so that long before daybreak the expedition could be well on the way, the object being to surprise the stockade and its defenders, and burn the bamboo fortification and the prahus.

The force was to consist of fifty soldiers, twenty-five marines, and fifty blue-jackets, who were to embark in the steamer's boats, two of which were provided with small breech-loading pieces running on slides, and under the charge of the sailors.

Water, provisions, plenty of spare ammunition, all were handed down, and two hours after midnight, the boats that were to convey the soldiers ranged up alongside the landing-place, and in due time the embarkation took place, the soldiers being under the command of Captain Smithers, the sailors under that of the first lieutenant of the "Startler."

A guide had been found in the person of a native fisherman, who, upon coming to the island the day before, had been detained, so that he should not communicate with the shore, and so give warning of the expedition. Not that there was any fear, for the Malay was in a high state of delight at the idea of the rajah meeting his match.

From this man they learned that for many years past Rajah Gangtang had been a perfect scourge to the river. He was famous for his piracies and his daring. Sultan Hamet dreaded him; and it was only to strengthen his position against the warlike rajah, who was too strong for him, that Hamet had entered into his alliance with the British, and invited the presence of a resident and the troops.

This was satisfactory, for the idea of the sultan proving treacherous was a suggestion of a complicated knot that it would take no end of policy to undo. Whereas, if it was all true about Rajah Gantang, his defeat and the breaking up of his power would be hailed with delight, and work greatly towards the pacification of a country terribly broken up by petty quarrels, strengthen Hamet's position, and give inimical chiefs a lesson on the power of the British forces that they were not likely to forget.

It was soon after two o'clock that the soldiers were mustered down to the boats, and silently took their places, just as through the mist, and with muffled oars, three more boats came slowly abreast of them, and after a brief colloquy moved off, with instructions that there should be no talking on board.

Fortunately for the expedition, though it was misty it was not so dark but that the leaders could follow the little light sampan of the Malay fisherman, who, apparently without any difficulty, sent his frail boat onward against the stream.

It was a weird procession through the mist, which gave the boats a fantastic, unreal appearance, while the shores looked, where the fog broke or floated up, strange, dark, and full of mystery. Every now and then there was a low echoing splash in the water, which told of some great reptile disturbed from its resting-place upon a muddy bank. Then those in the boats heard strange cries coming from a distance in the jungle, to be answered by other calls, some farther distant, some near at hand, telling that the various nocturnal creatures were busy securing food before the sun should drive them to their hiding-places in the darkest recesses of the forest.

"What's that?" whispered Bob Roberts to old Dick, who was beside him in the foremost boat.

"Sounds like something swimming, sir. There, you can hear it blowing."

"Do you think one of the boats has upset," whispered Bob, excitedly, as he leaned over the gunwale and tried to pierce the mist.

"'Taint likely, sir. Wouldn't they shout if they was turned up! Leastwise our chaps would; there's no counting for what soldiers might do, though. I shouldn't say as they'd let their selves drown without a squeak. That there's a tiger swimming 'crost the river, that's what that is."

"Get out," exclaimed the middy; "just as if a great cat would take to the water. Hist! I say, Doctor Bolter!"

"Yes," was whispered back from the next boat.

"Would tigers swim?"

"Yes. There's one trying to cross the river now."

"What did I tell you, Mr Roberts?" growled old Dick, softly.

"Here, give me your rifle, marine;" said Bob, excitedly. "I should like a shot at a tiger."

"Silence in that boat!" said Captain Smithers sharply; and the oars went on dipping softly, while Bob Roberts sat and listened till the panting noise of the swimming creature died away.

"I wonder whether Ensign Long's in the expedition?" said Bob, after a pause.

"Yes, sir; please I see him," said one of the sailors. "He got into one of the boats, wrapped up in a big grey great-coat."

"I hope he won't get wounded this time," said Bob. And the men all laughed; for Ensign Long's wound was a subject that afforded them no little amusement.

Then the procession went on, the boats gliding along in wonderful silence. Sometimes a glimpse of the dark foliage told them that they were a little too near either bank, but on the whole the Malay led them a very correct course along the centre of the stream, which wound here and there, sometimes contracting its banks, sometimes widening out, but always running swift, deep, and strongly, downward towards the sea.

The mist grew thicker, and hung so low down upon the water that at last the boats had to proceed very slowly, a rope being paid out from one to the other, so that there should be no mistake, otherwise it was quite within the range of possibility that one or the other would go astray, and be wanting at some critical time. A similar plan was carried out with the sampan, during the latter part of the journey, for it was often invisible; and so at last they felt their way onward in silence, till the Malay allowed his sampan to drift alongside the bows of the leading boat, and whispered to the interpreter his conviction that they were close up to the stockade.

"Might be anywhere," muttered the midshipman.

"Yes, sir, it's a thick 'un," growled old Dick; "and if I was in command o' this here expedition, I should give orders for all the Jacks to out cutlashes and cut the fog in pieces, while the sogers and marines forked it over with their bay'nets."

"Silence, there!" came from one of the officers, just as a faint breeze began to spring up, as if to solve the difficulty; breaking the fog into patches, and then forcing a way right through, so that it was swept to right and left of the river, passing under the trees.

The change was almost magical, for at the end of ten minutes the river was quite clear, and by the glittering starlight they could see the stockade on their right, while moored in front of it were two large prahus.

The boats closed in for the officer in command to give his final orders for the attack, and every man's heart beat fast with excitement, as he clutched his weapons.

They had no knowledge of the enemy's strength; but trusting to a night surprise, they felt satisfied of being able to put him to flight; so two boats were sent to board the prahus, while the three others made for the stockade, one to attack in front, while the others landed on either side, to take it in the rear, expecting an easy task, for there was not a sign of life as far as they could see.

But if the leaders of the expedition counted upon trapping the Malays asleep, they were mistaken. There is too much of his native tiger in the Malays' nature for such a march to be stolen upon them; and, just as the boats separated, and began rapidly to advance, the silence was broken by the deafening clangour of a gong, lights appeared suddenly in the stockade and in both the prahus, and to the astonishment of the attacking force, there was the flashing of muskets, the louder roar of the lelahs or small brass guns, and the surface of the river was splashed up in all directions by the bullets.

Fortunately the aim was bad, and the boats had separated, so that no one was injured, as, with a loud cheer, the sailors made their oars bend, the waters lapped and splashed beneath the bows of the boats, and soldier and marine waited eagerly for the command to fire.

But this was not given; for Captain Smithers felt that if the task was to be done, it must be achieved at the point of the bayonet; so, bidding his men be steady, he waited till the boat he was in crashed amongst the thick reeds and grass growing along the water's edge; and then leaping out, lead his little company through the dense undergrowth, round to where he expected to find the entrance to the stockade, from which a lively fire was now being kept up, while a deep-toned roar told that the large gun in the boat attacking the face of the stockade had begun to speak.

The party Ensign Long was with, under one of the lieutenants, had to make for the other side of the stockade, while the boat in which was Bob Roberts, being manned entirely by sailors and marines, had to attack the largest prahu.

The men were sanguine and full of spirit, their only regret being that they had so far to go before they could reach the sides of the long prahu, which they found now on the move, her anchor having been slipped, so that she was slowly floating down the stream, as she kept up a lively fire against the boat.

It seemed long, but not a minute could have elapsed before the boat was alongside, the bowman driving a Malay head over heels with the boat-hook, and then making fast, while the sailors let their well-secured oars swing, seized their rifles, and began to spring up the sides.

"Up with you, my lads," roared Bob Roberts, who was armed with a cutlass far too large for him to handle in comfort. But it was easy enough to say, "Up with you!" while it was excessively difficult to obey. Man after man tried to climb the side of the prahu, but only to slip back into the boat; while those who had better success found it impossible to surmount the stout bamboo basket-work or matting, with which the sides were protected from assault.

Through this, spear after spear was thrust; and after several ineffectual attempts to reach the deck, the sailors and marines began to retaliate by thrusting bayonet and cutlass through in return. A few shots were fired, but there was nothing to aim at; though the Malays were not of that opinion, for they kept loading and firing the two lelahs on board, making a great deal of noise, but necessarily doing no mischief.

"Back into the boat, my lads," cried the lieutenant in command, as they floated down with the prahu, which evidently swarmed with men; "we'll try round the other side."

"Let me board them first, Mr Johnson," cried Bob excitedly.

"No, no, my lad," was the reply. "What the men cannot do, you cannot."

In the excitement of the men firing and making a fresh effort, as the boat was worked round the stem of the prahu, the lieutenant lost sight of Bob Roberts, who, after feeling terribly alarmed for the first few inmates, had become accustomed to the firing and shouting, and then grown so excited and angry that he felt as if he could not stay in his place. Getting hold of a rifle, laid down by one of the men who tried to board the prahu, he had given vent to some of his excitement by loading and firing as fast as he could, sending bullet after bullet whistling through the tough screen, but doing no mischief to a soul; and still the prahu floated steadily down the stream, getting farther and farther away from where the firing was on the increase; the boats' guns sending an echoing report to roll along the surface of the water, and giving ample notice to those at the residency that the business was going on.

As the boat Bob Roberts was in reached the other side of the prahu, the Malays, uttering loud yells, rushed over, and once more there was a desultory attack kept up and repelled; for do all they could, not a sailor was able to surmount the tall screen.

Several wounds had been received from the limbings, and the men believed that they had pretty well retaliated with the bayonet, but they could see nothing; and checked as they had been, again and again, they were growing disheartened, and thinking what else they could do, when a loud yelling from the prahu, and the reports of several muskets, told of something fresh.

"Where's Mr Roberts?" said the lieutenant, suddenly.

"Here he is, sir," replied old Dick; and in the same breath, "No he ain't, sir. He was here just now."

"Look out, my lads! Seize those sweeps," said the lieutenant, as several long oars were now thrust out beneath the bamboo screen, and the Malays stabbed at the boat with them, trying to drive a hole through her bottom.

Several of the sailors seized the long oars on the instant, and hung on, while some of their messmates tried to fire through the holes, with the result that long spears were now thrust through, and desperate stabs made at the attacking party.

It was a wretched desultory fight, and the lieutenant was almost at his wits' end, for his spirit forbade his giving up, and all the time, no matter how bravely his men tried, they could not get on board the prahu.

Just then it was observed by the men who held on by the sweeps, that a brass lelah was being thrust through a hole, and brought to bear upon them, when the result would have been death to several, and the sinking of the boat, if it was fired. The danger was, however, averted by old Dick, who seized a boat-hook, and hitching it on the prahu's side, gave so sturdy a haul that he drew the boat some six feet along, and closer alongside.

He was just in time, for as the boat grated against the prahu there was a sharp ringing report, and the water was thrown up close astern.

A sharp volley from the boat replied to this, probably with as good results; and then thrusting with spear and bayonet went on in the darkness.

"Confound it all, my lads! we must get aboard her somehow," cried the lieutenant, stamping his foot with rage, as he stood up in the boat. "Here, make ready some of you, and follow me. Dick Dunnage, you keep her fast with the boat-hook."

As he spoke the lieutenant parried a thrust with his sword, and replied to it with a shot from his revolver, letting both weapons then hang from his wrists by sword-knot and lanyard as, seizing one of the sweeps, he began to clamber up, followed by a dozen of the men. There was a confused roar of shouts, yells, and cheers mingled, as those left in the boat ceased firing, so as not to injure the boarding party, who made a desperate effort now to climb over the bamboo screen, little thinking that the missing midshipman had boldly climbed up a little ahead of where they were, mounted to the great bamboo spar that held up the screen, and then with a miserably ineffective weapon, to wit, his pocket-knife, set to work as he sat astride it, and sawn away at the rattans that held it up.

It was a brave act, but an unlucky one. He had nearly succeeded in getting through, and he would have shouted out a warning, but that would have brought upon him the spears of the Malays; so he cut away, and had been so successful that, as the boarding party made their desperate dash, down came the great bamboo with a rush. The screen went outwards, over the sailors, who fell back beneath it into the boat, while Bob Roberts felt himself describing a half circle in the air, before plunging out of semi-darkness into that which was total, as he went down, yards away from the boat, into the cold black water, one thought alone filling his mind, and that thought was—crocodiles.

Chapter Ten
How Bob Roberts was not Drowned

For a few minutes it was a question of whether the boat would be swamped or no, as she lay beneath the great bamboo screen, which completely paralysed the efforts of the crew. The prahu was still floating with the stream, and the boat being dragged along in her wake, while, awaking now to a sense of their assailants' position, the Malays hurriedly thrust out sweeps, and others fired, and hurled their spears, a couple of dozen of which stuck in the bamboo mat. Dick in the stern, and a couple of the men in the bows, however, began a steady fire at the prahu, loading as rapidly as they could, while the men amidships cast off the awkward canopy, and, half stunned, but panting with rage and excitement, the lieutenant once more gave his orders.

"Oars, lads!" he cried, "and give way. We shall have 'em yet."

"Boat ahoy!" came from out the darkness.

"Why, that's young Roberts, sir," cried Dick. "Ahoy-oy-oy."

"Help here!" came from the stern again.

"We shall lose the prahu," cried the lieutenant.

"But we must have Mr Roberts, sir," cried old Dick, excitedly. "Give the word, sir—starn all—and we'll overtake her arterwards."

"Starn all, my lads, and do your best."

"Ahoy!" came once more, faintly, out of the darkness.

"We're going away from him," cried the lieutenant. "Pull round, my lads," he cried, seizing the tiller. "Now then, steady. Be smart there with a boat-hook. Roberts, ahoy!"

"Help, help," came again, from somewhere astern now, for the poor fellow was growing weak.

For as he had plunged down, with the thought of the great reptiles uppermost in his mind, Bob Roberts had felt a chill of horror run through him that seemed for the moment to rob him of all power; but as he rose to the surface again, and felt that he could breathe, he struck out manfully in the direction of the firing; but in his confusion, after swimming for a minute, he found from the noise behind that he was making for the stockade, and he turned hastily to swim after the boat.

It was no light task, dressed as he was. He had a sword in his belt, and on the other side a revolver, and his first thought was to rid himself of them; but a strange feeling of dislike to parting with his weapons made him put off the act of throwing them away until he should feel that he was sinking; so, guided by the flashes of the pieces that were being fired, he swam lustily in the direction in which he felt the boat must be.

He called for help several times, but his voice was not heard by those to whom he appealed; and as he felt himself being left behind, a cold chill of horror once more seized upon him, making his limbs seem heavy as lead, and paralysing his efforts in a way that was terribly suggestive of death.

Thoughts of the great slimy monsters being at hand to seize upon him, sent his blood rushing to his face in a way that made him giddy, and for a few moments he felt half mad with fear; but calling upon his manhood, he mastered the nervous trepidation.

"'Taint English—'taint game," he cried aloud, with the water at his lip; and checking the frantic desire to beat the surface with his hands in the natural last effort of a drowning creature, he swam steadily on, hailing the boat at intervals, but more and more feebly, as his despair increased; for he felt that he was only a lad, and that his life was a mere nothing compared to a successful capture of the prahu.

"They have gone after her," he groaned, as he uttered a despairing hail. And then the bright light of hope seemed to cross the darkness, for he heard a shout in reply, and then other answering hails to his cry for help, and he knew now that it was only a question of holding out till the boat could reach his side.

Shouts came again and again out of the darkness, and he answered— each time more feebly, for his strength was ebbing fast. He could see the stars flashing in the water, and he fancied he could hear the splash of oars, and the sounds of voices; then, too, he heard the crackle of distant musketry, and the roar of one of the boat-guns. Then, as if he were in a dream, he could hear some one close at hand hailing him—but he could not answer now, only swim feebly on, with his clothes, and the weapons, and cartridges in his pouch, dragging him down.

Then the stars above, and the stars on the water, seemed to be blotted out, and he was in utter darkness—strangling, but swimming still, beneath the stream. Then he seemed to see the stars again in a dim way, and he heard a shout; but he could not reply, for all was dark once more; and lastly, in a dim misty state he felt a spasm, and a sensation of being dragged beneath the water, and he thought that one of the reptiles of the river had seized him; and then he knew that he was lying in the bottom of the boat, and someone was pouring brandy between his lips.

"I just ketched the glint of his white face under the water," said a voice which seemed to be Dick's, "and ketched hold of his jacket. It was a near touch, and no mistake."

"Give way, my lads, give way!" was the next thing Bob Roberts heard; and as if in a dream he made out that they were rowing fast in chase of the prahu, which, with all her sweeps out on either side, was going rapidly through the water, her object being to get down to the tidal way at the lower part of the river, where there were mangrove-fringed creeks and inlets by the hundred, offering her a secure hiding-place from her indefatigable assailant.

"We shan't never ketch her, sir," growled Dick.

"No," replied the lieutenant, sharply, "but we'll hang on to her to the last. How far are we now from the steamer?"

"Not two miles, I should think, sir."

"Make ready then, marines," he cried, "and fire after her; hit her, if you can. Two fire at a time—mind, slowly and steadily. They will hear it on board, and be on the look-out, and if they don't sink her as she goes by them, why, it's a wonder."

Almost directly after there was the report of a couple of rifles, and then two more at half-minute intervals, while right on ahead, in the darkness, they could hear the heavy beat of the prahu's sweeps, and knew that she was going more rapidly than they.

"How are you now, Roberts?" said the lieutenant, kindly.

"Coming round, Mr Johnson," said Bob. "Thank-ye for picking me up."

"Keep your thanks for to-morrow, Roberts," said the lieutenant, bitterly. "How vexatious to make such a mess of the affair?"

"There's another one a-coming, sir," said Dick, softly. "You can hear the oars beating right behind us, sir."

The lieutenant listened.

"There must be a great curve in the river here," he said, "one that we did not notice in the fog."

"Then it's a precious big curve, sir, that's all I can say," exclaimed old Dick; "for if that ain't t'other prahu coming down, with all sweeps out, I'm a Dutchman."

"They never can have failed the same as we have," exclaimed the lieutenant, listening. "No—yes—no. You are right, Dick, my man. Cease firing there. Make ready, my lads, and we'll plump every shot we have into this one as she comes abreast, and then lay the boat alongside, and board her in the confusion. Be ready, my lads, and then, you know, down with your rifles. Cutlasses must do it afterwards."

A few minutes of intense excitement followed, during which time every man sat with his finger on the trigger, listening to the regular beat of the prahu's long oars as she came sweeping down at a rapid rate, evidently bent upon making her escape, like her consort, out to sea.

"If we only had a bow gun," muttered the lieutenant. "No you be still, Roberts," he continued; "you are weak and done up."

"I think I could manage a rifle now, Mr Johnson," said the lad, with his teeth chattering from cold.

"I don't," was the abrupt reply. "Now, my lads, not a sound; we have a disgrace to wipe out, and this prahu must be ours."

By this time the long swift boat was rapidly approaching, quite invisible to the little party of English, but audible enough; and they waited eagerly till it seemed as if she was bearing down upon them, when, with a short, sharp warning first to be ready, the lieutenant gave the word *Fire!* when about fifteen rifles went off almost like one, their flashes lighting up the darkness for an instant, and displaying close upon them the long dark prahu, with a long bank of oars, coming down fast.

"Oars! Give way!" shouted the lieutenant; and almost as he spoke, the prahu changed her course so rapidly that there was but little rowing needed, for instead of avoiding them, the vessel came right at the English boat, trying to run her down, being so nearly successful that she ripped her down to the water's edge just by the bows. There was a crash of breaking oars; but the Malay boat dashed rapidly away, leaving the English helpless and sinking on the river.

"Catch this boat cloak," cried the lieutenant who was ready enough in the emergency. "Stuff it in, and one of you sit back against it."

"It'll take two on us, sir," cried the man, who rapidly obeyed orders, and to some extent checked the rush of water.

"Two of you begin baling," cried the lieutenant next; and then, as he saw that all their efforts would only just keep them afloat, "There, my lads," he said, "we've done our best. One more volley and then I think we had better run her ashore."

Another volley was fired, to give warning to the steamer that there was something extraordinary on the way, and then the boat's head was turned to the shore; but as they found that by constant baling they could just keep afloat, the lieutenant altered their direction, and they rowed on, with the gunwale nearly level with the water's edge, and proceeding very slowly, but ever carried by the stream nearer to the steamer and the isle.

"A nice night's work, Roberts," said the lieutenant dolefully, as they sat deep in the water that washed from side to side; "lost both prahus, and got the boat crippled."

"But we haven't lost any men, sir," said Bob, by way of comforting him.

"No; but several of the poor lads are wounded. There's only one thing that would give me any comfort for my ill-luck, Roberts, and that is to hear—"

"There's the 'Startler' a-talking to one, sir," cried Dick, forgetting discipline in his excitement, as the boom of a big gun not very far-off met their ears. "There she goes again, sir," he continued, as there was another shot, and another, and another, all showing that the captain had heard the firing and been prepared.

A couple more shots were heard, and then all was silent till the boat slowly drifted by the lights of the island, answering the sentries' challenges, and then sighting the lights and open portholes of the steamer, to whose side they managed to struggle, answering the challenges as they approached.

In spite of all their efforts, it was doubtful whether the boat could have floated another minute, but on reaching the side the falls were hooked on, and she was slowly run up to the davits, with the water rushing out, the lieutenant then reporting his ill-success to the captain.

"Not one man killed, though," he said.

"How many wounded?"

"Six, sir, but only slightly."

"Mr Johnson, I hope the other boats have done better," said the captain. "I'm afraid you will not get any promotion on the strength of this job."

"No, sir," said the lieutenant dolefully. "But did you sink either of the prahus?"

"Sink them, no," said the captain, testily. "I don't believe they were either of them touched; they went by us like the wind. There, go below all of you, and get into dry clothes." The captain went forward to see that the look-out was doing its best; while the prahus were safely making their way to a mud creek, where the chiefs who commanded them felt that they could laugh at any force the English might send to redeem the failure of the past night; and to work such mischief in the future as was little imagined at the time.

Chapter Eleven
How Bob Roberts had a Lesson on Common Sense

The sun rose over the dense forest, turning the river mists into gauzy veils, that floated rapidly away, leaving the rapid stream sparkling in the soft morning breeze. The brightly-coloured parroquets flew shrieking from bank to bank; and in the thick jungle, across from the end of the island, the noisy chattering of a party of monkeys could be heard.

But bright as was the scene in all the gorgeous tints of tropic scenery, no one on the isle or in the steamer had a thought for anything but the expedition. At the residency, Rachel Linton and her cousin had watched the starting of the boats in the dim starlight, and they had sat ever since at their window, listening for tidings. The noise of the distant firing had reached them, making their breath come short as they started at each volley. Even by the very faintly-heard pattering of the small arms, broken occasionally by the loud report of boat-gun or lelah, they knew that quite a sharp fight must be raging.

Twice over they were visited by the major's wife, for the major could not rest, but kept going to the steamer to consult with Captain Horton as to whether they had done everything possible to ensure success.

Mrs Major Sandars found the two ladies pale and anxious to a degree; and though she refrained from saying so, she shook her head, telling herself that this excess of anxiety was due to something more than the absence of a father and uncle, especially as the resident was not a fighting man.

She sat with them for long at a time, trying to comfort them, as she saw their agitation, and then grew as anxious herself, especially when the tide of the little war swept their way, and she heard the volleys bred from the boat, as the two prahus came down the stream.

At last, just as a couple of Malay fishermen had been engaged to help pilot the steamer up the river, where Captain Horton had determined to go in quest of the missing expedition, the sentry at the point of the island challenged, and the ship's boats were seen coming round a point, the sun gleaming brightly on the barrels of the rifles, while the white jackets and frocks of the soldiers and sailors gave life to a scene that was one series of gloriously tinted greens.

Glasses were brought to bear, and it was evident that it was no dejected beaten party returning, for no sooner did they see that they were observed than the men began cheering, their shouts bringing the Malays flocking down to the river side, where several chiefs were seen embarking in a naga, or dragon-boat, eager, though looking very stolid, to hear the news.

It was on the whole good, for on the party landing it was to announce that they had, after a sharp fight, captured the stockade, driving the Malays, who were headed by the Rajah Gantang himself, to take refuge in another stockade, in a ravine some three miles inland, and then the river fort was set on fire.

The officer who had attacked the second prahu had met with similar ill-success to Lieutenant Johnson, and upon relating the incidents of the fight, found but little sympathy from the late occupants of the other boat, who were rather rejoiced to find they had not been excelled.

The escape of the second prahu was followed by a short council; and several Malays being found ready enough to act as guides to the stockade to which the rajah and his men had fled, it was decided to follow him up, and read him a second severe lesson.

It was a risky proceeding, for the guides might prove treacherous and lead them into an ambush; but after giving them notice that they would receive no mercy if they proved false, a small portion of the little force was left in charge of the boats, and, lightly equipped, the men went off in search of the second stronghold.

It proved to be an arduous task, for the way was through one of the jungle-paths, with walls of dense vegetation right and left, of the most impenetrable nature. Every here and there, too, the enemy had cut down a tree, so that it fell with the branches towards the pursuers, who were compelled to force a way through the dense mass that choked the narrow path.

But these impediments were laughed at by the Jacks, who hacked and hewed, and soon made a passage, through which, in the darkness of the forest, the little force crept on till they halted, panting, for the Malay guides to go on first, and act the part of scouts.

"Perhaps to give warning of our coming," said Captain Smithers.

"No," said Tom Long, "I don't think that. I should say that they have had spies out all along the path, and that they know our position to an inch."

"You are right, Long," said Captain Smithers, as, one after the other, several reports rang out. "They are firing on our friendly Malays."

So it proved, for the men came running back to say that they had been fired upon as soon as they neared the stockade; and now, as there was no chance of a surprise, the men were divided, and, each party under its leader, started off to try and flank the place.

This was something new to the Malays, who looked upon it as unfair fighting, and the result was, that after five minutes' sharp, hand-to-hand engagement, the rajah and his men once more took to the woods, and the second stockade was burned.

This was so satisfactory a termination, that it seemed to make up for the loss of the two prahus. These, however, Captain Horton said the ship's boats would soon hunt out; and the Malay chiefs went back to the sultan, to announce to him the defeat of his old enemy; while at the island every one was occupied about the hospital and the wounded men, who, poor fellows, were carefully lifted ashore, the doctor saying that the sailors would be far better on the island, in a tent beneath the shady trees, than on shipboard.

"Ten wounded, major," he said sharply, "and not a man dangerously. I'll soon set them right. Steady there, my boys; lift them carefully."

A goodly group had assembled by the landing-place when the men were brought ashore, the ladies being ready with fruit and cool drink for the poor fellows; and Bob Roberts, who had come to the landing-place with Captain Horton in the gig, felt quite envious.

An hour or two's sleep had set him right, and he felt none the worse for his adventure; but there was Tom Long being lifted carefully ashore by two of the sailors, and Rachel Linton and Mary Sinclair eagerly waiting on the youth, for he had received a real wound this time, and looked most interestingly pale.

"Just like my luck," grumbled Bob. "He gets comfortably wounded, and they will be taking him fruit and flowers every day. I shouldn't wonder if they had him carried up to the residency, so that he would be handy, and—hang me if it ain't too bad. Oh! 'pon my word, I can't stand this; they are having him carried up to the house. Just my luck. I get a contemptible ducking, and no one wants to wait upon me."

Bob ground his teeth and looked on, while Tom Long was sympathised with and talked to on his way up to the residency, where, after swallowing his wrath, as the middy expressed it, he got leave to go up and see his friend.

"My friend!" he said, half aloud, as he walked on through the brilliant sunshine. "Lor', how I do hate that fellow! I wish I had had the kris. I'd have given the Malay such a oner as he wouldn't have forgotten in a hurry. Poor old Tommy, though I I hope he isn't hurt much. How do you do, Miss Linton?" he said stiffly, as he encountered Rachel Linton in the verandah.

"Quite well, I thank you, Mr Roberts," said Rachel, imitating his pompous stiffness, and curtseying profoundly; "how do you do?"

"Oh! I say; don't, Miss Linton. What a jolly shame it is," he cried, throwing off all form. "You always laugh and poke fun at me."

"Not I, Mr Roberts," she replied. "When you are stiff and formal, I shape my conduct to suit yours; when you come as the nice, frank, manly boy that we are always so glad to see, I am sure I never laugh at you then."

"Boy? Yes, of course, you always treat me like a boy," said Bob, dolefully. "Is a fellow never going to be a man?"

"Far too soon, I should think," said Miss Linton, holding out her hand.

"Oh! I'm only a boy," said Bob, stuffing his hands in his pockets, and looking so sadly injured, and in so comical a way, that Miss Linton could hardly refrain from laughing.

"Such a boy as I'm sure we are all very proud of," said Miss Linton. "We have heard from my father and Lieutenant Johnson how bravely you behaved last night."

"Gammon!" said Bob, blushing scarlet. "I only behaved like a boy. How is the wounded man you have had brought up here—Mr Ensign Long?"

"Poor boy!" said Rachel Linton quietly; "he has a nasty wound."

"Say that again, Miss Linton," cried Bob excitedly; "it does me good."

"He has a nasty wound. Are you so pleased, then, that your friend is badly hurt?" said Miss Linton gravely.

"No, no; of course not. I mean the other," cried Bob.

"Why, what did I say?"

"You said 'Poor boy!'" exclaimed the middy.

"Of course I did," said Miss Linton, raising her eyebrows.

"Say it again, please," said Bob.

"Poor boy! I am very sorry for him."

"That does me a deal of good," cried Bob excitedly. "You know I can't stand it, Miss Linton, for you to think of him as a man and of me as only a boy."

"Why, you silly, foolish boy!" she said, laying her hand upon his shoulder, and gazing full in his face, "of course I think of you both as what you are—a pair of very brave lads, who will some day grow to be officers of whom England will be very proud."

"If—if I'm not a man now," said Bob, in a low, husky voice, "I shall never grow to be one."

"Not grow to be a man? Why, what do you mean?" said Miss Linton.

"I don't know," faltered Bob, "only that it's precious miserable, and—and I wish one of the jolly old Malays would stick his old kris right through my heart, for there don't seem anything worth living for when one can't have what one wants."

Rachel Linton gazed at him half sad and half amused.

"Do you wish me to think of you, Robert Roberts, with respect and esteem?"

"I'd give all the world to be one of your dogs, Miss Linton, or your bird."

"Do you mean to be a goose?" said Miss Linton, laughing. "There, I did not mean to hurt your feelings," she added frankly; "but come, now, give up all this silly nonsense, and try to remember that you are after all but a boy, whom I want to look upon as a very dear friend."

"Do you really?" said Bob.

"I do, really," said Miss Linton, holding out her hand; "a friend whom I can believe in and trust, out in this dangerous place, and one who will not make my life wretched by being silly, romantic, and sentimental."

Bob gripped the hand extended to him, and held it for a few moments.

"There," he said firmly, as he seemed to shake himself together, "I see it now. It's all right, Miss Linton; and it's better to be a brick of a boy than a weak, puling noodle of a man, isn't it?"

"Indeed it is," cried Miss Linton, laughing merrily.

"There, I'm your man—I mean I'm your boy," cried Bob; "and I'll let you see that I'm a very different fellow to what you think. Now I want to go and see poor old Tom Long. I am sorry he's hurt."

"You are now more like the Bob Roberts, midshipman," said Miss Linton, "whom I saw first some months ago, than I have seen for a long time."

"All right," said Bob; "now let's go and see the other poor boy."

"Come along, then," she said, smiling; "but I'm afraid that Tom Long will not be so easy to convince that he has not yet arrived at years of discretion."

As she spoke Miss Linton softly opened the door unseen, and let Bob Roberts enter a cool and airy well-shaded room, closing the door upon him, and herself gliding away.

Chapter Twelve
A Discussion upon Wounds

"Avast there! what cheer, my hearty? Heave ahead, my military swab. How goes it!" cried Bob, as Tom raised himself a little on his couch, evidently very glad to see his old companion.

"Oh, not quite killed," he said. "Gently; don't shake a fellow to pieces."

"Where's the wound?" cried Bob. "Ain't going to send in the number of your mess, are you?"

"No, I'm not," cried Tom Long, flushing up; "and if I ever do come across the chief fellow who gave me such a nasty dig, he'll remember it to the end of his days."

"What was it—a spear or a kris?" said Bob.

"Kris, right through my left shoulder. Doctor Bolter says if it had been four inches lower it would have been fatal."

"Bother!" cried Bob. "If it had been four inches higher it would have missed you altogether."

"Yes, of course," said Tom; "but it's precious unpleasant to have a fellow stick his skewer right through you."

"Well, I don't know," said Bob, who had made up his mind that the proper thing was to try and cheer the ensign, and not to let him think he was very bad. "I think I'd just as soon have it right through as only half-way."

"Oh, it's nothing to laugh at, I can tell you," said Tom Long, "I don't see why you mightn't just as well have had it as me. You always get off all right."

"I didn't last night, or rather this morning," said Bob. "I was right into the prahu we tried to take—first man, sir—I mean boy, sir; and I was sawing away at a mat with my knife, when all came down by the run, and I was pitched into the river."

"And picked out," said the ensign impatiently.

"Yes, but not before I'd been swimming for a quarter of an hour—good measure. Oh, I say, Tom, didn't I think of the crocodiles!"

"You're such a cheeky little beggar, I wonder they didn't get you," said Tom, who looked feverish and excited. "I say, Bob Roberts, you know what that chap, that Kling fellow, said to us about the krises."

"Yes, of course. What then?"

"Do you think they are poisoned?"

"No, not a bit. Do you?"

"Yes," said the young ensign; "and I am sure this one was, for I can feel the wound throbbing and stabbing, and a curious sensation running to my finger ends."

"Well, so one did when one had a bad cut," said Bob sharply. "Bah! poisoned! it's all rubbish. Why, if you had been poisoned you'd have been sleepy and stupid."

"I feel so now."

"What—stupid?" said Bob, grinning. "Well that's natural: you always were?"

"I can't get up and cane you, Bob Roberts," said the ensign, slowly.

"Of course you can't, old man. But there, don't you worry; that kris wasn't poisoned, or you'd feel very different to what you do now."

"Think so?"

"Sure of it."

"How do you know?" said Tom Long, peevishly. "You were never wounded by a poisoned weapon."

"No, but I've seen somebody else, and watched him."

"What was he wounded with?"

"Serpent's tooth," said Bob; "Private Gray."

"Why, that's a different thing altogether," said Long.

"No it isn't, Mr Clevershakes. The snake's poison goes into the blood, don't it, same as that of a kris, and the symptoms would be just the same."

Tom Long seemed to think there was something in this, and he lay thinking for a minute.

"How did Gray look?" he said. "I don't remember."

"Just the same as you don't look," said Bob, sharply; "so don't be a stupid and frighten yourself worse. Malay krises are not poisoned, and it's all a cock-and-bull story."

"What is?" said Doctor Bolter, entering the room.

"About krises being poisoned, doctor."

Doctor Bolter felt his patient's pulse.

"Have you been putting him up to thinking his wound was poisoned?" he said, angrily.

"No, doctor," said Tom Long, quietly; "it was my idea, and I feel sure it is."

"Tom Long," said Doctor Bolter, "you're only a boy, and if you weren't so ill, I'd box your ears. You've been frightening yourself into a belief that you are poisoned, and here's your pulse up, the dickens knows how high. Now look here, sir, what's the use of your placing yourself in the hands of a surgeon, and then pretending to know better yourself?"

"I don't pretend, doctor."

"Yes, you do, sir. You set up a theory of your own that your blood is poisoned, in opposition to mine that it is not."

"But are you sure it is not, doctor?"

"Am I sure? Why, by this time if that kris had been poisoned you would have had lock-jaw."

"And Locke on the Understanding," put in Bob.

"Yes," laughed the doctor; "and been locked up altogether. There, there, my dear boy, keep yourself quiet, and trust me to bring you round. You, Bob Roberts, don't let him talk, and don't talk much yourself. You'd better go to sleep, Long."

"Wound pains me too much, doctor. It throbs so. Isn't that a sign of poison?"

"I'll go and mix you up a dose of poison that shall send you to sleep for twelve hours, my fine fellow, if you don't stop all that nonsense. Your wound is not poisoned, neither is that of any other man who came back from the expedition; and if it's any satisfaction to you to know it, you've got the ugliest dig of any man—I mean boy—amongst the wounded."

The doctor arranged the matting-screen so as to admit more air, and bustled towards the door—but stopped short on hearing a buzzing sound at the open window, went back on tiptoe, and cleverly captured a large insect.

"A splendid longicorn," he said, fishing a pill-box from his pocket, and carefully imprisoning his captive. "Ah, my dear boys, what a pity it is that you do not take to collecting while you are young! What much better men you would make!"

"There," said Bob, as soon as they were alone, "how do you feel about your poison now?"

"He says it is not, just to cheer me up," said Tom Long, dolefully. "I say, Bob Roberts, if I die—"

"If you what?" cried Bob, in a tone of disgust.

"I say, if I die."

"Oh, ah, of course. Now then, let's have it. Do you want me to write a verse for your tombstone?"

"They'd pitch me overboard," said Long, dolefully.

"Not they," said Bob. "This promising young officer, who had taken it into his head that he had been wounded by a poisoned kris, was buried under a palm tree, to the great relief of all who knew him, for they found him the most conceited—"

"Bob Roberts!"

"Consequential—"

"I tell you what it is—"

"Cocky—"

"I never heard—"

"Unpleasant fellow that ever wore Her Majesty's uniform."

"Just wait till I get well, Master Bob Roberts," said Tom Long, excitedly, "and if I don't make you pay for all this, my name's not what it is."

"Thought you had made up your mind to die," said Bob, laughing. "There, it won't do, young man; so now go to sleep. I've got another half-hour, and I'll sit here and keep the flies from visiting your noble corpus too roughly; and when you wake up, if you find I am not here it is because I am gone. D'ye hear?"

"Yes," said Tom Long, drowsily; and in five minutes he was fast asleep, seeing which Bob sat till the last minute, and then went out on tiptoe to run and learn whether the boat was waiting by the landing-stage.

Chapter Thirteen
An Unpleasant Interruption

The feeling of satisfaction was very general at the lesson given the rajah; and though his two prahus had escaped, his power had received a most severe blow.

Sultan Hamet was sincere enough in his demonstrations of pleasure, sending presents five or six times a day to the resident, the various officers, and, above all, fruit for the wounded men.

The presents were but of little value, but they showed the Malay's gratitude, and the officers were very pleased with what they looked upon as curiosities. Even Bob Roberts and Tom Long were not forgotten, each receiving an ivory-mounted kris, the young chief Ali being the bearer.

The resident, however, felt that the sultan was not meeting him in quite a proper spirit, and he was rather suspicious, till a fresh embassy of the principal chiefs arrived, and brought a formal invitation for the resident and the officers to visit him upon a fixed day.

As before, an imposing force was got ready, and once more the march to what Bob had nick-named Palm Tree Palace, took place, the middy coming afterwards to Tom Long's room, and telling him how the affair had gone off.

"It was no end of a game," he said to the young ensign, who was rapidly gaining strength, the fancy that his wound was poisoned having passed away. "We started just as we did last time, and marched through the jungle till we came to the sultan's barns, where the men were drawn up, and no end of the niggers came to wait on them, bringing them a kind of drink made of rice, and plenty of fruit and things, while we officers had to go into the sultan's dining-room—a place hung round with cotton print—and there we all sat down, cross-legged, like a lot of jolly tailors, with the sultan up at the top, the major on one side, and our skipper on the other."

"But they didn't sit down cross-legged?" said Tom Long.

"Didn't they, my boy? But they just did; and it was a game to see our skipper letting himself down gently for fear of cracking his best white uniform sit-in-ems. Your major split some stitches somewhere, for I heard them go. Then there was the doctor; you should have seen him! He came to an anchor right enough, but when he tried to square his yards—I mean his legs—he nearly went over backwards, and looked savage enough to eat me, because I laughed."

"Poor old doctor!" said Tom Long, smiling.

"Oh, we were all in difficulties, being cast upon our beam-ends as it were; but we got settled down in our berths at last, and then the dinner began."

"Was it good?" said Tom Long, whose appetite was growing as he began to get better.

"Jolly!" said Bob, "capital! I say, though, how hot this place is."

"Yes," said the ensign, "the lamp makes it hot; but the window is wide open."

Bob glanced out into the darkness, to see the dark gleaming leaves, and the bright fire-flies dancing in the air, while right before them lay the smooth river, reflecting the brilliant stars.

"There was no cloth; but it was no end of fun. Mr Sultan is going in for English manners and customs, and he mixes them up with his own most gloriously. By way of ornaments there was a common black japanned cruet-stand, with some trumpery bottles. There was one of those brown earthenware teapots, and an old willow-pattern soup tureen, without cover or stand, but full of flowers. Besides which, there were knives and forks, and spoons, regular cheap Sheffield kitchen ones, and as rusty as an old ring-bolt."

"Indeed!" said Tom Long.

"I looked at our officers, and they had hard work to keep solemn; and I half expected to see a pound of sausages, and some potatoes in their skins, for the banquet. But wait a bit; those were the English things brought out in compliment to us. Mr Sultan had plenty of things of his own, some of silver, some of gold. He had some beautiful china too; and the feed itself—tlat!" said Bob, smacking his lips. "I wish you had been there."

"I wish I had," sighed Tom Long. "Getting well's worse than being wounded."

"Never mind; you'll soon be all right," continued Bob. "Well, we had some good fish, nicely cooked, and some stunning curry; the best I ever ate; and we had sambals, as they call 'em, with it."

"What the dickens are sambals?" said Tom Long.

"Well, it's either pickles or curry, whichever you like to call it," continued Bob. "These sambals are so many little saucers on a silver tray, and they are to eat with your curry. One had smashed up cocoa-nut in milk; another chillies; another dried shrimps, chutney, green ginger, no end of things of that kind—and jolly good they were! Then we had rice in all sorts of shapes, and some toddy and rice wine, and some sweets of sago, and cocoa-nut and sugar."

"But you didn't eat all those things?" said Tom Long, peevishly.

"Didn't I, my boy? but I just did. I thought once that the sultan might be going to poison us all; and, as they say there's safety in a big dose, and death in a small, I went in for a regular big go. But I say, the fruits! they were tip-top: mangosteens and guavas, and mangoes, and cocoa-nuts, and durians, and some of the best bananas I ever ate in my life."

"You didn't try one of those filthy durians again?"

"Bless 'em, that I did; and I mean to try 'em again and again, as long as a heart beats in the bosom of yours very faithfully, Bob Roberts. They're glorious!"

"Bah!"

"That's right," said Bob. "You say 'Bah!' and I'll eat the durians. But I didn't tell you about the drinks. We had coffee, and pipes, and cigars, and said pretty things to each other; and then the sultan told Mr Linton he was going to bring out some choice English nectar in our honour."

"And did he?"

"He just did, my boy. A nigger came round with a little silver tray, covered with tiny gold cups in which was something thick and red."

"Liqueur, I suppose," said Tom Long, uneasily.

"Wait a wee, dear boy," said Bob. "Here's the pyson at last, I says to myself; and when my turn came, I did as the others did, bowed to the sultan, feeling just like a tombola, and nearly going over; then I drank—and what do you think it was?"

"I don't know; go on."

"Raspberry vinegar, and—ah!"

Tom Long started back, looking deadly white in the feeble light of the lamp; for, as Bob ejaculated loudly, a Malay spear whizzed past his ear, and stuck in the wooden partition behind him, having evidently been thrown through the window by some lurking foe.

Chapter Fourteen
How Bob Roberts made a Firm Friend

Bob Roberts seized his sword and dashed to the window, leaping boldly out, and shouting for help; and as he did so he heard the bushes rapidly parted, the crackling of twigs on ahead, and then, as he neared the river in pursuit of the assailant, there was a loud splash, followed by the challenge of a sentry and the report of his piece.

A brisk time of excitement followed, during which a thorough search was made, but no one was found; and it was evident that the spear had been thrown by an enemy who had come alone; but the incident was sufficient to create a general feeling of uneasiness at the residency. The sentries were doubled, and orders were given that the place should be carefully patrolled; for though the English were upon an island, the Malays were such expert swimmers that they could start up stream and let themselves float down to the head of the island and land.

It was some few days before Bob Roberts was able to pay another visit to the residency, for he had been out twice with the steamer's boats, in search of the two escaped Malay prahus, each time on insufficient information; and after a weary pull through a winding mangrove creek, had come back without seeing them.

Meantime the relations with the Malays were daily growing in friendliness. A brisk trade with the shore was carried on, and sampans from far up the river came laden with fruit, fish, and rice; some brought poultry, and green sugar-cane for eating; others cocoa-nuts, and quaint articles for barter. But somehow there was an uneasy feeling on the island, that though the sultan and his people were friendly, some of the rajahs detested the English, as being likely to put a stop to their piratical practices, the destruction of Rajah Gantang's stockade, while it gave plenty of satisfaction in some parts, being looked upon with disfavour in others.

"Pretty well all right again, old man?" said Bob, sauntering in one day, to find the ensign reading.

"Yes, I'm stronger by a good deal than I was," said Tom Long, holding out his hand.

"No more limbings pitched in at the window, eh?"

"No," said Tom Long with a slight shudder; "I hope that sort of thing is not going to happen again."

"To which I say ditto," said Bob. "But I say, I know who pitched that spear at you."

"You do?"

"Yes, it was that Malay chap you offended with the durian."

"Then he must be taken and punished."

"First catch your brown hare, master officer of infantry," said Bob, smiling. "He won't set foot here again, depend upon it, unless he slinks in at night. By George, what a malicious lot they must be, to act like that!"

"Yes, it's not pleasant," said Tom Long, with an involuntary shudder, as, in imagination, he saw the dark face of his enemy always on the watch for an opportunity to assassinate him.

"I never finished my account of the trip to the sultan's," said Bob, at last.

"Was there anything more to tell?"

"Yes, one thing," replied Bob; "the best of the whole lot."

"What was it?"

"Don't get riled if I tell you."

"Pooh! how can it rile me?"

"Oh, I don't know; only it may. It was a proposal made by the sultan to Mr Linton." ￢

"Proposal! What proposal?"

"Well, I'll tell you; only don't go into fits. It was after we'd been sitting smoking for a bit, and just before we were coming away. Master Sultan had shown us all his best things—his gold and silver, and his slaves, and the dingy beauties with great earrings, and bangles on their arms and legs, who have the honour of being his wives; and at last he said something to Mr Linton, who understands his lingo as well as you and I do French."

"Well, but what did he propose?" said Long, eagerly.

"I got to know afterwards from Captain Smithers," continued Bob, "that he said he had been thinking very seriously about his position in connexion with the English, and that he saw how a strong alliance would be best for all; that it would settle him in his government, and make it a very excellent match for the English, who would be able to get tin and rice from the sultan's people, and gold."

"You're as prosy as an old woman," said Tom Long, impatiently.

"Yes, it's an accomplishment of mine," said Bob coolly. "Well, as I was telling you, he said the proper thing was a very strong alliance; and the resident said we had already made one. He said he wanted a stronger one; and he thought the best thing would be for him to marry Miss Linton and her cousin, and then it would be all right."

"Why, confound his insolence!" said Tom Long, starting up.

"No, no, you must say something else," cried Bob. "I said that as soon as I heard it."

"Did not Mr Linton knock him down?" cried Tom Long.

"No, he did not. He heard him out, and said it must be a matter of consideration; and then we came away."

"But it's monstrous!" cried Tom Long.

"Of course it is," said Bob, coolly; "but don't you see it was of no use to break with the fellow at once. It was a case of diplomacy. We don't want to quarrel with Master Sultan Hamet: we want to keep friends."

"But it was such an insult to the ladies!"

"He looked as if he thought he was doing them an honour, Master Long, so it wouldn't have done to fall out with him. There, don't look so fierce, we've got a difficult game to play here, and our great point is not to quarrel with the Malays, unless we want spears thrown in at every dark window while we stay."

Tom Long sat biting his nails, for Bob had touched him in a very tender part, and he knew it. In fact, the middy rather enjoyed his companion's vexation, for he had begun, since his memorable conversation with Miss Linton, to look upon his feelings towards her with a more matter-of-fact eye.

"I shall have to get about at once," said Tom Long, speaking as if his weight in the scale would completely make Sultan Hamet kick the beam; but upon seeing the mirthful look in Bob Roberts' eye, he changed the subject, and began talking about how he longed to be out and about again.

"I thought we should get no end of fishing and shooting out here," he said, "and we've had none as yet."

"Get well, then, and we'll have a try for some," Rob suggested. "There must be plenty;" and with the understanding that the ensign was to declare himself fit to be off the doctor's hands as soon as possible, Bob Roberts returned to the steamer, and then finding it terribly close, he did what he had acquired a habit of doing when the weather was very hot, found a snug shady place on deck, and went off to sleep.

That was very easy in those latitudes. Whether the sun shone or whether it was gloomy, black, and precursive of a thunder-storm, an European had only to sit down in a rocking chair, or swing in a hammock, and he went off into a delicious slumber almost on the instant.

So far so good; the difficulty was to keep asleep; and so Bob Roberts found.

He had settled himself in a low basket-work chair, beneath a stout piece of awning which shed a mellow twilight upon the deck, and loosening his collar, he had dropped off at once; but hardly was he asleep before "burr-urr-urr boom-oom-oom, boozz-oozz-oozz" came a great fly, banging itself against the awning, sailing round and round, now up, now down, as if Bob's head were the centre of its attraction, and he could not get farther away. Now it seemed to have made up its mind to beat itself to pieces against the canvas, and now to try how near it could go to the midshipman's nose without touching, and keeping up all the time such an aggravating, irritating buzz that it woke Bob directly.

There was plenty of room for the ridiculous insect to have flown right out from beneath the awning and over the flashing river to the jungle; but no, that did not seem to suit its ideas, and it kept on with its monotonous buzz, round and round, and round and round.

Half awake, half asleep, Bob fidgeted a little, changed his position, and with his eyes shut hit out sharply at his tormentor, but of course without effect.

He turned over, turned back; laid his head on one side; then on the other; and at last, as the miserable buzzing noise continued, he jumped up in a rage, picked up a book for a weapon, and followed the fly about, trying to get a fair blow—but all in vain. He hit at it flying, settled on the canvas roof; on the arms of chairs, and on the deck, and twice upon a rope—but all in vain: the wretched insect kept up its irritating buzz, till, hot, panting, his brows throbbing with the exertion, Bob made a furious dash at it, and with one tremendous blow crushed it flat.

The middy drew a long breath, wiped the perspiration from his forehead, and, panting and weary, threw himself back in the chair, and closed his eyes.

He was a clever sleeper, Bob Roberts. Like the Irishman who went to sleep for two or three days, when Bob went to sleep, he "paid attintion to it." In a few seconds then he was fast, and — truth must be told — with his mouth open, and a very unpleasant noise arising therefrom.

Vain hope of rest. Even as he threw himself back, a little many-legged creature, about two inches long, was industriously making its way over the deck towards where one of the middy's limbs lay outstretched, and in a few seconds it had mounted his shoe, examined it with a pair of long thin antenna, and then given the leather a pinch with a pair of hooked claws at its tail.

Apparently dissatisfied, the long thin yellow insect ran on to the sleeper's sock, carefully examined its texture, tasted it with its tail, and still not satisfied, proceeded to walk up one of the very wide open duck trouser legs, that must have been to it like the entrance to some grand tunnel, temptingly inviting investigation.

The insect disappeared; Bob snored, and there was the loud buzzing murmur of men's voices, talking drowsily together, when, as if suddenly electrified, Bob leaped up with a sharp cry, slapped his leg vigorously, and stood shaking his trousers till the long thin insect tumbled on to the white deck, and was duly crushed.

"Scissors! how it stings!" cried Bob, rubbing the place. "O Lor'! what a place this is to be sure. Who the dickens can get a nod?"

Bob Roberts was determined upon having one evidently, for having given the obnoxious remains another stamp, he took a look round, to see if any other pest, winged or legged, had been brought from the shore, and seeing nothing, he again settled himself down, gave a turn or two and a twist to get himself comfortable, ending by sitting with his legs stretched straight out, his head thrown back, and his nose pointed straight up at the awning.

This time Bob went off fast asleep; his cap fell on to the deck, but it did not disturb him; and he was evidently making up for lost time, when a very industrious spider, who had made his home in the awning, came boldly out of a fold by a seam of the canvas, and with busy legs proceeded to examine the state and tension of some threads, which it had previously stretched as the basis of a web upon a geometrical plan, expressly to catch mosquitoes.

Apparently satisfied, the spider set to work busily, its dark, heavy body showing plainly against the yellowish canvas; and in a very short time a main rope was attached to the roof, and the architect of fly-nets began slowly to descend in search of a point to which the other end of the said main-stay could be attacked.

Now fate had so arranged it, that the point exactly beneath the spider as it slowly descended was the tip of Bob Roberts' nose, and to this point in the course of a minute the insect nearly arrived.

It may be thought that its next act would be to alight and fix its rope; but this was not so easy, for the soft zephyr-like breaths the middy exhaled drove the swinging architect to and fro. Now it came near, now it was driven away; but at last it got near enough to grasp at the sleeper's most prominent feature, just brushing it with its legs, and setting up an irritating tickling that made Bob snort and scratch his face.

The spider swung to and fro for some seconds, and then there was another terrible tickle, to which Bob responded by fiercely rubbing the offending organ.

The spider was driven to a distance by this; but it was back again directly, with its legs stretched out, tickling as before.

Bob was not asleep, and he was not awake, and he could neither sink into oblivion, nor thoroughly rouse himself. All he could do was to bestow an irritable scratch at his nose, and the spider came back again.

At last, spider or no spider, he dropped into a strange dreamy state, in which he believed that Tom Long came and loomed over him on purpose to bend down and tickle him, out of spite and jealousy, with the long thin feather from a paroquet's tail.

"Don't! Bother!" said Bob, in his sleep; but the tickling went on, and he felt ready to leap up and strike his tormentor; but he seemed to be held down by some strange power which kept him from moving, and the tickling still went on.

Then he could hear voices talking, and people seemed to be about, laughing at and enjoying the trick that was being played upon him; and then he started into wakefulness, for a voice exclaimed, —

"Come, Mr Roberts, are you going to wake up?"

It was Lieutenant Johnson who spoke; and on the middy jumping up, he found standing by him, with the lieutenant, the dark-faced youth who had met them and acted as guide on the occasion when they made their first visit to the sultan's home.

He was dressed similarly to the way in which he made his first appearance before the English party; that is to say, he wore the silken jacket and sarong of the Malay chiefs, with a natty little embroidered cap, set jauntily upon his head like that of a cavalry soldier; but in addition he wore the trousers, white shirt-front, and patent leather boots of an Englishman, and the middy saw that he had a gold albert chain and straw-coloured kid gloves.

"This gentleman is the son of the Tumongong of Parang, Mr Roberts," said the lieutenant, "and he has come on board to see the ship. Take him round and show him everything, especially the armoury, and let him understand the power of the guns. Captain Horton wishes it."

The lieutenant looked meaningly at the middy, who saluted, and then nodded his head in a way that showed he comprehended his task.

"The skipper wants these people to know that it is of no good to try and tackle us," thought Bob. "Yes, sir," he said aloud, "I'll take him round;" and then the lieutenant, who had been interrupted in a nap, saluted the young chief; who salaamed to him gravely, and the two young men were left alone, gazing straight at one another, each apparently trying to read the other's thoughts.

"This is a jolly nice sort of a game," said Bob to himself! "How am I to make him understand? What a jolly fool old Johnson is. Now, my sun-brown-o cockywax, comment vous portez-vous? as we say in French. Me no understandy curse Malay's lingo not at all-oh. Bismillah! wallah! Come oh! and have a bottle oh! of Bass's ale oh!"

"With much pleasure," said the young Malay, laughing. "I am thirsty."

Bob Roberts turned as red as a turkey-cock with vexation.

"What! Can you understand English?" he stammered.

"Rather!" was the reply. "I couldn't make out all you said—not quite," he added, laughing meaningly.

"Oh! I say, I am sorry," said Bob frankly. "I didn't know you could understand a word."

"It's all right," said the young Malay, showing his white teeth, and speaking fair idiomatic English, though with a peculiar accent. "I've been a great deal at Penang and Singapore. I like English ways."

"I say, you know," cried Bob, holding out his hand, "it was only my fun. I wouldn't have chaffed you like that for a moment if I had thought you could understand."

"No, I suppose not," said the young Malay. "Never mind, I wanted to see you. That's why I came. Where's the young soldier?"

"What Tom—I mean Ensign Long?"

"Yes, En-sign Long."

"Knocked up. Ill with his wound. He got hurt up the river."

"I did not know it was he," said the young Malay. "Poor fellow!"

"He was in an awful state," said Bob. "Got a kris through his shoulder, and thought it was poisoned."

"What, the kris? Oh, no. That is nonsense. Our people don't poison their krises and limbings. The Sakais poison their arrows."

"The whiches?" said Bob.

"The Sakais—the wild people of the hills and jungle. Naked—wear no clothes."

"Yes," said Bob drily. "I knew naked meant wearing no clothes. So you Malay folks are not savages, but have got savages somewhere near."

"Savages? wild people," said the young man, with a little flush appearing through his tawny skin. "The Malay chiefs are gentlemen. We only are simple in our ways and living."

"Oh! that's it, is it?" said Bob. "Well, come and have this drop of Bass. I can't stand fizz."

"Fizz?" said the visitor; "what is fizz?"

"Champagne."

"Oh, yes! I know; frothing, bubbling wine, with a pop cork."

"Yes, that's it," said Bob, grinning, "with a pop cork;" and leading the way below, he got a bottle of Bass and a couple of glasses, which they sat down and discussed.

"Have a cigar?" said the young Malay, producing a handsome French-made case.

"Thanky," said Bob. "What are these? Manillas?"

"No; from Deli, in Sumatra," said his visitor. And then they lit-up by the open window of the gun-room, and sat and smoked for a few minutes in silence, each watching the other.

"I say," said Bob at last, "this is jolly rum, you know. Why you are quite an Englishman, young fellow."

"I like English ways," said the young chief, flushing; "some of them. If I were sultan, I'd take to all the best English customs, and make them take the place of all our bad ones. Then we should be great."

"Yes," said Bob; "I suppose so."

"Ah," said the young man, sadly, "you laugh. But I could improve our people."

"Yes, of course," said Bob, hastily. "Now come and see round the ship."

"No, no, let us sit and talk," said the young Malay. "I have seen plenty of ships. I know all about them."

"Just as you like," said Bob. "Then let's go and sit on deck, under the awning. It's awfully hot here."

"You think it hot?"

"Yes; don't you?" said Bob.

"No, not at all," said the young Malay, smiling; and rising he followed the middy on deck.

"That's better," said Bob; "sit down in that cane chair. I say, what's your name?"

"Ah; what is yours?"

"Robert Roberts; commonly known to my intimates as Bob."

"Intimates? what are intimates?"

"Best friends," said Bob.

"Yes, I understand. May I be an intimate?"

"To be sure you may," said Bob, holding out his hand, which the other eagerly grasped. "But no larks, you know."

"Larks! what is larks?" said Ali, eagerly.

"I mean, no sticking that kris of yours into a fellow on the sly."

"Nonsense! What bosh!" cried the young Malay.

"Bosh, eh?" said Bob, laughing. "I say, Master Ali, you are civilised, and no mistake. It is only our very educated people who say *Bosh*!"

"You took the word from us," said the young Malay. "Bosh is good eastern language, and means *nothing*."

"I've heard it was Turkish," said Bob, drily.

"Well, Turkish; the language of Roum. We look upon the Sultan of Roum and Stamboul as our greatest chief."

"Oh, I say," cried Bob; "I can't stand this, you know. I thought you were a young Malay chief, and you are talking like a professor. Look here, Ali, is there any good fishing here?"

"Yes, oh yes. I'll take you in my boat, and my men shall catch plenty."

"No, no," said Bob. "You take me in the boat, and I'll catch the fish. But is there any shooting?"

"Shooting!" said the young Malay, laughing; "everything; bird that flies, bird that swims, tigers, buffalo, deer."

"Where?" cried Bob, excitedly.

"In the great forest—the jungle. Will you come?"

"Will I come?" cried Bob. "Won't I! I say," he went on, excitedly, "you can't shoot, can you?"

"I practise sometimes," said the young Malay, quietly.

"What with? A blow-pipe?"

"Yes, I can use the sumpitan," said the young Malay, nodding; "but I use a revolver or a rifle."

"I believe I'm half asleep," muttered Bob. "Haven't got a gun, have you?"

"Yes; an English gentleman changed with me. I gave him ivory and gold, and he gave me his double gun."

"Not a breechloader?" said Bob.

"Yes, a breechloader—a Purdey he called it, and a bag of cartridges."

"Oh, I say," cried Bob; "this is rich, you know. I am sorry I was such an idiot with you at first. But do you mean it? If I get a day ashore, will you take me where there's some good shooting?"

"Oh, yes, plenty;" was the reply.

Bob Roberts was thoughtful for a few moments.

"I say," he said at last, "I wish Tom Long were here."

"En-sign Long?" said Ali.

"Yes. He's a very cocky fellow, you know; but he's a good one at bottom."

"Should I like him?"

"Yes, when you got to know him; but he only shows some fellows his clothes."

"I don't want to see his clothes," said Ali, smiling.

"I mean, some people never get to know what's inside him," said Bob.

"What is 'inside him'?" said Ali, whom these mysteries of the English tongue somewhat puzzled. "Do you mean what he has had to eat?"

"No, no;" said Bob, laughing. "I mean his heart."

"Show people his heart?" said Ali, thoughtfully. "Oh yes, I see; I understand. You mean he is cold outside, and proud, and does not show people what he really thinks—like a Malay?"

"Yes, that's what I mean," said Bob, smiling. "But that's like a Malay, is it? They say one thing, and mean another, do they?"

"Yes," said Ali, gravely—"to their enemies—to the people who try to cheat, and deceive them. To their real friends they are very true, and full of faith. But it is time now that I should go."

"I say, though, stop a minute," said Bob sharply. "Are your people really good friends to us?"

"Yes," said the visitor, "I hope so. I believe so. They are strange at first, and do not like English ways, like I. Afterwards they will do the same as I do. Good-bye."

"But about our shooting?" said Bob. "May I bring Tom Long?"

"I should like to know En-sign Long. He is very brave, is he not?"

"Pretty bobbish, I believe," said the middy.

"Is he bobbish, too, like you. Are you not Bob Bobbish?"

"No, no, I'm Bob Roberts," said the middy, laughing. "I mean, Tom Long is as brave as most fellows."

There was a short consultation then as to time and place of meeting; after which the young Malay passed over the side into his boat, rowed by four followers, and was quickly pulled ashore.

Chapter Fifteen
How the Sultan was put off with Words

There was a good deal of communication now between the sultan and the resident, and rumours began flying about that the former proposed paying a visit to the residency; but the days glided by, and it did not take place. The men who had been wounded were rapidly recovering; and after several attempts to find the missing prahus, it was announced one evening, in a quiet way, that there was to be another expedition down the river, for information had been brought in by a Malay boatman, who had been employed to act as a scout, that the two vessels were lying-up in a creek on the left bank of the river. It would therefore be quite easy for the steamer to float down stream off where they lay, and either send in boats to the attack or to shatter them by sweeping the mangroves with the steamer's great guns, for the prahus lay behind a thick grove of these trees some twenty or thirty yards across, quite sufficient for a screen, but worse than useless as a protection if the heavy guns were once brought to bear.

Messages had come again and again from the sultan, urging that the power of the rajah should be thoroughly crushed; in fact, his requests almost took the tone of a command.

There was a disposition to resent this, but it was felt better to temporise, and word was sent to the sultan by a trusty messenger that something would be done.

The result of this was another visit from the leading chiefs, who rather startled the resident by the message they brought, which was to the effect that their master thought it would be better that his marriage to the two Englishwomen should take place at once; and what did Mr Linton think of the next day?

Mr Linton thought, but he did not tell the sultan's ambassadors so, that he would consult Major Sandars and Captain Horton; and this he did while the messengers waited.

Major Sandars blew his nose very loudly, and said he should like to kick the villain.

Captain Horton said that nothing would give him greater pleasure than to have this Mr Hamet tied up and to give him six dozen.

"This is all very well, gentlemen," said Mr Linton, smiling; "but it does not help me out of my difficulty. What am I to say so as not to offend this man?"

"Oh, you must offend him," said the major. "I can see nothing for it, but to send him word that the English ladies are greatly honoured by the sultan's proposal, but that they cannot accept it."

Captain Horton nodded approval, and the resident agreed that they could do nothing better; so the message was delivered to the sultan's ambassadors, who looked exceedingly depressed upon hearing it, and as if they would have gladly exchanged places with somebody else.

"Those fellows expect to get into trouble," said the major, as he noticed the change.

He was quite right, for the two chiefs took their departure, looking as if they expected to be introduced by their wrathful ruler to the execution kris as soon as they returned.

The troops had been expecting orders for a trip down the river in search of the two prahus, but the command came upon them, as such matters usually do, just when it was least expected. One company, under Captain Smithers, was ordered to embark, but to Tom Long's great disgust, he found he was not included.

He hurried to the doctor's quarters, and found that gentleman busy with a case of instruments, open before him.

"Look here, Long," he said; "did you ever see such a wretched country as this? Everything rusts; look at my instruments."

"Yes, sir, it is terrible; such fine steel too."

"Fine steel? There isn't a better case in the army. I could do anything with these tools."

Tom Long shuddered as he glanced at the long, fearfully keen knives, and the saw—so horribly suggestive of taking off arms and legs.

Doctor Bolter saw it, and smiled to himself.

"Come to say good-bye, Long?" he said, as he stuffed some lint into a pouch, with some bandages. "I'm not a lighting man, and don't mean to be killed."

"No, sir. I came to ask you to let me go—to give me a certificate, saying I am quite well enough."

"But you are not, my dear boy. You are too weak."

"Weak, sir? No, I feel as strong as a lion. Let me go, doctor."

"What nonsense, my dear lad! I'm not the commandant. Ask the major."

"No, sir," said Tom Long. "You are not the commandant by name, but from the major downwards you do just as you like with us. Hang me if I'd have drunk such filthy stuff as you gave me, by the major's orders. I'd sooner have lost my commission."

"Ha, ha, ha!—Ha, ha, ha!" laughed the doctor. "That's very good, Long, very good indeed. I suppose I do get the better of all of you in turn. Ha, ha, ha! But look here, my dear boy, I don't think you are well enough yet."

"Do let me go, doctor," pleaded Tom. "There, I don't want to *fight*, but let me go with you and help you. This dreadful do-nothing sort of life seems to make me worse."

"Idleness is bad for any man," said the doctor.

Tom Long felt flattered at being called a man, but still looked pleadingly at the doctor.

"I could take care of your instruments, sir, and hand you what you wanted if there were any of our fellows hurt."

"Humph! yes, you could do that," said the doctor. "But look here," he said, gazing searchingly into the youth's face; "did you take your medicine to-day?"

"Yes, sir, three times," cried Tom, eagerly; for, after neglecting it for two days previously, he had taken it that day by way of a salve to his conscience.

"Then you shall go," said the doctor. "Be quick. Get your great-coat— and mind, you are to be my assistant."

Tom Long ran back to his quarters, and doctor's assistant or no, he buckled on his sword, and stuck his revolver in its case, before putting on his grey great-coat; meeting the detachment on its way down to the boat.

"Hallo, Long, what are you doing here?" said Captain Smithers. "You are not detailed for duty."

"No," said the doctor, sharply, "he is coming on hospital service."

There was no time for argument, so they marched on down to the "Startler's" boats, which were waiting, and at once put off silently, the swift stream bearing them quickly to the steamer's side, as she lay there with her steam up, but not a light visible to tell those upon the shore of the projected expedition. There was the low dull hiss and snort of the escaping steam; and one versed in such matters would have noticed that the steamer had let go her moorings at the stem, and swung round in the stream, holding on hard by the stern, ready to slip the cable and start.

But Captain Horton felt pretty secure of getting away unobserved; and trusting to the keen eyes of a couple of Malay boatmen, he calculated upon getting the steamer just abreast of the mangrove creek where the prahus lay, and then dealing with them and their crews as he pleased.

The distance down was about ten miles; and the stream was so swift, that in a couple of hours the steamer would have run down without the aid of her screw; but it was proposed to steam for about two-thirds of the distance, and then drift in silence, with a turn of the screw now and then to keep her head right.

The river was so deep, and clear of obstruction, that there was nothing to fear in their journey down, while fortunately the night, though not illuminated by the moon, was tolerably light.

The arrangements were soon made, and directly the boats were hoisted up the cable was slipped from the great buoy, and the steamer drifted down stream, the steam power being kept in abeyance until they were some distance below the campong.

In his character of doctor's assistant, Tom Long did not mix with the officers in command of the little detachment, and was standing aloof leaning over the bulwarks, and gazing at the fire-flies on the shore, when he heard a familiar voice close by.

"Think those Malay chaps will be able to see the creek on a night like this, Dick?"

"See it, Master Roberts, sir? Why, I could see it myself if I tried, and knowed where to look for it. Bless yer 'art, they Malay chaps have got eyes like cats, and can see in the dark."

"Oh yes, I dare say," said Bob. "Well, all I can say is, I hope we shall knock the prahus into splinters. I do owe those fellows a grudge for being chucked overboard as I was. It makes me feel wet now to think of it."

"Yes, that 'ere war a rum 'un, Master Roberts, sir," said Dick, solemnly. "Now, look here, sir, you being a boy like, and not wanted, if I was you, I'd just go down below, get on my perch, and tuck myself up and go to roost where I should be quite safe."

"Thank you, Dick," said Bob, quietly; "I'm going to stop on deck, and then go with the party ashore. We'll leave the old men and old women on board to take charge of the ship till we come back."

"That's as good as saying I'm a reg'lar old woman, Master Roberts, sir," said Dick, grinning.

Bob did not condescend to reply, but walked aft a little way, to where he could see a dark figure half-leaning, half-sitting in the darkness upon a gun, and looking over the bulwarks.

"Here, you sir," he said sharply, "come away from that gun. Why are you not with the detachment forward there?"

"Oh, you be hanged!" said a familiar voice.

"What? Tom Long?"

"That's my name, Mr Roberts," said the dark figure.

"Why, I thought you were in hospital yet."

"I'm on hospital service," replied Tom. "I got the doctor to bring me."

"I say—I am glad," said Bob. "Eh?"

He stopped short, for Tom Long had pinched his arm.

"Isn't that a long low vessel moored there under the bank?" said Tom.

Bob looked long and attentively.

"I think so—two of them," he said. "I'll tell the officer of the watch."

He turned aft and pointed out the dimly seen objects.

"Yes, I think they are prahus moored to the trees," he said, examining them through the glass.

The officer reported what he had seen to the captain, who also inspected them through a night-glass.

"Yes, coasting boats, I think. We'll overhaul them as we come back, we must not stop now."

The vessel was now steaming steadily down stream, not quickly, for there were too many turns, but sufficiently fast to bring them rapidly near their goal.

"Let's see; I want to have a talk to you, Tom Long, about a trip ashore—shooting," said Bob.

"Silence there, young gentleman," said the officer of the watch sternly, and then Bob was called suddenly away, so that he had no opportunity for a quiet chat with the young ensign.

Meanwhile the heavy throb throb of the steamer was the only noise heard save some weird cry of animal or bird in the dense jungle on either side. But every now and then as the waves and wash of the steamer rolled ashore, churning up the mud, they startled the dull, heavy alligators into activity, sending them scurrying off the muddy banks into deep water, to await the passing of the, to them, large water monster, whose great bulk dwarfed them into insignificance the most extreme.

Lower and lower down stream went the steamer with the dense black line of jungle on either side, till at the suggestion of the Malay pilots the steam was turned off, a couple of boats lowered, and the position of the vessel being reversed, she was allowed to float down head to stream, for quite another half-hour, when the word having been given, a small anchor that had been hanging down in the water was let go, without so much as a plash, the stout hemp cable ran quietly out, and the vessel was checked just off the narrow mouth of a creek, which seemed to run up amidst the palms and undergrowth, for there were no mangroves till the tidal waters were reached.

There was a little rapid passing to and fro here, and a couple of boats were silently lowered down, to go a quarter of a mile below to watch the other entrance to the creek, for the Malays were too fox-like not to have a hole for exit as well as one for entry. But everything was done in the most noiseless manner, so that when three more boats full of soldiers, marines, and sailors rowed off for the creek, no one would have imagined that they had slipped off on a deadly errand, or that the steamer was cleared for action, the guns shotted and every man ready to let loose a deadly hail that should cut down the jungle like a scythe amidst the corn.

But the British officers had yet to learn that the Malays were more than their equals in cunning. No sooner had the steamer passed on into the bank of mist and darkness that overhung the river, than there was a rustle, a splash, the rattling noise of large oars being thrust out, and in a couple of minutes the two long snaky prahus they had passed crammed with fighting men were gliding up stream towards the residency, where certainly there were sentries on guard, but no dread of an enemy at hand.

The boats then had pushed off from the steamer, which lay ready to help them, and rowing out of the swift waters of the river they began to ascend the dark and muddy creek, when Bob Roberts, who was with the lieutenant and part of the soldiers in the same boat suddenly whispered—

"Hark! wasn't that distant firing?"

They listened, but could hear nothing, and the lieutenant was about to order the men to pull more sharply, when Bob touched his arm again.

"I'm sure that's firing, sir," he said.

"Nonsense, Roberts! absurd! Sit still and be silent. What firing could it be? We are ten miles from the residency."

"I can't help it, sir, if we are twenty," said Bob, sharply. "I'm sure it was firing, and there it goes again."

"Silence, sir," said the lieutenant, angrily. "Give way, my lads, give way."

The ship's boats glided on over the smooth water, the men rowing with muffled oars; and so steadily that the blades seemed to be dipping in without making a splash.

The creek grew narrower, so that they had to keep right in the middle to avoid letting the oar blades brush the reeds, and so they rowed on, but without seeing anything resembling a prahu.

As to their direction, that they could not tell, but the shape of the creek they believed to be that of a bow—at least so the Malays had described it; and as the two ends of the bow must rest upon the river, they were sure, unless they struck up some narrow tortuous way, to come out at the other mouth and join the boats.

They went on very cautiously, with the midshipman anxious to talk to Tom Long, who sat beside him, but forbidden now to utter so much as a whisper. The oars dipped and rose, dipped and rose, without a sound, and sometimes a reed or water plant rustled slightly as it brushed the sides of the boats.

That in which the lieutenant was in command led the weird procession, Captain Smithers being in the next, while the third, nearly full of marines, every man with his loaded rifle between his knees, was close behind.

Still there was no sign of the prahus, and to the lieutenant's great annoyance, he found that in the darkness they must have turned up the sluggish stream that flowed into the creek, and missed the continuation, which was probably masked with reeds.

He felt ready to stamp with vexation, but controlling himself he passed the word, and the boats backed down the stream, that in which the officer in command was seated naturally being the last of the three.

"Wouldn't it have been better to have brought the Malays, sir?" said Bob.

"Yes, of course; but the cowards were afraid to come, my good lad," said the lieutenant.

"There, sir," whispered Bob again, "isn't that firing?"

"If you say another word to me about your confounded firing," said the lieutenant sharply, "I'll have you gagged, sir."

"I don't want to talk about it, sir," grumbled Bob, "but I'm sure there's something wrong up yonder."

"And I'm sure there's something wrong here, Mr Roberts," said the lieutenant, "and that's enough for me to attend to."

They went back in silence for some time, and then Tom Long, whose eyes were unusually good, pointed to a part of the reed-bed on the right.

"Is not that the continuation of the creek, sir?"

"Yes, to be sure, so it is," said the lieutenant. "We can see it coming this way. It's masked by those trees the other way. Steady, my lads; steady. Let us go first."

The creek was wider here, so the boats turned, and retook their former positions; but still there was no sign of the prahus.

"Those scoundrels must have led us wrong," muttered the lieutenant; "there's nothing here. Why, yonder's the open river, isn't it; or is it a wider space? Yes, thank goodness; there are the prahus after all."

He waited till the other boats closed up, and then whispered his final orders, appointing two boats to attack one of the prahus while he made for the other alone.

"Now then," he whispered, "are you all ready? A bold dash, my lads, and they are ours."

"Please, sir," said old Dick.

"What is it?" cried the lieutenant, angrily.

"Them's our own two boats. I'd swear to 'em."

"And I'm sure that's *firing*," cried Bob, aloud.

"Yes," said Tom Long, speaking excitedly; "those were the two prahus we passed on the way down."

"And they are attacking the residency," cried Bob.

Even as he spoke there was a shot fired from the steamer to recall the boats, and the men bent to their stout ashen oars with all their might, the lieutenant as he leaped on board being met by Captain Horton with—

"These Malay tigers are a little too cunning for us, Johnson. Those were the prahus we passed on the way down."

"Yes, sir, another slip; but we may have them yet."

Chapter Sixteen
How Private Sim took a Nap, and found it Unpleasant

A general feeling of uneasiness had been excited as soon as it was known that the "Startler" had left her moorings to go in search of the two escaped prahus. Mr Linton did not feel happy in his own mind, though he did not communicate his fears to a soul.

Still he might have spoken openly, for it would not have caused greater terrors in the breasts of his daughter and niece, who were for some reason or another too full of vague fears to retire to rest. It did not occur to them to associate their sensations with the departure of the steamer. In fact if they had so done, they would not have harboured the thought for a moment, knowing as they did how well-protected they were by the sturdy little garrison of troops, only about a third of which had gone upon the expedition.

Both Tom Long and Bob Roberts might have been conceited enough to think that the uneasiness of the ladies was entirely upon their account, and they would have been terribly upset to know that not a single thought concerning them had crossed the minds of either since the departure.

It was, in fact, a vague feeling of general uneasiness, such as might have been suffered at any time by those who were comparatively alone in the midst of a notoriously hostile, and even treacherous people, some of whom were friendly to the English, though the majority bore them the most intense hate.

Even the Major was out of spirits, and told Mrs Major that he would after all a great deal rather be at home, than out in such a treacherous, krising, throat-cutting place as Parang.

"And a very nice thing to say too," said Mrs Major Sandars, "just as we are going to bed. I shall now lie awake all night thinking, and keep seeing brown men climbing in through the blinds, and be uneasy as can be."

"Don't talk nonsense," said the Major, gruffly. "But really I've a good mind to have the sentries increased in number."

"I really would, if I were you," said Mrs Major.

"No; second thoughts are best. There is no occasion to harass the men with extra duty; and, besides, I'm nearly undressed."

So the Major and Mrs Major went to bed, as did the majority of those at the station, excepting, of course, the officer and the guard.

There was one man though who shared the feeling of uneasiness. Earlier in the night he had been disappointed at not being called upon to form one of the little company for the expedition, for he was raging with desire to in some way distinguish himself. He was a mere private soldier, but he told himself that the way to honour was open; and though a long and wearisome one for a private, still he might win his way to promotion—corporal, sergeant—some day, perhaps, ensign; and so on, till he became, maybe, adjutant of his regiment.

He could not sleep that evening, and crushing down the feelings that oppressed him, he told himself it was the heat, and dressing lightly, he went out into the comparative coolness of the night.

He had not gone far before he was reminded that there was watchfulness around; for he was challenged by first one and then another sentry, who, however, in turn, let him pass, on finding who it was. And so he wandered restlessly here and there amidst the trees, longing to go in one direction, but fighting hard against the desire; as he told himself with a bitter smile that some of the old poison of the water-snake must still be in his blood, and be the cause of all this restlessness and pain.

He had wandered here and there for some time, seating himself amidst the trees, and then going down to the landing-place to gaze at the calm swift river that eddied and gurgled amidst the water-washed boats and masses of rush at the edge of the island, wondering the while whether possibly at some time or another the effect of the constant washing of the water might not be to completely sweep away the island. "Not in our time of possession," he said to himself; and turning slowly away he stood hesitating for a while, and then, in spite of his self-restraint he took the path leading to Mr Linton's house, to convince himself, so he mentally said, that the place was quite safe.

The "place" in his brain really meant one solitary being in that house, for if he felt assured that Rachel Linton was sleeping peacefully, and with no overhanging danger, he said that he should be satisfied.

He went on then cautiously, getting nearer and nearer to the house, and feeling surprised that he was not challenged by a sentry, till he was quite close up, and then his heart began to beat fast, for he fancied he heard whispering voices, and at last, after intense listening, he was quite sure.

Here then was the danger; not such danger as he had fancifully imagined—the swimming of tigers from the mainland, or some noxious reptile; it was from man that the peril was to come.

He stole on again, making not a sound. And now he recalled how some Malay had swum to the island and hurled a spear in through one of the residency windows.

"Good heavens!" he muttered; "and I am quite unarmed." As this thought occurred to him, he could hear the whispering continued; and mingled with it there seemed to come a sound of hard breathing, like a sleeper close at hand.

It was so—the sentry asleep; and following the sound two or three yards, Adam Gray bent over a prostrate form, and caught up the rifle with fixed bayonet, seeing at the same moment that it was Private Sim.

He was about to kick the fellow, but he thought that by so doing he should be spreading the alarm, perhaps prematurely; so he walked cautiously forward towards where the whispering seemed to be.

It was so dark amidst the trees that he could hardly make out his position; but directly after it seemed to him that the sounds came from an upper window; and as the thought struck him he stepped upon a piece of dry cane, which snapped beneath his feet.

To bring his rifle to the present was the work of an instant; and as he did so a quick voice exclaimed,—"Who is there? Is that the sentry?"

"Yes, ma'am," he replied; feeling the blood tingle in his face, as he recognised the voice.

"We thought we heard the hard breathing of some beast, or some one asleep," said Rachel Linton, with her voice shaking a little as she spoke, "and we were afraid."

"There was—there is some one asleep here, ma'am;" said Gray, trying to speak calmly and quietly; "but I am on duty now."

"It is Private Gray, Rachel, whom you attended to," said another voice. "Let us go in now, we shall be quite safe."

"Yes," said Rachel, in a low voice, meant only for herself; but heard plainly in the utter silence of that night, "we shall be quite safe now."

"Good-night, sentry," said Mary Sinclair.

"Good-night, ma'am," replied Gray; and he stood and heard the shutter blind closed with a bitter feeling of annoyance at his heart.

"My name seems to have driven her away," he muttered. "At any rate, though, I am of some use," he said soon after; "she feels safe when I am by."

All was perfectly still now, except the heavy breathing of Private Sim; and Gray stood thinking what he should do.

Should he wake up Sim?

No; if he did, he would have to leave him on duty, when he would go to sleep again, and something horrible might happen.

What was to happen? he asked himself.

That, he could not say; but on one thing he determined at once, and that was, to take Private Sim's place and to keep guard.

But then Sim's lapse of duty would be found out, and he would be severely punished.

Richly he deserved it; but perhaps a severe taking to task might suffice to awaken him to a sense of his duty; and therefore Gray felt that he would be lenient, and not betray him, though it was horrible to think that the lives of all on the island might be betrayed to death by the neglect of such a fellow as this.

Private Gray was a man of quick decision, and his mind was made up at once. He would keep on duty till it was time for the guard to be changed, and then he would wake up Sim, and see that a responsible man took his place.

"The lazy, untrustworthy scoundrel!" he muttered, as he shouldered the rifle and walked up and down for a few minutes along the sentry's post. But matters were not to be ordered as he intended, for he had not been on duty very long before he heard a sound from the river that made him start and listen attentively.

"Nothing!" he said to himself after a few seconds' attention; and he once more resumed his slow march up and down, the motion seeming to calm him, for when standing still his thoughts tortured him.

"There it is again," he said to himself suddenly. "It is a boat of some kind."

Plainly enough now he had heard the peculiar creak given by an oar rubbing against wood, and this was repeated again and again.

He strained his eyes in the direction from which it came, but could see nothing for the trees. Feeling, though, that he ought to act, he went to where Private Sim still lay sleeping heavily and gave him a lusty kick, with the effect of making him start to his feet.

"I only—oh, it's you Private Gray," he said, huskily. "I thought it was the sergeant."

"You untrustworthy villain!" whispered Gray. "Silence, this moment. Take your rifle, and keep watch till I return."

"Who are you talking to like that?" said Sim, in a bullying tone.

"You, sir," replied Gray, in a low, authoritative manner, which made the man shrink. "Do you wish me to report that I found you sleeping at your post? Silence! no words. There is a large boat of some kind approaching; be on the look-out and challenge, and fire if necessary."

Private Sim did not answer, but stood on the alert, while Gray ran back in the direction of the fort.

Before he was half-way there, though, he heard the challenge of a sentry on his right, followed by a faint cry and a heavy fall.

The challenge was repeated by another sentry farther away, and this time there was the report of a sentry's rifle; and directly after came from behind him, where he had left Private Sim, the report of another piece.

He knew it must be Sim, and as danger was there, his first impulse was to run back to the help of the ladies and the resident. His second thought told him that he was unarmed, and such an act would be madness. It must take some time for an enemy to break into the place, and before then the soldiers would have turned out.

In fact the bugle rang out as he hurried on through the darkness, being compelled-to turn back twice; for he heard the trampling of feet and rustling of the leaves as people forced their way through, and he was obliged to make somewhat of a détour.

Even then somebody struck at him, a blow which he returned with his fist, sending his assailant staggering back amidst the bushes, while he ran on, to hear a limbing whistle by his ear.

Shot after shot had meanwhile been fired, fully giving the alarm, and by the time Gray reached the fort, after an extremely perilous run—for the way seemed to swarm with enemies; and even now he did not know whether he was wounded or no, for he had felt two heavy blows in the chest and back—he found the men falling in, and catching his rifle and belts from the stand he joined them.

Major Sandars was with them, in nothing but his shirt and trousers and bare feet, but he had not forgotten his sword, and in a few short words he made his arrangements for the defence of the fort, while, to Gray's great delight, he detailed a party of a dozen men, under a lieutenant, to go down to the residency.

"You must act according to circumstances, Mr Ellis," he said quietly. "It is impossible to tell who or how many our assailants are; but the darkness that favours them will also favour you. Your orders are to get somehow to the residency, and hold it or bring its occupants away, according to circumstances."

The lieutenant saluted, and the dozen men, among whom was Gray, were marched to the gate.

There was not one among them who had done more than slip on his trousers, so that they were in light fighting trim; and as soon as they were outside the gate, the lieutenant gave the word, "Quick march—double!" and away they went in single file along the narrow path.

Before they could reach the residency their pulses began to throb, for there were the sharp, quick reports of a revolver, fired six times in succession. Then a rifle spoke, and another followed by a desultory firing as if in reply.

Then from behind came the loud, heavy report of a brass lelah, fired evidently from some boat on the river; then another, and another, with more desultory firing.

"Come along my lads; our fellows will talk to them directly." There was a crashing volley just then.

"I told you so. That's English, my lads. Steady, steady; don't get out of breath. As we get out of the wood here, form up directly in the open, and wait till we can see by the firing where the enemy is. Then we'll give him a volley, and charge at once right for the verandah, where we'll take our places, and act as is afterwards necessary."

The men followed their leader's commands to the letter, formed up in a little line outside the path, and stood there waiting in the darkness, watching the flashing of a revolver fired from one of the residency windows, and the quick streaks of light from a party of the enemy, whoever that enemy might be, just in front.

"Ready!" cried the lieutenant; and as he gave his command there was the quick rattle of the pieces, then a ringing little volley, the cry *Forward!* and on the party dashed with a hearty hurrah, which had the effect of stopping the fire from the residency, Mr Linton and his servant, who had been defending the place, recognising the voices of friends.

The little line, with fixed bayonets, dashed over and swept down a cluster of Malays who tried to meet their attack with spears before taking to flight, and the next moment, it seemed to Gray, he was standing with his comrades in the verandah, reloading.

"Any one down?" cried the lieutenant, sharply.

"No, sir; no, sir," was repeated on all sides.

"All right then, my boys; make cover of anything—posts, flower vases, anything you can; and we must hold on. Fire where you have a chance; but don't waste a shot."

The opening of a door changed the plans, for Mr Linton's voice was heard saying,—"Come in quickly; and we can fire from the windows." This little evolution was soon performed, but under fire, for the Malays sent a desultory series of shots, in company with flying spears, though without any effect, while as soon as the rest of the upper windows were thrown open the men knelt down behind what was an excellent breast-work, and maintained a steady fire wherever they saw a flash.

Meanwhile there was some sharp volley firing from the direction of the fort, in reply to that of the enemy's brass lelahs. This was soon after followed by the heavy roar of a larger gun on board one of the prahus, to which the occupants of the little fort could not reply, on account of the darkness, and the fact that one of the attacking prahus was between them and the campong, while the other was so sheltered by trees that it would have been folly to have fired.

The attack was weak in the extreme—the Malays running forward, firing a shot or two, and then retreating to cover; and this was kept up for a considerable time, the enemy evidently thinking that as the defenders were weak through the departure of the steamer, they would soon give in.

It was evident that they were staggered by the defence, for they had no doubt hoped to surprise both fort and residency. In token of this, the attacking party retreated two or three times over, as if to ask for advice or fresh orders from their boats—orders that were pretty decisive, for they came on each time more keenly than before, the last time with bundles of inflammable wood and reeds, with which they boldly advanced to the verandah of the residency, throwing them down and then rapidly retreating.

Lieutenant Ellis no sooner became aware of this, though, than he got his men out from a side window, formed up, waited their time till the Malays came on, shouting, with a burning torch of inflammable resin, and then gave them a volley, followed by a charge.

The enemy gave way at once, but only for a few moments; then their numbers seemed to become augmented, and with a tremendous rush they bore back the little party of soldiers step by step. Numbers fell, but they paid no heed to this; and the lieutenant began to wish earnestly that they were safe back within the walls of the residency, when there was a roar like thunder, then the beating of gongs on both sides of the island. Then another roar, and another, and the Englishmen began to cheer and pursue, for the Malays were rushing in the direction of the gongs.

But it was no time for pursuing this crowd of Malays into narrow paths through dark woods. They had maintained their defence till the steamer had returned, and now she was firing regularly, gun after gun, in the direction of the prahus, but doing no harm, the darkness giving them no opportunity for taking aim.

The firing of the steamer's big Armstrongs had, however, the effect of causing a *sauve qui peut* style of retreat amidst the Malays; and at the end of ten minutes the sweeps of the prahus were in full work, and the whole party rapidly making their way up the river once more to some fresh hiding-place, from which they could issue to deal ruin and destruction wherever they pleased.

Chapter Seventeen
How Dick buys a Rajah, and his first Luff objects

The rapid rate at which the two prahus went away from the island after the attacking party had scrambled in was sufficient to show those on board the "Startler" how impossible it would be to overtake them by means of boats. The only way would be to surprise their crews, or to sink them with the guns of the steamer next time they tried to pass down the river.

Congratulations in plenty were exchanged as soon as the communications were effected, though a good deal of annoyance was felt at being again out-manoeuvred by the Malay cunning.

One thing was very evident, and that was that there would be no safety for the residency while so daring a chieftain as Rajah Gantang was at liberty, with his two cleverly managed prahus.

No further alarms took place during the night, and in the morning the amount of damage done was found to be nothing more than a little carpentering and painting would restore. The real damage done was to the British prestige, which, in spite of the brave defence, had received a blow in the eyes of the Malays.

Judging the matter fairly next morning, Mr Linton and the officers came to the conclusion, after a careful inspection, that though it would have been necessary for the occupants of the residency to have fled to the little fort, half-a-dozen such desultory attacks would have done the latter no real harm.

"No," said Major Sandars, aloud; "for my part, if provisioned, I should see no difficulty in holding our place against half-a-dozen rajahs. There is only one way in which we could be hit."

"And that is?" said Captain Horton.

"By a surprise such as they treated us to last night. There is no other way in which they could harm us."

Adam Gray heard his words, and in silence made an addition to them.

"They could harm us by treachery, or by the neglect of our sentries."

The dark scene of the previous night flashed across his mind as he thought this, and he recalled Private Sim's recumbent form amidst the grass, wondering the while whether he ought not to relate what had taken place, and so obtain for the fellow the punishment he deserved.

Finally, he made up his mind to let matters take their course, after giving Sim to understand that he should report him if such a thing came under his notice again.

The sultan sent word that he was most grieved to hear of this new attack, and begged the resident to spare no pains to root the rajah and his followers off the face of the earth. He assured Mr Linton, by his messengers, that he felt the insult as bitterly as if it had been offered to himself; while even now, surrounded as he was by faithful followers, he never dared sleep twice in the same place in his house, for fear that an envoy of the rajah should pass a kris up between the bamboos that formed the flooring, and assassinate him.

The message sent back was that no effort should be spared to rid the river of so dangerous a neighbour; but opportunity failed to offer for carrying out the promise.

Anywhere within a mile or two of the sultan's campong the people were ready enough to give information to the English, when a boat was sent to cruise about and endeavour to find where the rajah had hidden; but beyond that distance they were met with stern looks of distrust, and it was evident to the officers in charge that the rajah was perfectly safe, his influence being too great amongst the people for any one to act as informer.

This added a good deal to the feeling of insecurity felt at the residency; and to counteract this the ship's carpenters were set to work to contrive stout shutters with loopholes for barricading, and also make the doors more secure.

The fort with its little barrack was already pretty safe, and of course so long as the steamer lay there, any attacking prahus could be literally blown out of the river; but there was always the risk of the steamer being called away, and in view of this Mr Linton increased the arms and ammunition at his house, and also asked for an extra sentry.

In a few days the night attack had lost the greater part of its terrors, for the steamer was not likely to be moved at present, and boats were almost constantly out patrolling the river in search of the enemy.

Every sampan or prahu that came down the stream was stopped, boarded, and searched, at first greatly to the annoyance of their occupants. Several times over efforts were made to slip by, but the report of a heavy gun fired across their bows brought the Malays to their senses, and they humbly submitted to the overhauling.

These boats were for the most part laden with rice, fruit, or slabs of tin, and of these every rajah up the river made a practice of taking toll for payment of his permission to pass down the stream.

The occupants of a prahu then might already have paid tax two or three times, and the appearance of this new power in the river was resented strongly; but when it was found that no tin was taken from them, and that when rice, or fruit, or poultry was taken, the full market value was paid in dollars, a strong friendly feeling sprang up mingled with respect.

The news soon spread, and from that time whenever a trading boat came down from the upper country, the sight of an English boat was sufficient to make the Malays lie on their oars or pole, and await the coming of the English officer to board.

There came quite a calm over the little settlement about this time. The rajah was not heard of, and information, true or false, was brought in that the prahus were high up the stream, where they had been rowed during a flood, and taken up a tributary of the main river, where, on the cessation of the flood, they remained grounded and out of reach.

The sultan seemed to have forgotten his disappointment about the ladies, and the soldiers and sailors were enjoying a time of indolent ease, their greatest excitement being a little drill. Provisions were plentiful, fruit abundant, with as much native tobacco as the men liked to buy, at a most moderate price, and in spite of the steamy heat the people were perfectly happy.

Ali, the young chief, had been again to see Bob Roberts on board; but as yet the visit had not been returned, the attack upon the residency having put a stop to all leave for the time being; but as the officers were getting less strict, the middy was looking forward to the day when he could go ashore. In the meanwhile he indulged himself with a little fishing from out the chains.

Doctor Bolter was about the happiest man at the island, for now that he had got his sanitary matters put right, and his wounded men well, he had ample time for following his favourite pursuit of natural history.

The sailors were in a high state of delight over what they called the "Bolter's weakness," and out of gratitude to him for many a little bit of doctoring, they took him everything they could get hold of that flew, crept, crawled, ran, or swam, bothering him almost to death. For Jack could not see the necessity for refraining from presenting the doctor with a fire-fly, because Tom had taken him a dozen the day before, and Bill two dozen the day before that.

"Wasn't his flies as good as Bill's, or Tom's? Well, then, mind yer own business, and let him mind his."

Dick came back from the shore beaming one day, with a large black monkey under his arm, held by a stout piece of chain, and a dog collar round its loins.

"Hallo, Dick," said one of his messmates, Bill Black, as soon as he climbed on board. "Where did you find your little brother?"

"'Tain't no brother o' mine," said Dick seriously; "he's a Black, and his name's Joseph, ain't it Joey?"

The monkey wrinkled its forehead, and its restless eyes ran over one after the other of the group as the sailors gathered round, who now began laughing.

"Well, he's a handsome chap at all events," said Bill, putting out his hand to pat the monkey on the head.

"Don't touch him, lad," growled Dick, by way of caution; "he bites."

"Get out," said Bill. "Now then, old man, how are you?"

"Chick—chack—squitter—witter—chack," cried the monkey, snapping at the sailor's hand and giving it a sharp nip.

"There, I told you so," said Dick.

"Hallo, what have you got there, Dick?" said Bob Roberts, coming up, attracted by the laughing.

"Native gentleman, sir, I bought for four dollars," said Dick, seriously. "He's a rar-jah I think, only he hadn't time to get his toggery and his kris afore he come aboard."

"Didn't know the native gentlemen had tails," said Bob, smiling. "Hallo, old chap, how are you? Have a bite?"

He held out half a biscuit that he happened to have in his jacket pocket, and the monkey looked at him curiously, as it held out one long thin black hand, flinchingly, as if expecting to be teased.

Twice it essayed to get the biscuit, but always flinched, till Bob took a step more in advance, when the animal snatched the coveted morsel and began to eat it ravenously.

"Why, it's half-starved, Dick," said the middy.

"Yes, sir, he tried to get a piece of Bill Black's finger, but Bill cut up rough, and wouldn't let him have it."

Here there was a fresh burst of laughter, in which Bill, whose finger was, after all, only pinched, heartily joined.

"What are you going to do with him, Dick?" said Bob Roberts.

"Well, sir," said Dick, with a dry wrinkle or two extra on his mahogany physiognomy, "I was going to ask the skipper if he'd like to have the gent for a new middy, seeing as you, sir, have got to be quite a grown man now."

"Don't you be cheeky, Dick," said Bob, indignantly.

"No, sir, I won't," said the old sailor humbly; "but on second thoughts, which is allers the best, Mr Roberts, sir, I thought as the skipper wouldn't have a uniform as would fit him, so I said as I'd take him on to the island, where they'd soon make a sojer of him."

"Now look here, Dick," said Bob, "I take no end of impudence from you, but let there be some end to it. Now then, have you done joking?"

"Yes, sir, but he would look well in a red jacket, wouldn't he?"

"What are you going to do with the monkey?" said Bob, peremptorily.

"Well, sir," said Dick, seeing that he had gone far enough, "I was up in the campong there, and I bought him of one of the niggers as used him to pick cokey-nuts."

"Oh, yes, of course," said Bob, derisively.

"He will," said Dick; "and I bought him because, I says to myself, I says: Here's just the sorter thing our doctor would be glad to have, and he'd pin a long name to him directly, and say as he's a Blackskinnius Monkinius, or something of the kind."

"And are you going to take it to the doctor?" said Bob.

"Yes, sir, now, directly I've showed you how he can pick cokey-nuts. Bill Black, mate, just step down and bring that ball o' stout fishing-line out o' the locker, will you?"

The sailor addressed went down, and returned directly after to Dick, who undid the chain, and tied one end of the stout fishing cord to the monkey's strap.

The little animal had been munching away at the biscuit in a quaint semi-human fashion; but as soon as Dick had fastened one end of the cord to the belt, it seemed to know what was wanted, for it squatted upon the deck, looking intelligently up in the sailor's face.

"There, ain't he an old un?" said Dick. "Now then, Yusuf, be kraja."

As the monkey heard the last two words, it sprang up the rigging to one of the great blocks, which in his mind represented the cocoa-nuts it was to bring down, and seizing one it tried hard to twist it off, chattering angrily, till Dick gave the cord a jerk, when the animal bounded to another block, and tried hard to fetch it off, going so far as to gnaw at the rope that held it, till Dick gave the cord another jerk, when it came down.

"Well done, old man," said Dick, patting the animal, which kept close to his leg, as if feeling that it must find protection of him, when Dick took it under his arm.

"Are you going now, Dick?" said Bob, eagerly.

"Yes, sir."

"Wait a moment, and let me see if I can get leave. Why, look here; the doctor's coming aboard."

True enough, Doctor Bolter was seen in a sampan rowed by one of the Malays, and a minute or two later he was on deck.

"Monkey, eh?" he said sharply, as he saw the animal. "*Semnopithecus Maurus*, I should say. What are you going to do with it?"

"Dick was going to give it to you, sir," said Bob, smiling.

"Give it—to me?" cried the doctor. "Thanks; no, my man, I must draw the line somewhere. Keep it on board. Climb the rigging, and that sort of thing. Here, you Roberts, tell the captain I'm here."

Bob went off, and then brought a message to the doctor, who went into the cabin. On returning to where Dick was standing, that worthy was scratching in a melancholy way at his head.

"I'm 'bout done over this here monkey, sir," he said. "I can't go and get the chap to take him back."

"Keep him, and make a pet of him, Dick," said the middy, holding out a lump of sugar to the subject of their conversation.

"No, sir, that wouldn't do. The skipper wouldn't stand it; and besides, if the monkey was mine the chaps would lead him such a life, teaching him to smoke tobacco and drink grog. Will you have him, sir?"

"No, Dick," was the reply. "I've no money to spend on monkeys."

"I didn't mean that, sir," said Dick. "I meant it for a present for the doctor. Will you have him as a present, and take care of him?"

"Of course I will, Dick, but I don't like taking it."

"Why, bless your 'art, Mr Roberts, sir, you'd be doing me a kindness by taking of it. You take it, and you can larn him all sorts of tricks. Why, look at the pretty crittur, how he takes to you!"

"Pretty crittur, indeed!" cried Bob. "You mean how he takes to the sugar. Here, come along, old man. Come, rouse up."

To Bob's surprise the monkey got up, and came close to him, while upon Dick making a motion as if to refasten the chain, the animal snarled and snapped at him.

"There now, look at that," cried Dick. "You see you'll have to take it, Master Roberts, sir."

"I'll take him for a day or two," said Bob; "but I expect the skipper won't let me keep it."

"Lor' bless you, sir, he'll let you keep it, see if he don't," said the old sailor, and his words proved true.

Chapter Eighteen
How Bob Roberts went a-fishing

Bob Roberts liked having the monkey, but there was a sore side to the matter; it was unpleasant to hear that the first lieutenant had said that one monkey was enough in the ship, and they did not want two.

"It's as good as telling me to my face that I'm a monkey," said Bob to himself. "Now look here, I shall just go and ask him to lend me the dinghy to sit in and fish, and old Dick to manage it; and if he says no, I shall just tell him that his remark about the monkey was precious ungentlemanly."

So Bob went up to the first lieutenant and preferred his request, fully anticipating a refusal, but to his surprise the officer in question was all that was urbane and pleasant.

"Fishing from the dinghy, eh, Roberts?" he said, smiling.

"Yes, sir, I thought I might catch a basket if I fished from the dinghy. I lose so many hauling them up the side into the chains."

"To be sure—yes—of course," said the lieutenant. "On one condition, Roberts, you can have it."

"What's that, sir?"

"Two conditions, I should say," replied the lieutenant. "The boat is to be properly cleaned afterwards, and we are to have a dish of fresh fish for the gun-room dinner."

"Certainly, sir," said Bob, laughing, "if I catch them."

"You must catch them," said the lieutenant. "Ah, I remember the days when I used to be fond of going up the Thames fishing, and—there, be off with you as soon as you like."

The first lieutenant smiled as he felt that he had been about to prose over his old days; and Bob having obtained leave for Dick to be his companion, and to manage the boat if he should elect to go up or down the river, instead of lying astern hitched on to a ring-bolt, was soon over the side, with plenty of hooks and lines and bait.

"This here's a rum sorter game, Mr Roberts, sir," said old Dick, as soon as he had fastened the boat's painter to a ring in the stem part of the great steamer. "I'm afraid I shan't be strong enough for the job."

Dick glanced at the great muscles in his sun-browned arms with a smile of pride, and then stared at the middy, who turned upon him sharply.

"Now look here, old Dicky," he said, "you've come here to manage the dinghy for me, and not to preach and drive away all the fishes. So just light your pipe and sit still and hold your tongue, and if I find you are not strong enough to do that, I'll hail the steamer, and ask them to send me down another hand."

Old Dick chuckled and grinned, and without more ado took out and filled a short black pipe, which he lit with a burning glass, and then sat contentedly sucking at it, while Bob, who had provided himself with a bamboo about ten feet long—a natural fishing-rod in one piece—fitted on a thin line, baited his hook, and began to fish in the deep stream.

The sun poured down his rays like a shower of burning silver, and in spite of the puggaree with which he had provided himself, Bob found the heat almost too much for him, and looked enviously at old Dick, who lay back in the bows of the little cockle-shell of a boat, with his knees in, his chin pointing upwards, and his arms resting on the sides, literally basking in the hot glow.

The line kept floating down with the stream, and Bob kept pulling it up and dropping it in again close to the boat, but there was no sharp tug at the bait; and after half an hour of this work a peculiar drowsy feeling began to come over the middy, the bright flashing river ran on, and the palms and attap-thatched houses on the shore began to run on too, and all looked misty and strange, till the rod was about to fall from his hand, his nodding head to rest itself upon his chest, and the first lieutenant's basket of fish to vanish into the realm of imagination—when there was a tremendous tug, and Bob started into wakefulness, with his bamboo bending nearly double, and some large fish making the line hiss through the water as it darted here and there.

The contest was short and furious. Any doubts in the middy's mind as to the existence of fish in the river were gone, for he had hooked a monster. Now it was rushing up towards the surface, now diving down so deeply that the top of Bob's bamboo dipped in the water, and then it was sailing up and down stream, anywhere in fact, but never giving the excited lad a chance of seeing what it was like.

"Had I better go in arter him, sir?" said Dick, grinning.

"I don't know, Dick. I think—oh, I say, look at that!"

That was Bob's line hanging limply from his straight bamboo, for there was a furious rush, a dull twang, and the fish had gone.

"He was a big 'un, sir," said Dick, refilling his pipe. "Never mind. Try another, sir; better luck next time."

Bob sighed as he fitted on a fresh lead and hook, and was soon fishing once more, thoroughly awake now; and to his great delight he felt a sharp tug at his line, and striking, found that he had hooked a fish of a manageable size, which he soon hauled into the boat, and recognised as the *ikan sambilang*, a fish frequently sold to them by the Malays, and esteemed quite a delicacy.

"It's a rum-looking one," said Dick, examining the captive as Bob put on a fresh bait. "It's just like one of the eel pouts as we boys used to ketch down in the drains in Yorkshire."

"In the drains, Dick?"

"Oh, I don't mean your drains. I mean land drains as take the water off a country. We used to catch lots on 'em, thick, short, fat fellows, but they hadn't got a lot of long beards like these here. What, another already!"

"Yes, and a big one too," said Bob, excitedly, as he lugged out, after a sharp tussle, a handsome fish, with glistening scales, and a sharp back fin, bearing some resemblance to a perch.

"That's the way, sir," said Dick, smoking contentedly in the bows. "I like fishing arter all."

Bob smiled, and went on catching the little barbed fish, rapidly, and every now and then a good-sized fellow of a different kind. Two or three of the men came and leaned over the side to watch them for a few minutes, but the heat seemed too much for their interest to be kept up, and they soon disappeared.

There was a little audience on the further bank, though, which watched Bob's fishing without ceasing, though unseen by the young fisherman. This audience consisted of three half-nude Malays, lying in a sampan hidden amidst the reeds of the river's side, and these men seemed greatly interested in all that was going on, till, as the evening drew near, Bob, who had captured at least sixty fish of various sizes, sat at last completely overcome by the heat, and following Dick's example, for that worthy had gone off fast asleep, and Bob's bamboo dipped in the water, the line unbaited, and offering no temptations to the hungry perch. That was the time for which the Malays in the sampan had been waiting, and one of them glided over the side like a short thick snake, reached the shore, and then making his way up stream for some little distance, he softly plunged in, with nothing but a kris in his lingouti, or string round the waist used by the natives to support their loin cloths, and after swimming boldly out for some distance, turned over, and floated with just his nose above the water.

The stream did all he required, for the Malay had calculated his distance to a nicety, so that he was borne unseen right to the steamer's bows, and then floated along her side, and round the stem, where a few strokes brought him into the eddy.

Dick and the fisherman slept on soundly, so that they did not see a brown hand holding a keen kris raised from the water to divide the boat's painter, neither did they see that the same hand held on by the cut rope, and that the dinghy was floating, with its strange companion, swiftly down the stream.

At the end of five minutes it had been swept round a bend, and was out of sight of the steamer.

So likewise was the sampan from which the Malay had come, while one of its occupants steered it into the dinghy's course, and the other crouched in the forward part with a keen-headed limbing or spear.

Chapter Nineteen
How Bob and Old Dick finished their Day

The very motion of the boat lulled its occupants into a deeper sleep as they glided on and on down the swift deep river, with the tall waving palms and the dark undergrowth ever slipping by the travellers, who had embarked now upon a journey whose end was death.

The sampan floated quietly on in attendance, and the Malay, whose hand was twisted in the boat's painter, kept beneath the bows of the little boat with merely his face above water, the dinghy now floating down stern foremost, and, having been guided into the swiftest part of the stream, always faster and faster towards its journey's end.

Utterly unconscious of danger, and dreaming comfortably of being in a land of unlimited do-nothingism, Dick's head lay across the gunwale of the boat in terrible proximity to the Malay's kris; while Bob, with his chin on his chest, was far away in his old home, in a punt of which he had lost the pole, and it was being whirled along faster and faster through the shallows towards the mill down at the bend of the river.

He was very comfortable, and in spite of an uneasy position his sleep was very sweet, unconscious as he was of anything having the semblance of danger.

And now the dinghy was a good half mile below where the steamer was moored. They had passed the last house standing on its stout bamboo props, some distance above, and the river had curved twice in its bed, so that they had long been concealed from any one upon the deck, and still the Malays hesitated, or rather waited the time to make their spring. They had no special enmity against the occupants of the dinghy in particular, but they were three of the most daring followers of Rajah Gantang, who had assumed the part of fishermen in a sampan, with a rough cast net, so as to hang about the neighbourhood of the "Startler," and pick up information for their chief, who, so far from being, with his two prahus, *hors de combat*, was merely lying-up in a creek hidden by bamboos and palms, awaiting his time to take deadly vengeance upon the destroyers of his stockade and miners of his income from the passing boats.

The opportunity of cutting off a couple of the hated infidels who had forced themselves into the peaceful country, where their rajah, like many another, had been free to carry on a happy lawless existence, cutting throats, selling slaves, committing acts of piracy, and indulging in every vile and sensuous custom, was one not to be lost. Rajah Gantang wanted no peace, or order, or prosperity in the land where he could seize on the wretched people, and make them pay him in gold, tin, rice, poultry, fruit, or any precious commodity, for the right to pass down the river, which he, and a few more of his stamp, looked upon as theirs by right; so that his three followers were certain to receive praise and reward for the proof they might be able to show of the death of a couple of the giaours.

For the Malays are good Mohammedans, and look upon the slaying of a Christian as a most meritorious act, but at the same time they were too cautious to endanger their plot or their own lives by undue haste.

Hence it came about that the dinghy was allowed to drift down a good three quarters of a mile before the Malays made any attempt, when, as the sampan closed up, and the man in her bows raised his limbing to throw, the savage in the water reached up one hand to Dick's shoulder, and struck at him with the other.

The blow from the kris and the hurling of the spear took place at one and the same moment, but the touch of the Malay's hand upon his shoulder made Dick leap up with such a sudden start that the aim was baffled, and the boat rocked so violently that the spear whizzed by Bob Roberts' head, and plunged into the water.

In a moment more Dick had seized the little scull that lay in the dinghy, and struck the Malay in the river so severe a blow on the head that the man went under, to rise again a few yards away, and then paddle feebly towards the sampan, whose occupants, spear in hand, now made a desperate attack upon those they meant to make their prey.

Bob Roberts never quite knew how it all took place, but he had a lively recollection of old Dick standing up in the boat, sweeping the little oar round his head, and striking fiercely at the men who thrust at him with their spears.

It was a most unequal encounter, for while the Malays were upon comparatively substantial ground, the dinghy rocked to and fro, and it only needed the hand of the half-drowned Malay to catch at the side, in a frantic effort to save his life, to send it right over, and Bob and the English sailor into the stream.

Bob felt that his minutes were numbered, for as he struck out for the shore the Malays in the sampan uttered a savage yell, and came in pursuit.

"SENT IT OVER, AND BOB AND THE SAILOR INTO THE STREAM."

Dick swam to his side on the instant, and the dinghy went floating away with the half-drowned Malay, while now the sampan was close after them, and as one of their enemies rowed, the other stood in the bows ready to thrust at them with his spear.

"Swim away, my lad," cried old Dick, hoarsely, "and get ashore, I'm only an old 'un, and I'll get a grip of his spiker if I can."

"No, no, Dick, keep with me," panted Bob, who saw in Dick's words a determination on the brave old fellow's part to sacrifice his life that he might live.

"No, my lad, it's no use. Swim on," cried Dick, "they're here. Tell the skipper I did my dooty like a man."

As he bravely shouted these words in his excitement, he turned to face his enemies, the Malay with the limbing thrusting savagely at him.

But Dick was quick enough to strike the limbing aside, and grasp it with both hands, when a struggle for its possession took place.

It was a futile effort, though, upon Dick's part, for the other Malay dropped his oar, and picking up another spear, came to his comrade's help.

Bob was paralysed, and the desire was upon him to shut his eyes, and escape seeing the death of the brave old sailor, who was giving his life to save his young officer; but in place of closing his eyes, the middy felt that he was forced to hold them open, and fixed them upon the terrible scene; and his lips parted to utter a cry of warning, when, just as the third Malay was about to deliver his thrust, to avert which Dick was powerless, there was a sharp whizzing noise through the air, accompanied by a loud report, and then another whizzing, and a second report.

Bob turned his head to see the smoke rising from above a good-sized naga, or dragon-boat, coming up the stream, and at the sight thereof the Malays seized their oars, gave the sampan a sharp impulse which brought them within reach of their comrade, and after helping him on board, they rowed off with all their might, with the dragon-boat coming up fast.

But the naga had to stop and pick up the middy and Dick who had swum, as soon as they were free from enemies, towards the dinghy, which they reached as the dragon-boat came up.

"Are you hurt?" said a voice in English, and a delicate hand was stretched down from the naga's side to help Bob in, where, as he sank down panting, he recognised Ali, the young Malay chief.

"No: only half-drowned. But Dick—save Dick."

"I'm all right, Mr Roberts, sir," said the old sailor, hoarsely; "and the dinghy's made fast astern."

"But are you speared, Dick?" said the middy.

"Not as I knows on, sir. I ain't felt nothing at present, but I don't say as I ain't got a hole in me somewheres."

"They'll get away," said Ali, just then, as he stood up with a double gun in his hand. "Only small shot," he said, tapping the stock. "I have no bullets."

As he spoke he clapped the piece to his shoulder and fired twice rapidly, as the Malays in the sampan seemed to dive through a screen of reeds into some creek beyond.

The pattering hail of straggling small shot hastened their movements, and then Bob proceeded to thank the young chief for saving their lives, explaining to him, as far as he knew, how it was that they had fallen into such a plight.

"You must take more care," said Ali, in a low voice. "Our people would not harm you; we are friends, but plenty hate you much. But you are safe."

"Yes," said Bob, who, with all the elasticity of youth, was fast recovering himself, "we are quite safe; and the fish are there too. I say, though, old chap, I am so much obliged."

"Oh, no," said the young Malay, laughing, as he coloured through his brown skin; "it is nothing. I saw a wretch trying to do harm, and I fired at him with small duck shot. You would do the same."

"Yes, and with bigger shot too if I had a chance," said Bob excitedly, as he proceeded to wring all the water he could out of his clothes, for now the excitement was over he felt slightly chilly.

Meanwhile the boatmen were rowing steadily up stream, it having been seen to be useless to attempt pursuit of the Malays in the sampan, and they were rapidly nearing the steamer.

"'Scuse me, Mr Roberts, sir," said Dick, who was very wet and spongy, "but your knife's littler than mine, and if you'd pick a few o' these here small shot outer my arms, I'd feel obliged."

Examination showed that Dick had received quite a dozen shots in his arms and chest. They had just buried themselves beneath the skin, and were easily extracted by means of an open knife, after which Dick declared himself to be much better.

"They've give them Malay chaps a tickling, I know," he cried, laughing. "I'm such a thick-skinned 'un, I am, that they only just got through. I'll bet an even penny they've gone a good inch into them niggers."

The boat now reached the steamer, where, after a warm and hearty parting, Bob stepped into the dinghy with Dick, and the remains of the painter were made fast to the cut fragment hanging from the ring.

"Now, if you'll take my advice, Mr Roberts," said the old sailor, "you'll step up and get to your berth, and change your togs, while I get out the fish and wash the dinghy. Being wet won't hurt me. What's more is, as I shouldn't say nought about the scrimmage; specially as we're not hurt, or you won't get leave again."

"But you are hurt, Dick."

"Bah! Don't call that hurt, dear lad. I'm as right as nine-pence. You go on, and think about what I've said."

"I will, Dick," said Bob; "but take care of the fish."

"Ay, ay, sir."

"But I say, Dick."

"Ay, ay, sir."

"How did the dinghy get loose? You must have gone to sleep."

Dick rubbed his ear. "Well, sir, suttunly I think I must have shut one eye; but how the dinghy got loose is more than I can say, unless them spiteful niggers cut us adrift. But you get aboard. We ain't been missed."

But Dick was wrong: they had been missed, and the sentry had reported the coming of the naga-boat; so that as soon as Bob had changed his wet clothes for dry, he had to go to the captain's cabin and relate the whole affair. Those on board merely supposing that they had gone down the river to fish, it was a remark made aloud by the young chief Ali that had started a train of ideas in the first lieutenant's head that something was wrong.

"Ah," said Captain Horton, "that was well done of the young chief. But it seems to me that we've a lot of ugly scoundrels about to deal with, and we must take care, gentlemen, we must take care."

"Yes, Captain Horton," said the first lieutenant, "and we will. But are there no fish there for us, Roberts, eh?" he continued.

"Yes, sir, there are," said Bob. "I've caught you a capital dish. And very nearly got turned into ground bait for my pains," he said to himself, as he went out to find Dick. "I say, Dick," he said, as he met him with the basket of fish, "did you think about crocodiles when you were in the water?"

"No, sir, never once; there was too much to think about beside."

"So there was, Dick," said Bob. "There's sixpence: go and ask them to give you a glass of grog to keep out the cold, but first change your things. I'll take the fish."

"Right, sir," said Dick: but he finished the dinghy first, said that there'd be a row about the cut painter, and then had his glass of grog before he changed his things.

Chapter Twenty
A Run after a Rajah

Fresh news reached the residency the next day from the sultan, who sent word that he had had a very threatening letter from Rajah Gantang, declaring that if he did not break at once with the English, ruin, destruction, and death would be his fate before many months had passed.

This threatening language had completely upset the sultan, so the chief who bore the message said, and he begged that his friends and allies, the English, would not let him suffer for his fidelity to them; and when asked what he wished done, the chief replied that while Rajah Gantang lived there would be no peace, for the rajah's emissaries were in every part of the country, ready to carry news, to rise on their lord's behalf, even to assassinate, should their orders be to that extent.

The result of all this was a promise that the rajah should be found, if possible, though how it was to be done the resident could not say.

Just in the nick of time a good-sized prahu came down the river, and on anchoring by the steamer her captain went on board, with a pitiful tale of how he had been treated higher up the river.

Believing the rajah's power to be broken, he had been on his way down, laden with a good cargo of tin, when he was summoned by a prahu to stop. This he refused to do, not knowing who summoned him, when he was attacked by a party from the prahu, two of those on board were killed, and he himself severely wounded.

In proof of his assertions he displayed a spear wound in his arm and the stab of a kris in his shoulder.

Doctor Bolter was sent for, and the master of the prahu had his wounds dressed, after which he implored the help of Captain Horton to recover the slabs of tin that had been taken from his boat, almost ruining him, so severe was the loss.

The news that one of the prahus was about, up the river, set the ship's company on the *qui vive* once more. The master of the prahu, having been robbed of his cargo, had no farther aim, and was glad enough to offer his services as guide. When asked as to the depth of the river, he declared that the steamer could ascend for another twenty miles, so it was decided to make a fresh expedition against this disturber of the country; but the whole of the plans were kept a profound secret, lest the time and arrangements of the party should again be conveyed to the rajah by some one or other of his spies.

Preparations were quietly made, then, and fifty men from the island taken on board the steamer, a few at a time, so as not to attract notice; and when at last the expeditionary party started, the occupants of the residency were dining with Major and Mrs Sandars at the officers' quarters, where they quietly stayed.

Steam had been got up before dark, and every preparation made, for this time the "Startler" was to go up stream: and at last, when night rapidly succeeded day, as it does in the tropics, the steamer lay waiting for the rising of the moon, and then her screw slowly revolved, and she began to feel her way gently against the swift stream—the people of the campong only seeing her at nightfall moored as usual, and not awaking to the fact that she had gone until the morning, of course far too late to give any warning to the rajah if they were so disposed.

Patiently and almost silently the great steamer forced its way on for quite a mile, when, there being no fear now of being heard, the propeller revolved more rapidly, and the waves made by the vessel ran washing the roots of the trees on either side.

The moon was just at its full, and seemed as it rose to silver the tops of the trees, while it left the river in utter darkness, though it marked out its course through the dense jungle where it seemed to have to cut its way, the great trees growing to the water's edge, and overhanging the stream.

A rapid rate was impossible, on account of the way in which the river wound about; but it kept so wide and deep that there was but little difficulty in its navigation, especially as not a single craft of any kind was encountered.

The master of the prahu pointed out a couple of campongs as they passed them, on the banks; but they might have been villages of the dead, so silent and unoccupied did they seem, as the steamer slowly glided by.

The moon rose higher and higher, till the river was like a broad path of silver, and along this they continued their course with a man constantly sounding from the chains, but always to show an average depth of about four fathoms, with a thick, soft, muddy bottom, upon which the steamer could have met with no harm had she taken the ground.

Silence had been ordered, but as the Jacks and soldiers sat beneath the shelter of the bulwarks, or leaned over and watched the smooth, silvery river, they conversed in low whispers about the expedition, and wondered what luck was to attend them now.

The plan was evident to all, it was intended to spare the men all the risk they could, by getting the steamer within range of the prahus, and sinking them with her big guns. If this could not be done, through the shallowing of the river, of course the boats would have to continue the journey up stream; but even then it was Captain Horton's intention to make use of the boat-guns as much as possible, and save the men from the disadvantages of boarding vessels that were so carefully protected.

Higher up the river still, and past the stockade, whose remains showed plainly in the soft moonlight. Ever and again strange noises could be heard from the jungle on either side, as the various denizens of the thick tangle of vegetation were alarmed by the throb and rush of the steamer, with its strange wave that rushed up to the bank, and startled many a nocturnal creature from its lurking-place, where it lay watching in search of prey.

To Bob Roberts' great delight, he found that Tom Long was one of the party, for, being declared well enough by the doctor, he had put in a sort of claim, as having been of the last force, to a right to belong to this.

This was conceded to him by Major Sandars, and he was burning to distinguish himself, if he could obtain a chance.

Very formidable he seemed, with his sword ground to the keenest possible edge, and a revolver in his belt; though in appearance Bob Roberts was scarcely less offensive in the way of weapons, as he took pains to show his friend.

It must have been close upon midnight, when the man in the chains, who had continued to take soundings, announced by degrees the shallowing of the river.

For quite twenty miles it had kept to its muddy bottom and uniform depth, but during the past half-hour the mud had given place to clean-washed gravel, the depth grew less, and at last the anchor was let go, for it was not considered safe to proceed farther. But it was not until there was less than a foot of water beneath the vessel that the order was given; while even then there was so much way upon the steamer that she touched upon the gravel lightly before she gradually settled back and swung to her cable.

Quickly and silently four boats were lowered, each containing twenty men, and at the word of command the party, under the joint command of Lieutenant Johnson and Captain Smithers, pushed off, with the good wishes of all left on board.

The master of the prahu was in the foremost boat, and according to his account they were still about a couple of miles below where the attack took place, he having been mistaken about the steamer's draught of water. His opinion was that both the prahus would be found lying in the Qualla, or mouth of a river higher up, and towards this point the boats steadily ascended without any undue bustle, for the object of the officers in charge was to get the men up to the point fresh and ready for the task in hand.

Each boat carried a gun running on slides, and upon the proper service of these guns depended a good deal of the success of the expedition.

They had been rowing steadily on for above half an hour, when suddenly from their left a bright line of light cut the black darkness of the forest, and was followed by a sharp report.

For a moment the course of the boats was checked, and one was directed to pull in and see who the enemy might be, but directly after there was another report a couple of hundred yards higher up, and then another, and another.

"Catch a weasel asleep," said Lieutenant Johnson, grimly; "that signal will run right up to the prahus. We've got to deal with some one who has his wits about him."

So indeed it proved; for a quarter of an hour later, as they still pushed steadily on in line, there came a warning from the first boat in the shape of a dull heavy report, and the other boats sheered out of the right line, ready to deliver their own fire.

For plainly enough, though wearing a grey shadowy appearance, a couple of prahus could be seen coming swiftly down the stream, the long rows of oars on either side beating the water with a wonderfully regular stroke, and sending them along at quite a startling rate.

Shot after shot was fired, but with what effect the occupants of the boats could not tell, for no heed was paid to the firing, save that the prahus seemed to increase their speed, and were steered so as to run down the enemy that tried to check their way.

It was a matter of little more than a minute from the first sighting of the vessels, each of which was five or six times the size of the largest boats, and their disappearance round the point below, with the water foaming behind them, and the English boats in full pursuit. Several shots had been fired, for each boat found its opportunity at last, and the firing was kept up till the enemy had gone.

The attempt to overtake them was, however, felt to be hopeless, for the prahus went at least two yards to the boats' one; all the officers could hope was, that one of the shots had done irreparable mischief, or that, warned by the firing, the steamer would sink them as they passed.

More they could not have done; for to have remained still was to have been sunk, the prahus dashing down at a fearful rate, and evidently seeking a collision; so, angry and disappointed, the pursuit was kept up, every ear being attent for the first shot sent at the enemy's boats by the steamer; but they waited in vain, for when at last they came within challenging distance, it was to find that no prahus had been seen.

"Was a strict watch kept, sir?" asked Lieutenant Johnson, sharply.

"Yes, of course," said Captain Horton. "I have been on deck with my night-glass ever since you started, and as soon as we heard your guns the men stood ready, lanyard in hand, to fire at any vessel that tried to pass."

"Then they must have gone off through some side stream, and come out into the river lower down."

Captain Horton stamped his foot with rage, but nothing could be done until morning; for if the steamer had set off at once, it might have been only to pass the prahus in the darkness of some creek.

Morning then was impatiently awaited, and at the first streak of daylight a couple of boats at once set off, to find a side branch of the river about a mile above the steamer, and that it came out in the main stream once more, half a mile lower down.

They rowed through it to find the current swift and deep, though the place resembled a narrow canal. It was a short cut off through a bend of the river, and at last, vexed and discomfited, the steamer went rapidly back, to learn that the prahus had passed the island at daybreak, and had fired a few defiant shots from their lelahs as they rapidly went by.

"Never mind, Tom Long," said Bob, as the former shivered in his great-coat, for the early morning was damp and cold, "only take time, and we shall put salt on their tails yet."

"No, sir," said old Dick, shaking his head seriously, "it strikes me as you never won't catch them as manages them two swift boats. They're too clever for us, they are. But only think of two big bits of Her Majesty's army and navy like us being set at nought by this here savage prince."

"Wait a bit, Dick, and you'll see," said Bob. "It strikes me that I'm the man for settling Mr Rajah Gantang; and if it does come to me to do so, why let him look out."

"Ay, ay, sir; and his men too. I owe 'em one for that boat affair. The cowards! when a fellow was asleep!"

"Ah," said Tom Long, discontentedly, "it's all very well to talk, but I want my breakfast;" and he made haste off to his quarters as soon as the steamer's boats had set the military part of the expeditionary party ashore.

Chapter Twenty One
How Abdullah showed the
Smooth Side of his Ways

It was decided after this to wait patiently for an opportunity to capture Rajah Gantang, or to destroy his prahus; and meanwhile life at the residency went on very pleasantly. The men at the fort had settled down into an easy-going existence, and under the doctor's guidance a careful examination was made of the little island, to clear it of everything in the shape of noxious reptile and insect, as far as was possible.

The example of the Malays was followed by the construction of a large bathing-place for the men, which being carefully stockaded round with stout bamboos, allowed the free flow of the river-water, without the addition of any four-footed creatures, in the shape of crocodiles, which were far too common to be pleasant, especially where lower down the river the salt water mingled with the fresh. In fact, it was dangerous there for a hand to be dragged in the water beside a boat, the hideous creatures being ready to make a dash at it, darting through the stream as they did with great velocity, by a stroke of their powerful tails.

The great desire on the part of the men was to go ashore, but, in the majority of cases, this was sternly refused. Here and there, though, an officer had a shooting-trip, but it was thought better to wait until the confidence of the natives had been more thoroughly won, and the disaffected party of Rajah Gantang dismissed.

The sultan seemed to have quite forgotten his rejection by the ladies, and was most liberal in his presentations of fruit and fresh provisions. Every morning a boat came off with a load, the fore part being generally crammed with freshly-cut flowers; and later on in the day the resident's boat would be sent ashore to return the compliment. Tom Long generally had the honour of being the escort, and marching a fatigue party up to the sultan's residence with something likely to gratify his highness.

There used to be hearty laughter amongst the officers at the quaintness of the presents, and sometimes Tom Long would have been glad to evade his duty had he dared; for, he confided to Bob Roberts—

"It is so confoundedly ridiculous, you know. I don't mind taking him up a little case of a dozen champagne pints, but what do you think I had to take yesterday?"

"I don't know," said Bob, laughing; "a pound of candles, perhaps."

"No, not yesterday," cried Tom Long; "but I did have to take him a packet of composite candles, one day. Only fancy, you know, an officer in Her Majesty's service marching with a fatigue party, up to a palm-thatched barn, to take a coffee-coloured savage a packet of candles for a present!"

"Mustn't look a gift horse in the mouth," said Bob, philosophically. "Present's a present, whether it's a pound of candles or a gold chain."

"Bah! It's disgusting," said Tom Long. "It's enough to make a man want to part with his commission."

"What'll you take for it, Tom Long? I think I should like a change. Or come, I'll swap with you. I'll turn ensign, and you take a go at the sea?"

"Don't be absurd."

"Certainly not; but come, you didn't tell me what you took up yesterday."

"No," exclaimed Tom Long, flushing with annoyance; "but I will tell you, for it's a scandal and a disgrace to the service, and Mr Linton ought to be informed against. I actually, sir, had to march those men all along through that jungle with a box."

"Box of what?" said Bob; "dominoes?"

"No, sir," cried Tom Long. "A box containing two bottles of pickles."

"Ha, ha, ha, ha!" roared Bob. "What were they? Walnuts, or onions?"

"Neither," said Tom, with great dignity; "one was piccalilli, and the other mixed."

"Well, I dare say he was very glad of them," said Bob. "I consider a good bottle of pickles, out in this benighted place, one of the greatest luxuries one could have."

"Yes," said Tom Long, who had on a supercilious fit that day, "I suppose it would satisfy you."

"All right, my noble friend," thought Bob to himself; "I'll take you down for that some day."

They strolled out and about the fort together for a time, and then out to the upper end of the island; for though longing to go to the lower portion where the residency stood, both of them carefully avoided that part. But it so happened that soon after, when they directed their steps towards the landing-place, they found that the ladies were there, in company with the major's wife, talking to a couple of Malays in a sampan laden with fruit and flowers.

The ladies were making liberal purchases of the delicious fruit and sweet-scented flowers, when, to the astonishment of Bob Roberts, he saw that one of the Malays was the man who had made so fierce an attack upon Tom Long over the durian affair.

Seeing this they both stepped forward, when the Malay recognised him, said a few hasty words to his companion, and they both leaped ashore, the man of the kris salaaming profoundly, and remaining half prostrate before the young ensign.

"Dullah asks pardon of his excellency," said the other man in good English. "He thought him an enemy who had insulted him, and he drew his kris. He asks now that his excellency will forgive him."

"Yes, yes," said the offending Malay, without raising his head or his pleading hands; and then he repeated what seemed to be the whole of his stock of English, "Yes, yes."

"Dullah asks your excellencies to forgive him, and to let him bring fruit and flowers, and to make offerings to the English princes he has offended."

"Oh, I say, Tom Long," said Bob; "that's a little too strong, isn't it? English princes!"

"What are we to do about the fellow?" said Tom Long; "tell the sentry to turn him off?"

"No; what's the good?" said Bob. "Here, leave it to me. I'll settle him."

He glanced merrily at Rachel Linton as he spoke, seeming quite at ease in her society now; while Tom Long appeared to be buttoned up in his stiffest uniform, though he was in undress white.

"Go on, then," said Tom Long in a whisper, "but don't say anything stupid; the ladies can hear every word."

"All right," said Bob. "Look here, old cockolorum," he continued to the Malay who interpreted, "what has become of that Kling who was here before?"

"Gone Mirzapore, most excellent prince," said the man.

"Come, that'll do," said Bob impatiently; "drop all that eastern sugar wordings, my fine fellow, and look here!"

The Malay salaamed again.

"My friend here isn't an English prince. We are English officers. And my friend here says you may tell Mr Abdullah there that he does not bear any malice against him for the attack. If he asks pardon, that is enough."

This being interpreted to Abdullah, who remained humbly bent, he started up, and catching Tom Long's hands, kissed them both, and afterwards Bob's, very much to that young gentleman's disgust, though Tom received the salute with a good deal of dignity, posing himself to look to the best advantage in the presence of the ladies.

"There, that'll do now," said Bob. "It's all right, only tell Mr Abdullah not to be so handy with his kris again, and that I—Mr Roberts, of Her Majesty's ship 'Startler'—think he ought to present us with some durians."

This was duly interpreted to the Malay, who drew back, gazing keenly from the ensign to the middy, and back again, his dark eyes seeming to flash, as he said something in his native tongue to the interpreter.

"Dullah say you throw durian again in his face, and it make him mad."

"No, no, old fellow, nothing of the kind," said Bob, laying his hand on Abdullah's shoulder. "That's all past."

The Malay judged his meaning from his looks, and not from his words. Then smiling, he leaped back into the boat, and returned laden with the finest fruit he had, which he offered to the young officers with no little grace and dignity, smiling pleasantly the while, but manifesting nothing little or servile.

The ladies looked on so wonderingly, that Bob had to leave the durians and explain, returning directly after, though, to the Malays, and obtaining a splendid bunch of the sweet flowers of the waringhan tree, which he carried back to the ladies, who smiled, thanked him, and took their departure.

"I never saw such a fellow as you are, Roberts," said the ensign, sulkily, as Bob returned; "you always seem to know what to say or do when ladies are present. I don't!"

"Native modesty, ability, and natural gifts, my dear fellow," said Bob; "and I'm precious glad they are gone, for I want to have a go at those durians."

Abdullah had already opened one, which he presented to Bob, who took it and made a terrible onslaught; and then, with a doubting look in his dark eyes, the Malay opened a second durian, hesitated, and then, evidently mastering his pride, offered it to Tom Long.

The latter drew back, shaking his head, and the Malay looked hurt and annoyed.

"Tell him I don't like durians, Bob Roberts," said Tom, nervously, "or we shall have another row."

"Here, hi! old cockolorum!" cried Bob, with his mouth full as he turned to the Malay, "tell Mr Abdullah there, that his durians are 'licious—luscious—'licious, but Mr Long likes mangosteens better."

This was interpreted, and Abdullah's doubting look changed as he hurried back to the boat, and returned with a basket full of delicious fruit, which he offered Tom Long with a bow; and then, finding they were accepted, he stood smiling with his head bent, while Bob went on devouring durian at a terrible rate.

"I say, Tom Long," said Bob, making a very unpleasant noise with his mouth.

"What is it?" said the ensign, who was deep in the mysterious flavour of the delicious mangosteen.

"I never believed in old Darwin, and his development, and evolution, and that sort of thing, till now."

"Why now?" said Tom Long.

"Because I feel such a pig," said Bob, attacking another durian. "Look here, old man, if you'll put me up in a durian tree, I don't want anything else thankey; you may have all the honour and glory. Oh! I say, this one's lovely! it's just like nectar made with custard, with an old shoe put in for flavour, and all stirred up with a paint brush. How are you getting on?"

"Bravely," said Tom Long.

The two young officers went on eating till they caught sight of the doctor in the distance—a sight so suggestive of making themselves ill that they gave up with a sigh or two, and went away, Tom Long offering to pay liberally for the fruit, notwithstanding a hint from his companion that he should be content to accept it as a present.

Both the Malays drew back very proudly, but Bob Roberts healed the breach in etiquette by quietly taking out his case, and offering a cigar to each of the Malays in turn.

These were taken with a smile, and accompanied by a thoroughly friendly look at parting.

"They're rum fellows, those Malays," said Bob, "and want a lot of managing. They are gentlemen at heart, and savages at body. That's my opinion of them."

"And my opinion is," said Tom Long, "that they are a precious unpleasant treacherous set of people, that it is downright cruelty to expect a gentleman to live amongst."

Up to this point no Malay, not even a servant, had been admitted to live upon the island, though the want of natives for assistance and to supply food had been keenly felt.

During the last few days, however, the resident had begun to relax this stringent rule, and a fisherman had been permitted to set up his hut and keep his boats at the upper end of the island, with the consequence that in place of a very intermittent supply, there was plenty of fish at the mess table.

Now as soon as the young officers had gone, Abdullah and his Malay companion sought audience, basket in hand, of the resident, who, after talking to them for a time, walked down to the landing-place, saw their ample supply of fruit and flowers, and ended by granting them a site by the water's edge, where they might set up their hut, and secure their boat, the understanding upon which the grant was made being that an ample supply was to be kept up for the use of the officers and men.

"Capital fellow, Linton," said the doctor. "Nothing like fruit in moderation to keep men in health. But isn't it risky to have these fellows on the isle?"

"I have thought of that," said Mr Linton; "but by being too exclusive we shall defeat our own ends. We must receive the principal part of the Malays in a friendly way, and it is only by a more open policy that this can be done. If we admit any wolves amongst the sheep they must meet with the wolves' fate. So far I think I have done well."

"Well, yes, perhaps you are right," said the doctor. But both gentlemen would have altered their opinions exceedingly if they had seen a long low boat, painted of a dark grey, and manned by six men, float gently down stream that night, and, unseen by the sentries, stop beside the sampan of Abdullah and his Malay companion.

Here there was a short consultation, Abdullah crawling over the gunwale into the long low boat, where he lay down, side by side with the man who steered.

Their conversation was long, and the others in the boat lay down while it was going on, so that had the boat been seen by an unusually watchful sentry it would have appeared to be empty, and moored to a bamboo stake thrust into the mud.

But the dark silent boat was not seen by the nearest sentry, either when it floated down, or when it was cautiously turned and paddled up stream once more, till, out of hearing, the oars went down with a noisy splash, and the long narrow vessel literally dashed through the river.

The reason it was not seen was simple enough.

Private Sim was on duty that night, and he had been once more fast asleep.

Chapter Twenty Two
The Crew of the Captain's Gig

There was a good deal of the schoolboy left in the young representatives of Her Majesty's two services; not that this is strange, for a good deal of his schoolboyhood clings to a man even in middle life. Bob Roberts had a tiff with Long, made vow after vow that he would never speak to the ensign again; declaring him to be a consequential cocky scarlet pouter pigeon, with as much strut in him as a bantam.

On the other hand, Tom Long declared the middy to be a most offensive little rascal, with impertinence enough in him for a dozen men. He was determined to cut him dead—that he was, and he would have no more to do with him.

Result the very next day:

Bob Roberts hurried down into the captain's gig, sitting there very eager and excited; for they were going to the island, and he had a plan in his head.

The captain came to the side and down the ladder, the gig was pushed off, the crew's oars fell into the bright river with one splash, and as they did so Bob Roberts forgot all the respect due to his commander, by suddenly catching him by the arm.

"Look, look, sir. See that?"

"No, Mr Roberts," said the captain rather sternly, "but I felt it."

"I beg your pardon, sir," said Bob, saluting. "It was a great crocodile, and the splash of the men's oars frightened it."

"Oh, indeed," said the captain dryly; and he took out a despatch and began to read.

Dick, who was coxswain of the gig, screwed up his mahogany visage, and Bob pretended to look terribly alarmed, and so the boat was rowed over the sparkling waters to the bamboo landing-stage, when the captain got out, and Bob was left in charge of the boat.

Bob jumped up as soon as the captain had entered the residency, and began to fidget about.

"I wish I knew how long the skipper would be, Dick," he said. "I want to go ashore. No, I don't," he said, correcting himself. "I got in a row once for that. But look here, Dick, suppose you go and find Mr Long."

"All right, sir," said Dick, with alacrity. "I'll go."

"Oh no, you don't," cried Bob, recollecting himself again; "that fly won't take the same cock salmon twice, Master Dick."

"I don't understand you, sir," growled Dick, rubbing his ear.

"Oh no, I suppose not," said Bob. "You didn't go ashore for me once with a message, and then get up to the canteen and forgot to come back again, did you?"

"Lor', now you mention it, sir, so I did," said Dick. "It was that day as I met Sergeant Lund, and he says, 'Why, Dick, old man,' he says, 'you look as dry and thirsty,' he says, 'as a fish. Come and have some lime juice and water,' and I did, and talking together about the 'Startler' and her guns, and earth-works, made me quite forget how the time went by. But lor', Mr Roberts, sir, what a memory you have to be sure."

"Yes," said Bob, sticking his cap on one side, and cocking his eye knowingly at the old salt; "a fellow just needs to have a good memory. I say, Dick, that lime juice and water was precious strong that day, wasn't it?"

"No, sir, not a bit," said the old sailor, stolidly. "But now I come to recollect, the sun did make me awful giddy."

"All right, Dick," said the midshipman; "run the boat a little more under the shade of those trees, and we'll keep you out of the sun to-day."

Old Dick growled, and picked up the boat-hook to draw the gig further along to where there was a dense cool shade. Then as he laid the boat-hook down and retook his place, he began to chuckle.

"You're a sharp 'un, Mr Roberts, that you are," he said, laughing. "Well, I'll own it; that was a bit of a slip that day. Send one o' the tothers ashore then with your message."

"No, I'll be blessed if I do," said Bob. "I'll never give way an inch again about a boat's crew; I haven't forgotten that little game at Aden, where I sent one chap ashore to get me some cold water to drink, and he didn't come back; and another volunteered to go and fetch him, and I let him go, and he didn't come back; and then I had to send another, and another—eight of 'em, every one vowing he'd bring the rest back; and at last I sat alone in that boat without a crew, and the first lieutenant came, and a nice wigging I had. No, Master Dick, I've been at sea too long now to be tricked by those games, and I mean to have the strictest discipline whenever I'm in command."

The men in the forepart of the boat overheard all this, and began to look very gloomy.

"Couldn't you let one on us go and get a bucket o' water, sir? it's precious hot," said the man who pulled bow oar, and he touched his forelock.

"No, Mr Joe Cripps, I couldn't," said Bob, sharply; "but I tell you what you all may do; put your heads over the side, and drink as much of this clear river-water as you like. We're not at sea, man."

"More we aren't, sir," said the man, glancing round at his companions, who laughed.

"Look here," said Bob, "Dick will keep an eye on the shore, and I'll tell the sentry there to pass the word. You may all smoke if you like, only look smart, and put away your pipes if the captain's coming."

"Thanky, sir," chorussed the men, and pipes were quickly produced by all save Dick, who helped himself to a fresh quid.

"I say, sentry," cried Bob, "pass the word on there—I want to see Mr Long."

"Yes, sir," was the reply, and the white-coated sentry walked to the end of his beat, and made a sign to the next sentry, who came to the end of his beat, heard what was wanted, and passed the message on, so that at the end of a few minutes Ensign Long came slowly down to the landing-place, with an umbrella held up to keep off the sun, and found the boat's crew smoking, and Bob Roberts, with his cap tilted over his eyes, sitting in the bottom of the gig, with his legs over the side, so exactly arranged that the water rippled round the soles of his shoes, and pleasantly cooled his feet.

"Did you wish to speak to me, Mr Roberts?" said Long, stiffly.

"Hallo, Tom, old man! Here, jump in! I've got some news for you."

Ensign Long looked very stand-offish; but the eager face of Bob, the only one about his own age of whom he could make a companion, was too much for him; and as Bob got up and made a place for him, Mr Ensign Long unbent a little, and really as well as metaphorically undid a button or two, and got into the captain's gig.

"I say, look here, Tom, old man, what's the use of us two always falling out, when we could be so jolly together?" said Bob.

"I don't quite understand you," said Tom Long, stiffly. "I am not of a quarrelsome disposition, as any of my brother officers will tell you."

"Then it must be me then who is such a quarrelsome beast, and there's my hand, and we won't fall out any more."

Ensign Long undid a few more buttons, for it was very hot, and condescended to shake hands.

"I'm sure it's not my wish to be bad friends," said Ensign Long. "I think the members of the two services ought to be like brothers."

"So do I," said Bob. "I say, sentry, keep a sharp look-out for the captain, and I'll stand a glass for you at the canteen next time I come ashore."

"Yes, sir," said the sentry. "But p'raps, sir, I mayn't see you next time you come ashore."

"There's an artful one for you, Tom," cried Bob, getting his hot wet hand into his pocket with no little difficulty, and throwing the man a fourpenny piece. "Now, look here, Tom," he continued, as the man cleverly caught the tiny piece and thrust it in his pocket, Ensign Long carefully closing his ear and looking in the other direction the while, "you and I might have no end of games if we could only keep friends."

"Well, let's keep friends, then," said Tom Long.

"Agreed," said Bob, "and the first one of us who turns disagreeable, the other is to punch his head."

"No, I can't agree to that," said Tom, thoughtfully, "because we could not settle who was in the wrong."

"Then we'd punch one another's heads," said Bob; "but never mind about that. Look here."

Ensign Long undid a few more buttons, of which he had a great many down the front of his mess waistcoat, just like a row of gold-coated pills, and then he proceeded to *look there*, that is to say mentally, at what his companion had to say.

"Do you know that young Malay chap, who came on board yesterday with his father, the Bang-the-gong, or Tumongong, or whatever he calls himself?"

"Yes, I saw him; he came afterwards to the fort, and was shown round."

"Didn't you speak to him?"

"Not I. Don't care much for these niggers."

"Oh! but he's no end of a good chap," said Bob. "He can't help being brown. I took him down to the gun-room, and we smoked and talked; he can speak English like fun."

"Indeed!"

"Yes, indeed; and I tell you what it is, he's worth knowing. He's quite a prince, and as jolly as can be. He says there's out-and-out shooting in the jungle, and if we'll go ashore and have a turn with him, he'll take us where we can have a regular good day."

"What does the young savage shoot with," said Long, disdainfully, "a bow and arrow?"

"Bow and arrow be hanged! Why, don't I tell you he is quite a prince? and he's regularly English in his ways. Some one made him a present of a Purdey breechloader, and he uses Eley cartridges. What do you think of that?"

"Very disgusting that men should take to such adjuncts to civilisation before they leave off wearing those savage plaid petticoats."

"I believe they are a tribe of Scotsmen, who came out here in the year one and turned brown," said Bob, laughing. "Those sarongs are just like kilts."

"Yes," said Tom Long, "and the krises are just the same as dirks."

"Well, bother all that!" cried Bob. "I told him we'd both come to-morrow, and bring guns, and he's going to get some prog, and half-a-dozen beaters; and we'll have a jolly day."

"But," said Tom Long, dropping his official ways, and speaking excitedly, "he didn't ask me!"

"He said he'd be delighted to know you. He likes Englishmen."

"But we can't get leave."

"Can't we?" cried Bob. "I can. If the skipper says no, I think I can work him round; and I'm sure you can manage it. Look here, you ask Doctor Bolter to manage it for you, and say we'll bring him all the specimens we can shoot."

"By Jove, Bob, what a jolly idea!" cried Tom Long—an officer no longer, but a regular boy again. "We'll get leave to-night, and start early."

"That we will."

"But are you sure that young Tumongong would be glad to see me too?"

"Ali Latee, his name is, and I've got to call him Al already, and he called me Bob. Glad? of course he will. I said you'd come too; and I told such a whopper, Tom."

"What did you say?"

"I told him you were my dearest friend."

"Well, so I am, Bob; only you will get so restive."

"Yes, I always was a restive little beggar," said Bob. "To-morrow morning then, and—"

"Captain coming, sir."

"Landing-place at daybreak, Tom. Cut," whispered Bob; and the young ensign rose and leaped ashore, buttoning up his little golden-pill buttons, as Captain Horton came down the path, and answered his salute with a friendly nod.

The next minute the water was flashing like fiery silver from the blades of the oars, and the gig returned to the steamer's side, where Bob began to prepare for the next day's trip, taking it for granted that he could get leave.

Chapter Twenty Three
How Bob Roberts and Tom
Long asked for Leave

Very great things come from very small germs, and for a long time afterwards Captain Horton bitterly regretted that he had been in so easy and amiable a frame of mind that he had accorded Bob Roberts the holiday he desired.

He had dined well, and was in that happy state of content that comes upon a man who is not old, and whose digestion is good.

It was a glorious night, and the captain was seated on deck at a little table bearing a shaded lamp and his cup of coffee, when Bob respectfully approached, cap in hand.

"If you please, sir—"

"Who's that? Oh! Roberts. Here; go down to the cabin, Roberts, and fetch my cap. I don't want to catch cold."

"Yes, sir."

"Hi! stop, my boy! Here; lend me your cap till you come back."

It was a very undignified proceeding, but Captain Horton had a horror of colds in the head, and would far rather have been undignified than catch one. So he took the little, natty gold-laced cap held out to him, and stuck it upon his pate.

"Bless my soul!" he exclaimed. "What a stupid little head you've got, Roberts."

"Yes, sir," said the lad sharply, "very; but it will grow, sir."

"Then I hope it won't grow more stupid, boy. There, be quick!"

Bob ran down to the captain's cabin, and obtained the required piece of headgear, with which he returned to the quarter-deck, where the captain was sipping his coffee, apparently oblivious of the fact that he had sent for his cap.

"Your cap, sir."

"Oh, ah! to be sure! yes, of course. Thank you, Roberts. Exchange is no robbery, as we used to say at Harrow. You needn't wait."

"Thank you, sir; no, sir, but—"

"Now what is it, Roberts? You know I don't like to be troubled after dinner."

"Yes, sir; but I beg your pardon, sir. Might I have leave to go ashore to-morrow?"

"Yes—no. What, in the name of goodness, do you mean, Mr Roberts, by coming and asking me? Go to the first lieutenant."

"Please, sir, I'm very sorry to trouble you, but he's dining at the residency."

"Then why didn't you wait till he came back?"

"Because, sir, please sir, Mr Wilson's always cross when he has been out to dine. He's not like you, sir."

The captain started up in his chair, and gazed full in the lad's face.

"You're a nice boy, Roberts," he said; "but don't you try any of that impudent flattery on with me again."

"No, sir. I beg pardon, sir, but may I go?"

"Wait till the first lieutenant comes back, sir, and ask him."

"But please, sir, it's important."

"What is?"

"That I should have leave to-morrow, sir."

"Where are you going, then?"

"Please, sir, I *was* going shooting."

"Oh!" said his captain, laughing; "then that's what you call important, eh? Well, I don't know what to say. Have there been any complaints against you lately?"

"Two or three, sir," said Bob; "but I have been trying very hard, sir," he added earnestly, "to do my duty."

"Humph!" said the captain. "Well, I was a youngster myself once. I suppose you'd be very much disappointed if I said *no*?"

"Yes, sir; very much."

"Humph! Who's going with you?"

"Ensign Long, sir, if he can get leave."

"Well, Roberts, you can go; but be careful with your guns. And look here, don't do anything to annoy the Malays. Don't go near their religious places, or get trespassing."

"No, sir, I'll be very careful."

"Any one else going?"

"Ali Latee, sir, the Tumongong's son."

"Very well. Be off!"

"Yes, sir, thank you, sir," cried Bob joyously, and he hurried away.

Ensign Long felt perfectly sure that if he went direct to the major, and asked for leave to go ashore shooting, it would be refused. He would have gone and asked Captain Smithers to intercede for him, but the captain was always short, and ready to be annoyed at nearly everything said; so he concluded that Bob Roberts' idea was the best, and he went straight to Doctor Bolter, who was in his room, in his shirt and trousers, both his sleeves rolled up, busily pinning out some gorgeous butterflies that he had secured.

"Ah, Long!" he said, as the youth entered; "how are you? just hand me that sheet of cork."

"Quite well, sir, thank you."

"Oh! are you? I'll look at your tongue directly. Hand me one of those long thin pins."

The pin was handed.

"Now put a finger on that piece of card. Gently, my dear boy, gently; the down upon these things is so exquisitely fine that the least touch spoils them. Look at that Atlas moth by your elbow. Isn't it lovely?"

"Magnificent, sir," said Long, taking up a shallow tray, and really admiring the monstrous moth pinned out therein.

"Ah, my lad! I wish I could see you turning a little attention to natural history, now we are in this perfect paradise for a collector. How much better for you than lounging about all day under the trees. Now then, put out your tongue."

"But I'm quite well, Doctor Bolter."

"Put—out—your—tongue—sir. Confound it all, sir, I've no time to waste!"

As he spoke he took up the lamp, and held it close to Tom Long's face, so that the light might fall upon the protruded organ.

"Hah!" ejaculated Doctor Bolter, resuming his seat.

"But I really am quite well, sir," remonstrated Tom Long.

"Don't tell me, sir, that you are quite well. Do you think I don't know when a man's well, and when he is not? You are just a little wee bit feverish."

He felt the youth's pulse, and nodded his head sagely.

"Too much idleness and good living is what is the matter with you, sir. Why don't you collect?"

"How can I, sir," said Tom, "when I'm shut up in this island?"

"Go ashore. Here, I'll give you some collecting boxes, and lend you a vasculum and a net. Go and get me some butterflies."

"Well, sir, if it's all the same to you," said Tom, taking advantage of the wind blowing in the right direction, "shooting's more in my way. Suppose I shot you some birds?"

"Better still," said the doctor, enthusiastically. "Nothing I should like better. I want a few trogons, and the blue-billed gaper. Then you might get me the green chatterer, and any new birds you could see."

"Yes, sir."

"And look here, Long; the woods here are the chosen resort of the great argus pheasant. I don't suppose you would be able to come across one, but if you do—"

"Down him," said Tom Long.

"Exactly," said the doctor. "There, my lad, I won't give you any medicine, but prescribe a little short exercise."

"Thank you, sir," said Tom, trying hard to restrain his eagerness. "Might I have a run to-morrow? I have felt very languid to-day."

"To be sure. I'll see the major and get leave of absence for you. Be careful, though. Don't overheat yourself; and mind and not get into any scrape with the Malays."

"I'll mind, sir," said Tom.

"That's right. Be very careful not to spoil the plumage of the birds. You can make a Malay boy carry them tied by the beaks to a stick. Stop a minute;

as you are here, you may as well cut up these cards for me in thin strips. I'll go and ask the major the while."

Tom set to work at the cards with a pair of scissors, and the doctor donned his undress coat, went out and returned with the requisite permission.

"By the way, look here, Long; if you'll promise to be very careful, I'll lend you my double gun."

"I'll take the greatest care of it, sir," was the reply.

"Good! There it is; so now be off; and to-morrow night I shall expect a nice lot of specimens to skin."

So Tom Long went off with the gun, and the doctor helped to turn the residency into an abode where danger usurped the place of safety, and peace was to be succeeded by the horrors of war.

Chapter Twenty Four
A Jaunt in the Jungle, with an Awkward End

Tom Long rather overslept himself, but it was pretty early when he started from his quarters, to encounter Captain Smithers soon after, looking anxious and annoyed. He nodded shortly, and the young ensign went on through what was quite a wilderness of beauty, to meet, next, Rachel Linton and Mary Sinclair, who had been flower-gathering, and who stopped for a few minutes' conversation with him, the former nearly spoiling the expedition by turning the foolish youth's thoughts in quite a contrary direction from collecting or shooting.

But Rachel Linton quietly wished him success, and Tom went off telling himself that it would look foolish if he did not go.

He had not far to go to the landing-place now; but in the little space close by the resident's garden he encountered Private Gray, who saluted him, and sent Tom on thinking that he wished he was as old, and good-looking, and as manly, as the young soldier he had just passed. And then he felt very miserable and dejected, and wished he was anything but what he was, until he saw Bob Roberts, sitting in the "Startler's" dinghy by the landing-place, and forgot all about everything but the shooting excursion.

"Come along! You are a chap," shouted Bob. "I've been waiting over half an hour."

"Met the ladies," said Tom, "and was obliged to speak."

"Oh, you met the ladies, did you?" said Bob, looking at him suspiciously. "Well, never mind; jump aboard. Got plenty of cartridges?"

"Yes, heaps; and some food too."

"So have I," cried Bob. "Now, then, pull away, Dick. Set us ashore under those trees. Hooray, Tom; look! There's young Bang-gong there, waiting with a couple of niggers."

Dick pulled steadily at the sculls, and the little dinghy breasted the water like a duck, soon crossing the intervening space, when the two lads landed with their ammunition and stores, shook hands with the handsome dark young chief who confronted them, and at once started off for the jungle, while Dick stood refilling his right cheek with tobacco, before rowing the dinghy back to the steamer.

"Ah!" he said, as he once more took the sculls, "they never asked me to go, too. Now you see if by the time they get back to-night they hain't been in about as pretty a bit o' mischief as was ever hatched."

Old Dick had no intention of setting himself up as a prophet of evil, for his remark was made more out of spite than anything else, it having struck the old fellow that a good idle ashore would be very pleasant, especially with plenty to eat and drink, and a fair supply of tobacco.

"It wouldn't be very hard work to carry all the game they shoot," he said, chuckling; "and one might get a good nap under a shady tree."

But Dick's hopes were blighted, and instead of shade under trees, he had to row back to where the "Startler" was blistering in the hot sunshine, and take his part in the regular duties of the day.

Meanwhile the two lads with their companion were striding along beneath the shade of the trees, with the naval and military services of her most gracious Majesty completely forgotten, and their elastic young minds bent entirely upon the expedition. They looked flushed and eager, and the Tumongong's son, Ali, was just as full of excitement.

The latter was about the age of the young English officers, and their coming was to him delightful. For his father was wise enough to foresee the course of events—how the old barbarism of the Malay was dying out, to give place to the busy civilisation taught by the white men from the west; and he felt sure that the most civilised and advanced of the young chieftains would occupy the best positions in the future. Hence then he had sent his son for long spells at a time to Singapore and Penang, to mingle with the English, and pick up such education as he could obtain.

Ali, being a clever boy, had exceeded his father's expectations, having arrived at the age of eighteen, with a good knowledge of English, in which tongue he could write and converse; and in addition he had imbibed a sufficiency of our manners and customs to make him pass muster very well amongst a party of gentlemen.

Bob Roberts and he were sworn friends directly, for there was something in their dispositions which made them assimilate, Ali being full of life and fun, which, since his return to Parang, he had been obliged to suppress, and take up the stiff stately formality of the Malays about him, of whom many of the chiefs looked unfavourably at the youth who had so quickly taken up and made friends with the people they looked upon as so many usurpers.

No sooner were the three lads out of sight of the attap-thatched roofs and the island, the fort and steamer, than all formality was thrown to the winds, and they tramped on chattering away like children. Tom, however, walked on rather stiffly for a few minutes, but the sight of a good broad rivulet was too much for him; drill, discipline, the strict deportment of an officer and a gentleman, whose scarlet and undress uniforms had cost a great deal of money, and in which, to tell the truth, he had been very fond of attiring himself when alone with his looking-glass, all were forgotten, and the bottled-up schoolboy vitality that was in his breast seethed up like so much old-fashioned ginger beer.

"Follow my leader!" he cried, handing his gun to one of the Malays, whose eyes rolled with pleasure as he saw sentimental Tom Long take a sharp run, leap well from the near bank, and land on the other side of the stream, but he had to catch at some bamboos to save himself from falling back into the water.

"With a cheerly hi ho," shouted Bob Roberts, dropping his gun on a bush. "Look out, soldier."

The words were on his lips as he ran, and in his leap alighted on the other side in so bad a place that he had to catch at Tom to save himself from falling, and for a few seconds there was a sharp scuffle amongst the bamboos before they were safe.

"Look out, Ali," shouted Bob, on seeing their companion coming; "it's bad landing."

But Ali was already in full career; as light and active of foot as a deer, he made a quick rush and a leap, and landed in safety quite a yard beyond the young officers.

"Well done! Hooray!" cried Bob, who had not the slightest objection to seeing himself surpassed; while the two Malays in charge of the guns and impediments on the other side stared at each other in astonishment, and in a whisper asked if the young chief had gone out of his mind.

"Now then, Sambo-Jumbo," cried Bob, "over with those guns. Come along, they are not loaded."

The two Malays stared, and Ali said a few words to them in their native tongue, when they immediately gathered up the guns, and, being bare-legged, waded across the stream, which was about four yards wide.

The last man came over with a rush as he neared the bank, for suddenly from a reed-bed above them there was a wallow and a flounder with a tremendous disturbance in the water, as something shot down towards the main stream.

"A crocodile," said Ali, as the young Englishmen directed at him a wondering gaze.

"Crocodile!" cried Bob, snatching his gun from the attendant, and hastily thrusting in cartridges, after which he ran along the stream till checked by the tangled growth.

"No good," said Ali, laughing at his eagerness. "Gone."

The reptile was gone sure enough, and it was doubtful which was the more frightened, it or the Malays; so they went on along a narrow jungle-path, that was walled up on either side by dense vegetation, which seemed to have been kept hacked back by the heavy knives of the working Malays. To have gone off to right or left would have been impossible, so tangled and matted with canes and creepers was the undergrowth, Bob waking up to the fact that here was the natural home of the cane so familiar to schoolboys; the unfamiliar part being, that keeping to nearly the same diameter, these canes ran one, two, and even three hundred feet in length, creeping, climbing, undulating, now running up the side of some pillar-like tree to a convenient branch, over which it passed to hang down again in a loop till it reached some other tree, in and out of whose branches it would wind.

As they went on farther they were in a soft green twilight with at rare intervals the sharp bright rays of the sun, like golden arrows, darting through the dense shade, and a patch of luxuriantly growing pitcher-plants or orchids, more beautiful than any that had previously met their eyes.

"Mind the elephant-holes!" cried Ali, who was behind.

"All right," said Tom Long, who was leading the way. "Oh, my gracious!"

There was a loud *splash* and a wallowing noise, followed by a loud suck as of some one pulling a leg out of thick mud; and this proved to be the case, for on Bob running forward, and turning a corner of the winding path, there was Tom, just extricating himself from an elephant-hole.

For they were in a land where wheeled carriages were almost unknown, all portage being done either by boats on the many streams, or on the backs of elephants and buffaloes, by the former of whom the few jungle-paths were terribly cut up, partly by the creatures' weight, but more particularly from the fact that, no matter how many passed along a track, or how wet and swampy it might be, the sagacious creatures believed in the way being safe where any of their kind had been before, and invariably placed their great round feet in the same holes; the effect being that these elephant-holes were often three or four feet deep, and half full of mud and water.

The two Malays were called into requisition, and by means of green leaves removed a good deal of the mud, but the mishap did not add much to the lad's comfort. However, he took it in very good part, and they went on for some distance, to where a side track, that was apparently but little used, turned off to the left, and the Malays, drawing their heavy knives, went first to clear away some of the twining creepers that hung from side to side.

So beautiful was the jungle that for a time the two English lads forgot all about their guns, as they stopped hard by some watercourse to admire the graceful lace-fronded fern or the wonderful displays of moss hanging from the more ancient trees.

But at last the weight of their guns reminded them that they had come to shoot, and they drew Ali's attention to the fact.

"Wait a little," he said, smiling. "We shall soon be in a clearer part. You can't shoot here."

As he said—so it proved, for after another half-hour's walking, during which they had become bathed in perspiration from the moist heat, there was less tangled growth, and the magnificent trees grew more distant one from the other. They were of kinds quite unknown to the little party, who, though seeking birds, could not help admiring the vast monarchs of the primeval forest.

"This looks more hopeful," cried Bob, who so far had only heard the occasional note of a bird which was invisible. Now he saw one or two flit across the sunny glade in advance.

"Yes, there are birds here; but take care, there are serpents too."

Tom Long winced a little at this last announcement, for he had a honour of the twining creatures; and as his memory ran back to the narrow escape of Adam Gray, from the sea snake, he asked with some little trepidation,—

"Poisonous?"

"Oh, yes, some of them! But you need not be alarmed, they hurry off as soon as they hear our steps."

"But," said Tom, to Bob's very great delight, for he could see his companion's alarm, "how about the boa-constrictors?"

"Pythons your people call them," said Ali. "Yes, there are plenty of them in the wet places."

"Dangerous?"

"No," said Ali, "I never knew them to be—only to the little pigs."

"But ain't they very large?"

"Oh, yes," was the reply, "big as my leg, and so long."

He made a mark on the soft earth with one foot, and then took seven paces, where he made a fresh mark, indicating a length of about eighteen feet.

"But they attack men sometimes, don't they?" said Tom, importantly.

"No, I never knew of such a thing," said Ali. "They steal the chickens, and swallow them whole."

Tom felt somewhat reassured, but all the same he walked delicately over the thick herbage and amongst the scrub, not knowing but that he might plant his foot at any time upon some writhing creature, whose venomous fangs would be inserted in his leg before he could leap aside; but no such accident befell him, neither had one of the party had a single shot, when Bob declared that he was too hungry to go farther, and going on alone to where a huge prostrate tree stretched its great trunk for many yards, he was about to sit down, when he stopped short, held out one hand to indicate silence, and beckoned with the other.

Ali ran softly up, and on seeing at what his friend pointed, he signalled to one of the Malays to come.

The man came up without a sound, caught sight of Bob's discovery—a black snake about five feet long, and going gently up, he, to the lad's horror, suddenly seized it by the tail, and with a rapid snatch drew the reptile through the left hand up to the neck, which the Malay grasped tightly, while the reptile writhed, hissed, and angrily twined itself round the man's bare brown arm.

"It isn't poisonous, then?" said Tom Long, coolly.

"Yes," replied Ali; "it is a cobra, one of our most dangerous snakes."

The Malay held it close for the lads to examine, which, after learning its deadly character, they were not particularly eager to do; but the native laughed, and seemed to think very little of the danger, ending by placing the reptile's neck upon the fallen tree, and decapitating it with one clean cut of the knife.

A halt was made here, and a hearty lunch was disposed of; after which, feeling rested and comparatively cool, they started once more, and before long the first shot was had at a blue-billed gaper, a lovely bird, with azure and golden bill, and jetty-black, white, and crimson plumage.

"One for the doctor!" exclaimed Tom Long; and the beautiful bird was safely stowed away.

Ali next brought down a paroquet, with long delicate tail, and delicious sunset hues blushing upon its plumage of pearly grey green.

Bob followed, with a shot at a green chatterer, a lovely little bird, all rich green and black, with a handsome crest.

Next followed sundry misses, and then with varying fortune they secured a dozen really beautifully-plumaged birds for the doctor.

"And now," exclaimed Bob, "I think we ought to get something for the pot."

"For the pot?" said Ali, looking puzzled, for anything verging on sporting slang was to him as so much Greek.

"I mean for cooking and eating."

Ali laughed, and said something to his followers, who led the way on to a more densely wooded part nearer the river, whose proximity was indicated by the change in the character of the vegetation.

"Stop a minute, though," exclaimed Tom Long. "I can't stand this any more. Here's something been biting me ever so!"

He made a halt, and began to examine his ankles and legs.

"Why, look here?" he cried; "I'm bleeding like fun!"

Like fun or no, he was certainly bleeding freely, and the cause was not far to seek. In fact, as he turned up the legs of his trousers four bloated little leeches, satiated with their horrid repast, dropped off his skin, and he caught a couple more feasting upon him right royally.

"You should have tied your trousers round your ankles, and put on your boots outside them," said Ali; "but it won't hurt you."

"Won't hurt!" exclaimed Tom Long, indignantly; "but it does hurt. Why, I'm bleeding horribly."

At a stream close by, however, his wounds were bathed, the bleeding checked, and then a few shots were had at the jungle-fowl, two brace of which, a little bigger than ordinary bantams, were secured before the little party halted in a clearing close to the river.

Here were half-a-dozen native houses, one and all built upon bamboo piles, so as to raise the dwellers well above the damp ground, the possibility of flood, and out of the reach of any wild creatures that might be wandering by night.

There was something exceedingly homelike in the appearance of the places, each with its scrap of garden and fruit-trees; while the occupant of the principal hut insisted upon the whole party coming to partake of rest and refreshment before continuing their way.

"Oh! we don't want to go in," said Tom Long, peevishly.

"Well, no, I don't want to go in," said Bob, "but the old fellow will be offended if we do not; and we want to make friends, not enemies."

Ali nodded, and they sat down in the bamboo-floored hut, through whose open door they saw their host busy sending a Malay boy up one of his cocoa-nut trees, the boy rapidly ascending the lofty palm by means of nicks already cut in the tree for the purpose.

Three great nuts, in their husk-like envelopes, fell directly with a thud, and these the friendly Malay opened and placed before his visitors.

"This is very different to the cocoa-nut we boys used to buy at school," said Bob, as he revelled in the delicious sub-acid cream of the nut, and then partook of rice, with a kind of sugary confection which was very popular amongst the people.

Homely as the outside of the huts had appeared, both the lads could not help noticing how similar the habits of these simple Malays in this out-of-the-way part of the world were to those of people at home.

For instance, beneath the eaves hung a couple of cages, neatly made of bamboo, in one of which was a pair of the little lovebird paroquets side by side upon a perch; and in the other a minah, a starling-like bird, that kept leaping from perch to perch, and repeating with a very clear enunciation several Malay words.

Thoroughly rested at last, the little party set off again—their host refusing all compensation, and once more they plunged into the thickest of the jungle, though very little success attended their guns.

This was hardly noticed, though, for there was always something fresh to see—huge butterflies of wondrous colours flitting through the more open glades, strange vegetable forms, beautifully graceful bamboos, clustering in the moister parts, where some stream ran unseen amidst the dense undergrowth, while at last they reached a river of such surpassing beauty, with its overhanging ferns, in the deep ravine in which it ran, that both the strangers paused to admire, while the Malays looked on with good-humoured wonder at their enthusiasm.

But very little of the sluggish stream was seen for the dense emerald growth, and the water itself was more like a chain of pools, which seemed to be likely haunts of fish; and forgetting heat and weariness, both the young Englishmen began to divide the reeds and long grass and ferns with the barrels of their guns, so as to peer down into the water.

Ali, evidently to please them, displayed quite as much interest as they; while the two Malays squatted down, and taking out sirih leaves, spread upon them a little lime paste from a box, rolled in them a scrap of betel-nut, and began to indulge in a quiet chew.

The lads were only a few yards apart, and Bob Roberts cautiously approached a deep still pool, when he heard upon his right a splash and a rush, accompanied by a wild cry for aid.

For the moment he was paralysed by the strange horror of the cry; but, recovering himself, he rushed through the long reeds and ferns, to look upon a sight which, for the time, almost robbed him of the power to act.

Chapter Twenty Five
How Bob and Tom bagged Strange Game

The young midshipman saw at a glance what had happened, and the sight of the deadly struggle going on roused him from the stupor that had assailed him.

It was evident that Ali had been holding by one hand to the branch of a tree, and was leaning over just such a pool as that which had caught the attention of Bob, when a crocodile, taking advantage of his unguarded approach, had seized him by the leg just above the knee.

Ali had at once dropped his gun, seized the branch with the other hand, and clung for life as he uttered the cry for help, while the reptile tugged viciously, and shook him violently, to make him loose his hold.

Had the creature succeeded, the young Malay chief's fate had been sealed, for in another moment he would have been drawn down into the deep pool, with a few bubbles ascending through the agitated water to show where he lay.

The time seemed long to the brave young fellow as he held on for dear life; and it seemed long to Bob Roberts before he could act; but it was but a matter of moments before he had reached Ali's side, with his gun cocked; and placing the piece close to the reptile's eye as it glared savagely at him, and seemed about to leave one victim to seize another, he fired both barrels in rapid succession.

There was a tremendous splash as the smoke hung before him for a few moments, then as it rose the young middy saw nothing but the troubled water before him, and Ali lying panting, and with his eyes starting, close by his side.

By this time Tom Long and the two Malays had come up, eager with questions, to which Ali answered faintly, and gladly partook of a little spirits from the young ensign's flask.

"I ought to have known better," he said, "but I did not think of the danger. It will be a warning for you both. These rivers swarm with the brutes."

"But your leg?" cried Bob, kneeling down.

"A little torn; that's all," said the young Malay, stoically. "My sarong and the trousers have saved it, I think."

All the same though it was bleeding freely, and with a rough kind of surgery Bob's handkerchief was used to bind it up.

"I'm not much hurt," said Ali then; and to prove his words he rose, limped a step or two forward, and picked up his gun, while Bob proceeded to slip a couple more cartridges in his own, gazing once more eagerly into the pool, but seeing nothing but a little blood-stained water.

He turned sharply round, for something touched him, and there stood Ali, looking at him in a peculiar manner, and holding out one hand, which Bob took, thinking the other felt faint.

"I can't talk now," said Ali, hoarsely; "but you saved my life. I shall never forget it."

"Oh, nonsense, old fellow," cried Bob. "But, I say; what a brute! He must have been twenty feet long."

"Oh, no," said Ali, smiling faintly, "not ten. The small ones are the most vicious and dangerous. Let us go."

"But can you walk?" said Bob. "Have a cigar."

"Yes; I will smoke," said the young Malay, as he walked bravely on, though evidently in pain; and lighting a cigar, he talked in the most unconcerned way about the creature's sudden attack.

"Such things are very common," he said. "Down by the big river they seize the women who go for water, and carry off the girls who bathe. There are monsters, ten, twenty, and twenty-five feet long; but we are so used to them that it does not occur to us to take care."

They were now walking over the ground they had that morning traversed, Ali seeming so much at ease, and smiling so nonchalantly, that his companions ceased to trouble him with advice and proposals that he should be carried.

At last they came to a spot where a fresh track turned off, and Ali paused.

"You will not think me rude," he said, speaking with all the ease of a polished gentleman, "if I leave you here? Ismael will take you the nearest way down to the island. Yusuf will go with me. My leg is bad."

"Then let us carry you," cried Bob. "Here, we'll soon cut down some bamboos and make a frame."

"No, no, it is not so bad as that," cried the young man, firmly; "and I would rather walk. This is a nearer way, and you will do as I ask, please."

The two youths hesitated, but Ali was so firm, and his utterances so decided, that although unwillingly, they felt constrained to obey his wishes.

"No, no," exclaimed Bob, "let me go with you, old fellow. Let us both come."

"Do you wish to serve me more than you have already done?" said Ali, quietly.

"Yes, I do, 'pon my word," replied Bob.

"Then please say 'good-bye.' I am very nearly at home."

There was nothing more to be said, so the young Englishmen shook hands and parted from their companion, after he had promised to send word by Yusuf the next day how he was.

"I don't half feel satisfied," said Bob, trudging along behind the Malay who was their guide. "I think we ought to have gone with him, Tom."

"I feel so too," was the reply, "but what could we do? Perhaps he was not so very much hurt after all."

They were tired now, and the heat of the afternoon seemed greater than ever, so that they longed to get out of the stifling forest to the open banks of the river. But they were as yet far away, and their guide made a cut along the side of a patch of marshy ground, looking back from time to time to see if they followed.

"Snipe, by all that's wonderful!" cried Bob, firing two barrels almost as he spoke, and bringing down four birds out of a flock that bore some resemblance to, but were double the size of, snipes.

Tom raised his piece for a shot, but he was too late; and Yusuf smiled and showed his teeth as he ran and picked up the birds, tied their legs together with some grass, and added them to the jungle-fowl he was carrying.

"Well, they won't be able to laugh at us," said Bob. "We shan't go back empty. Hallo! what the dickens now?"

For a couple of scantily clad Malay girls, their sarongs torn and ragged with forcing their way through the bushes, came panting up, uttering loud cries, and flinging themselves down at the astonished youths' feet, clung to their legs, while Yusuf began to abuse them angrily, and kicking one, was about to thrust away the other with his foot.

"You leave them alone, will you?" said Bob, giving him a rap on the head with his gun-barrel. "I wish to goodness I knew what was the Malay for *cowardly beast,* and you should have it, young fellow."

The Malay's hand flew to his kris as he threw down the birds, and it flashed in the sunshine directly.

"Ah! would you bite?" cried Bob, presenting his gun at the other's breast, when the man shrank away, with his eyes half-closed, and a peculiarly tigerish aspect about him as he drew his lips from his white teeth, but kept at a respectful distance, knowing as he did how ably the young sailor could use his gun.

Just then the girls renewed their cries and lamentations, clinging wildly to the youths as if for protection, as half-a-dozen Malays, armed with krises and the long limbings, or spears, that they can use with such deadly force, came running up, and made as if to seize upon the two girls.

"Keep off, will you! Confound your impudence, what do you mean?" roared Bob, slewing round his gun to face the newcomers. "I say, Tom, what fools we do seem not to be able to speak this stupid lingo! What are they jabbering about?"

"Hang me, if I know," said Tom, whose face was flushed with heat and excitement. "All I can make out is that they want these two Malay ladies who have come to us to protect them."

"Then, as my old nurse used to say, 'want will be their master,'" said Bob, angrily; "for they're not going to have them."

The leader of the Malay party volubly said something to the two English, and then said some angry words to the two girls, who clung more tightly to their protectors, as he caught each by her shoulder.

Bob brought the barrel of his gun down heavily on the Malay's head, in the same fashion as he had served Yusuf, who was now missing, having suddenly glided away.

The Malay leaped back, tore out his kris, and made at his assailant; but the presented barrels of the two guns kept him back, as they did his companions, who had presented their limbings as their leader drew his kris, while now the girls leaped bravely up, and interposed their bodies between the two youths and the threatened danger.

"That's very prettily done, my dears," said Bob; "but you are both of you horribly in the way if we should shoot, and it isn't the fashion in England. Place aux Messieurs in a case like this. There, you stand behind me."

He gently placed the girl behind him, keeping his gun the while pointed at the Malays, and Tom Long followed his example.

"Shall we shoot, Bob Roberts?" said the ensign, hoarsely.

"No," said Bob, whose voice sounded just as hoarse. "Not unless they try to do us mischief. This is the time for a strategical retreat, as they are three to one, and we may at any time be cut off. I say, Tom, I feel in such a horrible state of squirm; don't you?"

"Never was so frightened in my life," replied Tom, "but pray don't show it."

"Show it?" replied Bob sharply; "hang 'em, no; they should cut me to pieces first. But I say, old fellow, I never thought I was such a coward before."

"More did I," replied Tom. "Suppose they understand what we're saying!"

"Not they; no more than we can them. I say, I have it! These are two slaves trying to escape, and these chaps want to get them back."

"Then we'll take them right away to the fort," cried Tom. "Look out!" he added, as, after speaking to his followers, the chief Malay made another angry advance with the men.

"Now look here, Mr Café-au-lait," said Bob, raising his gun this time to his shoulder, as he spoke aloud, "if you don't sheer off, I'll let fly at you a regular broadside. Be ready, Tom."

"Ready!" was the sharp reply, "when you say Fire."

"Right," replied Bob. "Now then, old check-petticoat, are you going to call off your men?"

For answer the Malay pointed to the two trembling girls, and signed to his men to advance with their spears.

"I'm horribly alarmed, Tom!" cried Bob, "but retreating now is showing the white feather, and we shall be whopped. Now then, don't fire, but let's make a dash at them."

The Malays were only about three yards off, having before retreated five or six, but now they had diminished the distance, when the two lads, with their pieces at their shoulders, stepped boldly forward, with the result that the Malays broke and fled, their leader first; and out of bravado Tom Long fired a shot over their heads to quicken their steps, while Bob burst into a hearty fit of laughter.

"Look here!" he said. "Here's a game! Only look, sojer!"

"What is it!" cried Tom, drawing out the empty cartridge case and putting in a new one. "Why, you don't mean to say—"

"But I just do mean to say it!" cried Bob, stamping about and laughing as he opened the breech of his gun, and drew out two empty cases, to replace with full.

"Not loaded!"

"No," cried Bob, "That moment, you know, I shot at the snipes, and hadn't time to load again. Did you ever see such a game, keeping those chaps off with an empty gun? Oh, I say, don't!"

This last was in consequence of the energetic action taken by the two poor girls, who, seeing themselves now safe, began to demonstrate their gratitude by hysterical cries and sobs, seizing and kissing the lads' hands, and finally placing their arms round them and kissing their cheeks.

"Oh, this is awful!" cried Tom Long, who was blushing like a girl.

"I shall be compelled to tell my mamma!" said Bob. "There, there, it's all right. Come, give me your hand, Semiramis, or Cleopatra, or whatever your name is, and let us make haste down to the river before it is too late."

The girl seemed to understand him, and ceased sobbing as she prepared to continue the flight, the other clinging to Tom Long's left hand.

"I say, though, let's have the birds," said Bob, stooping to pick them up; but the girl snatched them from him, to carry them herself.

"Yes, Tom, old fellow; no doubt about it, they're slaves. Come along, or we shall be cut off. It's not polite to let the ladies carry the baggage, but as we are the escort we must be prepared to fight."

"I say!" cried Tom Long, "do you know the way?"

"Not I," said Bob; "don't you?"

"Not the ghost of an idea!" cried Tom.

The girls were watching them, and evidently in a state of great excitement were trying to comprehend their words; but as soon as they saw their indecision, and their bold start off in the direction they imagined to be correct, then the slave girls understood their dilemma and stopped them, gesticulating and shaking their heads as they pointed in a quite fresh direction.

"They know where the ship lies, see if they don't," said Bob. "Let's trust them."

"But suppose they lead us wrong?" replied Tom.

"Not they," cried Bob. "They'll lead us right away. Come along, my fair specimens of chocolate à vanille; and the sooner we are safe under the British flag, the better I shall like it."

The girls started off at a sharp walk, and then made signs that they should run.

"All right," said Bob, nodding his head. "Double there, in the infantry brigade! Naval brigade to the front! Forward!"

He broke into a trot, and the little party ran sharply on, to the great delight of the two escaped slaves, who, as Bob had prophesied, led them straight away to the side of the river, which they reached without encountering a soul.

"I'm about knocked up," said Bob, panting. "It's disgusting to find these girls can beat us hollow at running."

"The doctor's specimens are all shaken up into a regular mash!" said Tom Long, peeping into the vasculum hung by a strap from his shoulder.

"Never mind," replied Bob. "Here's the boat coming. I shall come with you straight; or no: let's take them on board the 'Startler'?"

"No, no!" said Tom, "they must come to the fort."

"No, no, to the 'Startler,' I tell you."

"No, no, to the fort."

"Then we'll split the difference, and take them to the residency," said Bob; and as the boat touched the shore they stood back for the girls to leap in, and then crouch down with their arms around each other's neck, sobbing with joy as they felt that now they were safe.

There was no little excitement as the two girls were landed, and Mr Linton seemed puzzled as to what he should do; but the poor creatures were safe now under the protection of the British flag; and Bob Roberts and Tom Long proceeded to the doctor's quarters for a thorough wash and change, having fully verified old Dick's prophecy that they would be in mischief before the day was out.

Chapter Twenty Six
How the two Companions were knocked off their Perch

If they had not been English, the probabilities are that Bob Roberts and Tom Long would have hugged each other. As it was they seemed to think it quite the correct thing to shake hands over and over again, and then walk up and down under the palm-trees of the enclosure, flushed, excited, and as full of swagger as they could possibly be.

"Blest if they don't look like a couple o' young game cocks who have just killed their birds," said old Dick to Billy Mustard. "My word, they are cocky! But where are you going, old man?"

"To fetch my instrument," said Billy.

"What, yer fiddle? What do you want that 'ere for?"

"The young gents wants it," said Billy.

So with a nod he went into his quarters, to return with his beloved violin in its green baize bag, which he bore to where Bob and Tom were now seated at one of the tables beneath a shady tree.

On the strength of their adventure they were indulging themselves with bitter beer, into which they dropped lumps of ice, and as soon as Billy Mustard came, the violin was brought out, tuned, and the harmonious sound produced had the effect of soon gathering together an audience in the soft mellow hour before sunset.

Several officers seated themselves at the table, and followed the youngsters' example; soldiers and sailors gathered at a little distance beneath the trees; and unseen by the party below, Rachel Linton and Mary Sinclair appeared at a mat-shaded window.

"Tom Long's going to sing 'The Englishman,'" shouted Bob Roberts suddenly, and there was a loud tapping upon the rough deal table.

"No, no, I really can't, 'pon honour," said the ensign, looking very much more flushed than before.

"Yes, yes, he is," said Bob, addressing those around. "He is—in honour of the occasion; and gentlemen, let's sing out the chorus so loudly that those niggers in the campong can hear our sentiments, and shiver in their shoes, where they've got any."

"Hear! hear!" said a young lieutenant.

"But really, you know, I hav'n't a voice," exclaimed the ensign in expostulation.

"Gammon!" cried Bob. "He can sing like a bird, gentlemen. Silence, please, for our national song, 'The Englishman'!"

"I can't sing it—indeed I can't," cried the ensign.

"Oh, yes, you can; go on," said the young lieutenant who had previously spoken.

"To be sure he will," cried Bob Roberts. "Heave ahead, Tom, and I'll help whenever I can. It's your duty to sing it, for the niggers to hear our sentiments with regard to slavery!"

"Hear, hear!" cried several of the officers, laughing; and the men gave a cheer.

"Slavery and the British flag!" cried Bob Roberts, who was getting excited. "No man, or woman either, who has once sought protection beneath the folds of the glorious red white and blue, can ever return to slavery!"

"Hear, hear, hear!" shouted the officers again, and the men threw up their caps, cried "Hoorar!" and the sentry on the roof presented arms.

"Now then, play up, Private Mustard—'The Englishman,'" cried Bob Roberts. "Get ready, Tom, and run it out with all your might!"

"Must I?" said the ensign, nervously.

"To be sure you must. Wait a minute, though, and let him play the introduction."

Billy Mustard gave the bow a preliminary scrape, and the audience grew larger.

"What key shall I play it in, sir?" said Billy.

"Any key you like," cried Bob, excitedly. "Play it in a whole bunch of keys, my lad, only go ahead, or we shall forget all the words."

Off went the fiddle with a flourish over the first strain of the well-known song, and then, after a couple of efforts to sing, Tom Long broke down, and

Bob Roberts took up the strain, singing it in a cheery rollicking boyish way, growing more confident every moment, and proving that he had a musical tenor voice. Then as he reached the end of the first verse, he waved his puggaree on high, jumped upon the table to the upsetting of a couple of glasses, and led the chorus, which was lustily trolled out by all present.

On went Bob Roberts, declaring how the flag waved on every sea, and should never float over a slave, throwing so much enthusiasm into the song that to a man all rose, and literally roared the chorus, ending with three cheers, and one cheer more for the poor girls; and as Bob Roberts stood upon the table flushed and hot, he felt quite a hero, and ready to go on that very night and rescue half-a-dozen more poor slave girls from tyranny, if they would only appeal to him for help.

"Three cheers for Mr Roberts," shouted Dick, the sailor, as Billy Mustard was confiding to a friend that "a fiddle soon got outer toon in that climate."

"Yes, and three cheers for Mr Long," shouted Bob. "Come up here, Tom, old man; you did more than I did."

Tom Long was prevailed upon to mount the table, where he bowed again and again as the men cheered; when, as a lull came in the cheering, Billy Mustard, whose fiddle had been musically whispering to itself in answer to the well-drawn bow, suddenly made himself heard in the strain of "Rule Britannia," which was sung in chorus with vigour, especially when the singers declared that Britons never, *never, never* should be slaves; which rang out far over the attap roofs of the drowsy campong.

So satisfied were the singers that they followed up with the National Anthem, which was just concluded when the resident sent one of his servants to express a hope that the noise was nearly at an end.

"Well, I think we have been going it," said Bob Roberts, jumping down. "Come along, Tom. I've got two splendid cigars—real Manillas."

Tom Long, to whom this public recognition had been extremely painful, was only too glad to join his companion on a form beneath a tree, where the two genuine Manillas were lit, and for a quarter of an hour the youths smoked on complacently, when just as the exultation of the public singing was giving way to a peculiar sensation of depression and sickness, and each longed to throw away half his cigar, but did not dare, Adam Gray came up to where they were seated, gradually growing pale and wan.

"Ah, Gray," said the ensign, "what is it?"

"The major, sir, requests that you will favour him with your company directly."

"My company?" cried the ensign; "what's the matter?"

"Don't know, sir; but I think it's something about those slave girls. And Captain Horton requested me to tell you to come too, sir," he continued, turning to Bob Roberts.

"We're going to get promotion, I know, Tom," said the middy.

"No, no," said the ensign, dolefully, "it's a good wigging."

Bob Roberts, although feeling far from exalted now, did not in anywise believe in the possibility of receiving what his companion euphoniously termed a "wigging," and with a good deal of his customary independent, and rather impudent, swagger he followed the orderly to a cool lamp-lit room, where sat in solemn conclave, the resident, Major Sandars, and Captain Horton.

"That will do, Gray," said Major Sandars, as the youths entered, and saluted the three officers seated like judges at a table, "but be within hearing."

"Might ask us to sit down," thought Bob, as he saw from the aspect of the three gentlemen that something serious was afloat.

But the new arrivals were not asked to sit down, and they stood before the table feeling very guilty, and like a couple of prisoners; though of what they had been guilty, and why they were brought there, they could not imagine.

"It's only their serious way," thought Bob; "they are going to compliment us."

He stared at the shaded lamp, round which four or five moths and a big beetle were wildly circling in a frantic desire to commit suicide, but kept from a fiery end by gauze wire over the chimney.

"What fools moths and beetles are!" thought Bob, and then his attention was taken up by the officers.

"Will you speak, Major Sandars?" said the resident.

"No, I think it should come from you, Mr Linton. What do you say, Captain Horton?"

"I quite agree with you, Major Sandars," said the captain stiffly.

"What the dickens have we been doing?" thought Bob; and then he stared hard at the resident, and wished heartily that Rachel Linton's father had not been chosen to give him what he felt sure was a setting down for some reason or another.

"As you will, gentlemen," said the resident firmly, and he then placed his elbows on the table and joined his fingers, while the light from the lamp shone full upon his forehead.

"Mr Ensign Long—Mr Midshipman Roberts," he began. "He might have placed me first," thought Bob. "I wish someone would catch those wretched moths."

"You have been out on an expedition to-day?"

He waited for an answer, and as Tom Long had been placed first, Bob waited, too; but as his companion did not speak, Bob exclaimed quickly—

"Yes, sir, snipe shooting;" and as the resident bowed his head, Bob added, "two brace."

"Confound you—you young dogs!" cried Captain Horton, "and you brought a brace of something else. I beg your pardon, Mr Linton; go on."

Mr Linton bowed, while Bob uttered a barely audible whistle, and glanced at his companion.

"Then it's about those two girls," he thought.

"It seems, young gentlemen," continued the resident, "that while you were out, you met two young Malay girls?"

"Yes, sir."

"Who had run away from their master?"

"From their owner, as he seemed to consider himself, sir," said Bob, who, to use his own words, felt as if all the fat was in the fire now, and blazed up accordingly. "You see, sir," he said quickly, "we were watching for something that we saw in the reeds, close to the boggy ground, you know, and Tom here thought it was pig, but I thought it might be a deer. So we stood quite still till we heard sounds in the distance, when out jumped two dark creatures, and I was going to fire, when we saw that they were girls."

"And they ran up to us," said Tom Long.

"Like winking," said Bob, "and threw themselves on their knees, and clung to our legs, and wouldn't let go. Then up came half-a-dozen of the niggers—"

"I think, Mr Roberts, we will call people by their right names," said the resident, quietly; "suppose we say Malays."

"Yes, sir, Malays; and laid hold of the girls to drag them away. They screamed out, and that roused us, and we sent the nig— Malays staggering back. For you see, sir, as Englishmen—"

"English what—Mr Roberts?" said Captain Horton.

"Men, sir. I'm a midshipman, sir," said Bob, sharply; and the captain grunted out something that sounded like "impudent young puppy!" but he did not look angry.

"Go on, Mr Roberts," said the resident.

"Well, sir, being English—boys—big boys, who felt like men just then—" said Bob, rather sarcastically.

"That's not bad, Mr Roberts," said Major Sandars, with a glance at the naval captain.

"Well, sir, as the poor girls had regularly appealed to us to protect them, and the nig— Malays, sir, whipped out their krises, we presented arms, and would have given them a peppering of snipe shot if they hadn't sheered off when we brought the two poor weeping slave girls under the protection of the British flag, and set them free. Didn't we, Tom?"

"Yes," said Tom Long, looking nervously at the resident, and wondering what Rachel Linton thought about their feat.

There was a dead silence for a few moments, during which Bob Roberts wiped his streaming forehead, for he felt uncomfortably hot. Then the resident began—

"I think I am speaking the sentiments of my friends here, young gentlemen, when I say that you both behaved just as two brave British lads would be expected to behave under the circumstances."

"Yes," said Major Sandars, "Ensign Long, I felt sure, would not be wanting, if called upon."

Tom Long's face grew the colour of his best uniform.

"Very plucky act," said Captain Horton; and he nodded in so friendly a way at the middy, that Bob felt quite beaming.

"But," continued the resident, speaking very slowly, and as if weighing every word he said, "what is very beautiful in sentiment, and very brave and manly if judged according to our own best feelings, young gentlemen, becomes very awkward sometimes if viewed through the spectacles of diplomacy."

"I—I don't understand you, sir," faltered Bob.

"Let me be explicit then, young gentlemen. You both were, it seems, granted leave of absence to-day, for indulging in a little innocent sport, but by your brave, though very indiscreet conduct, you have, I fear, completely overset the friendly relations that we have been trying so hard to establish with these extremely sensitive people."

"But, sir," began Bob, "the poor girls—"

"Yes, I know all that," said the resident quietly; "but slavery is a domestic institution among these people, and to-morrow I feel sure that I shall have a visit from some of the sultan's chief men, demanding that these poor girls be given up."

"But they can't be now, sir," said Tom Long.

"No, Mr Long, we cannot return the poor girls to a state of slavery; but do you not see into what an awkward position your act has brought us?"

"I'm very sorry, sir."

"Yes, but sorrow will not mend it. We have been, and are, living on the edge of a volcano here, young gentlemen, and the slightest thing may cause an eruption. This act of yours, I greatly fear, will bring the flames about our heads."

Bob Roberts turned pale, as he thought of the ladies.

"But they'd never dare, sir," he began.

"Dare? I believe the Malays are quite daring enough to attack us, should they feel disposed. But there, we need not discuss that matter. You young gentlemen have, however, been very jubilant over your rescue of these poor girls, and you have been summoned here to warn you, while your respective officers take into consideration what punishment is awarded to you, that your noisy demonstrations are very much out of place."

"Punishment, sir!" said Bob, who looked aghast.

"Yes," said the resident sharply, "punishment. You do not seem to realise, young gentleman, that your act to-day has fired a train. Besides which, it is a question of such import that I must make it the basis of a special despatch to the colonial secretary at Whitehall."

Bob Roberts turned round and stared at Tom Long, but the latter was staring at Major Sandars.

"I don't think I need say any more, young gentlemen," said the resident quietly, "and I fervently hope that I may be able to peaceably settle this matter; but it is quite on the cards that it may be the cause of a deadly strife. And I sincerely trust that whatever may be the upshot of this affair, it may be a warning to you, as young English officers, to think a little more, and consider, before you take any serious step in your careers; for sometimes a very slight error may result in the loss of life. In this case, yours has not been a slight error, but a grave one."

"Though we all own as quite true," said Captain Horton, "that we don't see how you could have acted differently; eh, Sandars?"

"Yes, yes, of course. But, hang it all, Long, how could you go and get into such a confounded pickle? It's too bad, sir, 'pon my soul, sir; it is too bad—much too bad."

"Are we to be under arrest, sir?" said Bob Roberts, rather blankly.

"Not if you'll both promise to keep within bounds," said Captain Horton. "No nonsense."

"No, sir," said Bob glumly.

"Of course not, sir," said Tom.

"That will do then, young gentlemen," said the resident gravely; and the two youths went blankly off to their several quarters.

"Poor boys! I'm sorry for them," said the resident sadly.

"Yes, it's a confounded nuisance, Linton," said Major Sandars, "but you must diplomatise, and set all right somehow or another."

"That's a fine boy, that Roberts," said Captain Horton. "I'll try my best, gentlemen," said the resident, "for all our sakes; but we have a curious people to deal with, and I fear that this may turn out a very serious affair."

Chapter Twenty Seven
How Diplomacy worked in a Malay State

The Parang river looked like a belt of damasked silver studded with diamonds the next morning, while the waving feathery palms were of the brightest green. Mingled with these, on the shore farthest from the town, were the dadap trees, whose ripe scarlet blossoms stood out in rich relief as they gave colour to a landscape already dotted with the blooms of the chumpaka, both yellow and white, shedding a sweet scent that Doctor Bolter said was like Cape jasmin, but which Bob Roberts declared to resemble tea made with lavender water.

The "Startler," with her deck as white as hands could make it, lay looking smart and bright in her moorings below the island, her yards perfectly square, her sides glistening with fresh paint, her brass rails, bell, and guns flashing back the sun's rays, and the awnings spread over the deck almost as white as snow.

Here and there the Jacks, in their duck frocks and straws, were paddling about barefooted in the sunshine, giving the last touches to the rails and glass of the skylights.

On the island the resident's house and the barrack fort looked more like some ornamented set of buildings for summer pleasure, than a couple of places designed as a stronghold and retreat in case of danger. For the ditch and the earthwork were now carpeted with verdant growth, while the abattis, having been made of green wood, was putting forth fresh shoots.

Both the resident and Major Sandars had been desirous of retaining all the shade possible, for the protection of the men; therefore, save where they were likely to afford harbour to the enemy, trees and bushes had been spared. The men too, having plenty of time at disposal, had been encouraged to take to gardening, and with Doctor Bolter for head instructor, the place had been made to present the appearance of a nursery ground, where one bed rivalled another in the perfection of its growing vegetables. Neat, well-kept walks led up to the fort and the resident's house, which daily grew brighter and more picturesque, with its ornamented reed-woven walls, and carefully thatched roof of attap. The broad verandah, with its punkahs, was made gay with beautiful creepers, climbing the pillars of palm and bamboo, and festooning the edges, some of these being jasmines of great size and beauty; while rough rotan baskets hung at intervals, full of moss and dead wood, on which flourished the wonderful orchids and pitcher-plants that were the delight of the ladies of the residency.

By the help of Doctor Bolter and Adam Gray, a large cask had been cut in half, and decorated on the outsides and edges with rough bark, in whose interstices were planted orchids, and the pretty maiden-hair fern; while upon these being both mounted upon a short rough stump, they formed a couple of rustic vases of huge size, standing just inside the broad verandah, on either side of the entrance door, and looked, when filled with water, and supplied with aquatic plants, no slight additions to the beauty of the place.

Upon one of his excursions with net and can Doctor Bolter had succeeded in capturing several of the beautiful little chaetadons, or shooting-fish; tiny little broad fellows, beautifully banded, whose peculiarity was the adroitness with which they would lie in wait for any unfortunate fly that settled on the edge of an aquatic leaf, and then fire—or rather, water—off at it a tiny globule, with such unerring aim, that the insect was generally brought down into the water and swallowed. Three or four would sometimes sail round one after the other shooting at a fly in turn till it was knocked off, when a rush took place for the dainty prize.

But the river and the little jungle streams abounded with miniature fish of great beauty, their peculiarity being the way in which they were coloured, some being of a most gorgeous scarlet, with broad bands of vivid blue across their sides.

All on board the "Startler" was the perfection of neatness, and from a friendly rivalry the residency and fort were as smart and neat; perhaps never did they look to greater perfection than on the day after the adventure of Bob Roberts and Tom Long.

The morning drill was over, and the sun was growing intensely hot, when there was heard the sound of a gong in the distance, and one of the sentries announced the coming of a boat.

As it drew near it was seen to be one belonging to the sultan, with a couple of his principal officers therein.

They landed, each in his gay silken sarong, in whose folds the handle of the kris was carefully wrapped, to indicate that they were bound on a friendly mission, and leaving their men at the bamboo landing-stage fitted up by the sailors, they made their way to the residency.

No sooner had the news been given to Mr Linton of the approach of the sultan's boat than a signal was hoisted, whose effect was that the captain's gig was lowered down, and he arrived at the stage directly after, joining Major Sandars who had been fetched by an orderly, both officers being in full uniform.

"I say, Tom," said Bob Roberts to his companion, who had come across to the ship a short time before, "if I were you I'd go back and fig myself. I shall put on my best duds, for you see if we ar'n't sent for to meet those two coffee-coloured swells."

Tom Long, who was rather low-spirited about the matter, took the middy's advice, and went back to the island, where the visitors had already been ushered into the resident's reception room, the captain and major dropping in directly after as if by accident.

It was the most friendly of visits. The two officers were the tumongong, or chief magistrate, and the muntri, or chief adviser, of the sultan; and nothing could have been more amiable than their demeanour as they conversed with Mr Linton, who from time to time interpreted to the two British officers.

Was there anything the sultan could do in the way of providing better supplies of rice, fruit, and meat? A great fish expedition was about to be set afoot, and more would be brought down the river and kept in floating tanks. If the resident would only speak, everything possible should be done.

Nothing was required, so thanks were returned; when the tumongong smiled most agreeably, and said that he must now come to the chief object of his visit. The fact was, the sultan had decided to have a great tiger-hunt. Much mischief had of late been done by tigers. Several poor fellows, especially Chinamen, had been carried off from the rice-fields, and the sultan had decided to get together all his elephants, with a large number of beaters, and have a great hunt. Would the British officers bring their rifles and help? Elephants should be placed at their disposal, the largest the country produced, and every thing done to make the hunt a success.

"Then it's a mare's nest after all, Sandars," said Captain Horton. "They're not going to take any notice of those boys' tricks. What do you say; shall we go?"

"I should enjoy it immensely," said the major. "I long for a shot at a tiger."

"Wait a little, gentlemen," said the resident, smiling; "the interview is not at an end. What shall I reply about the hunting-party?"

"Oh, we shall be delighted to go. You'll go too?" said Captain Horton, answering for both.

"If matters are pleasantly settled," said Mr Linton. Then turning to the two Malay officers, whose dark restless eyes had been scanning the faces in turn, he said that they would be most happy to accept the sultan's invitation.

The officers were delighted, and declared that the sultan's joy would know no bounds.

They had previously declined all refreshments, but now that their business was at an end they accepted cigars, and laughed and chatted, evidently enjoying the visit immensely, and accepting a proposal to walk round the grounds with alacrity.

As they went into the verandah, the resident found a couple of the sultan's men waiting, with a present of the choicest fruit the country produced; huge durians, and fine mangosteens, with the most select kinds of plantain known for the delicacy of their flavour.

The visitors took an almost childish delight in the fish in the two fonts, and smiled with pleasure at the sight of the large selection of flowers; but a keen observer would have noticed that as they walked round the fort and earth-works, the muntri eagerly scanned every preparation for defence, though apparently more attracted by the uniforms of the sentries than anything else.

As they were crossing the little parade ground, with its well-trampled soil, on their way back to their boat, Tom Long was encountered, on his way to the mess-room.

He started on coming upon the little party so suddenly, but saluted and went on.

Oddly enough that brought to the muntri's memory a little affair that had happened on the previous day. Two young officers of the ship had been ashore shooting birds, and they found a party of the country people behaving rather ill to a couple of slave girls, and naturally enough, like all young men would, they took the girls under their protection, and brought them to the residency. Was it not so?

"Yes," the resident replied; "and they are now with the ladies."

That was so good and kind, and so like the English, who were a great and generous nation. The sultan had been terribly annoyed at his people behaving so ill to the poor girls, the muntri continued, and they had been punished, which was quite right—was it not?

The resident perfectly agreed with the muntri, who smiled content, while the tumongong looked hurt and sad.

He was so glad that Rajah Linton was satisfied at what the sultan had done, and the sultan would be greatly happy at his acts meeting such approval from the chief of the great queen. So that was settled. He thanked the resident more than he could tell, and he would give him no more trouble about the two poor girls, but take them back in the boat.

This was very cleverly done, but the sultan's officers had to deal with an equally clever man, one who was well versed in oriental wiles and diplomacy. Mr Linton was in no wise taken aback, since he had been waiting for this, and therefore was quite prepared to reply firmly that such a proceeding was impossible. The two girls had been brought beneath the British flag, and hence were slaves no longer. He could not therefore give them up.

Of course the resident meant that he could not send them back then, the muntri observed, smiling. Perhaps the poor girls were ill with their fright, and the rajah resident would send them back when they were better.

The resident assured his visitors that such a course was impossible, for according to the British laws the girls were now free, and could not be forced to go back.

The two officers did not press the matter, but began to ask questions about a breech-loading cannon, and were greatly surprised at the ease with which it was charged.

They had by this time finished their cigars, and being near the landing-stage, they took a most effusive leave of the three officers, entered their boat, and were rowed away.

"Well, then," said Captain Horton, as soon as he heard the parts of the conversation that he had not understood, "that game's over, and they are beaten at diplomacy?"

"Yes," said Major Sandars. "I envy you your command of countenance, and knowledge of the language, Linton."

"Game? over?" said Mr Linton, smiling sadly. "No, my dear sirs, that is only the first move our adversaries have made—king's pawn two squares forward; to which I have replied with queen's pawn one square forward."

"And that's a bad move, isn't it, Horton?" exclaimed Major Sandars.

"So the chess books make one think," said the captain.

"It all depends upon your adversary and your game," said the resident, smiling. "Gentlemen, I hope I have done right."

"And what are you going to do now?" said Captain Horton.

"Wait to see our adversary's next move. Meanwhile, gentlemen, extra caution will do no harm, for we have touched the Malays in one of their most sensitive places."

"We? You mean those young scamps of boys," said Captain Horton.

"Oh, it's *we* all the same," said Major Sandars. "Well, what's to be done?"

"I should, without seeming to do anything, put on a few extra sentries, Major Sandars," said the resident; "and, Captain Horton, I should be ready for action at a moment's notice, and be cautious about who came on board, and what prahus anchored near."

"Quite right—quite right, Linton," said Captain Horton. "You had no business to be a civilian. You ought to have been in the service."

The resident smiled, and they separated, as Mr Linton said, to wait for the enemy's next move.

Chapter Twenty Eight
How Sultan Hamet visited his Friends

The enemy, as the resident termed the sultan's party, made no move for a couple of days, during which all went on as usual. There was the usual morning parade in the fort, and the soldiers gardened, idled, smoked, and told one another it was "jolly hot" —a fact that needed no telling. On board the "Startler" the men were beat to quarters, and went through their drill in the cool of the morning, before hammock rails, the sentries' rifles, and the breeches of the glistening guns grew too hot to be touched with impunity. So hot was it, that, like the burnt child who fears the fire, Bob Roberts was exceedingly cautious about placing his hands in any spot where they were likely to be defiled by the pitch that cannot be touched without those consequences; for from between seams, and the strands of well-laid cables, it oozed, and even bubbled out, beneath the ardent wooing of the tropic sun.

It was a listless life, but a pleasant one, for such strict discipline was observed, and stringent rules laid down by the medical officer of the corvette and the detachment, that the men kept in excellent health. They had plenty of amusements; fruit was abundant, and they had taken quite a taste for the coarse country tobacco, which many of the soldiers smoked after the Malay fashion, rolled up à la cigarette in the roko, or outer sheath of the palm leaf or the plantain. Some, too, adopted the Malay's plan of rapidly cutting a pipe from a short joint of bamboo, which, with a hole bored in the side for the insertion of a thin reed or quill, formed a pipe much affected by the Jacks when they took their tobacco in smoke, instead of by the unpleasantly moist masticating process.

At the residency all went on as usual; sometimes the ladies received, and there was the sound of music and singing in the pleasantly lit-up verandah; sometimes Captain Horton sent his gig, and the agreeable little reunions were held on board the "Startler," in an improvised tent, draped with the ship's colours, while the lights were reflected on the smooth surface of the hurrying stream, and the Malays on shore watched the figures that passed to and fro till the party was over.

Captain Horton and Major Sandars both thought the rajah's party had forgotten the affair; but the resident held to his opinion, which was strengthened by the imploring manner in which the two girls, who had attached themselves as attendants on Rachel Linton and her cousin, begged him not to let them be fetched away.

"Suppose I did let them have you back," said the resident to them one day in their native tongue, "what would happen?"

One of the girls, a tall, dark, graceful creature, but with the protruding lips, high cheekbones, and flat distended nose of the Malay, rose with contracted eyebrows, took her companion, forced her upon her knees, and then drawing an imaginary kris, she placed the point on the girl's shoulder, and struck the hilt with her right hand as if driving it perpendicularly down into her heart.

"They would kill us—so!" she exclaimed, "and throw our bodies in the water to the crocodiles!"

The other girl shuddered, and raised her frightened eyes to the faces of the ladies as if imploring them to intercede—and not in vain.

"But they will not trouble about you now;" said the resident, tentatively.

"Yes, yes," they both exclaimed, "they will send a naga and many men, but you will not let us go?"

"No," said the resident, quietly. "*We* shall not give you up," and he went away thoughtfully to his room, to continue writing the despatch he had commenced some days before.

That same evening the two principal officers came to have a chat, and over their cigars Major Sandars introduced the subject of the doubled sentries.

"There is no longer any need for this," he said. "Let's see, Linton, it is now a week since those two fellows came. Don't you think, Horton, it is an unnecessary precaution?"

"Well, to be frank," said Captain Horton, "I do; and I shall be glad to give up our strict discipline on board."

"What do you think, Captain Smithers?" said the resident to that officer, who was present.

"I cannot help agreeing with the major," he replied. "I see no reason for these extra precautions."

"Then I am in the minority," said the resident, smiling.

"Look out there, gentlemen," he said, pointing through the open window. "What do you see?"

"You tell him, Smithers," said the major, "I'm too hot and tired to do more than breathe."

"I can see the bright river with the lights of the steamer glistening on its surface; the fire-flies are darting amongst the trees; the stars look soft and mellow; altogether it is a delightful picture, that reminds one of being in some delicious summer retreat on the banks of dear old Father Thames."

"Captain Smithers," said the resident, gravely, "it is indeed a beautiful picture; the river flows peacefully on with the lights reflected from its bosom; but you know as well as I, that if a man attempted to breast those treacherous waters, he would, before he had swum many yards, have been drawn down by one of the hideous reptiles that swarm in the Parang. That river is to my mind a type of the Malay feeling towards us—the intruders upon his soil. So little am I satisfied with what seems to me to be a deceitful calm, that I have serious thoughts of asking you to increase the sentries."

"Nonsense, my dear Linton," said Captain Horton; "we shall hear no more of the affair."

"We shall hear more," said the resident. "Wait and see."

The resident was right; for the next day the sultan's principal naga, or dragon-boat, with its uncouth figure-head, was seen coming swiftly down the stream, propelled by about thirty rowers, all clad in rich yellow jackets—the royal colour—and nattily-made scarlet caps. Their lower limbs were bare, save where covered by their scarlet and yellow sarongs. The men rowed well together; and as the word was passed by the sentries the officer on duty could plainly make out beneath the matting awning reaching nearly from end to end of the boat, the figures of the sultan and several of his officers.

The sultan was easily distinguishable; for while his chief officers strictly adhered to their native costume, he wore a gorgeous semi-military uniform, that had specially been built—so Bob Roberts termed it—for him in England. It was one mass of rich embroidery, crossed by a jewelled belt, bearing a sabre set with precious stones, and upon his head he wore a little Astrakhan fur *kepi*, surmounted by an egret's plume, like a feathery fountain from a diamond jet.

Orders were given for the guard to turn out, and the resident and Major Sandars hurriedly prepared to meet their distinguished guest, who, however, did not stop at the island, but went straight on to the corvette, where he was received by a guard of marines, the captain awaiting his visitor upon the quarter-deck.

The visit was but short, for at the end of a few minutes Captain Horton accompanied the sultan on board the naga, and the long low vessel was swiftly turned, and rowed with no little skill to the island landing-place, where a sufficiently imposing military force, under Captain Smithers, was ready to receive him, the sultan walking up to the residency verandah, between a double line of infantry with bayonets fixed.

The eastern potentate's opal eyeballs rolled from side to side as, looking rather awkward in his ill-fitting European dress, he tried hard to emulate the dignity of his bronze followers in baju and sarong, each man with the handle of his kris carefully covered by a silken fold.

On landing here, the sultan was followed by his kris and sword-bearers, each having his appointed station behind the monarch, holding the weapons by the sheath, with the hilt against the right shoulder, so that a very respectable procession, full of colour and glow, was formed from the landing-place to the residency.

The most incongruous part of the following was the appearance of the officer who bore an umbrella to keep the rays of the sun from his liege's head; but as in place of one of the gorgeous, gold-fringed, scarlet-clothed sunshades generally used for that purpose, this was an unmistakeable London-made chaise gingham, with a decidedly Gampish look, it robbed its master of some of his dignity, though he was so busily employed in trying to carry his richly-jewelled sabre with the ease of the English officers, and at the same time to show the splendid weapon to the best advantage, that he saw not the want of dignity in his umbrella, and walked awkwardly to where Mr Linton received him in company with Major Sandars, and such officers as could hurry on the uniforms they so scrupulously avoided in that torrid clime.

Tom Long, who paid more attention to the embellishment of his person than any man in the detachment, was one of the officers present, and although nervous about the Sultan's visit, and feeling certain that it had to do with the rescue of the slave girls, he could not help a smile at the umbrella, and a congratulatory sensation that Bob Roberts was not present, for he would have been sure to laugh, when an extension of the risible muscles might have been taken as an insult not to be endured.

The august visitors were received in the wide verandah on account of their number, where the sultan took the seat placed for him; five of his principal men, including the former ambassadors, stood behind him; the rest, sword and umbrella-bearers, carriers of the potentate's golden betel-box and spittoon, squatted down on their heels, and were as motionless as so many images of bronze.

The various British officers remained with the resident, standing, out of respect to the sultan, whose heavy dark features seemed to express satisfaction; and he at once proceeded in a rather forced, excited manner to inform the resident that he had only been having a water-excursion, and had thought how much he should like to see his good friends at the residency.

The resident was delighted, of course, at this mark of condescension, and hastened to assure the sultan of the fact.

The latter then proceeded to announce that his grand tiger-hunt would take place in a fortnight's time, and begged that all the officers would accept his invitation.

As spokesman and interpreter, the resident assured his august visitor that as many as possible would be there; when in addition the sultan asked that a great many soldiers might be sent as well, to help keep the tigers from breaking back when the hunt was on.

To this, Mr Linton, by Major Sandars' permission, readily assented; and then, knowing of old his visitor's taste in such matters, some champagne was produced. At the sight of the gold-foiled bottles the rajah's eyes glistened, and he readily partook of a tumbler twice filled for him; after which he walked into the house with the resident, as an excuse for not being present when his followers partook of some of the wine.

At length, after a walk round the fort, which was willingly accorded to him, that he might see that the residency and its protectors were well on the *qui vive*, the sultan took his departure, begging earnestly that all who could would come to the hunting expedition. Then the soldiers presented arms, and the little procession, gay of aspect, proceeded down to the bamboo landing-stage, where the visitor embarked with his following, and seated himself beneath the reed awning of his boat. Word was given, and the yellow and scarlet rowers bent to their oars, sending the long light naga vigorously up stream, one blaze of brilliant colour in the morning sun, till it disappeared round a verdant point about half-a-mile ahead.

"Well, Linton," said Major Sandars, "what do you say to it now?"

"Ah, to be sure," said Captain Horton. "Isn't the storm blown over?"

"Really, gentlemen, it looks like it," said the resident, "and I must confess that I am heartily glad to find that I have been wrong."

"Wrong? yes," said the Major. "Those fellows are no more fools than we are, and knowing what they do of the strength of our guns, and the discipline of our men, they would as soon think of measuring force with us, as of flying. Smithers, march the men back into quarters out of this raging sunshine, and to-night only put on the usual guard. What shall you do, Horton?"

"Only have the customary watch," was the reply.

Tom Long conveyed to Bob Roberts an account of what had taken place, and the reduction of the guard at night; to which that sage young midshipman replied, that the British Lion was only going to withdraw his claws within their sheaths, but the claws were there still; and that it would be exceedingly uncomfortable for any Malay gentleman on shore if the said BL was to put his claws out once more.

"But I say, Tom," he exclaimed, "get the major to let you go to the tiger-hunt."

"Do you think you can get leave?" said the ensign.

"I mean to try it on, my boy. The cap is sure to be huffy, on account of our last affair; but nothing venture, nothing gain, and I mean to go, somehow or another, so tigers beware. What are you laughing at?"

"The idea of you shooting a tiger," said Tom Long. "That's all."

"I daresay I could if I tried," said Bob shortly.

"I daresay you could," said Long, "but we'll see. We have to get leave first."

"That's soon got," said Bob Roberts. "Depend upon it, I shall be there."

"And I, too," said Tom Long; and the young fellows parted, each of them in secret vowing that he would have the skin of the tiger he meant to shoot, carefully dressed, lined with blue satin and scarlet cloth, and present it to Rachel Linton as a tribute of respect.

But the tiger had first of all to be shot.

Chapter Twenty Nine
How Ali fell into a Trap

They were very delightful days at the residency for the English party. The heat was certainly great, but the arrangements made as soon as they were settled down, warded that off to a great extent. The men enjoyed the life most thoroughly, especially as for sanitary reasons Doctor Bolter forbade that either the soldiers or the Jacks should be exposed to too much exertion.

The days were days of unclouded sunshine as a rule, and when this rule was broken, the change was to a heavy thunder-storm, with a refreshing rain, and then the skies were once more blue.

Fruit and flowers, and various other supplies, were brought now in abundance, especially since Dullah had been allowed to set up a trading station at the island. He monopolised the whole business, the various boats that came rowing straight to him; but he did it all in so pleasant a manner, that no one could complain. To the English people he was suavity itself. His courtesy—his gentlemanly bearing was the talk of the whole place; and regularly every morning one of his Malay slaves or bond-servants used to carry up and lay in the residency verandah a large bunch of deliciously fresh orchids, or pitcher-plants, or a great branch of some sweet-scented flowering shrub, for which he always received the ladies' thanks in a calm, courteous way that quite won their confidence.

Dullah's reed hut, with its bamboo-supported verandah, became quite a favourite resort, and he very soon provided it with a frontage each way. In the one verandah he arranged to supply the resident, the ladies, and officers; and in the other the soldiers and sailors, and received his supplies from the boats.

Sometimes the ladies walked down to buy fruit, sometimes it was the officers; but the two best customers were Tom Long and Bob Roberts, the former spending a great deal in flowers, to send to the residency—a very bad investment by the way—for the rapid rate at which they faded was astounding. Once his duty—as he called it—done, in sending a bunch of flowers, Tom Long used to indulge himself with fruit.

Bob Roberts had given up sending flowers, so he had more money to spend upon his noble self in fruit, and he spent it where he was pretty well sure to encounter Tom Long, whenever he could get leave to run across to the island.

Bob's way of addressing Dullah was neither refined nor polite, for it was always, "Hallo, old cock," and at first Dullah looked very serious; but as soon as his aide and companion interpreted to him the words, he smiled and seemed perfectly satisfied, always greeting the young midshipman with a display of his white teeth, for he considered his comparison to a fighting-cock, of which birds the Malays are passionately fond, quite a compliment.

The result was that for a small sum Bob was always sure of a choice durian, which he feasted upon with great gusto, while Tom Long came and treated himself to mangosteens.

Dullah always behaved to the young ensign with the greatest politeness, that young gentleman returning it with a sort of courteous condescension which said plainly enough that Dullah was to consider himself a being of an inferior race.

But Dullah accepted it all in the calmest manner, smilingly removing the malodorous durians which Bob maliciously contrived to place near the seat Tom Long always occupied, and waiting upon the ensign as if he were a grandee of the first water.

And here, as a matter of course, the subject of the approaching tiger-hunt was discussed, Dullah, by means of his companion, becoming quite animated about the matter, and enlarging as to the number and beauty of the tigers that would be shot.

Both Tom Long and the middy were having a fruit feast one day, when Ali, who had been off to the steamer, and then came on to the island, made his appearance in search of his two friends, Dullah quietly disappearing into the back of his hut, to attend to some of the sailors who had come in, while his companion waited upon the young officers.

Of course the tiger-hunt was the principal subject of discussion, and Ali promised to arrange to have one of the largest of the sultan's elephants fitted with a roomy howdah, so that they three could be together.

"I can manage that," he said, "through my father, and we'll have a grand day."

"But shall we get any tigers?" asked Bob.

"No fear of that," was the reply. "I'll contrive that we shall be in the best part of the hunt."

"That will be close to the sultan, of course?"

Ali's dark eyes were raised inquiringly to the speaker's face, but seeing that this was not meant sarcastically, he said drily,—"No; I shall arrange to be as far away from the sultan's elephant as I can."

Bob looked at him keenly.

"What, isn't he fond of tigers?" he said sharply.

"My father is the sultan's officer, and greatly in his confidence," said the young man quietly. "I don't think the sultan is very fond of hunting, though."

Just at this moment, unseen, of course, by the three young men, Dullah was whispering to a rough-looking, half-naked Malay, into whose hands he placed a little roll of paper, which the man secured in the fold of his sarong, dropped into a sampan, and then hastily paddled to the mainland, where he plunged into the wood and disappeared.

Meanwhile the three friends sat chatting, and Ali expressed his sorrow about the adventure the two young Englishmen had had with the slave girls.

"Where are they now?" he quietly asked.

"Oh, Miss Linton and her cousin have quite adopted them," said Bob. "But surely you don't think we did wrong."

"Speaking as the son of the Tumongong, I say yes," replied Ali; "but as one who has imbibed English notions and ideas, I am bound to say that what you did only makes me feel more thoroughly how it is time we had a complete revolution in Parang."

"I say," said Bob, "you'll get stuck-up for high treason, young fellow, if you talk about revolution."

"No fear,"—said Ali, laughing quietly. "My ideas are pretty well-known; but I am too insignificant a fellow for what I say to be noticed. Now if it was my father—"

"Yes—if it was your father," said Bob, "I suppose they would kris him?"

Ali nodded, and after a quiet cigar under the trees, during which he complained more than once of the wrench the seizure by the crocodile had given to his muscles, he bade them good-bye, promising to have everything ready for the tiger-hunt, and, leaping into his boat, was rowed away.

Ali had about a mile to walk along one of the jungle-paths to reach his father's house, and he was going along very thoughtfully under the trees, quite alone—for he had left his men behind, to look after and secure the boat. It was comparatively cool in the shade, and he began thinking about the two young men he had left, and contrasting their civilised life with his. The savagery and barbarism by which he was surrounded disgusted him; and knowing well as he did, how the sultan and the various rajahs of the little states lived by oppressing and grinding down the wretched people around, he longed for the time when a complete change should come about, bringing with it just laws, and a salutary rule for his country. His own life troubled him in no small degree, for he saw nothing in the future but the career of a Malay chief, a ruler over slaves, living a life of voluptuous idleness, and such an existence he looked upon with horror.

Could he not enter the British service in some way? he asked himself, and rise to a life of usefulness, in which he might do some good for the helpless, ground-down people amongst whom he was born?

Such a life, he told himself, would be worth living, and— What was that?

His hand involuntarily flew to his kris, as he heard a rustle amidst the tangled cane just ahead, and he advanced cautiously lest it should be some beast of prey, or one of the great serpents that had their existence amidst the dense undergrowth.

There it was again; a quick sharp rustle amidst the trees, as of something hastily escaping, and his hand fell to his side, and he watched eagerly in advance, not hearing a cat-like step behind him, as a swarthy Malay came in his tracks, sprang upon the young man's back, and pinioned his arms in an instant.

Ali uttered a hoarse cry, and strove to draw his kris, but the effort was vain. Three more Malays darted from their hiding-places, and in a few minutes he was securely bound, with a portion of his sarong thrust into his mouth to keep him from crying for help; another Malay, who had been pulling a long rattan on ahead to imitate the sound of an escaping animal, coming from his hiding-place and smiling at the success of the ruse.

"What does it mean?" Ali asked himself; but he was puzzled and confused, and his captors gave him no opportunity for further thought, but hurried him right away into the depths of the jungle through a long narrow winding track that was little used.

"Why, this leads to the sultan's old house, where the inchees were killed!" thought Ali. "Surely they are not going to kill me?"

A shudder ran through him, and a strange sense of horror seemed to freeze his limbs as he was half thrust half earned along through the jungle, his captors having at times to use their heavy parangs to cut back the canes and various creepers that had made a tangle across the unfrequented track.

It was as the young chief had surmised. They were taking him to the deserted house that had been formerly occupied by former inchees or princesses of the Malay people, who, for some political reason, had been cruelly assassinated by order of the present sultan, they having been krissed, and their bodies thrown into the river.

Was this to be his fate? he asked himself; and if it was, in what way had he offended?

The answer came to him at once. It was evident that the intercourse he had held with the English was not liked, and now in his own mind he began to have misgivings about the resident and his party. Sultan Hamet was, he knew, both cruel and treacherous. Was the position of the English people safe?

Yes, he felt they were safe. He was the offender; and once more a shudder of fear ran through him at the thought of his young life being crushed out so soon; just, too, when he was so full of hopeful prospects and aspirations.

His manhood asserted itself, though, directly. He was the son of a chief, he told himself; and these treacherous wretches who had seized him should see that he was no coward.

Then he began to think of his father, and wondered whether it would be possible to communicate with him before he was killed.

Then he felt a little more hopeful, for perhaps, after all, the instructions to his captors might not be to slay him. If it was, and he could only get his hands free, their task should not be so easy as they thought for.

For two long hours was he forced through the tangled jungle, and every minute he became more convinced that his captors were bound for the place of whose existence he knew, having once come upon it during a shooting expedition, and, in spite of his followers' horror, persisted in examining the ruins nearly choked even then with the rapid jungle growth.

At last they reached the place, and the young man's searching eye at once saw that some attempts had been made at cutting down the tangled trees.

But very little time was afforded him to gratify his curiosity. He was rudely thrust forward, and then half dragged, half carried up the rough steps, some of which were broken away, and then pushed into the great centre room of what had been a large Malay house.

It was very dark, for the holes in the roof had become choked with creepers, which had formed a new thatch in place of the old attap top. The bamboos that formed the floor were slippery here and there with damp moss and fungus, and in several places they were rotted away; but there was plenty to afford a fair space of flooring, and in a momentary glance Ali saw that the inner or women's room of the house was dry, and not so much ruined as the place where he stood.

"Did they kris the poor prisoners here?" he asked himself; and then his thoughts flew to the bright river upon which his boat had so often skimmed; to the clean, trim corvette, with its bright paint, smart sailors, and Bob Roberts, the merry, cheery young English lad. Then he thought of the residency, with the sweet graceful ladies, the pleasant officers, always so frank and hospitable; of Tom Long, whom he liked in spite of the ensign's pride and stand-offishness; and lastly he asked himself what they would think of him for not keeping faith with them about the hunt, and whether they would ever know that he had been treacherously krissed in that out-of-the-way place.

A grim smile crossed his lip as he wished that he might be thrown afterwards in the river, and his body float down to be seen by the English people, so that they might know why he had stopped away.

And then a thrill ran through him, for a couple of his captors seized him, and in the dim green light of the place, with a few thin pencils of sunshine striking straight through like silver threads from roof to floor, he saw a third man draw his deadly kris.

Chapter Thirty
How Private Gray proved Suspicious

Adam Gray left the men in the mess-room that night, chatting about the coming tiger-hunt, and wondering who would be selected to accompany the expedition. He could not help thinking, as he shouldered his rifle, and was marched off by a sergeant with half-a-dozen more, to relieve guard, that he should like to be one of the party himself. In happy bygone days he had been fond of sport, and in a trip to North America were well-remembered perils and pleasant adventures. And now this talk of the tiger-hunt had roused in him a strong interest, and set him recalling days when he was very different to what he was now.

"It's no good to sigh," he said to himself, and the measured tramp, tramp of the marching men sounded solemn and strange in the darkness, rousing him once more to a sense of his position.

"If I'm to go, I go," he said bitterly. "That will be as my superiors please; and if I do go, it will not be as a hunter."

In spite of himself; however, as soon as guard had been relieved, and he was left in charge of a post not far from Dullah's hut, his thoughts went back to his early career, and he grew at times quite excited as he compared it with the life he was living now.

Then his thoughts wandered to the residency, and from thence back to the day when he was bitten by the sea snake, and lay there upon the deck tended by Miss Linton.

These thoughts agitated him, so that he set off pacing briskly up and down for a couple of hours, and then, his brain calmed by the exercise, he stood still under the shadow of a great palm, with whose trunk, as he stood back close to it, his form so assimilated in the darkness that at a couple of yards distance he was invisible.

His post was close to the river, so close that he walked upon the very edge of the bank, which was in places undermined by the swift current. This post had been cleared from the thick jungle. It was but a narrow piece, some two yards wide, and forty long, and this it was his duty to pace during his long watch, to guard that side of the island from a landing foe.

Midnight had passed, and all was very still. There was a splash from time to time in the stream, telling of the movement of some reptile or great fish, and now and then, from the far-distant parts of the jungle across the water, he could hear the cry of some wild beast. Now and then he watched the fire-flies scintillating amidst the leaves, and thought of how different life was out in this far-off tropic land to that in dear old England.

He had been thinking quite an hour without stirring; but though his memory strayed here and there, his eyes were watchful, and he scanned from time to time the broad smooth surface of the stream in search of passing boats.

At last he fancied he detected something dark moving along, but it went by so smoothly that it might have been the trunk of some tree, or even the back of a great crocodile, for there was no splash of oars.

He had almost forgotten the incident, when he started slightly and listened, thinking he could hear a whispering, and this was repeated.

He listened intently, but though he felt sure that he could hear voices, still that need not mean danger, for sound passes so easily across the water, that the noise might have come from down lower in the island, or even from the shore across the river.

The whispering ceased, and then he listened in vain for a time, and at last he was just thinking of pacing up and down once more, when certainly there was a faint splash, and on looking in the direction he could see on the dark water what seemed like a dim shadow gliding along.

It might have been a boat or the shadow of a boat, he could not be sure. In fact, there were moments when he doubted whether it was not some ocular illusion brought about by too intently gazing through the gloom.

And there he stood, hesitating as to whether he should fire and give the alarm.

But the next moment he reasonably enough asked himself why he should do so, for there was nothing alarming in the fact of a tiny sampan gliding over the river. It might be only a fisherman on his way to some favourite spot, or perhaps one of the Malays bound up the river, or possibly after all a mere deception.

There seemed to be nothing to merit the alarm being raised, and he stood watching once more the spot where the boat had disappeared. Still he did not resume his march up and down, but recalled the night of the attack, and began to consider how easy it would be for a crafty enemy to land and take them by surprise some gloomy night. Dark-skinned, and lithe of action as cats, they could easily surprise and kris the sentries. In his own case, for instance, what would be easier than for an enemy to lurk on the edge of the thick jungly patch by which the path ran, and there stab him as he passed?

"It would be very easy," he thought. "Yes; and if I stand here much longer I shall begin to think that I am doing so because I dare not walk beside that dark piece of wood. Still I dare do it, and I will."

As if out of bravado, he immediately began to pace his allotted post once more, and he had hardly gone half-way when a sharp sound upon his left made him bring his piece down to the present, and wait with bayonet fixed what he looked upon as a certain attack.

Again he hesitated about firing and giving the alarm, for fear of incurring ridicule and perhaps reprimand. He knew in his heart that he was nervous and excitable, being troubled lest any ill should befall the occupants of the residency, and being in such an excited state made him ready to imagine everything he saw to mean danger.

So he stood there, ready to repel any attack made upon him, and as he remained upon his guard the rustling noise increased, and he momentarily expected to see the leaves parted and some dark figure rush out; but still he was kept in suspense, for nothing appeared.

At last he came to the conclusion that it was some restless bird or animal disturbed by his presence, and told himself that the noise made was magnified by his own fancies; and, rather glad that he had not given the alarm, he continued to march up and down, passing to and fro in close proximity to a dark Malay, whose hand clasped a wavy, dull-bladed kris, that the holder seemed waiting to thrust into his chest the moment an opportunity occurred, or so soon as the sentry should have given the alarm.

At last the weary watch came to an end, for the tramp of the relief was heard, and Sergeant Lund marched up his little party of men, heard Gray's report of the rustling noise, and the dark shadow on the river; said "Humph!" in a gruff way; a fresh man was placed on sentry, and Adam Gray was marched back with the other tired men who were picked up on the round into the little fort.

Chapter Thirty One
How Some could go and Some must stay

The day of the tiger-hunt was at last close at hand. A vast deal of communication and counter communication had taken place with the sultan, whose people were making great preparations for the event.

The sultan was constantly sending messengers, and asking that stores might be given him with plenty of ammunition. Not, though, in any mean begging spirit, for whenever a couple of his chiefs came with some request they were accompanied by a train of followers bearing presents—food, supplies of the finest rice, sugar-cane, and fruit; buffaloes and poultry; slabs of tin, little bags of gold dust, specimens of the native work; an abundance, in short, of useful and valuable things, all of which were accepted; though there was a grim feeling in the mind of Mr Linton that pretty well everything had been taken by force from some of the sultan's miserable subjects.

Still the policy was, to be on the best of terms with the sultan, and to hope to introduce reforms in his rule by degrees. The resident took the old school copy-book moral into consideration, that example was better than precept, and knowing full well that any sweeping code of rules and regulations would produce distaste, certain hatred, and perhaps a rising against the English rule, he determined to introduce little improvements by degrees, each to be, he hoped, tiny seeds from which would grow grand and substantial trees.

The tiger-hunt was being prepared for evidently with childlike delight, and instead of its being a few hours' expedition, it proved that it was to be an affair of a week. Tents were to be taken, huts to be formed, and quite a large district swept of the dangerous beasts. For as the sultan informed the English officers, the tigers had been unmolested for quite two years, and saving one or two taken in pitfalls, they had escaped almost scot free. The consequence of this was, that several poor Malays had been carried off from their rice-fields, and at least a dozen unfortunate Chinamen from the neighbourhood of some tin mines a few miles away.

"I never meant to enter into such an extensive affair, gentlemen," said the resident to Major Sandars and Captain Horton after dinner one day, when they had all been entertained at the mess-room. "I almost think we ought to draw back before it is too late."

"Well, I don't know," said Major Sandars. "It will please the sultan if we take a lot of men, and this is rather a stagnating life. I frankly tell you I should be very glad of the outing, and I am sure it would do good to the men."

"I quite agree with you, Sandars," said Captain Horton; and Bob Roberts and Tom Long, who were opposite one another at the bottom of the table, exchanged glances. "I want a change, and I should be glad to give my lads a turn up the country. Drill's all very well, but it gets wearisome. What do you say, Smithers?"

"I must confess to being eager to go," was the reply. "It seems to me the only gentleman who does not care for the trip is Mr Linton."

"My dear fellow, you never made a greater mistake in your life," said Mr Linton, laughing. "Nothing would please me better than to be off for a couple of months, with a brace of good rifles, and an elephant, with plenty of beaters. I could even manage to exist for three months without reading a report, or writing a despatch."

Here there was a hearty laugh, and Mr Linton went on,—"There is one voice silent—the most important one, it seems to me. Come, doctor, what do you say? may we all go up the country and live in tents?"

"Hah!" said Doctor Bolter, "now you have me on the hip. I want to go myself; horribly."

"Ha, ha, ha, ha!" laughed every one in chorus.

"I want to see those black monkeys like our friend Mr Bob Roberts has for a pet. I say I want to see them in their native state. I want to get a specimen of the pink rhinoceros, and some of the *Longicorns. Nymphalis Calydonia* is to be found here, and I must shoot a few specimens of *Cymbirhynchus Macrorhynchus*, besides supplying my *hortus siccus* with a complete series of *Nepenthes*."

"For goodness' sake, doctor, don't go on like that," cried Captain Horton. "If you want to be cheerful to that extent, give us a recitation in pure Malay."

"Ah, you may all laugh," said the doctor; "but I'm not ashamed of being a modest naturalist."

"Modest!" said Major Sandars. "Do you call that modest, to talk big like that? But come, tell us, may we go safely?"

"That's what I can't quite settle," said the doctor. "I don't know what to say to you. A week's hunting picnic would be very nice."

"Splendid," said everybody.

"And you'd have a good supply of tents? I can't have my men sleeping in the open air."

"Abundance of everything," said Major Sandars. "Regular commissariat stores—mess tent, and the rest of it."

"Stop a minute," said the doctor, "not so fast. You see, what I'm afraid of is fever."

"We all are," said Captain Horton. "Never mind, take a barrel and keep a strong solution of quinine always on tap for us. Now then, may we go? You see if it was on duty we shouldn't study a moment, but as it's a case of pleasuring—"

"And keeping up good relations with the sultan," said the resident.

"And freeing the country from a pest," said Captain Horton.

"Tigers are pests enough," said the doctor, "but intermittent or jungle fever is to my mind the pest of the country."

"Yes, of course, doctor," said the resident; "but what do you think, may we go?"

The doctor sat tapping the table with a dessert knife.

"Will you all promise me faithfully not to drink a drop of water that has not been filtered?" he said.

"*Yes*, yes, yes," came from all down the table.

"I'll promise, doctor, not to drink any water at all," said Bob Roberts in a low voice, that was heard, though, by the doctor.

"It strikes me, young gentleman, that you won't get anything stronger," he said. "Well, gentlemen, if you'll all promise to abide by my rules, I'll say *yes; you may go.*"

A long quiet conversation was afterwards held, and finally it was decided that quite half the men should go, and on the eve of the expedition the final preparations had been made, tents and stores had been sent ashore ready for a start at daybreak.

The river had been scoured by the corvette's boats, and no trace of Rajah Gantang's prahus found; in fact, nothing had been heard of him or them for many days; and all being esteemed satisfactory and safe on that score, what remained to do was to settle who should stay and protect the residency and the corvette, and who should go.

As far as the men were concerned, this was soon settled; for the order was given to fall in, and they were soon ranged in line, every man anxious in the extreme as to his fate. The next order was for the even numbered to take two paces back, and the next for the rear-rank men to fall out; they were the lucky ones, and in a high state of delight.

With the officers it was more difficult. However, that was soon settled. Captain Horton said that he should go; and gave the corvette in charge of Lieutenant Johnson. Major Sandars followed his example by appointing Captain Smithers to the task of taking command of the fort; and to his great disgust Tom Long found that he was not to be of the select.

The resident had not intended to go, but so pressing a request that he would come had arrived from the sultan, that he felt bound to make one of the party. On the eve of the start the principal talk was of the qualities and powers of the various rifles and shot guns that had been brought out to be cleaned and oiled.

Tom Long was solacing himself out in the open air with a strong rank cigar that had been given him by a brother officer, and very poorly it made him feel. But he put that all down to the major's account for depriving him of his treat.

"I'll be even with him, though," he said, breaking out into the habit of talking aloud. "I won't forget it."

The night was very dark and starless, and he stood leaning up against a tree, when he heard the splash of oars from the landing-place, a short sharp order, and then the rattling of a ring-bolt.

"Some one from the steamer, I suppose," he growled. "Gun borrowing, I'll be bound. They don't have mine, whoever wants it."

"Here you, sir," said a familiar voice, as a figure came up through the darkness. "Where's Major Sandars—at the officers' quarters or the residency? Do you hear? Why don't you speak?"

"That path leads to the officers' quarters, Mr Robert Roberts, and the other leads, as you well know, to the residency. Now go and find out for yourself, and don't air your salt-junk bluster on shore."

"Salt-junk bluster be bothered," said Bob sharply. "How the dickens was I to know it was you standing stuck-up against that tree like two tent poles in a roll of canvass? Here, I've come from the skipper to see if the major's got any spare leggings, for fear of the noble captain getting any thorns in his legs."

"Hang the captain!" growled Tom.

"Hang the major, then!" said Bob sharply.

"You may hang them both, if you like," said Tom.

"I should like to kris them all over, till they looked like skewered chickens ready for the spit," said Bob. "I say, ain't it an awful shame?"

"Shame, yes," said Tom Long, slightly mollified by his companion's sympathy. "I don't see why one of us two should be left out of the party. It isn't much pleasure we get."

"No," said Bob sharply; "but I think if one of us was to go it ought to have been this young person."

"Well, but you are going, aren't you?" said Tom Long.

"Not I," said Bob. "I'm second officer on board HMS 'Startler' till they come back, that's all."

"But, my dear Bob, I thought you were going. Old Dick, who was ashore an hour ago, told me you were."

"Then old Dick told you a cram," said Bob. "He said you were going, though."

"I'll kick old Dick first time I see him," cried Tom Long. "I'm not going. Smithers and I are to be in charge of the fort."

"You are not going?" cried Bob incredulously.

"No!"

"Oh, I am glad."

"Thanky," said Tom.

"No, I don't mean that," said Bob. "I mean I'm glad I'm not going, now you are not."

"I say, Bob, do you mean that?" said Tom Long excitedly, and dropping all his stiffness.

"Of course I do," said Bob. "What's the fun of going without a friend?"

"Bob, you're a regular little brick," said Tom Long. "Shake hands. 'Pon my word I shall end by liking you."

Bob shook hands, and laughed.

"Oh, I say, though," he exclaimed. "Poor old Ali! Won't he be cut up, just?"

"Yes, he won't like it," said Tom Long thoughtfully. "And he was to have a big elephant all ready for us."

"Yes," said Bob. "But I say, I wonder we haven't heard from him since that day he was here."

"Yes, he might have sent a message of some kind."

"He's been up the country with a butterfly net to catch an elephant for us," said Bob, laughing.

"And now he'll have it all to himself," said Tom.

"I'll bet half a rupee that he don't," said Bob.

"Oh, yes, he will," said Tom. "I rather like him, though. He isn't a bad sort of nigger."

"Don't call the fellows *niggers*," said Bob impatiently; "they don't like it."

"Then they mustn't call us *giaours* and *dogs*," said Tom impatiently.

"Look here," cried Bob, "I must go on after these leggings for the skipper; but, I say, Tom, as I said before, I'll bet half a rupee that Ali don't go to the hunt when he finds we are to stay."

"Stuff!"

"Well, it may be stuff; but you see if he don't stop behind, and, as soon as they are all off, come across here."

"I wish he would," said Tom. "It'll be dull enough."

"If he does, we'll have a good turn at the fish," said Bob. "Good night, if I don't see you again."

"I say," said Bob, turning round and speaking out of the darkness.

"Well?"

"I don't wish 'em any harm; but I hope they won't see a blessed tiger all the time they're away."

"So do I," said Tom. "Good night!"

"Good night!" And Bob found the major; borrowed the pair of canvas leggings, with which he returned to the boat, and was rowed back to the corvette, where he had the pleasure of going over the captain's shooting gear, and helping him to fill his cartridge cases, and the like.

"You'll have to go on a trip yourself Roberts, by-and-by," said the captain.

"Thank-ye, sir," said Bob. "When, sir, please?"

"When the soreness about rescuing those slave girls has worn off, Master Bob Roberts," said the captain, smiling. "I can't afford to have one of my most promising young officers krissed."

"All soft soap and flam," said Bob to himself, as he went out on deck. "Promising officer, indeed. Well, he's a promising officer, and I'll keep him to his promise, too; and old Ali, and Tom, and I will have another day to ourselves."

Chapter Thirty Two
How Mr Linton believed in a Precipice

It was a grand sight, and a stranger to the scene might have imagined that a little army was about to set off for the conquest of some petty king, instead of to attack the striped tiger in his stronghold.

The two parties from the steamer and the island were ashore before daybreak, to find an imposing gathering of the sultan's people coming down to meet them. There were over thirty elephants, large and small, with their attendants, and the beasts were furnished with showy cloths under their rattan basket howdahs.

The sultan was there in English dress; and his chiefs made a gaudy muster, wearing showy silken sarongs and bajus, as if it were to be a review day instead of a hunting trip, while the following, to the extent of several hundreds, were all armed with spear and kris. Here and there a showily clad Malay was seen to be armed with a gun or rifle, but for the most part their means of offence were confined to the native weapons.

The meeting was most cordial; but the sultan and his followers seemed somewhat taken aback to see the various officers in rough sporting costume, and the soldiers and sailors in anything but stiff, ordinary trim.

One thing, however, had been rigidly adhered to. Every man was well-armed, and carried a good supply of ball cartridge.

The sun was shining brightly, when at last the hunting-party was duly marshalled, and moved off right through the jungle by a well-beaten path, one which took them straight away from the river; and very effective the procession looked, with the great lumbering elephants moving so silently along, the gaily-dressed Malays forming bright patches of colour amidst the clean white duck frocks and trousers of the sailors, and the dull grey of the soldiers' linen tunics. There was, of course, fraternisation, and a disposition on the part of the Malays to freely mix with the Englishmen then; but the order had been that a certain amount of formation was to be maintained, so that, if necessary, the men might be ready to gather at any time round their officers. Not that any difficulty was apprehended, but it was felt to be better to keep up discipline, even when only engaged upon a shooting-trip, though every act that might be interpreted by the Malays into a want of confidence was carefully avoided.

The morning was sufficiently young as yet to enable a good march to be made without difficulty; but as the sun began to make his power felt wherever there was an opening amidst the trees, a halt was called in a beautiful park-like patch of ground, with huge spreading trees sufficient to shelter double their number. Here a capital lunch was served by the sultan's cooks, one that no doubt an English *chef* would have looked upon with contempt, but which, after a long morning tramp through the steaming heat of the jungle, was delightful.

Every one was in excellent spirits, the sultan having set aside a great deal of his formality, and smiling apparently with pleasure as he gazed around at the gratified countenances of his guests.

Then followed a siesta while the sun was at its greatest height, Doctor Bolter impressing upon all the officers that a quiet rest during the heat of the day was the one thing needful to make them bear the exertion of the journey; and then, as soon as he saw every one following his advice, he arranged his puggaree around his pith helmet, put some cartridges in his pocket, and went off into the jungle to shoot specimens, with no little success.

Ten miles were got over that evening, and then camp was pitched on the edge of an opening, close by a curious rounded mountain, which towered up in front of the setting sun, looking massive and grand with its smooth outline thrown up, as it were, against the saffron sky.

The scene was lovely in the extreme, and every touch given by the hunting-party seemed to add thereto, for white tents sprang up like magic against the dark green foliage; fires began to twinkle here and there; the large mess tent, that had been carried by one of the elephants, was well lit with lamps; and a white cloth spread with ample provisions and no few luxuries, ornamented by the freshly-cut flowers which grew in profusion, as if waiting to be cut by the servants, added no little to the brightness of the interior.

Outside all was apparently picturesque confusion, though in reality everything was in due order, from the men's tents to the ranging of the elephants, who, relieved of their loads, were quietly lifting up great bunches of grass and tucking them into their capacious jaws. Over all rose a loud hum of many voices, and soon to this was added the click of knives and forks from the English mess and the rattle of plates. Amongst the Malays great leaves did duty for the latter, and all was quieter.

Later on, watch was set, the sultan and his officers smiling gravely at the precautions taken by the English, assuming though that it was against the wild beasts of the jungle, and hastening to assure all concerned that they need have no fear, for no tiger would approach so busy a camp, especially as there were fires burning, which would be kept up all night.

"Let them think it's the tigers, and that we are afraid of them, if they like," said the doctor; "but I wouldn't slacken discipline in the slightest degree. Keep everything going just as if we were going through an enemy's country."

"I support that motion," said the resident quietly.

"But why?" said Captain Horton. "Surely we may relax a little now."

"No, Doctor Bolter is right," said the major, nodding. "It's a nuisance, Horton, of course, but you would not let your ship go without a good watch being set?"

"Well—no," said the captain thoughtfully, "I suppose not. We should keep that up even if we were in dock. Thank goodness, though! I have not any watch to keep to-night, for I'm tired as a dog."

"It has been a tiring day," said Major Sandars. "I wonder how Smithers is getting on. I hope he's taking care of the ladies."

"Yes," said Mr Linton gravely, "I hope he is taking care of the ladies."

"They're in good hands," said Captain Horton. "Johnson is a sternish fellow, and," he added laughing, "if any dangerous parties go near the island, Mr Midshipman Roberts will blow them right out of the water."

"Yes," said Major Sandars, indulging in a low chuckle, "he and Mr Ensign Long between them would be a match for all the rajahs on the river."

Mr Linton was the only one who did not smile, for just then, like a foreboding cloud, the dark thought came across his mind that it would be very, very terrible if advantage were taken by the Malays of the absence of so large a portion of the force; and try how he would to sleep that night, the thought kept intruding, that after all they were doing wrong in trusting themselves with the Malay sultan, who might, under his assumption of hospitality, be hatching some nefarious scheme against them all.

Through the thin canvas walls of the tent he could hear the low breathing of some of his friends, the snort of some elephant, and close by him there was the monotonous hum of the mosquitoes, trying hard to find a way through the fine gauze of the net; now and then came too an impatient muttering of a sleeper, or the distant cry of some creature in the jungle.

The only solacing thing he heard in the heat of those weary sleepless hours was the steady beat of some sentry's pace, and the click of his arms as he changed his piece from shoulder to shoulder.

He was the only unquiet one, for the others fell asleep almost on the instant, and several of them gave loud signs of their peaceful occupation.

At last Mr Linton could bear it no longer, and rising, he went softly to the tent door and peeped out, to pause there, wondering at the beauty of the scene, as the moon was just peering down over the jungle trees, and filling the camp with silvery light and black shadows. What was that glint of some arm?

He smiled at his uneasiness directly after, for there was the sharp steady beat of feet, a sergeant's guard came out of the black shadow, and he saw them relieve sentry, the glint he had seen being the moonbeams playing upon the soldier's piece.

He went back and lay down once more, feeling relieved, and falling off into a restful sleep, little thinking how that deadly peril was indeed hovering round the island he had left, and that he and his companions were going to march on and on, not to encounter tigers alone, but men even more cruel in their nature, and quite as free from remorse when dealing with those whom they looked upon as dogs.

Chapter Thirty Three
Private Gray has his Orders

The men on the corvette, with those who rowed back the empty boats, gave a loud cheer, which was answered from the island, as the hunting-party moved off in procession.

"Give them another, my lads," cried Bob Roberts excitedly; and the sailors, with whom he was a special favourite, responded heartily.

"Just another, my lads, to show them we are not a bit envious," cried Bob; and then another prolonged "Hurrah!" went up in the morning skies, the middy shouting with the best of them; and it was amusing to see Bob's calm, consequential ways as he stood there, completely ignoring Lieutenant Johnson, and taking upon himself the full command of the ship.

He glanced up aloft, and his look threatened an order to man the yards, when the lieutenant interfered.

"I think that will do, Mr Roberts," he said quietly, and Bob was taken rather aback.

"Yes, of course, sir," he said, "but the men are already loaded with a cheer, hadn't they better let it off?"

Lieutenant Johnson gazed full in the lad's face, half sternly, half amused at his quaint idea, and then nodded. Then there was another stentorian cheer, and what seemed like its echo from the island, when Bob smiled his satisfaction, strutting about the quarter-deck as he exclaimed, — "We can beat the soldiers hollow at cheering, sir, can't we?"

"Yes, Mr Roberts," said the lieutenant quietly; and then to the warrant officer near him, "Pipe down to breakfast, Mr Law; the men must want it."

"I know one man who wants his," said Bob, half aloud; and then he stared wistfully after the tail of the departing expedition, as the sun glinted on the spears, and a very dismal sensation of disappointment came over him.

"You'll make a good officer some day, Roberts," said the lieutenant, and Bob started, for he did not know he was so near.

"Thank you, sir—for the compliment," said Bob.

"But at present, my lad, you do imitate the bantam cock to such an extent that it irritates grown men."

"Do I, sir?" said Bob.

"You do indeed, my lad," said the lieutenant kindly.

"But I don't want to, sir, for nothing worries me more than to see Ensign Long coming all that strut and show off."

"Well, we won't quarrel about it, Roberts," said Lieutenant Johnson kindly. "You'll grow out of it in time. As it is, I'm captain for a few days, and you are my first lieutenant. So first lieutenant," he continued, clapping the lad on the shoulder, "come down and breakfast with me in the cabin, and we'll talk matters over."

Bob flushed with pleasure, and if the lieutenant had asked him to jump overboard just then, or stand on his head on the main truck, Bob would have tried to oblige him.

As it was, however, he followed his officer into the cabin, and made a hearty breakfast.

"I tell you what," said the lieutenant, who was a very quiet stern young officer—and he stopped short.

"Yes, captain," said Bob.

Lieutenant Johnson smiled.

"I tell you what," he said again, "nothing would give me greater pleasure than for Mr Rajah Gantang to bring down his prahus some time to-day, Lieutenant Roberts. I could blow that fellow out of the water with the greatest pleasure in life."

"Captain Johnson," said Bob, solemnly, "I could blow him in again with greater pleasure, for I haven't forgotten my swim for life."

"You feel quite a spite against him then, Roberts?"

"Spite's nothing to it," said Bob. "Didn't he and his people force me, a harmless, unoffending young fellow—"

"As ever contrived to board a prahu," said the lieutenant.

"Ah, well, that wasn't my doing," said Bob. "I was ordered to do my duty, and tried to do it. That was no reason why those chicory-brown rascals should cause me to be pitched into the river to the tender mercies of the crocodiles, who, I believe, shed tears because they couldn't catch me."

"Well, Roberts," said the lieutenant, "you need not make yourself uncomfortable, nor set up the bantam cock hackles round your neck, and you need not go to the grindstone to sharpen your spurs, for we shall not have the luck to see anything of the rajah, who by this time knows that it is his best policy to keep out of the way. Will you take any more breakfast?"

"No, thank you, sir," said Bob, rising, for this was a hint to go about his business; and he went on deck.

"Mornin', sir," said old Dick, pulling at his forelock, and giving one leg a kick out behind.

"Morning, Dick. Don't you wish you were along with the hunting-party?"

Old Dick walked to the side, sprinkled the water with a little tobacco juice, and came back.

"That's the same colour as them Malay chaps, sir," he said, "nasty dirty beggars."

"Dirty, Dick? Why they are always bathing and swimming."

"Yes," said Dick in a tone of disgust, "but they never use no soap."

"Well, what of that?" said Bob. "You don't suppose that makes any difference?"

"Makes no difference?" said the old sailor; "why it makes all the difference, sir. When I was a young 'un, my old mother used to lather the yaller soap over my young head till it looked like a yeast tub in a baker's cellar. Lor' a mussy! the way she used to shove the soap in my eyes and ears and work her fingers round in 'em, was a startler. She'd wash, and scrub, and rasp away, and then swab me dry with a rough towel—and it was a rough 'un, mind yer—till I shone again. Why, I was as white as a lily where I wasn't pink; and a young lady as come to stay at the squire's, down in our parts, blessed if she didn't put me in a picter she was painting, and call me a village beauty. It's the soap as does it, and a rale love of cleanliness. Bah, look at 'em! They're just about the colour o' gingerbread; while look at me!"

Bob looked at the old fellow searchingly, to see if he was joking, and then finding that he was perfectly sincere, the middy burst into a hearty roar of laughter.

For long years of exposure to sun and storm had burned and stained Dick into a mahogany brown, warmed up with red of the richest crimson. In fact, a Malay had rather the advantage of him in point of colour.

"Ah, you may laugh," he growled. "I dessay, sir, you thinks it's werry funny; but if you was to go and well soap a young Malay he'd come precious different, I can tell you."

"But somebody did try to wash a blackamoor white," said Bob. "Tom Hood says so, in one of his books."

"Well, and did they get him white, sir?" asked Dick.

"No, I think not," said Bob. "I almost forget, but I think they gave him such a bad cold that he died."

"That Tom Hood—was he any relation o' Admiral Hood, sir?"

"No, I think not, Dick."

"Then he wasn't much account being a landsman, I s'pose, and he didn't understand what he was about. He didn't use plenty o' soap."

"Oh yes, he did, Dick; because I remember he says, a lady gave some:—

"Mrs Hope,
A bar of soap."

"Then they didn't lather it well," said Dick decisively. "And it shows how ignorant they was when they let's the poor chap ketch cold arter it, and die. Why, bless your 'art, Mr Roberts, sir, if my old mother had had the job, he'd have had no cold. He'd have come out red hot, all of a glow, like as I used, and as white as a lily, or she'd have had all his skin off him."

"And so you really believe you could wash these Malay chaps white?"

"I do, sir. I'd holystone 'em till they was."

"It would be a long job, Dick," said Bob laughing. "But I say, don't you wish you had gone with the hunting-party?"

"Yah!" said Dick, assuming a look of great disgust and contempt, although he had been growling and acting, as his mates said, like a bear with a sore head, because he could not go. "Not I, sir, not I. Why, what have they gone to do? Shoot a big cat all brown stripes. I don't want to spend my time ketching cats. What's the good on 'em when they've got 'em? Only to take their skins. Now there is some sense in a bit of fishing."

"Especially when your crew in the boat goes to sleep, and let's you be surprised by the Malays."

"Ah, but don't you see, sir," said Dick, with his eyes twinkling, "that's a kind o' moral lesson for a young officer? Here was the case you see: the skipper goes to sleep, and don't look after his crew, who, nat'rally enough, thinks what the skipper does must be right, and they does the same."

"Oh! all right, master Dick," said the middy. "I'll take the lesson to heart. Don't you ever let me catch you asleep, that's all."

"No, sir," said the old sailor, grinning, "I won't. I've got too much of the weasel in me. But as I was saying, sir, there's some sense in a bit o' fishing, and I thought if so be you liked I'd get the lines ready."

"No, Dick, no," said Bob, firmly, as he recalled Lieutenant Johnson's words over the breakfast-table. "I've no time for fishing to-day. And besides, I'm in charge of the ship."

"Oh! indeed, sir," said Dick. "I beg pardon, sir."

"Look here, Dick," said Bob sharply, "don't you sneer at your officer because he makes free with you sometimes."

The middy turned and walked off, leaving Dick cutting himself a fresh plug of tobacco.

"He'll make a smart 'un by-and-by, that he will," muttered the old fellow, nodding his head admiringly; "and I'm sorry I said what I did to the high-sperretted little chap, for he's made of the real stuff, after all."

On the island, Tom Long was feeling quite as important as the middy. A keen sense of disappointment was troubling him, but he would not show it. He had several times over been looking at his gun, and thinking that it would carry a bullet as well as a rifle, and wishing that he could have game to try it. But soon afterwards he encountered pleasant Mrs Major Sandars.

"Ah! Mr Long," she cried, "I've just been seeing Miss Linton and Miss Sinclair. Now you know you have these deserted ladies and the whole of the women under your charge, and I hope you'll protect us."

"I shall do my utmost, madam," said Tom Long importantly. "You ladies needn't be under the smallest apprehension, for you will be as safe as if the major and Mr Linton were here."

"I shall tell Miss Linton so," said Mrs Major, smiling; and she nodded and went away, leaving the young ensign uncomfortable, as he felt a kind of suspicion that he had been speaking very consequentially, and making himself absurd.

"I wish I was either a man or a boy," he said to himself pettishly. "I feel just like a man, and yet people will treat me as if I were a boy. That Mrs Major was only talking to me patronisingly, and half-laughing at me. I can see it now. Oh! here's Smithers."

Captain Smithers came up, looking rather careworn and sad, and nodded in a friendly way at his junior.

"Well, Long," he said, "so we are commanders-in-chief just now. At least, I am. You'll have to be my colonel, major, and adjutant, all in one."

"I shall do my best to help you, Captain Smithers," said Tom Long stiffly.

"I know you will, my lad," was the reply; "but it will be no child's play, for we must be extra strict and watchful."

"Do you think there is anything to fear, Captain Smithers," said the ensign eagerly.

"To fear? No, Mr Long," said the captain. "We are English officers, and, as such, never mention such a thing; but there is a good deal to be anxious about—I mean the safety of all here."

"But you have no suspicion, sir—of danger?"

"Not the slightest. Still we will be as careful as if I felt sure that an enemy was close at hand."

There was something about that *we* that was very pleasant to the young ensign; and his heart warmed like a flower in sunshine.

"Of course, sir," he said eagerly. "I'll do the best I can."

"Thank you, Long, I am sure you will," said Captain Smithers. "By the way, you know, of course, that the ladies are coming to stay with Mrs Major, so that there will not be much cause for anxiety about the residency. Suppose we now take a quiet look round together; there is really no necessity, but we will go as a matter of duty."

Tom Long's self-esteem was flattered, the more especially as he could see that Captain Smithers was perfectly sincere, and looked to him, in all confidence, for aid in a time when a great responsibility was thrown upon his shoulders.

"If I don't let him see that I can act like a man, my name's not Long," he muttered to himself, as they walked on together.

"There's only—"

Captain Smithers, who was speaking, stopped short, and the ensign stared.

"I do not want to offend you, Long," he said, "but all I say to you is in strict confidence now, and you must be careful what you repeat."

"You may trust me, Captain Smithers," said the ensign quietly.

"Yes, I am sure I may," was the reply. "Look here, then. I was going to say that the only weak point in our arrangements here seems to be that!"

He nodded his head in the direction in which they were going, and the ensign stared.

"I mean about allowing that Malay, Abdullah, to set up his tent among us. He has such freedom of communicating with the banks of the river on both sides. He is a man, too, whom I rather distrust."

"Indeed?" said Long.

"Yes, I don't know why. But unless for some good and sufficient reason it would, I think, be bad policy to attempt to oust him."

"Yes," calmly said Long. "He is a violent fellow, too;" and he related the incident about their first meeting.

"If the major had known of this," said Captain Smithers, "he would never have allowed the man to settle here. You did wrong in not speaking of it, Long."

"He was so apologetic and gentlemanly afterwards," said the ensign, "that I did not care to speak about it, and upset the fellow's plans."

"Well, it is too late to talk about it now," replied Captain Smithers; "but I shall have his actions quietly watched. Let me see, who will be the man?"

"There's Private Gray yonder," suggested the ensign.

"I hate Private Gray!" exclaimed Captain Smithers, with a sudden burst of rage, of which he seemed to be ashamed the next moment, for he said hastily, — "It is a foolish antipathy, for Gray is a good, staunch man;" and making an effort to master himself, he made a sign to Gray to come to them.

"You are right, Long; Gray is the man. He is to be trusted."

The private came up, and stiffly saluted his officers, standing at attention.

"Gray," said Captain Smithers, "I want you to undertake a little task for me."

"Yes, sir."

"You will be off regular duty; another man will take your place. I want you, in a quiet, unostentatious manner, to keep an eye on Abdullah the fruit-seller. Don't let him suspect that you are watching him, for really there may be no cause; but he is the only native here who has free access to the island, and during the major's absence I wish to be especially strict."

"Yes, sir."

"You understand me? I trust entirely to your good sense and discrimination. You will do what you have to do in a quiet way, and report everything—even to the least suspicious proceeding—to me."

"Yes, sir."

"You shall be furnished with a permit, to pass you anywhere, and at all times."

"Thank you, sir."

"I'd go in undress uniform, and apparently without arms, but have a bayonet and a revolver under your jacket."

"Do you think there is danger, sir?" exclaimed the private hastily, forgetting himself for the moment.

"Private Gray, you have your orders."

Gray drew himself up stiffly and saluted.

"Begin at once, sir?"

"At once," said Captain Smithers. "I trust to your silence. No one but Mr Long knows of your mission."

Gray saluted again and went off, while the two officers continued their walk towards Dullah's hut.

The Malay came out as they approached, and with a deprecating gesture invited them to take a seat beneath his verandah and partake of fruit.

This, however, they declined to do, contenting themselves with returning his salute, and passing on.

There were two sampans moored close to Dullah's hut, each holding four Malays, but the boats themselves were filled with produce piled high, and the owners were evidently waiting to have dealings with their superior, the man who had been appointed to supply the English garrison of the island and the ship.

There was nothing suspicious to be seen here, neither did anything attract their attention as they continued their walk right round the island, everything being as calm and still as the sleepy shore which lay baking beneath the ardent rays of the sun, while the various houses looked comparatively cool beneath the shade of the palms and durian trees, with here and there a great ragged-leaved banana showing a huge bunch of its strange fruit.

Tired and hot, they were glad to return to their quarters, where Sergeant Lund was writing out a report, and occasionally frowning at Private Sim, who was lying under a tree fast asleep.

Chapter Thirty Four
A Hot Night on board the "Startler"

The young officers were pretty busy over their duties throughout the day, Bob Roberts to his great delight being left in sole charge of the steamer, while Lieutenant Johnson went to have a short consultation with Captain Smithers; and two hours later, when Captain Smithers accompanied the naval officer back, Ensign Long was in full command at the island.

The hot and sleep-inviting day had rolled slowly by; never had the river looked brighter and clearer, or more keenly reflected the rays of the sun. Far down in its pure depths the middy had watched the darting about of the fish, which seemed to seek the shadow beneath the steamer's hull for their playground.

This was noticed at stolen moments, for Bob was generally too full of his duties to think of the fish, or to do more than cast a longing glance at the dark shadows beneath the trees. For on board the heat was terrible, the pitch was oozing out of the seams, and blistering the paint; every piece of tarry cordage was soft and pliant, and very beads stood out upon the strands; while beneath the awnings there was a stuffy suffocating heat that was next to unbearable.

On the island the heat was less hard to be borne, the thick grove of palms and other trees whose roots were always moist, throwing out a grateful shade. Still the heat was severely felt, and the general impression was that the hunting-party had by far the worst of it.

The day glided by, and the sultry tropic night set in, with the great mellow stars glistening overhead reflected in the clear stream, and seeming to be repeated in the low undergrowth that fringed the shore. The watches were set, every precaution taken against surprise, and though no danger need be apprehended, Captain Smithers had the little fort quite ready to resist attack.

It was the same on board the steamer, the watch being visited at frequent intervals by the lieutenant and his subordinate, to the great surprise of the men, who wondered what made the "luff" so fidgety.

That night passed off without anything to disturb them; and the next day all was so dull and uniform that Bob Roberts, as he could not go ashore, was fain to amuse himself with his monkey, which he fed till it could eat no more, and then teased till it got into a passion, snapped at him, and took refuge in the rigging till its master's back was turned, when, to the great delight of the men, it leaped down on the middy's shoulder, and there seized the back of his jacket-collar and shook it vigorously, till seeing its opportunity it once more leaped up into the rigging, chattering fiercely, and showing its teeth as Bob threatened it and called it names.

Evening came on again, not too hot, but quite bad enough to make the middy glad to walk the deck in the loosest jacket he possessed. The watch had been set, the lights hung up, and all was very still; for, having had but little sleep the night before, Bob was too tired to talk, and now sat in the coolest place he could find, hitting out occasionally at a mosquito, and alternating that exercise with petting the monkey, which had made its submission by creeping down from the rigging at dinner-time, and approaching its master in a depressed mournful way, as if declaring its sorrow for its late sin, and readiness to do anything, if its master would forgive it. In fact, when the middy rose as if to beat it, the animal lay down on the deck, grovelling and whining piteously, as it watched his actions with one eye, that said as plainly as could be, "You don't mean it. I'm such a little thing that you would not hurt me."

Bob did not hurt it, but gave it one of Dullah's mangosteens instead, and peace was made.

Lieutenant Johnson joined the middy soon after he had given up seeking a nap on account of the heat, and came and leaned over the bulwark by his side, talking to him in a low voice, both feeling depressed and subdued.

"I wonder how our party is getting on?" said the lieutenant at last. "They'll have a storm to-night, and soaked tents."

"Yes; there's a flash," exclaimed Bob, as the distant forest seemed to be lit-up to its very depths by a quivering blaze of sheet lightning.

This was repeated, and with increased vividness, the pale blue light playing about in the horizon, and displaying the shapes of the great heavy clouds that overhung the mountains in the east.

"It's very beautiful to watch," said the lieutenant; "but suppose we take a walk forward."

They strolled along the deck, and on going right to the bows found the watch every man in his place; and returning aft spoke to the marine, who stood like a statue leaning upon his piece.

They sat down again, feeling no inclination to seek the cabin; and this feeling seemed to be shared by the men, who were sitting about, talking in low whispers, and watching the distant lashing lightning, whose lambent sheets seemed now to be playing incessantly.

"Is there anything the matter with you, sir?" said Bob at last.

"No, Roberts, only that I feel so restless and unsettled that I should like to jump overboard for a cool swim."

"That's just what I feel, sir," said Bob, "with a dash of monkey in it."

"A dash of monkey!"

"Yes, sir; as if I must run and jump about, or climb, or do something. It's the fidgets with this heat. Let's walk forward again, if you don't mind. I think it's cooler there."

"Cooler, Roberts? It seems to me as if the deck is thoroughly hot, and as if one's clothes were baking. I quite envy the lads, with their bare feet and open necks."

They strolled forward again, with the monkey softly following them; and when they stood leaning over the bulwarks, listening to the ripple of the water under the vessel's stem, the animal perched itself on one of the stays just above their heads.

They could almost have fancied they were at sea, gazing down at the phosphorescent water, so beautiful was the reflection of the stars in the smooth, dark current, as it glided swiftly along, rippling a little about the large buoy to which they were moored, and breaking the stars up, as it were, into a thousand tiny points, that divided into a double current and swept by the steamer's bows.

"What a night for a couple of prahus to come down and board us, sir!" said Bob.

"Rather unlucky for them, if they did," said the lieutenant quietly. "One good shot at them, or one of our biggest shells dropped into their hold, would crash through, and send them to the bottom. There's no such luck, Roberts."

"I suppose not, sir," said Bob; but, all the same, he could not help feeling that this was a kind of luck which he could very well dispense with on a dark night. He did not venture to say so, though.

"How quiet they seem on the island!" said the lieutenant at last. "Heigh-ho! ha hum! I wish we were there, Roberts, along with the ladies; a cup of tea and a little pleasant chat would be very agreeable."

"And some music," said Bob.

"And some music," said the lieutenant. "What's the matter with your monkey?"

"What's the matter, Charcoal?" said Bob; for the little animal had suddenly grown excited, chattering, and changing its place, coming down the stay, and then leaping on to the bulwark.

"He sees something in the water," said the lieutenant.

"Crocodile," said Bob; "they like monkey. Look out, Charcoal, or you'll be overboard."

This was on dimly seeing the monkey run along the bulwark, chattering excitedly.

"Help!" came in a hoarse tone from somewhere ahead.

"There's a man overboard," cried the lieutenant. "Pass the word there. Lower down the gig."

There was the sharp pipe of a whistle, and a scuffling of feet, for the hail had electrified the men; but meanwhile the cry was repeated.

"It's some one from the island swimming down to us," said the lieutenant. "Hold on, my lad," he cried, as the cry was repeated nearer and nearer, and then just ahead.

"Quick, sir," cried Bob, "he's holding on by the hawser, whoever he is;" and fully satisfied in his own mind that one of the soldiers had been bathing, and had been swept down by the current, he called out to the swimmer to hold on, but only to hear once more the one hoarse cry, "Help!" and with it a gurgling noise where the bright stars were broken up into a forked stream of tiny points.

So eager was he to cry out to the drowning man that help was coming, that he missed the chance of going himself, but leaned over the bows as the captain's gig, manned with a ready little crew, kissed the water, was unhooked, and ran swiftly along the side; then the oars splashed, and the little, light boat was rapidly rowed to where the great hawser was made fast.

It was so dark that Bob could only dimly make out the round buoy, towards which the gig passed over the water like a shadow.

"Can you see him?" cried the lieutenant, who was once more by Bob Roberts' side.

"No, sir; there's no one here," said the bow-man.

"Help! help!" came in a hoarse whisper just then, exactly below where the two officers leaned over; and they saw that a dark face that had risen to the surface was being swept quickly along by the steamer's side.

"Quick, my lads, here he is! Stern all!" cried the lieutenant; and the light gig was backed rapidly in quest of the drowning man; while Bob ran aft as hard as he could go, and climbed out into the mizzen chains, to stare down into the swift current, holding on by one hand.

But he could see nothing, and he was beginning, with throbbing heart, to believe that he was too late—that the wretched man had been swept away before he climbed over, when he caught sight of something just below the surface.

"Here, boat, quick!" he cried; and the bow-man struck his hook into the side, and sent the gig flying through the water.

"Where, sir? where?" cried he in the hoarse voice of Dick.

"There, just below there; I saw him."

For answer Dick leaned over the gig's bows, and thrust down his boat-hook.

"Give way, my lads," he cried, and again and again he thrust down his hook. Then a strange, choking feeling of horror seemed to seize upon the middy, and he felt dizzy as he gazed after the boat in the midst of that weird darkness, which made the event ten times more terrible than if it had been by day.

Just as his heart sank with dread, and he in fancy saw the dead body seized by one or other of the terrible reptiles that swarmed in the river, wondering the while which of the poor men it was, and why they had heard no alarm at the island, Dick's hoarse voice was heard some distance astern, exclaiming in triumph—

"I've got him, my lads! Give way!"

Chapter Thirty Five
How Ali made his Plans

There is a strange kind of stoicism about a Mohammedan that seems to give him an abundance of calmness when he comes face to face with death. He is a fatalist, and quietly says to himself what is to be will be, and he resigns himself to his fate.

The young chief Ali was imbued with all the doctrines of his people; but at the same time he had mixed so with the English that he had learned to look upon life as of too much value to be given up without a desperate struggle. One of his compatriots would have made a fight for his life, and when he had seen all go against him he would have given up without a murmur and looked his slayers indifferently in the face. Ali, however, did not intend to give up without another effort, and though he seemed indifferent, a terrible struggle was going on within his breast. Thoughts of his father, of his new friends, of the bright sunshine of youth, and the future that had been so full of hope, and in which he had meant to do so much to improve his country—all rose before his wandering eyes, and he had meant to seize the first opportunity to escape.

The approach of the kris-armed Malay, though, had been so sudden that all his calculations had been upset, and he had had no time to design a means of escape. He was tightly bound, held by two others, and this man was evidently under orders from the sultan to slay him.

It was useless to struggle, he knew—just as vain to waste his strength, and rob himself of his calmness; so that he felt bound to call up all his fortitude, and with it the fatalistic theories of his race, so that he might die as behoved the son of a great chief.

He drew himself up then, and stood gazing at the man with the kris as calm and motionless as if he had been made of bronze, and awaited the deadly stroke.

This, however, did not come; for in place of delivering a deadly thrust, the Malay roughly seized him by the shoulder, and began to saw away through the prisoner's bonds.

He was so firmly secured that this process took some time, during which Ali, by the strange revulsion that came upon him, felt as if he must fall prone upon his face from sheer giddiness; but by an effort he stood firm till his limbs were set free.

His wrists were painfully marked, and his arms felt numb and helpless, but his first thought, as soon as the ligatures that had held him were off, was how to escape.

His captors read this and smiled, each man drawing his kris and showing it menacingly, while their leader told him that he was a prisoner until the sultan's wishes were known.

"Are you not going to kill me?" said Ali passionately.

"Not yet," was the reply, "unless you try to escape, when we are to kill you like a dog, and throw you into the river."

"But why?" asked Ali; "what have I done?"

"I know nothing," was the surly reply.

"Does my father know of this?" cried Ali.

"I know nothing," said the Malay.

"But you will tell me what your instructions are, and where you are going to place me."

"I know nothing. I tell nothing," said the Malay. "Be silent. That is your prison. If you try to escape, you die."

Ali burned to ask more questions, but he felt that it would be useless, and that he, a chief's son, was only losing dignity by talking to the man, whom he recognised now as being the sultan's most unscrupulous follower, the scoundrel who did any piece of dirty work or atrocity. This was the man who, at his master's wish, dragged away any poor girl from her home to be the sultan's slave; who seized without scruple on gold, tin, rice, or any other produce of the country, in his master's name, and for his use. His hands had been often enough stained with blood, and while wondering at his life being spared so far, Ali had no hesitation in believing that any attempt at escape would be ruthlessly punished by a stab with the kris.

Obeying his captors, then, Ali went into the inner room of the ruined house, and seated himself wearily upon the floor, thinking the while of the hunting expedition, and of the light in which his conduct would be viewed by his friends.

Then he wondered whether his father would send in search of him; but his heart sank as he felt that, in all probability, the Tumongong would be carefully watched by the sultan's orders, and that any movement upon his son's behalf would result in his own death.

Then he began to feel that, if he was to escape, it must be through his own efforts; for he had so little faith in Hamet's nature, that he knew that his existence trembled upon a hair.

He was in an inner room of the house, little better in fact than a bamboo cage. The place was old, but he could see that here and there his prison had been mended with new green bamboos, especially about the flooring, through which he could see down to the earth, some twelve feet below, the sunlight shining up between the short bamboos, just as a few gleams of sunshine came through the attap roof.

There had been a window, but this had been filled in with stout bamboo cross-pieces, through and between which were woven long lengths of rattan; but the weak places had been made strong, and from old experience he knew that, unless armed with a heavy knife, it would be impossible to force a way through the tough wall of bamboo and woven cane.

The place was very gloomy, from the closing of the window; and as he glanced round he could see that his guards had been joined by half-a-dozen more, and that they were making themselves comfortable in the outer place, but in such a position that they could command a full view of his room.

Judging from appearances, they were preparing for a lengthened stay, for some of them were arranging cooking utensils; others placing pieces of dammar, a sort of fossil gum, of a pale blue tint, and very inflammable, ready for lighting up the part of the house where they were assembled.

After a time one of the number made ready the meal, for which his companions seemed to be impatiently waiting; and first of all a portion, consisting of broiled fish, some fruit, and sago, was brought to the prisoner, who, before partaking thereof, was rigorously searched, to see if he still bore any arms about his person. Satisfied upon this point, the Malays left him with his food, and proceeded to feast themselves, after which some began smoking, and some betel-chewing.

It was evident to Ali that he was to be kept a close prisoner; and as he lay there upon the bamboo floor, with his untouched food before him, he began to think out his position, and to calculate as to the possibility of escape.

How was it to be done?

His guards were so watchful that his slightest movements drew two or three pairs of eyes upon him, and he knew of old how quick they were of hearing. He felt assured that they would take it in turns to sleep, and hence he would have no opportunity of eluding their vigilance. Still he was hopeful, for there is an elasticity in the mind of youth which some things dash, when the spirit of middle or old age would be broken.

If he stayed where he was, sooner or later he felt sure that Hamet would be weary of the trouble he caused, and give orders for his death. So escape he must. But why should Hamet give orders for his death? Why should he wish him to be kept a close prisoner?

It was a puzzle that he could not solve; but at last, as he lay there thinking, the light broke more and more into the darkness of his mind.

It would be, he was sure, something to do with his intimacy with the English; and if so, Hamet's friendship was false.

Ali had suspected him for some time; and as he lay thinking, it seemed to him that he was correct in surmising that though Hamet was sincere enough, perhaps, when he made his first arrangements for the reception of a resident, the act had given such annoyance to several of the neighbouring Malay princes, notably to Rajah Gantang, that in his fear for his personal safety the sultan had repented of the arrangement, or had been coerced by those who might, he knew, in spite of the English being at hand, secretly have him assassinated.

This being the case, then, what should he do?

It was still a hard problem to solve, but as he went on thinking, Ali's brow grew damp, for he started upon a strange current of reasoning.

Sultan Hamet knew little of the English power. Certainly, they had good fighting men and guns; but they were small in number, and he might easily overcome them, and the people at Singapore or Penang would not dare to send more. If they did, the new contingent could be served the same as the old.

Ali's blood turned cold. Certain little things, which had only slightly roused his curiosity, now assumed an ominous significance; and as he thought, he started hastily into a sitting position.

This movement caused his guards to turn upon him; and seeing that he had excited their curiosity, he bent down over the supply of food placed for him, and began to eat as calmly as if nothing whatever troubled his spirit.

But all the same, he was wet with perspiration, and his heart beat painfully; for the light had come, and he saw plainly enough that something was wrong.

This was why he was a prisoner. Hamet knew of his intimacy with the young Englishmen, and feared that he would learn his plans and communicate them at the residency, perhaps to their defeat.

There was danger, then, threatening those whom he had made his friends. Hamet had yielded to the taunts of Rajah Gantang and others, and also given up to his own desire for revenge.

The resident had offered him a deadly insult in refusing to listen to the matrimonial proposal, and also in refusing to give up the slaves who had taken refuge with him.

Here was plenty of cause for hatred—a hatred that had been concealed under a mask of smiles; and now it was evident that Hamet meant to strike a blow at the English, destroying them, gaining possession of their arms and stores, and—the thought made him shudder as he pretended to be eating—get the two tenderly-nurtured ladies into his power.

How and when would this be done? Ali asked himself, and again came a flash of light, and he saw it all plainly enough. A trap had been laid for the English, and they were walking into it—that hunting-party!

It was all plain enough; the English force would be divided. A part would be marched to some suitable part of the jungle, miles away, and beyond the reach of their friends, where even the sounds of firing could not be heard, and then they would be set upon, and butchered in cold blood, most likely during their sleep.

This was the tiger-hunt, then, with the unfortunate English party being led directly into the tiger's lair!

It was terrible! The young man's face became convulsed with horror as he thought of the massacre that must ensue, and then of the surprise of those on the island and on the ship. Treachery, he knew, would be brought to bear in both cases, and here was he, knowing all, and yet unable to stir.

At all hazards, even that of death, he must make the venture, and warn those in peril; but where must he go first?

A moment decided that.

To the steamer and the island, and afterwards to the hunting-party; which would be easy enough to follow by their track, if they had gone.

In the eager impulse of the determination, he sprang to his feet to go, but as he did so three Malays sprang to their feet, and each man drew his kris.

Chapter Thirty Six
At the Prison in the Woods

The menacing act on the part of his captors brought Ali back to a sense of his position, and he stood there, gazing from one to the other, thinking what he should do.

Unarmed as he was, any attempt at violence was utter madness, and that he knew; so after a few moments' thought he made a sign for the chief man of the party to advance, which he did cautiously, and with his weapon held ready to strike.

Seeing his suspicion, Ali smiled, and threw himself on the floor, where, resting on one elbow, he began to appeal to the man to let him go, but only to find his words listened to in solemn silence.

The young chief then began to offer him bribes, one after the other, making the man's eyes glisten when he promised him his double gun; but directly after the man made a negative sign, merely told him to finish his meal, and returned to the outer room.

What was he to do? The more he thought of the suspicions that had entered his mind, the more certain did he become that he was right; and his sufferings became terrible, as in imagination he saw a treacherous attack made upon those he esteemed as friends, and the whole party put to death.

Could he not escape? It would not take him so very long to make his way to the river, where, if he could not seize upon a boat, he might swim down to the island, risking the crocodiles; though, somewhat unnerved by his late adventure, he felt a shudder run through him at the recollection of the grip of the loathsome beast.

Yes, he must get away, he said. He must elude the vigilance of the people who watched him, and by some means escape. Once in the jungle-path, with anything like a start, he did not feel much fear.

The hunt was to be on the next day but one, and that would give him ample time to devise some plan. He would require all his strength, so he must eat; and though the act went against him, he set to and ate of the food provided, then leaned back and half-closed his eyes, knowing full well that his every act was still watched by those who had made him a prisoner.

What should he do?

Bribery with the chief of the party was evidently useless, for though he had promised any price the man liked to name, he would not listen; though that was no cause for surprise, since if the man helped the young chief to escape, his own life would be forfeit, unless he could escape from the country.

But there were his followers, he might be able to win one of them to his side, could he get at him, and that could only be achieved by throwing the leader to some extent off his guard.

Even if he could enlist the sympathy of one of the others, Ali felt in no wise sure of success. Better, he thought, to trust to himself, and try to escape.

His anxiety grew momentarily greater, even though he knew the hunting-party would not set off until another day had elapsed, while, try hard as he would, he could devise no scheme that seemed likely to succeed.

Through his half-closed eyes he scanned every part of the closely-woven walls, to see if he could make out a weak place in his prison, but not one appeared; then turning, as if restlessly, he gazed up at the palm-thatched roof to see if there was any opening there; but even if there had been, he saw the hopelessness of trying, and at last he lay still with a dull feeling of despair creeping over him.

Night fell at last, and he saw his captors light a couple of dammar-torches, with whose light they were able to see distinctly his every act; and then he noticed that three of the men took up the task of watching him, while the others slept.

The hours rolled on, and, perfectly sleepless himself, Ali lay upon a couple of mats that had been brought him, listening to the heavy breathing of the men in the next room, and to the weird noises in the jungle, where the animals that had lain hidden all day were now prowling about, close to the ruined buildings, as if attracted by the presence of human beings in their midst.

Never had night seemed so long, or day so slow in coming; but at last as Ali lay watching he suddenly became aware that the dammar-torches, lit by each watching party in turn, were beginning to pale, and that it was once more day.

That day passed away in the most weary and monotonous manner. Sleepless as had been the young chief's night, he still felt no desire to close his eyes, but lay watching and thinking. Still no hopeful idea entered his head. The men were watched, he found, by their leader, who seemed to sleep so lightly that he was upon his feet the moment any of his followers moved.

Ali tried him again twice in the course of that day, but found him incorruptible; do what he would, the highest promises having no more effect than the lowest.

"No," he said once, grimly; "if I let you escape, all you gave me would not save my life."

"Who would dare to hurt you?" exclaimed Ali.

The man smiled sourly, and made no reply, but walked away.

That day glided by, and still no chance of escape. Food was brought, and Ali ate mechanically, feeling that he might need his strength when he did make the effort to get away; but still there seemed no chance. Walls, floor, roof, all were slight, and yet too strong for him to make any impression upon them, unless he could have had a few minutes to himself; then he would not have despaired of getting through. Sometimes he resolved to make a bold dash, run by his guards, and, leaping down by the entrance, trust to his swiftness to escape; but a few minutes' consideration taught him that such a plan must result in failure. His only hope was to elude the men.

Why did not his father try and save him? he asked himself; and then he sank back despairing again, wondering what he should do.

Then he tried his guard again upon another tack—would he, if he would not let him escape, bear a message to the residency island?

The man replied by a stern negative; and, as night came on, Ali determined to escape at all hazards.

The next morning the party would be starting for the hunt—a hunt from which, he felt sure, they would never return. Then it was certain that a treacherous attack would be made upon the ship and the island, and yet here he lay supine, knowing all this, and yet unable to act.

Night fell, and with the intention of making a bold rush through the outer room when half the watchers were asleep, Ali lay, watching hour after hour for an opportunity.

Time went on, and it seemed as if the leader would never lie down; he always seemed to have something more to say to his followers. But at last he threw himself on the floor, and seemed to sleep.

The time had come.

Three men sat there watching him, their swarthy faces glistening in the light of the torches. All was dark without, and the low growling noise of beasts was once more heard in close proximity to the place. Still they would not keep him back. He could risk an encounter with one of them, even death, sooner than this fearful torture.

At last he turned softly, and drew up one leg, watching his guards the while.

They did not hear him, and he drew up the other leg.

Still no notice was taken; and softly rising to his hands and knees, Ali remained motionless, nerving himself for the supreme effort.

The men were talking in a low voice, the sleepers breathed hard, and now was the moment. Rising then to his feet, he was about to make a rush across the room; he had even stooped to give impetus to his spring, when the chief of his guards leaped up, kris in hand, the others following the example, and Ali shrank back disheartened, and fully awake now to the fact that some one had been watching him all the time.

To struggle with them would only have been to throw away his life; so, with his heart full of despair, Ali allowed himself to be pressed back to his old position, where he lay down, his captor telling him savagely that the orders were to kill him if he attempted to escape.

"And we shall," said the Malay, "sooner than lose you."

His words were uttered in a tone of voice that told his hearer of the sincerity of that which was spoken. Ali knew the character of the Malays too well to entertain any doubt. There would not be the slightest compunction in the matter; and knowing this, he lay there watching the men, as they slowly settled down once more around the blazing dammar-torch they had replenished.

One coolly replaced his kris, and proceeded to get ready his betel for a fresh chew, calmly taking a sirih leaf, spreading upon it a little creamy lime from a tiny box, and rolling in it a scrap of nut, his red-stained teeth looking ogre-like in the torch-light.

Another set-to and prepared to smoke, making himself a pipe in a very few minutes out of a piece of green bamboo, cutting it off close to the joint, and then a little above it for a bowl, in one side of which he made a hole, and thrust in a little reed for a stem. In this sylvan pipe he placed some broken leaf of the coarse Malay tobacco, and began to smoke contentedly; while the third watcher helped himself to a piece of sugar-cane, and began peeling off the harsh, siliceous envelope, and then eating the sweet soft interior.

The leader had at once lain down, and seemed to have gone off to sleep; but of that Ali could not be sure.

He had failed; but Ali was not yet disheartened, and he lay there, thinking that he would risk life over and over again to warn his friends; but still he had to consider that if he lost his life he would not be serving them in the slightest degree, even if they should see his disfigured body float down.

What could he do?

If he had only possessed a little *toobah*, that creeping plant whose roots the Malays used for drugging the fish, some of that, he thought, infused in the food of his guards, would send them into a state of stupefaction, and give him time to escape.

He smiled directly after as he thought of this, and lay back wearily, thinking of what folly it was to form such bubble-like ideas; for of course it would have been impossible, even had he possessed the drug, to get it mingled with his captors' food.

No, he felt he must wait now, and trust to their dropping off to sleep, when he might still manage to crawl to the doorway, leap down, and dash into the jungle.

As he lay thinking, the hard breathing of a couple of the Malays could be plainly heard, and his hopes rose, for the others must grow weary, sooner or later, and fall asleep. The noises in the jungle increased; and as he lay with his cheek against the bamboo flooring, the sounds came up very plainly between the interstices. Now it was the heavy crashing of the reeds, the rustling of some animal going through the dense undergrowth, and then, unmistakeably, the low, snarling roar of a tiger. Now it was distant— now close at hand, and he knew that one of the great, cat-like creatures was answering another. How close it seemed! He could almost fancy that the tiger was beneath the house, hiding in the reedy grass that had sprung up amidst the ruins.

Two of the Malays moved about uneasily, and they lit a fresh torch, an act that set Ali thinking of cases he had known, in which tigers had sprung up eight or ten feet to the platform of a house, and seized and borne off its occupants one after the other.

If only one of the monsters would perform such a good office for him now, he would be able to escape in the midst of the confusion, perhaps into the jaws of another.

Well, if he did; what then? he asked himself. Better trust to chance in the jungle, than be left to the tender mercies of these men.

The roars came louder and nearer, close up at last, and the Malays seized their limbings, and stood with the keen points advanced towards the entrance; but their leader sulkily rose, took one of the dammar-torches, made it blaze a little, and going boldly towards the door, waited till a snarling roar came close at hand, when he hurled it with all his might in the tiger's direction.

There was a savage, deep-mouthed, hollow yell, and the crash of brittle reeds, telling that the tiger had rushed away, alarmed at the fire; when the man came slowly back, said something to his companions, who resumed their seats, while he seemed to lie down and go off to sleep.

Seemed, Ali felt; for after his late experience, he was sure that if any attempt were made to cross the room this watchful Malay would immediately rise to his feet and confront him.

Ali was intensely agitated. The expedition was to start the next morning, and if he did not warn them, they would be marching, he was sure, right into the jaws of death. Still the night was young as yet, and some opportunity might occur.

The light from the torches flickered and danced in the night air, and cast strange shadows about the place. From where he lay he could see the forms of his guards, huge and distorted, against the woven reed and bamboo walls, their every movement being magnified and strange. In his own part, from time to time he could see the bright green growth that had forced itself through the palm-thatch, and trace every bamboo rafter, save where, in places, all was in profound darkness.

How dreamy and strange it all seemed! There was the distant roaring of the tigers, growing more and more faint; the soft sighing of the night wind, and the rustle of the dry grass as some creature, on its nocturnal hunt for food, brushed through. Time was going by fast, but still the night was not nearly past, and the opportunity might come.

Surely, he thought, the leader was asleep now; he had moved uneasily two or three times, and was now lying motionless upon his back. One of the other men, too—the watchers—had let his chin sink upon his breast, and the other two looked heavy and dull.

His heart rose high with hope, for surely the chance of escape was going to be his.

The torches were growing dim, and if not soon replenished with fresh dammar, they would both be out; but no one stirred to touch them.

Ali waited, with every nerve drawn tight to its utmost strain, and he was ready for the rush, but he hung back, for fear too great precipitancy should spoil his chance; and he watched and watched, lying there till, to his great joy, one of the torches went completely out, and the other was failing.

Would either of the Malays move?

No, they were asleep; and the second torch gave out but a dim glimmer, as Ali rose, softly as a cat, and going on all fours, began to make what he felt was his final trial to get free.

He crept on nearer and nearer, but no one stirred. On he went, till he was close to his guards—so near that he could have stretched out a hand and touched them—but still no one moved. Their leader seemed now to be the most soundly asleep of the party, and so intensely excited did the fugitive become that it was all he could do to master himself and keep from rising up and rushing to the open door, through which the cool night wind now began to fan his cheeks.

He kept down the exciting feelings, though, by a mighty effort, and crawled softly on, as the second dammar-torch burned out, and all was darkness.

He passed the last man, and was now out well in the middle of the great room, with the open doorway before him, dimly seen like a square patch of star-lit sky. The hard breathing of the sleepers came regularly, and there was the low sighing of the wind without, then the softened, distant roar of a tiger, heard again and again, and repeated far more distantly. Then all was very still: the only noise being the faint rustle of his sarong, as he crept on nearer and nearer to the opening, from whence he meant to lower himself silently and make straight for the river, and try to find a boat.

It was hard work to keep crawling along there, inch by inch, lest the bamboos should creak. They bent and yielded to his weight over and over again, and twice over they gave so loud a noise that Ali paused, listening for the movement of his guards, meaning then to spring up and flee. Still no one moved, and in spite of his intense desire to make a bold rush, he crept on, knowing how great would be his advantage if he could get off without waking his guards, and free from the pursuit of a party following upon his track like a pack of hungry hounds.

Not two yards from the door now, and it seemed as if he would never reach it. His breath came thick and fast, and his heart throbbed so that he felt the bamboos over which he crawled vibrate, but still no one moved.

Another yard gained, and still all was darkness and silence, while the strain upon his nerves seemed greater than they could bear.

The last yard, and he grasped the bamboos to lower himself softly down, when there was a rush, a cry, a hurriedly-spoken order, and the Malays, who seemed to have divined that he was there, dashed across the floor in pursuit.

Ali told himself that he must not be taken, and dropping to the earth, he dashed across the reed and grass-grown space, and made for the jungle-path, meaning to follow it for a certain distance, and then strike off at the first opening across to the river.

To have attempted the jungle at once would have been utter madness, for he could not have forced his way a dozen yards through the tangled growth. All he could do was to trust to swiftness of foot and follow the track, and that was horribly overgrown. Thorns caught and tore his baju and sarong, rattan canes tripped him up, or were so woven across his path that he had to leap over them, when the upper boughs beat and lashed his face; but still he tore on, with his pursuers close behind. He could hear their shouts, and almost distinguish their breathing, as they panted on close behind him.

It was terrible work, and he felt himself at this disadvantage, that he was clearing the way down the little-used jungle-path for his pursuers, while every now and then he stepped into an elephant-hole, and nearly fell heavily. The tracks left by the huge beasts were in places very deep, but somehow Ali seemed to save himself just as he was on the point of falling.

On still through the intense darkness, and his pursuers close behind. The nearest, he seemed to feel, was the leader of the party; and as he listened to his heavy breathing, and fancied that the man was gaining upon him, the keen kris he held in his hand nearly grazed his shoulder.

A dozen times over, with the desperation of some hunted beast, Ali would have turned at bay and faced this man, but he knew that it meant death or capture, for the others were close behind, while he was quite unarmed.

And what did death or capture mean? The destruction or those whom he was trying to save.

Feeling this, he toiled on, with heart throbbing, his breath coming thickly, and his limbs growing more heavy moment by moment. At first he had bounded along like a frightened deer, but the terrible nature of the jungle through which he was struggling soon began to tell upon him, and the bounding pace settled down into a weary trot.

There was this, however, in his favour; the ground was very bad for his pursuers, and though eager to overtake him, they were not moved by the same intense desire as himself.

On still, and he was once more nearly down. Something lashed his face, then he tripped again once more, and the jungle, as he staggered up, seemed to grow more intensely dark. That vindictive enemy was close behind, and he had struck at him twice with his keen weapon. Then, as he panted on, he came upon first one and then another animal, which bounded away into close growth, while the poor hunted wretch could hardly drag one leg before the other.

Still he struggled on through the darkness, till feeling his pursuer close at hand, he roused all his remaining strength and leaped forward, caught his foot in a mass of interwoven creeping plants, and fell. He made one effort to rise, but his strength was gone, and he had only time to throw himself over and get his hands at liberty, as his pursuer threw himself down upon him, clutched him by the throat, and, raising his kris, was about to plunge it into the prostrate young man's breast.

But Ali was too quick. In spite of his weakness and the suffocating sensation caused by his position, he made a snatch at the descending arm, caught it, and stopped the blow, and then they both lay there panting and exhausted, chaser and chased, unable to do more than gaze into each other's eyes, as the jungle now began to grow lighter, and Ali could see the gleam of the deadly kris just above his head.

They were terrible moments; the oppression was so great that he could hardly breathe, and at the same time he felt himself growing weaker and weaker. There was the baleful glare of his enemy's eyes, and the gleam of the kris growing each moment nearer, and he powerless to arrest it. Only a few moments, and in spite of his brave resistance all would be over, and those he sought to save would be lost.

The thought of the friends at the residency nerved him to the final effort, and with a wild cry he drew himself up, and tried to throw his enemy from his chest—his enemy, whose eyes and weapon glared down at him so, and summoning all his strength, he felt that he had succeeded.

Panting heavily, Ali started up, but the gleam was about him still, for the bright rays of the morning sun were shining down through the attap roof, and with a moan of misery he sank back once more on finding that he had been overcome by weariness, and that this last painful episode was only a dream.

And his friends that he meant to save—what of them? Ali lay back and closed his eyes, for his misery seemed greater than he could bear.

Chapter Thirty Seven
How Ali made a Dash for Liberty

As Ali lay back there with closed eyes, it seemed impossible that he could have slept and dreamed all this, but it was plain enough now. He had but to unclose his eyes and see the Malays in the outer room, and listen to the twittering of the small birds, the screams of the parrots, and the cry uttered from time to time by some monkey.

Where was his manhood? he asked himself—where his keen desire to escape and help his friends? He felt half-maddened to think that he should have slept and neglected them, not sparing himself for a moment, and never once palliating what he called his crime by trying to recall the fact that he had not slept the previous night, and that he had been completely exhausted.

There was the fact staring him in the face; he had been lying there thinking of escaping, and listening to the cries of the prowling tigers, and— "Stop," he asked himself, "where did the reality end and dreaming begin? Did he see the Malay get up and hurl a torch out of the open door, and then come back and lie down?"

Yes, he felt sure that was true, but where that which he was watching shaded off into dreamland, he could not tell.

It was weak, perhaps, but the scalding tears rose and filled his eyes, and when he passionately dashed them away and sat up, he felt ready to make a fierce rush through his guard, and either escape or die.

He was on the point of risking all in some such mad attempt when two of the men came in, proceeded to make a careful inspection of the place where he was, and then sat down just in the opening, getting up soon afterwards, though, to make way for another, who brought in some food on fresh plantain leaves, rice freshly boiled with fowl, and curry made with freshly-grated cocoa-nut and peppers. There was an abundance of fruit, too, but Ali looked at it all with a feeling of disgust. He had no desire to eat.

The men left the food on its fresh green leaves before him, and went out to their own meal, while the prisoner sat thinking that the expedition had by this time started, for he had slept long in spite of his troublous dream. Then his thoughts turned to the steamer and Bob Roberts, whose frank, happy face was always before him, and then somehow he thought of the steamer and its powerful engine, and how it was kept going with fuel and water; and that set him thinking of himself. How was he to help his friends if he let himself get weak for want of food.

The result was, that he ate a few grains of rice, when the want of appetite disappeared, and he went on and made a very hearty meal. He felt annoyed, though, directly after, to find his captors smile as they came to remove the fragments of his feast.

Then began once more the terrible hours of anxiety, during which he paced up and down his prison like some wild beast, his guards squatting outside, and watching him in the most imperturbable manner, as they chewed their betel or varied it by smoking.

So long as he seemed disposed to make no effort to escape they were civil enough, one offering him, betel, another Java tobacco, an object much-prized by the Malays, but he did not take them, only fixed his eyes jealously upon their weapons, and longed to snatch them away, and in some desperate action to calm the suffering he endured.

Every now and then he listened, fancying he could hear the distant sound of firing, and he shuddered as he fancied that the massacre had already begun. But he was soon compelled to own that it was all fancy, and wearied out, he laid himself down again to try and scheme a way of escape.

The day slowly advanced, and the heat became intense in spite of the shadow in which he lay. A few light gleams came in through thin places in the roof, but they only seemed to make the room darker, for a couple of the Malays had been busy stopping up a small hole or two near the closed window. Now and then some busy fly or crawling beetle took his attention, or a nimble lizard in chase of an insect, and he thought of the native proverb as he saw how patiently the lizard crept along after its intended victim, and waited its time until with unerring certainty it could make its stroke.

He told himself that he must take a lesson from the quiet little reptile, and await his time.

And so the day wore on, every hour convincing him more and more of the impossibility of escape, unless some change should take place in the arrangements.

One gleam of hope came to him, and that was afforded by the restlessness of his guard. They seemed to be expecting some one, and watch was evidently kept for his arrival, but as the evening drew near there was no change, and the hope that the expected messenger might have been about to order them to convey him elsewhere—to a place perhaps affording a better chance of escape, died away.

True, the hope had been mingled with a sense of dread, for he felt that if a messenger had come he might have been bearer of an order to put him to death. But no one arrived, the sun was sinking fast, and his agony on the increase, for night was close at hand, with no prospect of his being able to convey the ill news he had to his friends.

The heat had been terrible to him in his excited state, and the evening breeze that now came whispering through the leaves seemed but little better. The men in the next room had twice over brought him food and water, and they were now busily preparing their dammar-torches, a couple of which were soon burning brightly, sending a warm glow like a golden band right across the prisoner's room, leaving both sides in the shade.

Worn-out with weariness of mind and body, Ali lay there at last, telling himself that he ought to follow the example of his compatriots, and calmly accept the inevitable.

But that he could not do, for he lay there fuming with impatience, and watching the outer room for a chance of escape. That did not come, for the party were more watchful than ever; and at last he sank back, feeling that all was over, and praying that warning might be given to those in danger, in some other way.

For the sake of coolness he was lying away from his mat, on the bamboo floor, between the rough pieces of which the night air came up, mingled with the sweet odours of the forest; and as he lay there, with his head throbbing from the mental excitement, while his guards were talking together in a low voice, Ali began to wonder whether he should hear the tiger prowling about the place that night. Then he began to think of the midshipman and the ensign, and he tried to comfort himself with the idea that the English were very brave, and might read Sultan Hamet a severe lesson instead of being beaten.

These thoughts were just crossing his mind, when he started, for it seemed to him that there was something rising close at hand, and then a faint touch.

This was evidently heard only by himself, for no one in the outer place had moved.

Ali felt a strange shudder pass through him, for the noise was just that which a large serpent would make as it forced its way between some old pieces of woodwork, and this was just the place for some monster to make its haunt. It had evidently been temporarily driven away, but had now in the silence of the evening returned to its home in the deserted house.

Ali was as brave as most young fellows of his age, but at the same time he shrank from contact with such a loathsome beast, and lay motionless, wondering whether it would pass him by, and then half-resolving to call the men to come with lights.

He was on the point of shouting to them, but he hesitated as his alarm might be foolish, and the noise be caused by some inoffensive creature.

He lay there listening, and as he did so he suddenly felt paralysed, for something touched his hand. The contact had such an effect upon him that he could not move.

It was a serpent, he was sure, for it felt cold and damp, and—there it was again, evidently coming up between the bamboos of the floor, and seeking about, and—Why, it was a hand, and it grasped his wrist! Ali wanted to call aloud, but he felt as if suffering from nightmare; to leap up, but he felt helpless, and lay bathed in perspiration. He knew what it was now; some miscreant beneath the house, seeking out where he lay.

He knew of plenty of cases where men had been assassinated by an enemy finding out where they slept in a room, and then quietly going beneath in the night and thrusting his kris between the bamboos.

This, then, was the way in which he was to be slain—as if it had been done by some stranger. One of his guards then must be beneath the house, though he had not heard one go out.

And yet, knowing all this, he could not stir, but lay as if stunned, till the blood that had been frozen seemed suddenly to start in rapid action, and his veins began to throb, for instead of the blade of a kris being thrust remorselessly into his side, the handle was softly pushed through against his hand.

This was a friend then below him, and had he had any doubt before, the soft pressure of a hand upon his told him that he was right, for there was a ring upon one finger that touched his, whose form he recognised. It was his father's ring, and he had come at the risk of losing his own life to save his son's.

For a few moments hand pressed hand. Then Ali's was drawn softly down between the bamboos, and two hands placed it under one of the long, split canes upon which he was lying, held it there, and then pressed it upwards.

Ali was puzzled. He dare not speak, neither did the Tumongong below venture so much as to whisper, but kept on forcing his son's hand upwards.

There was a faint creak, and then the light came into Ali's puzzled brain. It was plain enough now; this bamboo had been loosened at one end, for it gave way; and the young man's heart throbbed painfully, as he felt that the way of escape was open. He had but to wait his time, and then softly raise this one broad, split cane, to make space enough to let himself slide through into the open space beneath the post-supported house. Then the jungle was before him, and it was his own fault if he did not escape in the darkness.

He left off clasping the broad, split bamboo, and stretched out his hand once more to clasp that of his father, in expression of his thankfulness; but though he reached out in all directions, striving to grasp the loving hand that had brought help, there was nothing near, and Ali felt as if in a dream, till his other hand touched the kris that was now beneath his chest.

It was his right arm that was forced down between the bamboos, and he was consequently lying over upon his chest, when, to his horror, he heard a noise, and saw the principal of his guards seize a torch and enter the room, kris in hand.

For a moment Ali felt that he must spring up, kris in hand, and fight for his life. Fortunately he lay still and feigned sleep, his heart beating heavily, as he hoped to conceal the loosened bamboo with his body, as well as the kris.

The Malay looked curiously round the room, and held his dammar-torch on high, as he peered here and there. Not that he had heard a sound, but he was evidently suspicious, or else extra careful.

Ali lay motionless and breathing heavily, but with a choking sensation in his breast, as he felt that now, just when escape was open to him, he had been discovered. He was in such a state of excitement that he was ready to spring up and attack his guard, should he make any sign of having found out what had taken place; but though the man held the torch here and there, and walked round the room before coming back and bending down over Ali, as if to see whether he was asleep, he saw nothing.

Then a fresh dread assailed the prisoner. Why was this man bending over him, and did he mean evil against him?

Ali would have given anything to have been able to turn round and face his enemy, but to have made the slightest movement would have been to show that he had a kris beneath him, and his arm right through between the bamboos, so the young man lay perfectly still, mastered his emotion as best he could, and waited for what seemed an unreasonable space of time, till the Malay slowly moved off into the outer room, and sticking his torch in the floor, seated himself with his companions, and began to smoke.

Panting with excitement, Ali lay there in the darkness, and for some time not daring to move; but at last, watching the effect upon his guards the while, he made an uneasy movement and muttered a few unintelligible words.

The men looked up for a moment, but afterwards paid no heed; and finding this so, Ali secured the kris in the folds of his sarong, after softly withdrawing his arm from between the bamboos of the floor.

To his great delight, he found them very loose; and after waiting a reasonable time, and until his guards seemed to be settled, he softly raised the one that was loose, and rolled it, as it were, over on to the side, leaving a narrow opening through the floor.

Just as he did so, a low, snarling growl close at hand announced the return of the tiger.

This was terrible; for if he descended now, he was going from one danger to another, and his position was pitiable. At any moment the Malays might come in and see that the bamboo had been moved; and now all he had to do was to squeeze down through the opening, and glide away into the darkness.

There was the snarling growl again. The tiger evidently scented prey, and it came closer and closer. In fact, Ali felt that it was quite possible that the beast might spring up at the opening to seize him.

What could he do but wait?

His patience was rewarded; for as the great cat came prowling nearer, one of the Malays, who was uneasy at its presence, seized a torch, as had been done the past night; the others standing ready with their spears, advanced, and waiting until the animal seemed ready to make a spring at the door, he hurled the blazing piece of dammar, overturning the second torch in the act, one of his companions trampling it out, to save the floor from being set alight.

There was a snarling yell, once more followed by a loud shout from the Malays, when the tiger was heard to bound heavily away through the jungle, its yell being answered by another tiger some distance away.

Now was Ali's time. The Malays were talking, and trying to relight the torch, the place being in total darkness; and without a moment's hesitation the prisoner softly let himself down through the long narrow slit, lower and lower, till he reached his waist, where the kris stopped his further descent.

This was horrible, as he was as it were caught in the narrow hole, and he could not get the kris out from the folds of his silken sarong.

The Malays, though, were busy over their light; and freeing the weapon at last, he let himself glide down lower and lower, but not without noise, for there was hardly room for him to pass, and he began to tremble, lest his head should refuse to go through.

At any moment his guards might come in and find him in this helpless state, for he dared not hurry, but had to literally force his way down till he had only his head and shoulders above, his eyes glaring wildly in the direction of the outer room, where the Malays were talking.

By sheer force of muscle he sustained himself, as he hung at length with his head only in the room, and to his horror he found that it would not pass through; for he was opposite two of the knots of the bamboo, and strive how he would, he could not manage to get himself a little way along, to where the wood curved in.

Just then a light flashed upon his face, and he saw that his guards had succeeded in re-illumining their room; while to his horror, he now found that they were coming in to him.

With a tremendous effort, and feeling now that it was no time to study about noise, Ali forced himself a little way along, but in doing so slipped, and hung by his head, fixed between the bamboos, as the leader of his captors entered, uttered a shout, and made a bound forward to seize him.

That did it!

Had he come forward carefully, he could have seized his helpless prisoner; but this leap on the elastic, hollow canes bent one down, and set Ali free, his guard uttering a shout of rage as his captive literally slipped through his fingers, Ali's head disappearing from the light of the torch, and revealing the long narrow slit, looking dark and strange, in the floor.

"Quick, the door!" shouted the Malay, as he tried to force himself down through the slit—but had to struggle back, giving Ali moments to recover himself from the painful shock he had sustained; and when the man had reached the door, torch in hand, and leaped down to where his men were hurrying here and there, it was for the light to gleam for a moment on Ali's bright, silken baju, as he plunged into the jungle, forty yards away.

Chapter Thirty Eight
A Swim in the Night

As has been said, Ali suffered quite a shock from the jerk he received in escaping from his prison, and had his captors rushed down directly, his attempt would have resulted in failure; but the effort made by the Malay to follow him afforded the prisoner time to recover a little, to struggle up from where he had fallen, and to stagger off in a strange confused state, feeling all the while as if his head had been wrenched off.

Each moment, however, gave him force; he heard the shouts of the men as they leaped down from the platform; and as the light of the torch flashed upon his path, he seemed to regain his strength, and ran on with his guards in full pursuit.

The young man set his teeth hard, and grasped the weapon supplied to him by his father's hand. He was far from being bloodthirsty; contact with the English had softened and changed his nature, but in those fierce moments the feeling was upon him strong that he could slay or be slain sooner than give up his liberty once more.

He recalled his dream of the early morning as he dashed on, and wondered whether the leader was the first man in the pursuit, and whether they two would engage in deadly strife.

He glanced back, but he could not tell; and hurrying on, he kept recalling the difficulties he had encountered in his dream—elephant-holes—woven undergrowth—trailing canes—the hundred obstacles of a jungle, and wondered that he kept so well in the darkness to the path, and was able to progress at so swift a pace.

Not that it was swift, for he had to proceed very cautiously, but it was fast enough to enable him to keep well ahead of his pursuers, who had to make sure that they did not pass him on the way.

But this easy going was not to last, for he found the jungle track grew worse, and to his horror he found that his pursuers were gaining upon him rapidly. The light the first man carried enabled them to see a few yards in advance and make sure their steps, while he had what seemed like a black wall rising in front of him, into which he had to plunge as it were, and often and often found that he was straying from the track.

At last he strayed so far from it that his pursuers came up rapidly, their light showing him the path he had lost. He was about to make a rush for it, when the thought struck him that they might pass him unseen, and, crouching down, to his great delight he found that they did pass on—the whole party—leaving him to deliberate on what course he should pursue.

The simplest plan seemed to be to turn back, but that would be taking him away from the river, which he felt would be his saving to reach, and to gain that he must pursue the track his guards were upon.

After all, if he kept at a distance this was the safest plan. His enemies carried a light, and he would therefore be able to see them when they returned, if return they did; and to his great delight he remembered now that some distance ahead there was a track which led right away from the present one towards the river, making a shorter cut.

He did not stop to think, but at once followed the course taken by his guards, hastening his steps till he was pretty close behind—so close that he could hear their voices, and see the flaring of the torch through the undergrowth.

This went on for nearly an hour, when the Malays awakened fully to the fact that their prisoner had not gone in that direction, and they returned upon their track so suddenly that Ali had barely time to force his way in amongst the canes and crouch down, silent and breathless, before they were back, and were passing the place where the young man was hidden, when the bearer of the torch saw the broken canes and leaves, and drew attention thereto.

"Tiger!" said the man nearest to him, and he pointed to some footprints which were sufficiently recent to satisfy the other, and to Ali's great relief they passed on.

For a few moments he had felt that he was once more a prisoner, and now he breathed freely again, and waiting till the last rustle of the canes and undergrowth had died away with the faint gleam of the torch, he crept painfully out from amidst the thorny undergrowth, and continued his retreat.

He paused from time to time to listen, but all was silent now, and almost feeling his way through the dark forest, he pressed on, gladdened now and then by a glimpse of the starry sky, he continued his course, till he reached the edge of the river, rolling swift and dark through the midst of the dense forest.

All had heard the strange sounds on either side of the dark track he had come along, more than once shuddering slightly as he heard the cry of a tiger or the curious *coo-ai* of the argus pheasant, but nothing sounded so pleasant to him during his exciting retreat as the strange, low, untiring rush of the great river.

There was no noisy babbling, but a soft, low, hissing rush, as the swift stream hurried amidst the stones and water-washed roots of the trees upon the banks.

He had hoped to find a boat somewhere about the end of the track, where there was a wretched campong; but there did not seem to be a single sampan, and he tramped wearily down the bank, till he came near the houses opposite the island.

He dared go no further along the bank, lest he should be seized; and he stood in the shade of a tree at last, thinking of what he should do.

But one course was open to him, and that was to swim out into the swift stream, and make for the head of the island, where, to his great delight, all seemed perfectly still, and free from alarm. How long it would keep so, he could not say.

There was no other way for him, and being a swift swimmer he hesitated no longer, but throwing off his baju and sarong, he walked out as far as he could and swam boldly towards the head of the island, where he meant to land.

To his horror he found a couple of boats in the way, both of them well filled with men, and it was only by letting himself float down with the stream that he was able to pass them unnoticed. This, however, completely carried him out of his reckoning, for on striving once more to reach the head of the island, he was too low down, and was swept right away. He tried for the landing-place, but he could not near it, and in spite of his desperate efforts he was drawn on lower and lower by the heavy stream, so that he could not even grasp at the drooping trees at the lower end of the island, but found himself carried right away towards the lights of the corvette, where she lay a quarter of a mile lower down.

Knowing that he could not catch at anything on the smooth sides of the steamer, he made another frantic effort to reach the side of the island, but it was labour in vain, and at last, weak, exhausted, and with the water rising higher and higher about his lips, he felt that he was being carried right away, and that, unless help came, he would be drowned.

He grew excited and struggled harder, but only to weaken himself. He was confused by the darkness, and found that he had miscalculated his powers. The strain upon him during the past two days, and the efforts he had made that night, had been greater than he was aware of; and now, in spite of the sterling stuff of which he was made, the chill, dread thought came upon him that he was about to die.

The lights of the steamer seemed very near, and yet far-distant, for a blinding mist was before his eyes; and though he swam bravely, over and over again the swift current seemed to suck him down. He essayed to cry for help, but the water choked him; and at last he felt that all was over, that he should in another minute be swept past the steamer, when, trying to turn over and float, he went under, rose to the surface once more, struck against something and clutched at it, to find it slimy and hard to hold; but it enabled him to hold his head above water a few moments, while he cried for help — lost his hold, and was swept away once more, when all seemed dreamy and strange. The water thundered in his ears, his limbs were helpless, and it was as if he were being wafted into a strange and troublous sleep, when he knew no more, for all seemed blank.

Chapter Thirty Nine
How Ali brought News, and was not believed

There was plenty of excitement on board the steamer, as the falls were hooked on and the light gig was run up to the davits, the boat then being swung on board; and as lights were brought, the body of the man they had tried to save was laid upon the deck.

"Why, it's a nigger!" exclaimed Bob Roberts; and then, with a cry of horror, "Oh, Mr Johnson, it's old Ali! Here, quick! help, brandy! Oh, he's dead! he's dead!"

"No, he aren't, sir," said Dick gruffly; "leastwise, I don't think so."

"Carry him into the cabin," said Lieutenant Johnson sharply; and this being done, the poor fellow was stripped, briskly rubbed, and the customary plans adopted to restore respiration, Bob Roberts eagerly taking his turn, till, to his delight, as he watched Ali's arms being worked up and down, so as to empty and fill his chest, there was a faint flutter, a sigh, and the doubts as to the young Malay's life being spared were at an end.

"Hooray!" cried Bob, who was only in his shirt and trousers, his collar open, and his sleeves rolled right up to his shoulders. "Hooray!" he cried; and forgetting all his dignity as second officer in command of Her Majesty's ship, he indulged in a kind of triumphal dance, which ended with a flop, caused by his bringing one foot down flat on the cabin floor.

"I think that will do, Mr Roberts," said the lieutenant quietly; and Bob coloured up and looked confused.

"I felt so delighted, sir, to see the poor old chap better," he stammered.

"So I see," said the lieutenant. "There, put on your jacket, and give the men a glass of grog apiece for what they have done towards saving our friend here. Dick, there, has pretty well rubbed his skin off."

"Well, sir," said Dick in an ill-used tone, "I rubbed as hard as ever I could."

"That you did, Dick," said the middy.

"And he is coming to, sir," continued Dick.

"Yes," said the lieutenant, "a good sleep will set him right, I think. It is a pity the doctor has gone on the expedition; but we must do the best we can."

"Expedition!" said Bob sharply, "of course; but I thought Ali here had gone. He was going. Oh, I know; he has stopped behind because Tom Long and I were not going."

"Very likely," said the lieutenant drily; "but had you not better see about the men's refreshment?"

"Oh! yes, sir; of course," said Bob, hurrying on his light jacket; and Dick and a couple of men, who had been helping, followed him out of the cabin, smiling and wiping their lips in anticipation of the promised drink.

They had hardly left the cabin when Ali opened his eyes, and lay gazing up at the ceiling, then, in a curious, puzzled way, at the light, his mind struggling to recover itself and master his confusion.

A sigh and a few muttered words took the lieutenant to his side; and on seeing him Ali started, and said something to him in the Malay tongue.

"Are you better?" said the lieutenant kindly.

"Better?" he said, "better? Where am I? what place is this?"

"You are on board the steamer. We found you drowning in the river."

Ali clasped his forehead with his hands for a few moments, and then all seemed to come back like a flood.

"Yes," he said hoarsely, "I know now. I was swimming to the island."

"I see; and you were swept away," said the lieutenant kindly. "I think you had better lie down, and have a good sleep," he continued, as the young man struggled up.

"No, no!" cried Ali excitedly. "I recollect all now. Quick! call your men; there is great danger!"

"Come, come," said the lieutenant gently, "calm yourself. Try and sleep."

He laid his hand firmly on the young man's arm, but Ali caught his wrist.

"What, do you think," he cried, "that I am speaking no sense?"

"Well," said the lieutenant, smiling, "I think you are excited and ill."

"No, no," cried Ali. "Give me clothes; I will fight for you. There is danger!"

"Nonsense!" said the lieutenant. "There, lie down; and Roberts, your friend, you know, shall come and sit with you."

"Oh, listen to me!" cried Ali piteously. "I am not as you think. I swam off to warn you. Hamet has got half your men away by treachery. I am sure they are going to attack you. Quick! get ready; there is great, great danger! Give me clothes, and I'll fight for you!"

As he spoke excitedly, Bob Roberts entered the cabin, and stood listening.

"Come and speak to him, Roberts," said the lieutenant quietly. "Poor fellow! he is overdone, and it has flown to his head."

"Ah! You here?" cried Ali joyfully. "He will not believe me, Bob. Listen; there is going to be an attack made upon you—at the island, and here. They have got your men and officers away to lead them into a trap. I escaped to tell you."

"Oh! come, old chap, don't talk like that," cried Bob, taking his hand. "Don't talk such wild nonsense and bosh. Lie down and have a good sleep. I say, Mr Johnson, I wish old Bolter was here."

"You do not believe me!" cried Ali passionately. "What am I, that you treat me so? Is it that I always lie?"

"Lie? No, old boy," said Bob kindly; "but it isn't you talking. Your head's all in a muddle."

"Head? muddle? Not I!" cried Ali excitedly. "There! Hark! I told you so!"

As he spoke there was the sharp crack of a rifle, then another, and another, and a rattling scattered volley.

"Something wrong at the island, sir," reported one of the watch.

"By Jove! he's right!" cried the lieutenant, rushing out of the cabin. "Quick, Roberts!"

"Yes—clothes—my kris!" cried Ali joyfully. "I'll fight with you."

For answer Bob ran to his own berth, hastily threw the young Malay one of his spare suits; and then, quickly buckling on his sword, ran on deck, where the lieutenant was striding up and down, giving his orders.

"That's right, Roberts," he cried. "They're hard at work at the island."

The next moment Bob was running here and there, seeing that his superior's orders were executed. The drums had already beat to quarters, and with the wondrous business-like rapidity with which matters are done on board a man-of-war every man was at his place, the ports flew open, the magazine was unfastened, and while the moorings were cast off astern, and those ahead ready to be dropped at a moment's notice, the furnaces were roaring furiously, and every effort being made by the firemen to get up steam.

It was like the turning of a handle. There was no confusion; the whole machine was ready for action; guns loaded, and marines and sailors armed ready for any contingency that might befall the steamer.

Directly after, Ali came hurrying from the cabin, and made his way to where the middy was eagerly looking for his next order.

"Give me arms," he said; "I have lost my kris."

"And a good thing, too," said Bob sharply; "a murderous skewer! May I give him a sword, sir?"

"Yes, and a revolver, if he means to fight on our side," said Lieutenant Johnson sharply; and Bob hurriedly ordered the armourer to take the young Malay and supply what was needed. "They are making no signals at the island, Roberts," continued the lieutenant, "and I don't know what to do. I would man a boat and send on—"

"Under me, sir?" said Bob slowly.

"Of course, Mr Roberts; but we are so short-handed, I don't know what to do for the best. Ah! here is your friend. Now, sir; tell us in a few words what this all means."

Ali rapidly told him of his belief, and the lieutenant frowned.

"Certainly there is confirmation of what you say, sir," he said sternly, "but the story sounds wild and strange."

He gazed suspiciously at the young chief; but Ali did not blench in the slightest degree.

Just then the firing seemed to become furious on the island, and the lieutenant stamped his foot impatiently.

"How long is this steam going to be?" he cried. "How I hate being tied by the leg like this, Roberts."

"It's horrible, sir!" cried Roberts, who was stamping up and down the deck, when he was not trying to make out what was going on upon the island, by means of a small glass. "Let's do something, sir, or the people there will think we are not going to help them."

"What can we do, lieutenant," said the other, "except send a boat?"

"Let's fire a big gun, captain," said Bob; "that'll let 'em know we are all alive; and then send the boat. I'll be very careful, sir."

The lieutenant hesitated as he watched the island through his glass, and could see the flashes of the pieces as they were fired. In a short time steam would be up, and the vessel could pass right round the island and engage the prahus, if there were any attacking. Besides, he was very loth to reduce his already short ship's company.

"If it were not already so confoundedly dark," he exclaimed, "we could see what to do. Ah! at last, there goes the signal."

For just then there was a rushing noise, and a rocket went up from the island, far into the blackness of the night, burst, and the bright blue stars fell slowly, lighting up the palms and fruit-trees upon the island.

"Ready there with a rocket," exclaimed the lieutenant. "Be smart, Mr Roberts."

"Ay, ay, sir," was the reply; and with a mighty rush away on high sped the answering signal, to burst and fill the air above them with lambent light.

"That is better than your big gun, Roberts," said the lieutenant.

"No, sir, I don't think it is," said Bob, "for it won't frighten the niggers, and my gun would."

The night seemed to have come on darker than ever, and the rocket stars shone with wonderful brilliancy as they descended lower, and lower, and lower, some even to reach the water before they went out, and just as the last was floating down, Ali, who was close to the two officers, suddenly started, grasped Bob's arm, and exclaimed sharply,—

"Prahus!"

He was pointing with one hand down the stream, but on the middy gazing in the required direction it was too dark to see anything.

"I can see none," he said. "Where?"

"Two prahus coming up rapidly," said Ali; "be ready to fire."

"Not so fast, young sir," said the lieutenant. "Will that steam never be up? Roberts," he cried, "touch the trigger of that life-buoy."

The middy obeyed, and a life-buoy dropped over the side with a splash, a port-fire at the same moment bursting out into a brilliant blue glare, which, as the buoy floated down rapidly with the stream, lit-up the trees on either shore, made the water flash, but above all showed out plainly to all on board a couple of large prahus coming rapidly up the stream, the many sweeps out on either side making the water foam and flash in the blue light shed by the buoy.

"There!" said Ali excitedly, "they are Rajah Gantang's prahus. Fire at them."

"Not so fast, sir," said the lieutenant. "I must first be sure that they are enemies."

He was soon assured of that fact, for as the steamer was lit-up by the port-fire as well as the prahus, *bang, bang, bang, bang,* one after the other, came the reports of the brass guns the two long boats had on board, and a hail of small iron balls came whistling through the rigging.

"There's no doubt about it now," said the lieutenant grimly; and giving the orders as the prahus rapidly advanced, evidently with the intention of boarding, the two big guns on the port-side thundered out a reply, splashing the water all over one prahu, and going through the matting boarding-screen of the other; but otherwise doing no harm.

The prahus replied, and for a few minutes there was a sharp duel kept up, at the end of which time the oars were seen being swiftly plied, and the two boats went on up stream at a rapid rate, the steamer firing at them as long as they were visible by the lights they had on board.

"Was anything ever so vexatious?" cried the lieutenant. "Here we lie like a log upon the water. Will that steam never be up?"

Just then the welcome news was given, and the order was passed down to the engine-room; the screw began to revolve, and the men cheered as the vessel's head was freed from the buoy to which she had been moored, and they began to steam rapidly in the wake of the two prahus, whose lights had evidently passed to the left of the island.

Meanwhile a sharp engagement had evidently been going on in the neighbourhood of the little fort. Once or twice the nine-pounder they had there spoke out, but the principal part of the firing was that of rifles. Lights were seen from the deck, here and there amidst the trees, and were moving upon the shore, where the people were evidently in a state of alarm. Still the occupants of the island seemed to be making a good fight, and the lieutenant felt that he could not be doing them better service than by disposing of the two prahus, and to this end the steamer went on, its commander having a sharp look-out kept, and a man busy with the lead in the forepart of the vessel.

At the end of a few minutes the lights on the prahus were seen; the order, "Full speed ahead!" given, for they were now in the middle of the open reach of the river, and Lieutenant Johnson hoped to sink one or the other of his adversaries by using a little energy.

The shadowy shapes of the two boats were made out at the end of a minute, and a couple of guns were brought to bear upon them, the firing being replied to for a time, the flashes from the guns serving to light up the darkness of the night for a moment, while the roar of the big guns went rolling along the surface of the water, and was echoed from the trees upon the bank.

"Keep that lead going more quickly," shouted the lieutenant, as the last of the prahus, apparently unharmed, passed round the head of the island, placing the wooded land between her and the steamer, which followed rapidly in their wake.

The lieutenant's orders were obeyed, and the sounding shouted by the man who handled the lead line.

The river was very deep, but as no good chart existed, and it was dark, extra caution was being used, and all was going on well. In another minute she would have rounded the bend of the island and been in full chase of the fleet enemy, when just as the man had shouted out the depth, there was a sudden shock, which threw several men off their legs, and to the dismay of all, the steamer was tightly fixed upon a mudbank, every effort to release her only seeming to make her settle more firmly down. And this at a moment when her presence might serve to change the fortunes of the attack being made upon the residency.

Chapter Forty
How Private Gray went a-fishing

Private Gray had hard work to seem composed as he went away to execute his orders. The remarks of Captain Smithers had come like an endorsement of his own suspicions, and in imagination he saw the island given over to violence and rapine, as a large force of savage Malays who resented the coming of the English took advantage of the present state of weakness and carried all before them.

He felt as if a strange pallor was taking the place of the ruddy, sunburnt hue of his face, and he turned sick as he thought of Miss Linton and her cousin; of the major's wife, and those of several of the soldiers.

It would be horrible, he thought; but the next moment his strength of nerve returned, and feeling that the safety of all might depend upon the energy he displayed in his mission, he hurried on towards the fort.

As he went along under the shade of the trees, he recalled that which he had seen when on duty a night or two back, and wondered whether there was any cause for suspicion in the boat that he believed he had seen gliding over the dark river in so shadowy a way. Then he remembered the sounds he had heard; and lastly, he recalled various little things in Abdullah's behaviour, that, trifles in themselves, now seemed to be strangely significant.

By this time he reached the fort, on entering which he found Sergeant Lund perspiring profusely, as with big clumsy unsuited hands he fingered a pen, and wrote laboriously his report, while Private Sim, who had not declared himself ill for a week, lay back under a tree fast asleep.

He was a very unlovely man was Private Sim, especially when asleep, for at this time he opened his mouth very wide, and around it the busy flies were flitting, evidently taking it for the flower of some new kind of orchis or carnivorous plant, and they buzzed about and around it as if enjoying the fun of going as near as they could without quite getting into danger. That it was a fly-trap one big sage-looking insect seemed certain, for he settled on the tip of Private Sim's nose, and seemed to be engaged in making sudden flights and buzzings at young unwary flies as they came near and into danger, driving them away from the yawning cavern just below.

Gray smiled to himself as these ideas flashed across his brain, and then he walked up to the sergeant.

"Which—which—that—which—or which—but which—in which—for which—to which—phew! this is hot work. I wonder which would be best. Ah! Gray, sit down here a minute, my lad, and tell me what to say. I've been hours over this report."

"I am off on special business directly, sergeant," said Gray; "but let me see."

He read over the sergeant's report, and then dictated half-a-dozen lines, which that officer wrote down as quickly as he could. "I shall copy it out afterwards," he said, "neat and clean. Go on, my lad, go on."

Gray dictated a few more lines, which ended the report in a short, concise manner, and Sergeant Lund's face, which had been all in corrugations, smoothed itself into a satisfied smile.

"That's beautiful," he said, looking up at the private admiringly. "I shall copy that all out in a neat hand, and the thing's done. I say, Gray, how do you do it? Here, what takes me hours, only takes you minutes; and while it's hard labour to me to get it into shape, you run it off like string from a ball. Thanky, my lad, thanky. Now what can I do for you?"

"I want a bayonet and a revolver, with ammunition, directly," said Gray.

"What for?"

"Captain's orders, and private," said Gray, showing Captain Smithers' card, with a few lines pencilled thereon.

"Right," said the sergeant bluffly. "I'm not an inquisitive man. Come along, Gray."

He led the way into the part of the fort used as an armoury, and furnished the required weapons, which Gray proceeded to button up under his jacket.

"Oh! that's the game is it, my lad?" he said. "Then look here; don't take those clumsy tools; any one can see that you've got weapons hidden there. I'll lend you this little revolver; it's handier, and will do quite as much mischief. You can have this dirk, too, with the belt."

He brought out a handsome little revolver, about half the weight and size of the heavy military "Colt" previously supplied; and also a well-made, long, thin dirk, with a thin belt.

"There, my lad!" he said, buckling on the belt under Gray's jacket, and then thrusting the revolver into a little leather pouch. "There, you are now fitted up sensibly, and no one would be the wiser. Stop a moment, you must fill your pocket with cartridges. Let me have those things back safe, and I hope you won't have to use them; but being ready, my lad, is half the battle. You know I'm never ill."

"No, sergeant; you have excellent health."

"Right, my lad, I do; and I'll tell you why: I bought the biggest box of pills I could get before I left London. Four-and-six I gave for it, and I have never taken one. Diseases come, and they know as well as can be that I've got that box of big pills—reg'lar boluses—in my kit; and they say to themselves, 'This man's ready for action, with his magazine well stored!' and they go somewhere else."

"I see, sergeant," said Gray, smiling. "Good-bye!"

"Good-bye, my lad, good-bye. Here, nobody's looking. Sim's asleep. Shake hands, my lad, shake hands. You see, as your superior officer that's a bit of stooping on my part; but, between man and man, I, Sergeant Lund, look up to you, Private Gray, and always feel as if we ought to change places."

"Good-bye, sergeant," said Gray, shaking hands warmly with the sergeant, "and I echo your wish that I may not have to use the weapons; keep a sharp look-out."

"You leave that to me, private," said the bluff sergeant, and he nodded his head as Gray went off upon his mission.

It was rather an awkward one, for he wished to watch Abdullah without exciting his attention. Gray thought, however, that he might prove a match for the Malay, and as he wandered slowly along he began to consider what he should do?

The first idea that suggested itself was that he should go to Dullah and sit there and eat fruit; but he discarded the idea directly as too palpable a way of watching. He felt that the Malay would suspect him directly, as he was not a man who was in the habit of visiting the hut.

No; he must have some better plan than that, but no idea struck him for a few minutes, till happening to glance at the flowing river, the notion came, and going straight back he was soon after seen sauntering down to the river, armed with a long bamboo, a fishing-line, and some bait, with which he proceeded to fish as soon as he reached the river, but having no sport he began to grow impatient, fishing here and there, but always getting nearer to Dullah's hut, where he remained seated on the bank, fishing very perseveringly to all appearance, and occasionally landing a little barbel-like fellow, known by the natives as *Ikan Sambilang*, or fish of nine, from the number of little barbs beneath its mouth.

Gray fished on, never once turning his head to see what was going on at the hut, but making the keenest use of his ears. He made out, while landing a fish or re-baiting his hook, that there were a couple of sampans lying there, in which were some Malays who appeared to be basking in the sunshine; and soon after his quick ears told him plainly enough that some one, whom he believed to be Dullah, was approaching.

As the Malay came nearer, it was to find Gray's rod lying in the water, and the soldier, apparently overcome by the heat, sitting in a heap, with his chin down upon his chest, regardless of the fact that a little fish was upon its hook, tugging away to get free.

Dullah seemed about to speak to the intruder; but seeing this, he refrained, contenting himself with examining Gray closely, and then going slowly back.

"That will not do to report," thought Gray. "He saw me fishing, and he came to see what I had caught, and then went away. I must have something better than that."

However he had obtained a position whence, unsuspected, he could sit and watch what went on at the hut; for after satisfying himself as he had, it was not likely that the Malay would trouble himself any more about the presence of the private so near his place.

So Gray sat there, apparently fast asleep, all through the afternoon.

The night closed in as the sun went down rapidly, as is the case near the equator, and still Gray felt that he had nothing to report. Two men rose up once in the sampan nearest to Dullah's hut, but they appeared to lie down again amongst their fruit baskets; and Dullah himself, the last time Gray saw him, was seated peacefully smoking by his verandah.

As it became dark, Gray ran over in his mind the positions of the various sentries, and thought of how soon he could get help, should he need it; and then, after a little thought, he came to the conclusion that he ought to make his way to the fort, and tell Captain Smithers of his want of success.

Just then the glimmering of the stars in the water put an idea in his head. He paused for a moment, as the proceeding was so risky; but on consideration he felt that, if he carried out his plan, he would know for certain whether mischief was brewing. So, giving up his intention of going back to the fort at present, he proceeded to put his plan into execution.

Chapter Forty One
The Value of Private Sim

Where Adam Gray had been seated fishing the bank was about three feet above the surface of the water, and this clayey bank was either perpendicular, or so hollowed out beneath by the action of the river, that if any one had the courage to lower himself into the water, here about four feet deep, and to cling to the tangled vegetation, and wade along close to the overhanging bank, he could pass right up to Dullah's hut unperceived.

There was danger, of course; for the stream ran swiftly, and the venturesome wader might be swept away. A crocodile, too, might be lurking beneath the bank; but the business was so important that Gray resolutely set his face against the idea of danger, telling himself that it was his duty; and leaving his rod upon the bank, he quietly lowered himself into the river, the cold water sending a sharp shock through him as he stood, breast high, holding on by some tangled roots, while the water pressed against him, with no little force, as it ran.

He paused there for a few minutes listening, half fancying that he had heard a noise, and that the slight splash he made might have been noted by Dullah or the men on the sampans; and as he listened, sure enough there was a dull noise, as of a blow, followed by a little rustling, and then, just above his head, he could hear somebody breathing hard, as if after some exertion.

Gray did not stir; and fortunately he was quite concealed by the overhanging bank, as a Malay, down upon his hands and knees, leaned over the edge and looked up and down the river.

For the moment Gray felt that he must be seen, and his hand stole involuntarily towards his breast in search of a weapon; but he was in utter darkness beneath the bank, and the man's eyes were more directed outward.

The result was that the Malay, who, kris in hand, had crept cautiously from Dullah's hut right up through the undergrowth and long grass to where he believed the Englishman to be fishing, drew cautiously back, and crept once more away.

Gray remained motionless for a few moments, and then, convinced that this meant ill to him, he began to wade cautiously along towards where the sampans lay in the stream, some thirty yards away.

He moved very slowly, so as to make no plash in the water, which sometimes, as the river shallowed, came only to his waist, while at other times it nearly reached his chin; and had he not clung tightly to the water-washed roots and depending bushes, he must have been swept away.

Gray had gone about half the distance; and as he neared the sampans, whose forms he vainly tried to make out in the darkness, to his horror, he found that something was moving towards him in the water.

Quick as lightning he drew the long keen dirk from his belt, and stood ready to thrust, for it was either a crocodile or some large animal, he felt sure; but directly after he stood holding on by his left hand to a bunch of tangled root hanging from the bank, and felt his heart seem to stand still, for, to his surprise, he plainly made out that it was a man, wading in the opposite direction, and evidently for a similar purpose to his own.

It was, in fact, one of the Malays from the nearest sampan, who, while a companion had undertaken to stalk the Englishman from the shore, as he sat there asleep, had set off from the boat, meaning to get there at the same time as his friend, but had miscalculated the period it would take.

He was now coming along cautiously, and had nearly reached Gray in the darkness before he became aware of his presence.

As soon, though, as he made out that it was the Englishman who was before him, he made a lunge forward, striking at Gray with his kris; but the latter avoided the blow and prepared to close with his antagonist, feeling as he took a step back, that the result would probably be death for both, for they must be swept away by the swift stream.

Just then the Malay seemed to leap at him, but at the same moment he uttered a smothered cry, which was silenced directly by the rushing water, and Gray found that he was alone.

He needed no telling that one of the loathsome reptiles of the river had been close at hand, and had seized his enemy; his wonder was that he himself had not been the victim.

It was enough to paralyse the bravest heart, and for a few minutes Gray clung to the roots of the tree beside him, feeling sick and giddy, and as if some reptile was only waiting for his next movement to drag him down.

It was fortunate for him that he did not stir, for the Malay's cry had alarmed his companions, who could be heard talking quickly and in whispers, close at hand.

At first it seemed to Gray that they were coming to the help of their unfortunate companion, but this did not prove to be the case. They knew what had happened, from old experience, and accepted the accident as one of the misfortunes to which they were heirs, troubling themselves no more about the matter.

Recovering himself somewhat, but feeling all the time that any moment he might be seized, Gray crept once more slowly along, till he stood with the water nearly to his shoulders, beneath the overhanging bank, by Dullah's hut, and between it and the two sampans.

The place was admirably suited for concealment, for now little more than his head was above water, and that he had contrived should lie behind a screen of drooping verdure, which made his chilly hiding-place so dark that he could not have been seen twelve inches away.

Having escaped from the reptiles so far, he felt more hopeful; and as he stood there, behind his screen, he began to try and make his position valuable.

He had not long to wait for this. In less than a minute, a voice, that he took for Abdullah's, was whispering to some one on the river, and a sampan came so close in to the bank that had he stretched out his hand he could have touched the side.

It was a grief to him that he was not thoroughly conversant with the Malay tongue, but he had picked up a good deal, and had mastered a sufficiency to catch the import of the words he heard.

The principal was an order that the *orang* should come ashore, the order being given by Dullah.

What was the *orang*?

He puzzled for a few moments, as the sampan pushed off. *Orang-outang*! Was this after all a trading visit, and they were going to bring some great monkey ashore.

Orang-outang—man of the woods, of course. *Orang* meant man or men, and the men were to land. There was danger then, and men were to land. That was enough, and now he would go and give warning; but he could not move without being heard, and he had to remain listening, as there was the faint beat of oars, and then, though he could hardly see them, two long row-boats of great size seemed to come up out of the darkness, and he felt more than saw that they were full of men.

What was the sentry about? There was one so near that he ought to have seen or heard their coming, and Gray listened eagerly for the report of his piece giving the alarm.

But no report came, for the sentry had not heard. He had not been krissed, but as far as giving alarm was concerned he might have been dead; for the sentry close at hand was Private Sim, and he was fast asleep.

Chapter Forty Two
Why Dullah came to the Isle

Every moment that passed was more convincing to Adam Gray that Dullah was a traitor, and at the head of affairs for making a descent upon the island. In place of two long row-boats, each carrying some fifty or sixty men, it was evident now that there were four, and they were being cautiously forced up to the landing-place, where, under the orders of Dullah, several men ashore were ready to make them fast.

Directly after, coming like a revelation, Gray learned what a snake they had had concealed in the grass at the jungle-station; for as he listened, intently watching the while for an opportunity to escape, he heard Dullah's voice, and then those of his men addressing him as rajah. Directly after he heard a voice on one of the large boats asking for Rajah Gantang, which was replied to by Dullah.

There was the secret then of this man's presence on the island. It was Rajah Gantang himself who had come among them, to seek his opportunity for overthrowing the English, and now his opportunity had come.

Gray ground his teeth with rage at his impotence, and he tried to get away unperceived, as it became evident that the nearest sentry heard nothing. Still at any moment there might come the warning shot from his rifle; for though everything was very plain to him, hidden in the midst of the Malays, it was quite horrible that not a sound might reach the most attentive of sentries, especially as every word was spoken in a whisper.

It seemed impossible to get away without discovery. The slightest movement would have made his presence known, so closely had the boats come in.

Still no alarm was raised.

Then Gray began hoping that Captain Smithers or Ensign Long might be going the rounds, and his dread was lest they should fall into some trap. It was for him, then, to warn them, but how?

The water was very cold, and seemed to Gray to be the cause of the chill that struck to his heart as he stood there wondering, and listened to what was evidently a rapid debarkation.

Suddenly, as in imagination, he saw these merciless men gaining an entry to the fort and massacring all there, he recalled the fact that he possessed a pistol. A shot or two from that would give alarm to the sentries.

And bring certain death upon himself!

Well, he thought, as he paused for a few moments, why not? If he, by giving up his life could save those at the fort—his officers, comrades, the ladies, and the rest, ought he to hesitate—would he be doing more than his duty?

It was a hard struggle. Life was very sweet, and he had but to remain perfectly still to escape. Did he move, a dozen spears and krisses would be at his breast directly.

He smiled as he told himself he was not hesitating, but that all he wished to do was his duty; and without a moment's hesitation he drew the little revolver from its pouch, held it out as high as he could, and drew the trigger.

For answer there came a sharp click, and he knew that the water had damaged the cartridge.

He tried again, with no other result than the noise of the fall of the hammer; and then Dullah's, or Rajah Gantang's, voice was heard in a reproving tone as he bade his men be silent.

Gray tried again, but for the third time the cartridges, soaked as they were by being under water so long, refused to go off. But at his fifth and sixth pulls there were a couple of lines of light, and Gray felt astonished as he heard how loud were the reports the little weapon made.

For with a couple of bright flashes that seemed to the astonished Malays to come out of the surface of the river, there were as many echoing reports, and as they rang out they were answered by sentry after sentry about the island, the last shot being fired by Private Sim, close at hand, after which he ran for his life.

There was a sharp keen order at this, and the boats' heads were forced up to the bank, one of their prows crushing right in upon Gray even to touching him, but saving his life for the moment, as it concealed his position from the enemies, who were vainly trying to make out in the darkness who had given the alarm.

Gray had not a moment to lose; already spears were being thrust beneath the bank to right and left of him. His only chance was to dive right beneath the keel of the nearest boat and swim down the river for his life.

He did not pause to think of the risk—the alarm had been given, and he had the satisfaction of knowing that every one would be on the alert—as he dived down, passed beneath the keel of the first boat, and then beneath the next, keeping under water all he could till he was fifty yards or so from the nearest prahu, when he struck out for the shore.

The current ran very strong where he now was, and soon took him beyond reach of pursuit; but it had its disadvantages, for as he swam he felt that if he did not use every effort he would be swept right down the river. And now, too, came the dread of the crocodiles, and he swam on, expecting each moment to feel the teeth of one of the monsters, and to be snatched down into the depths of the river to a horrible death.

Meanwhile, shots were being fired on the island; he heard drum and bugle calling to the muster, and relieved of the fear that Captain Smithers would be surprised, he fought on manfully with the swift stream.

His efforts seemed in vain, for though he had contrived to get pretty close to the shore, the current ran so strong that he saw himself swept by the dark line of trees and into the stream below.

His only hope now seemed to be to make for the steamer, whose lights he could see below him; but involuntarily almost he turned and made a fresh effort to reach the island, when, to his great delight, he found himself in a strong eddy, and after five minutes' swimming he was able to catch at the overhanging branches of a tree and draw himself up close to the muddy bank, where he remained, panting for a few minutes, longing to draw himself out on to dry land, but too weak and exhausted, half paralysed too, as he thought of how the great reptiles had their haunts in the hollows beneath the river's banks.

At last, though, his heart beat less painfully, and he gently reached up one hand above the other, made a strong effort, and then lay panting beneath the trees, with the water running from him in a stream.

Safe from the water and the creatures that haunted the river, he had yet to thread his way through the ranks of human tigers who were now swarming about the island, as he could tell by the flashes and reports of the rifles that were being fired on either side.

He lay there for quite ten minutes, thinking of what would be his best plan to pursue, for he had a double peril to encounter—namely, the spears of the Malays, and the bullets of his comrades, who would be certain to fire at any one they saw approaching. Still nothing presented itself to his mind, and he at last began to move cautiously forward towards the little fort.

As he went on through the dense growth with which this part of the island was covered, he became aware that the Malays were making quite a furious attack upon the place, while it was just as evident that they were encountering a serious resistance. To his great delight now the field-piece began to speak, and he had seen the rocket go up, as a signal to the ship, the bright stars lighting up the patch of jungle where he lay to such an extent that he shrank close down beneath some shrubs, lest he should form a mark for the spear of some Malay.

Going so slowly and cautiously, it took him some time to get near the lines, and then he had to pause, for the flashes and reports of the rifles showed him where his enemies were lying, and twice over he nearly walked into the midst of a little group hiding amidst the trees.

He had taken the precaution of reloading the little revolver, though all the time feeling greatly in doubt as to whether the cartridges were not spoiled; and consequently he relied most of all upon his dirk, though he felt that his only chance would be to steal through the Malays, and then make a bold dash for the gate, shouting the password as he ran.

He was compelled to crawl as he drew near, for the bullets whistled through the trees, cutting off leaf and twig, and searching the jungle, as it were, for the enemy, who seemed all around him; for, go which way he would, there was always a party close at hand.

At last, though, he crawled behind some trees, with only an open space between him and the fort. He was waiting his opportunity; and the moment a sharp, scattered burst of firing was over, he rose and ran for his life.

Chapter Forty Three
Tom Long heads a Sally-Party

As Adam Gray ran through the darkness, a yell arose from behind him, telling him that his act had been seen, and, as if to prevent him, half-a-dozen spears came whizzing through the air, one of them so close that it grazed his arm; while, to make matters worse, the firing recommenced from the fort.

By dint of shouting strongly he made himself known, and the firing ceased, giving him time to run up to the breast-work, and then along it to the gateway, now doubly shut; but after a little parley he was admitted, and found himself in the presence of Captain Smithers and Ensign Long.

"Ah, Gray!" exclaimed the former, "I had given you up. Were those your shots that gave the alarm?"

Gray said they were, and in a few concise words told what he had seen.

"Yes," said Captain Smithers, "we are in for it; but our friends have a tougher job than they imagined."

During the next half-hour, while they were keeping the enemy at bay, they became aware of the fact that an engagement was going on between the steamer and some enemy unseen by them, though they immediately set it down as being with boats. The return signal had been seen, and there was no little comfort in the knowledge that the occupants of the steamer were at hand to co-operate with and help them, though they little thought of how soon the vessel would be rendered almost helpless.

With the daylight, which was most gladly welcomed, came the news that the corvette was ashore; and on Captain Smithers turning round to speak to Ensign Long, he found that young gentleman slapping his legs, bending down with laughter, and altogether behaving in an exceedingly indecorous manner for an officer and a gentleman.

"Why, Long!" exclaimed Captain Smithers, "what does this mean?"

Tom Long flushed up as red as a turkey-cock, and looked at his superior officer in the most shame-faced way.

"I—I—I—" he began.

"Why, I believe you were delighted to hear that the steamer was aground."

"Well, no, sir; not that the steamer is aground," said Tom. "I—I—was not sorry, though, that Roberts had made a mess of it. He is so bounceable, sir."

"I'm ashamed of you, Long!" said Captain Smithers severely. "This is no time for silly, boyish spite. Take ten men, and make your way down to within hailing distance of the vessel, and ask what they mean to do—hold the corvette, or come and take their chance with us? At once, sir, and act like a man."

Tom Long saluted, and getting Sergeant Lund and nine men, made his way out of the little sally-port, and led them along at the double, beneath the shelter of the fire from the fort, till they were opposite the dense grove of trees which lay between them and the steamer.

It was an awkward and a dangerous task, for not only was the piece of forest growth swarming with enemies, but from time to time a shot or two from the marines on board the vessel came whistling through the trees.

But Tom Long was smarting from his rebuke. He wanted to act like a man, and at heart he knew he had been behaving like a boy of a very petty disposition, so, with Captain Smithers' words yet ringing in his ears, he formed up his men, gave the word, and in skirmishing order they dashed through the trees, sending the Malays, after they had thrown a few spears, helter-skelter to right and left, save a few who were driven out in sight of the men on board the steamer, when a few shots sent them off into cover.

"Phew!" ejaculated Sergeant Lund, taking off his cap to wipe his wet forehead, and gazing admiringly at the ensign. "That's warm work, sir." And then he glanced at the men, who were delighted with what they called the ensign's pluck.

"Warm? yes, sergeant. Quick! some of you fire at those niggers; they are coming back."

A little volley at half-a-dozen Malays, who were showing menacingly on their left, sent them to the right-about, and then the men cheered, their cheer being answered from the steamer, which was only about thirty or forty yards from the shore.

"Ensign Long, ahoy!" cried Bob Roberts, leaping on to the bulwarks. "What cheer?"

"If you mean how are we getting on, and are we all safe, why don't you say so?" cried the ensign sharply.

"All right, sir. I'll write you a memorandum and a report," said Bob Roberts. "Now then, how are you?"

"Captain Smithers wants to know whether you are coming ashore or going to stay on board."

"Stay on board, Mr Long," said the lieutenant, who had come up. "Are you all well?"

"Yes, sir, all well."

"None wounded?"

"No, sir, not one as yet."

"Tell Captain Smithers that my duty is to stay here with the steamer; but if he is hard pressed I will either send him a party of sailors and marines, or else we will cover his retreat with his gun, if he will come and take refuge on board."

"Captain Smithers cannot leave his entrenched position, sir," said Tom Long stiffly; "but we can find room for you and your crew, if they like to come."

Tom Long said this so importantly that Bob Roberts began to laugh; and no doubt some sharp bandying about of words would have followed, had not Lieutenant Johnson said rather sternly,—

"Tell Captain Smithers, Mr Long, that a rocket sent up by night, or three calls of the bugle given sharply without any perceptible interval, will bring help from us; but ask him if any steps can be taken to help the expedition."

"Captain Smithers is of opinion, sir, that the expeditionary party is strong enough to take care of itself, and that it is our duty to—Oh!"

Tom Long blushed for it afterwards; but a well-thrown spear came so close to his ear that he could not avoid an involuntary cry. The next minute his little party were under cover of some trees, and slowly driving back a body of Malays, who, however, would have out-flanked them, but for a brisk fire kept up on them from the steamer, when they disappeared once more into the jungle, with which this part of the island was overgrown. When after a few more words with the occupants of the steamer, during which Lieutenant Johnson impressed upon the ensign that the best thing to be done was to act entirely on the defensive, the little sally-party started to return, the lieutenant promising to do all he could to cover their retreat.

The distance was not great, but full of peril; for the minute the Malays comprehended that Tom Long's party were going back, they began to swarm out of their lurking-places, and it now became evident that hundreds of fighting men must have landed on the island.

"Well, sir," said Sergeant Lund, wiping his face, as, after getting about half-way back, the little party found themselves hedged up in a little gully by Malay spears, whose holders kept themselves hidden behind the trees,— "well, sir, this is hot, and no mistake."

"Yes," said Tom Long, excitedly; "but be careful, my lads, don't waste a shot; you must be getting short."

"They've only about six rounds each, sir, now," said the sergeant; "but they've got the bayonets."

"Yes," said Tom, as he stood sword in one hand, revolver in the other; "but we mustn't let them get at us with their spears. I can't leave a man behind, sergeant."

"Then we'd better stop as we are for a few minutes, and get breath, sir, and then see which is the best way to go."

The sergeant hurried to a couple of the men who were exposing themselves a little too freely, and then returned to Tom Long, who was standing in the middle of two sides of a triangle composed of four men a side, and another forming the apex.

"I'd make a dash for it, sergeant," said the ensign, "only I should be sure to lose some of the boys; while if we stop here we shall get speared. It's a puzzle, isn't it? I say, I don't feel half so—so—"

"Scared, sir?"

"Well, yes; I didn't like to say frightened, sergeant," replied Tom, smiling, "because it sounds so queer."

"Ah, sir, you might say anything now before the lads, they wouldn't mind; and after the plucky way you led us on, they'd follow you anywhere. But hadn't we better let the enemy have a few shot, sir? They're closing in fast."

Tom Long was about to give the order for which his men were anxiously waiting, when he became aware of something going on in a clump of palms about forty yards away.

"What are they doing there, sergeant?" he said. "Look!"

"Getting ready for a rush, sir. Hadn't we better form square?"

"No; only close up a little," said Tom, sharply, as he set his teeth; for he knew that they were on the brink of a hand-to-hand encounter.

For though pretty well screened by the trees, it was evident that a large party of the Malays were getting ready for a rush, when *bang—crash*, there was the report of a gun from the steamer, followed almost instantly by the bursting of a shell in the very thick of the trees where the Malays had gathered, with the result that there was quite an opening rent in that part of the jungle, and the threatening party was scattered like chaff.

"That's what I calls the prettiest shot I ever see," said one of the men.

"Forward!" shouted Tom Long, and taking advantage of the momentary panic, he hurried his little party on at the double, with the result that by the time the Malays again menaced an attack, the sally-party were under cover of the guns at the fort, and a few minutes later, amidst the cheers of those they had left behind, Tom Long led his little party within the gates, not a man amongst them having received a scratch.

Chapter Forty Four
How Captain Smithers made Plans

There was plenty to do to make the little fort secure, and well the men worked. Double their number would not have been too strong a garrison, for the Malays mustered thickly now on all sides, save that nearest the ship, whose heavy guns had taught them the risk of making any display of their presence.

Captain Smithers would have gladly joined forces with Lieutenant Johnson, but he was not surprised at his reply, and he could only condole with him in respect to the accident that had occurred to the steamer, one which would partly place it *hors de combat* until some flood should cause a rise in the water of the river.

The men vied with each other in executing the orders that were given, and in a short time the mess-room and quarters were so strengthened that once within, the men felt that the only enemy they had to fear was fire, and that they hoped to avoid by means of their rifles, and, if needs be, their bayonets.

It was a terrible time for the women, many of whom had husbands with the expedition; but knowing as they did that the major's lady was in the same position as themselves, they tried hard to follow her calm and patient example.

It was only an outward calm though, for poor Mrs Major Sandars was suffering keenly, though she tried hard and successfully to speak words of comfort to Rachel Linton and her cousin, both of whom went about with her, talking to the soldiers' wives, and trying to amuse the children, who at times grew impatient at being forced to keep inside the walls of the barracks, the outer enclosure having been long declared unsafe.

Captain Smithers had sought the ladies, and spoken a few words of encouragement to them, gazing very hard at Miss Linton as he said, —

"You may rely upon us, Miss Linton. I would lay down my life sooner than harm should befall you."

"I am quite satisfied of that, Captain Smithers," said the lady, quietly. "I believe that of the meanest man here. In the meantime, I presume that you would like us all to keep within the walls."

"Yes, if you please, Miss Linton," said the young officer, coldly; and then, as he walked away, he muttered, "Yes, she believes that of the meanest soldier, and thinks as much of him as of me."

He walked across the open space to the lines where the men were placed, the intention being to hold them for the time, and if hard pressed, to retire within the barracks and there make their stand.

As he went to the nearest point a bullet whizzed by him, sufficiently near to show him that the Malays had not only good weapons among them, but men who could shoot straight; and he frowned as he felt that their chance would be but small if under some clever leader the Malays should make a bold effort to take the place.

On reaching the earth-works that surrounded the enclosure, every man was in his place, silent and watchful. The order had been given that no one was to fire except to check an advance, for though ammunition was abundant, Captain Smithers felt that it was impossible to tell how long they might be besieged, so he determined to economise as much as possible. Consequently, firing from the fort was only at intervals, and as the Malays relied principally upon their spears, the ball was not kept up with anything like vigour; but, all the same, certain movements on the part of the enemy warned the temporary commandant to be careful, as it would be craft more than open assault with which he would have to deal.

After completing his round and saying a few words to the men, he stood thinking on the side nearest the river, from which he was only separated by a space of about forty yards, and he could not help thinking how their position would be strengthened if the steamer could be got off and moored here, a trench being opened from stem and stern to connect it with the fort. This would be giving the latter a most powerful river front. Dullah's hut, which stood there, could easily be razed, and he knew that the water was deeper there than at any part of the river—quite sufficient to float the steamer.

It seemed a risky thing to do—to send again; but he felt that he ought to apprise Lieutenant Johnson of his ideas, and to request him to use every effort to get the steamer off.

"As if he would not do that for his own sake," he muttered directly after; and then he began to consider whom he should send.

Adam Gray immediately suggested himself to his mind, and his brow knitted as he felt that it was like trying to get rid of a man he disliked.

"He is the most trustworthy, and the best suited for the task," he said directly; and as the words left his lips he raised his eyes, and saw the object of his thoughts come with a dozen more men to relieve the party nearer him.

"Fall out, Gray," he said sharply; and Gray looked at him curiously as he stepped back out of the ranks.

"I want a message conveyed on board the steamer, Gray," said Captain Smithers. "She lies about fifty yards off the other side of the island, aground on the mud. Do you think you can reach her?"

"I shall do my best, sir," said Gray, quietly. "If I do not succeed, you will know it is because I am down."

"But you must not go down, Gray," said Captain Smithers, hastily. "You cannot be spared. This is a most important duty, and that is why I send you."

The private's eyes were fixed on those of his captain most searchingly, and the latter lowered his own before those of his inferior.

"I shall give you no written message, for fear that you may be taken, Gray," said Captain Smithers, hastily. "Take this verbal message, 'Captain Smithers begs, for the sake of all, that Lieutenant Johnson will strive to get the steamer off, and bring her round here, to moor her close up to the bank, alongside of Dullah's hut.' Do you understand?"

"Yes, sir," said Gray, and he repeated the words.

"That will do. Now go."

"At once, sir?"

"At once."

Gray saluted, and with his teeth pressing his lip started off upon another risky mission.

He met Ensign Long as he went back to the quarters, and on being questioned, he questioned in return, and obtained a few particulars, enough to make him determine to make his way up towards the head of the island, and there swim off, to try and get himself swept down to the steamer, hoping to be seen and get on board without mishap, and in this spirit, arming himself once more as on his former expedition, he set off.

Chapter Forty Five
Through Fire and Water

Private Gray was conscious that the ladies saw him start, and their eyes bade him succeed, or else it was his fancy. At all events the knowledge that he had their sympathy encouraged him, at a time when his heart was sore with the knowledge that Captain Smithers was selecting him for every dangerous service as if to get rid of him.

Sergeant Lund nodded sagely, on receiving the application for the revolver.

"All right, my lad," he said quietly. "I suppose I mustn't grumble at you for making it so rusty last time."

"No, sergeant; nor yet if I make it worse this time."

"Another risky journey then, eh? No, don't tell me, my lad. Go and do your duty; I'm not going to pump you."

"I know that, sergeant, but it is no breach of confidence to ask your advice."

"'Course not, my lad. There you are; fix 'em in tight. Now then, what is it? I'm good at some things, so long as you don't ask me to put 'em down in writing."

"If you wished to get to the steamer, sergeant, how would you proceed?"

"Oh, that's it, is it?" said the sergeant. "Well then, you've got a risky job, my lad. But you'll do it. Well, if it was me I should wait till night, if I could."

"And if you could not?"

"I should go just t'other way, to throw the Malay chaps off their scent. Then work round to the head of the island, slip into the water, and swim down."

"Exactly, sergeant," said Gray; and he turned off to go.

"He's as clever a young chap as ever I run against," said the sergeant, who, like a good many more people, fervently admired those who thought the same as he. "But what puzzles me more and more every day is how such a chap as him should come to be a common soldier. He's a gentleman, every inch of him. Why, didn't they get him to talk to the French officers when we landed at Ceylon, and the French frigate was there? and my word, how he did jabber away! He might have been a real mounseer. Well, 'taint no business of mine; so long as he gets his accoutrements clean, and a good coating of pipeclay on his belts, that's enough for me. I only wish there was more Grays and not so many Sims in the company."

Meanwhile Adam Gray was on his way to the far side of the fort, very quiet and thoughtful as he made his plans, the first part of which was to go quietly to the edge of the earthwork, wait for his opportunity, and drop into the dry ditch, from which he hoped to crawl unperceived to the cover of the trees, about a hundred yards away. The rest, he felt, must be left to chance.

As he reached the side he met Ensign Long, who came up to him, and to his great surprise shook hands.

"Captain Smithers has told me of your mission, Gray," he said; "I wish you every success."

"But you don't think, sir, that I shall succeed, and this is a friendly good-bye," said Gray, smiling.

"Well I—that is—I—'pon my word, Gray, you just hit what I was thinking about. You see I had such a narrow escape of it myself, that I couldn't help thinking of something of the kind."

"You tried it openly, sir; I'm going to try and steal a march upon the Malays."

"What, are you going over here?" said the ensign.

"Yes, sir, and there's a good opening now," said Gray, after a sharp look round. "Good-bye, sir; wish me luck."

As he spoke he glided as it were over the edge of the earthwork, and let himself roll into the ditch, whence he made his way to the edge on the other side, Ensign Long bidding the two nearest men cover the messenger with their rifles as long as he was in sight.

That was not for long, Gray crawling rapidly over the ground; and as those who watched scanned every shrub and tree for an enemy, they saw him reach the edge of the jungle and disappear.

It was into no haven of safety though that Gray had passed, for he had not gone twenty yards into the shadowy gloom, which was comparatively cool after the scorching sunshine in the opening that had been cleared of trees, before he heard voices on his left, and he had barely time to crouch down among the long grass before half-a-dozen Malays came along, one of whom saw the pressed down undergrowth and began to examine it curiously.

Another moment and he would have seen Gray, whose hand was thrust into his breast, but a word from one of his companions took off his attention, and he disappeared with them amongst the trees.

Gray drew a long breath as he once more started off, creeping on all fours, and at times crawling, so as to make sure of being unseen.

His journey of about half a mile, measured by his twisting and turning, was one series of hairbreadth escapes. A dozen times over he had to turn and come back over almost precisely the same ground to avoid a party of Malays, who seemed ready to spring out of the earth on all sides of him, but still, thanks to the thick growth, he was unseen. Such a journey on their first landing would have been impossible, but as the men were hardly ever allowed to go on the mainland, they had, by way of compensation, pretty free access to the jungle portion of the little island, and in consequence they had trampled down the dense vegetation, and forced paths here and there through the cane brakes when snake hunting.

At last, dripping with perspiration, Gray reached the head of the island, and lay half exhausted in a dense clump of canes, listening to the washing of the river as its waters divided a dozen or so of paces from where he lay.

He could not see the river on account of the thick growth, but it sounded very cool and pleasant; and now, having won his way thus far, he longed for the plunge and swim down to the steamer.

He reckoned that a minute's law would place him beyond the reach of spears, however ably thrown; and as to the enemy's rifles or muskets, he did not think they would be able to hit him as he swam with the rapid stream. Still he did not move, for he was so heated by his exertions that he dreaded risking cramp or shock from the sudden immersion.

Everything was so still in the hot afternoon sunshine, that the whirring noise of the insects seemed quite loud. Beautiful blue-billed gapers, all claret and black and white, flitted about, catching glossy metallic-looking beetles; little green chatterers, with their crested heads, flew from spray to spray; and tiny sun-birds, in their gorgeous mail of gold and bronze and purple, flew from flower to flower in search of honey. Now and then a scaly glistening lizard rustled by him, and twice over a snake crawled right across his body and away into the grass. Then a flock of the little lovebird paroquets came and settled in a tree hard by, piping, whistling, and chattering as they climbed and swung head downwards, or flew here and there; while upon some bushes close at hand sat a pair of the lovely rose-breasted trogons, with their grey reticulated wings and beautiful cinnamon backs.

It was a glorious scene for a lover of nature, so delicate were the many tints of green, so pure the sky above; while to add to the beauty of the place a flock of rose-tinted doves settled in the palms, and cooed as mellowly as if this were in some park in the young soldier's far-off home.

So lovely was everything around that Gray closed his eyes, and was ready to ask himself whether the idea of danger was not all a dream, and that it was but fancy to suppose that bloodthirsty men were swarming in the island, ready to slaughter the inhabitants to a man.

The sharp crack of a rifle, and then of half a dozen more, dissipated the dream, and with a sigh as he thought of the danger of those at the station, Gray unclosed his eyes, rose to his hands and knees from where he had been lying, and began to force his way softly amidst the canes.

It was no easy task till he came to a track, evidently that made by a crocodile in coming and going from the river. He paused for a moment, shuddering as he thought of his danger; then drawing the dirk, ready for a blow at the monster's eyes, should he encounter one, he crawled on, reached the water's edge in safety, parting the canes to peer up and down the river in search of danger, and seeing none.

From where he crouched the steamer was not visible, but he knew that a little bold swimming would soon show her lying below; and, all the while feeling very much like as if he were a frog about to plunge into a stream haunted by pike, he lowered himself towards the water, gazed for a moment into its depths, and then plunged in.

Down he went into the clear, cool stream, striking out so as to get well away from the bank as he did so, and then rising to the surface, to see, to his horror, that a good-sized boat, that had lain hidden amidst the reeds, was being pushed out, and with seven or eight occupants was coming in pursuit.

What was he to do? seek the shore again and take refuge in the jungle?

That seemed impossible; for he had plunged in so close to the boat that he would have been speared long before he could reach the place he had left, even if he had been able to swim against the stream.

Then, to his horror, he saw that the banks were perpendicular or else overhanging, and any attempt at climbing them from the water must have failed; for, as far as he could see, where he was being swept down not a tree laved an overhanging branch in the swift stream. There was only one course open to him, and that was to trust to the river, and swim for his life.

He had been taking this as his only chance as the above thoughts flashed through his brain; and now came in the value of his old school-day experience, when he had been one of the bravest swimmers of his age. In fact, as he swam on, recollections of the old alder and willow ait in the clear river came back, and he smiled as he turned upon his side and forced his way through the sparkling waters.

The position as he made the side-stroke was convenient, though not inspiriting; for as his cheek lay on the stream he could keep one eye upon his pursuers, who were now coming rapidly on. Fortunately for Gray, in their hurry and excitement the Malays had lost ground, so that the young soldier had a fair start before they bent regularly to their paddles. He could see, though, that a couple of men were standing upright in the boat, each with a foot upon the gunwale, and a spear poised in one hand, ready for hurling at the fugitive when within throwing distance.

Gray swam swiftly, but he saw that it was hopeless, and that he must soon be overtaken and perish. Still he did not despair, for his career had before now seemed as near its end. *Nil desperandum* was the motto of his life, and like some hunted hare he kept his eye upon his pursuers, meaning to try and dive the moment he saw an effort made to hurl a spear.

He might perhaps escape by diving. At all events, it was his only chance, and he swam on, with the boat now rapidly getting near.

Perhaps, he thought, they might not throw, but wait to thrust at him. If so, that would give him longer time; but no, there was no chance of that, for now he saw one of the Malays poise his spear, and draw himself back, to throw it with all his force.

Gray saw no more, but with a shuddering sensation, as he seemed to feel the deadly weapon pierce him between the shoulders, he made a tremendous effort, and dived down, swimming beneath the surface with all his might, till compelled to rise for breath.

As his head appeared above water a spear grazed his shoulder, and another passed just over his ear when he dived again, still pursuing the same tactics, and swimming beneath the surface.

Again he rose, and another spear splashed the water in his face, while the shaft of the next struck him a sharp rap, as the blade narrowly shaved his ear.

Down once more; but now he was weaker. The intense excitement and the need of breath exhausted him, and though he strove hard to keep down, his efforts began to prove vain. He had seen the last time that the boat was closer to him, and he felt sure that now on rising he should be within reach of one or other of the spearmen.

Still he made another effort to keep below, for though he was suffocating, and began to feel confused, weak, and helpless, these moments were moments of life, whereas the instant he reached the surface he knew that all was over.

In his confused, sense-benumbed state, he felt that after all he had done his duty, and he recalled the calm, trusting look directed at him by Miss Linton as he passed her that morning. Then the water above him grew lighter, and he rose to the surface, striking out but feebly now, as he saw the boat close at hand, heard a shout from the Malays, and saw one of the men in the bow lean over to thrust his spear into the helpless swimmer, now almost at his feet.

Chapter Forty Six
Shows how Bob Roberts gave a Hint, and the Malays got into Hot Water

Hunter and hunted had been alike too much occupied to note what had been going on elsewhere. Gray's anxious gaze when he rose to the surface had been directed backward at his pursuers, and for the time being the steamer and her occupants were forgotten. On the other hand, the Malays, keen on the scent of blood, intently watched the place where their quarry dived, and calculated where he would rise.

So it was then that just as one of the men in the prow of the boat was about to savagely stab the nerveless swimmer, whose glazing eye met his with more of defiance than menace therein, there was a rattling volley from half-a-dozen rifles, the two spearmen fell over the side, to be swept away by the stream, and their companions, on starting up and seeing one of the steamer's cutters coming rapidly on, to a man leaped overboard and swam for their lives, some making for the island, some for the opposite shore.

Adam Gray was so exhausted and surprised that it was some time before he realised that the danger was past, but that, unless he made a fresh effort, a new peril would await him, and he would lose his life by drowning.

Just then, though, the Malay boat was swept close to him, and he threw one arm over the side, holding on till he was dragged into the cutter, which was then rowed rapidly back to the steamer.

"That was a narrow squeak for you, Mr Soldier," said Bob Roberts. "My marines only spoke up just in time."

"I cannot find words to thank you now, sir," panted Gray, who was pale with exhaustion.

"All right!" said Bob; "and don't find any words to thank me by-and-by. I'm glad we were in time. You'd have done as much for any of us, my man."

"Of course, sir; of course," said Gray, huskily.

"Yes, of course you would; but how came you in the river?"

"I was swimming off with a message to Lieutenant Johnson, sir," replied Gray.

"Then if I were you I wouldn't go such a long way round next time," said Bob. "Steady there, marines. Let them see you cover them, and they'll rush off behind the trees."

This was in regard to some Malays who were showing themselves menacingly on the edge of the river; but the moment they saw that the marines' rifles were directed at them they ran to cover, and the cutter was soon alongside of the steamer, the falls were hooked on, and the boat swung by the davits, her mission being at an end.

Two anchors had been carried some distance out, steam got up, and with the screw going at high pressure and men at work at the capstan, every effort was being made to get the vessel out of her unpleasant position, but in vain.

Lieutenant Johnson heard the message brought by Gray, and then pointed to what was being done.

"I am making every effort," he said rather angrily. "Does Captain Smithers think I want to stay in this disgraceful position? You can tell him, though, that if I can get free I shall divide my time between chasing these rascally prahus and lying where he suggests."

The efforts went on, the men hauling and straining on the anchors, and the steam going furiously, but all in vain; the vessel would not move.

Then another plan was tried; all the ship's company were sent to one side of the bulwarks, and then run across to the other, to give a swaying motion to the vessel, so as to loosen the keel in the deep mud; but though the careening was effected, the steamer could not be moved, either ahead or astern.

Then the last plan was tried again, with the addition of the guns being run all over to the port-side, but still there was no change; and Lieutenant Johnson's brow knit with annoyance as he more fully realised the fact that they would be lying in that helpless position when the captain returned.

"The disgrace is enough to kill me, Roberts," he exclaimed.

"Let's set every sail, sir," said the middy; "there's a nice breeze coming down the river now, and that may send her over nearly upon her beam-ends."

"Yes!" exclaimed the lieutenant eagerly; and the order being given, the men ran up aloft, and sail after sail was lowered, Ali standing with folded arms watching the proceedings, and then turning to lean upon the bulwark and gaze down the river.

Just then Adam Gray saluted the lieutenant.

"Will you be good enough to have me set ashore now, sir?"

"Set you ashore, my man?" replied Lieutenant Johnson, "Why, you had better wait till night."

"I ought to get back with your message, sir."

"Wait a little while, and perhaps I can run you round to the other side of the island."

Gray, now that he had somewhat recovered, was eager to get back, but he could not quit the ship without the lieutenant's consent, and hence he waited patiently for the required permission, watching the steamer's sails drop down one by one, and fill and flap as the breeze rose and fell.

Now and then a dusky face could be seen amidst the palm-trees watching their proceedings, but it disappeared directly, and the clothing of the vessel with canvas went on without interruption, till pretty well every stitch was set save a studding-sail or two. Then a puff of hot air came, and the steamer bent well over, the sails being so trimmed that the vessel's course would have been astern had she shown any disposition to move; but though the steam was on full, and the men brought the capstan to bear on the cables, she did not budge an inch.

"Here, my lads, back with these guns," said the lieutenant; and for the next half-hour the men were busy replacing the heavy guns, when Ali, who since his escape had been remaining in sanctuary upon the steamer, suddenly gave the alarm.

"A prahu coming down," he exclaimed, running to the lieutenant and catching his arm, pointing out as he did so something moving round a reach of the river, and seen now and then where the growth was thin.

"Two prahus coming up stream," reported one of the look-out men.

"Look! look!" cried Ali, pointing up the river. "There is another—two more. They are coming to take the steamer," he cried.

"And we aground!" exclaimed the lieutenant, stamping his foot with rage as he gave the necessary orders. The drum beat to quarters directly; the magazine was opened; and the men ran eagerly to their posts; while

Ali went quietly into the cabin, and returned with a sword, revolver, and a spotting rifle, lent him by the lieutenant for shooting crocodiles.

"Are you going to fight?" exclaimed Bob Roberts, who looked flushed and excited.

"Yes," said Ali, "with this;" and he tapped the rifle.

"But against your own people?"

"Rajah Gantang's pirates are not my own people," said Ali, contemptuously. "Besides, the English are my friends, and if we could I would have gone to help those ashore."

"All right," said Bob, "then we will fight together. I say, it's going to be a hot affair, isn't it?"

"They think to take the steamer easily," said Ali, "as she is ashore, but you will not let them?"

"Let them!" said Lieutenant Johnson, "no, Mr Ali, we will not. We shall fight to the last, and the last will be that I'll blow the vessel up. I can't sink her, for she is aground."

Ali nodded his approval: he seemed in no wise moved at the prospect of the steamer being destroyed. And now he stood watching the coming of the great prahus, with their regular sweeps, twenty to thirty on each side, and alternated this with watching the loading of the guns and disposal of the men.

Just then an idea seemed to have struck Bob Roberts, who ran across the deck to where old Dick was standing ready by a gun.

"Here, Dick, I want you. Wilson, come and take his place."

"Ay, ay, sir!" cried the man; but old Dick growled.

"Don't take me away, Mr Roberts, sir," he said, querulously. "I was longing for a shot at them dirty pirates, and now I'm losing my chance."

"Look here, Dick," cried Bob, and he raised himself on tiptoe and whispered something to him, old Dick's soured face undergoing a complete change to one full of mirth. The wrinkles became puckers, and his eyes nearly closed, while his mouth seemed drawn out at the corners till nearly double its usual length.

"It will be just right, Dick," said the middy.

"To a T, Mr Roberts, sir. Well, you are a clever one, you are! Who'd ha' thought of that?"

"You be ready, Dick; I depend upon you, mind," cried the middy; and he ran back to his post.

The prahus were coming steadily on, up and down stream, and it could be seen from the steamer's deck that they were full of men, and bristling with spears, while any doubt as to the unfriendliness of their intentions was soon dispelled by the noise of beating gongs on board each vessel, the object being apparently to encourage each other and to excite alarm in the breasts of their foes, a result which in this case the noise decidedly failed in obtaining.

The men kept glancing anxiously at their commander, who seemed to be letting the prahus approach very closely, which appeared to be a bad policy, seeing that the Malays were about ten to one, and their object would doubtless be to board the steamer and engage in a hand-to-hand fight; but Lieutenant Johnson had made his plans, and was abiding his time. He himself carefully pointed the guns, depressing them somewhat, so that the shot should strike low; and then leaving the task in the hands of the captain of each piece, he waited the result.

The prahus were now within a couple of hundred yards of the steamer, and had begun firing iron shot from their little brass lelahs, when the first gun spoke out. There was a round puff of smoke and a deafening roar, and the shot struck the nearest right in the stem, tearing a great hole in her bows, and passing through her with such deadly effect that the prahu immediately began to sink, and her crew leaped overboard in confusion and began to swim ashore.

Grape-shot from the smaller guns or musketry from the marines would have destroyed numbers of the Malays struggling in the water, but looking upon them as out of the fight, Lieutenant Johnson left them to struggle, some to one bank, some to the other, and gave his orders merely to the men at the great guns.

It was one from the port-side that had wrought this mischief. Now one from the starboard spoke out. There was once more the great white ball of smoke, the deafening roar, and the shot struck the water about twenty yards from the nearest prahu, ricochetted, and passed clean through her, going down the river afterwards in a series of richochets.

This shot caused no little confusion on board, and several of the sweeps fell uselessly in the water; but the prahu still came on, with the occupants yelling and beating their gongs.

Another shot struck the water, and though well aimed for the next prahu, it rose and went over her, merely making a great gap in the matting-screen from behind which the Malays were keeping up a brisk but ineffectual fire.

Another shot at one of the prahus coming down stream; and this went clean over, and crashed through the palm-trees a quarter of a mile away. But the next shot produced a hearty cheer from the sailors, for it struck the slight vessel right on the water-line, made a tremendous gap, and must have caused terrible slaughter, for the Malays were thrown into confusion, the sweeps clashed one with the other, and all governance seemed gone, the prahu turning broadside on, and then floating slowly with the stream for a few yards before settling down and sinking, leaving her masts and the top of the mat screens visible, for the water was shallow where she sank.

The two prahus coming down stream were thus effectually disposed of; but the two coming up were now close at hand, and before another gun could be brought to bear their bows struck the sides of the steamer, grappling-irons were thrown over the bulwarks and into the chains, and yelling savagely their crews of fierce fighting men came swarming upon the deck.

It was sharp work leaving the guns and preparing for the boarders; but the sailors and marines were ready, and received the fierce, yelling crowd of Malays with a sharp fire and the point of the bayonet, while these latter attacked fiercely with kris and spear. Their charge was most daring, and they came on in such numbers, and fought with so great a display of courage, that the little party of Englishmen, in spite of their heroic defence, were driven back step by step, till Lieutenant Johnson began to bitterly regret that he had not signalled for help from the fort.

His heart sank within him as, in spite of his bravery and the example he set his men he saw them giving way on all sides.

Bob Roberts, young as he was, fought bravely and well, while Ali did good service with his rifle. But all seemed in vain; the Malays were gradually getting possession of the deck, and the question was arising in the lieutenant's mind whether it would not be wiser to take refuge in the cabin, and fire from thence as they could.

Men fell rapidly on either side, but while the Malays had three or four to leap into the places of those who went down, every wounded Englishman weakened the force terribly by his loss.

Still there was no sign of flinching, the men giving way solely from being forced back by the numbers that pressed upon them.

Three times over by a determined rally did the lieutenant strive to force the enemy back, but in vain; and the last time he nearly lost his life, for the Malays made at him at once, and in his efforts to avoid them he slipped and fell.

With a yell of triumph a couple of the enemy dashed at him spear in hand, when there was a sharp double report from a rifle, and one leaped in the air to fall flat on the deck beside his intended victim, the other staggered back and retreated to the rear.

Those shots were fired by the young chief Ali, who coolly reloaded his piece, and stood watching Bob Roberts, whose excitement was intense.

He had forgotten Dick and his instructions to the old sailor in the fierce passions of the fray, and poor old Dick had gone down almost at the first rush, to crawl afterwards under the bulwarks, where he bound up his head, and lay watching the fight as he strove more than once to join in.

But each time old Dick essayed to rise, a terrible sickness came over him, and he sank back trying to recall some order he had received from the midshipman, but unable to make out what it was.

He fainted away twice in his efforts to get up, and then lay back, sick at heart, and with just enough consciousness left to know that the fight was going against the English, and that he had it in his power to change the fortunes of the day.

"What was it Mr Roberts told him to do? What was it Mr Roberts told him to do?"

That was the question he wanted solved, but the sense had all seemed to escape out of the cut in his head, so he told himself, and the more he tried to recall what it was, the more did he grow confused, and at last he lay there helpless, listening to the yelling of the Malays, and the cheers and shouts of the comrades he could not help.

He could see clearly enough all that was going on, and feel bitterly every phase of ill fortune in the fight, while he regretted the powerless state in which he lay as he saw some companion worsted by the enemy.

"If I could only think what it was Mr Roberts told me to do, I might do it now," he muttered, "and that would help the poor lads."

His head was growing clearer, though, and he became more and more excited as he saw sailors, marines, and officers driven back, step by step, along the deck, with the prospect before them of being slain to a man, and the steamer taken.

That idea was horrible to Dick, and he thought of the captain, officers, and men away in the jungle, and what would be their feelings when they returned.

"If I could only help!" thought Dick. "Bravo, lad! Why he fights like a man," he muttered; "and there's that Mr Ali using his gun wonderfully, and him only a nigger; while I lie here with my orders on me, and do nothing to help my mates. Oh, if I only had strength," he groaned.

Still the fight went on, and to his horror Lieutenant Johnson saw that another prahu and a naga or dragon-boat were coming up to the attack, while in place of being able to repel them with a few shots from his guns, he and his men were hemmed-in by quite a mob of yelling Malays, every one of whom was thirsting for the Englishmen's blood.

All at once, in the thick of the fight, and just as he was panting, and too helpless to deliver another stroke, Bob Roberts recalled for a moment the orders he had given old Dick. But he felt that it was too late now, and stung by the disgrace of their position, he tried to reload his revolver, wondering whether Lieutenant Johnson would execute his threat of blowing up the ship.

Had the lieutenant been ever so disposed, though, he could not have accomplished his design, for a living wall of Malays was between him and the way down to the magazine, and he was weak and spent with his efforts, to such an extent that he could hardly raise his sword.

"It is all over," he thought to himself, "but we'll die fighting like Englishmen. Oh, my poor lads," he groaned, "my poor lads!" And he wondered whether he could have done anything else to lead them to victory instead of this bitter defeat.

It did indeed seem to be all over, for the fresh boats had reached the steamer, and their men were swarming over the side, when suddenly the remembrance of his orders flashed across old Dick's clouded brain, bringing with it renewed strength, for the faintness seemed to be driven away.

Abdullah, or rather Rajah Gantang, saw the fresh forces arriving, and he shouted to them to come on, stepping back half-a-dozen yards, and then leaping on to one of the wired skylights kris in hand.

Close beside him he saw a rough old wounded sailor screwing on something bright that looked like a copper pipe, and then seize hold of an iron spanner; and out of sheer thirst for blood the rajah, after waving to the new comers to come on, made a leap down at the old sailor, who faced him with what seemed to the rajah like a copper gun, presented, and fired—

No, that's wrong, he watered; for Bob Roberts' commands were at last executed, and a shower of scalding water from the boilers was sent by means of the hose and branch full in the rajah's face, driving him away yelling with agony, as Dick made a dash along the deck, the hose trailing after him, took the Malays in flank just as they were making their final dash at the hemmed-in defenders of the vessel, and the fortunes of the day were changed.

Whizz, squish, out flew the steaming water in a scalding shower, and in an instant the fierce crowd of Malays were turned into a set of agonised, dancing, maniacs, a dozen of them turning furiously on Dick, and rushing at him, kris and spear in hand; but with a grim smile on his rough visage, old Dick gave the copper branch a waving motion, and the scalding shower stopped the fiercest of them, drove them back, and as they fled the fresh party summoned by the rajah came running along the deck.

Dick did not flinch, but mentally praying that the supply might hold out, delivered the stream full in their faces as they came yelling up, and after a brave effort to withstand it for a few moments, sending them back, crushed and beaten, stamping, shrieking, leaping overboard, making frantic efforts to escape the pain, while Dick steadily followed them up, playing the boiling water amongst them, and literally cleaning the decks, amidst the cheering of the men.

"Quick there," cried Lieutenant Johnson, "A man there at the wheel—two! quick! two! She's afloat. Down there in the engine-room," he shouted, as he mounted the bridge, for a breeze had sprung up, and the mud that clung round the steamer's keel having been loosened by the firing, the motion of the vessel, and the pressure on the sails, the corvette had, unperceived, been afloat some minutes, and slowly floating down stream.

In another few seconds she was under full command; and as the men flew to the guns, the lieutenant took deadly revenge upon his fierce enemies by manoeuvring the steamer so that, in spite of the efforts of her crew with their sweeps; he literally sent her over the biggest of the three prahus, the stem of the steamer cutting it in two as if it had been made of paper, and then sinking the naga by a well-directed shot, the crews of both swimming easily towards the shore.

By this time the other two prahus were in full retreat up stream, evidently from a belief that the steamer would not follow; but in spite of his mishap in running aground, Lieutenant Johnson could not resist the temptation to administer the sternest punishment he could contrive; and with full steam on, he gave chase, firing at the two prahus as he went.

At the end of ten minutes one had been struck several times, and her captain ran her close in shore, he and his crew deserting her; while after avoiding only by a miracle at least a dozen shots, the last prahu suddenly turned in by a branch of the river and seemed to go right amongst the palm-trees, when, after a parting shot or two, the steamer proving quite unsuited for chase in such narrow, shallow waters, the lieutenant gave it up, his crew being too weak to continue the chase with the boats.

Chapter Forty Seven
How Bob Roberts burned the Prahu

The victory was dearly bought; for now that the breathless excitement was over, and there was time to make an examination, it was found that fully half the crew had injuries, more or less serious, the men, though, bearing their sufferings with the greatest fortitude as their two officers, for want of a doctor, bound up the wounds.

It almost seemed as if those who had most exposed themselves had come off best; for neither Lieutenant Johnson, Bob Roberts, Ali, nor Adam Gray, who had been brave even to recklessness, had received a scratch.

"I have only one regret about you, Gray," said Lieutenant Johnson, shaking his hand warmly.

"May I ask what that is, sir?" replied Gray.

"Yes, that you are not a sailor; that is all," said the lieutenant, smiling. "I shall not forget this affair. I believe you twice over saved my life."

"And you, too, friend Ali," continued the lieutenant, laying his hand upon the young chief's shoulder. "I have often called the Malays a set of treacherous wretches, but I find that there are Malays and Malays. Sir, I hope some day that you may rise to power, as in you England will always have a trusty ally."

Ali bowed gravely, and his eyes betokened the pleasure he felt as he thought of the possibility of his raising the people of this land to something better than the slothful, betel-chewing, piratical race they were.

The steamer was now rapidly making her way back, the men furling the sails, and the screw as it revolved sending a wave washing in amidst the roots of the trees on either side of the river; while, now that the present danger was over, the lieutenant went round to visit his patients, leaving Bob Roberts in command, and a man with the lead in the chains.

"I think the central channel is safe enough, Roberts," said the lieutenant; "but keep him heaving the lead."

"Trust me, sir," said Bob rather importantly.

"Yes, I'll trust you, Roberts," said the lieutenant. "I'll be frank with you, my lad, and tell you something that will please you, I know."

"What is it, sir?" said Bob eagerly.

"I don't think I shall ever look upon you again as a boy?"

Bob coloured with pleasure as soon as he was left alone; but his common sense prevailed the next moment.

"That's very kind of him," he thought, "but it's all gammon; I am only a boy yet. And there—hang it all! since Miss Linton spoke to me as she did, hang me if I care if I am!"

Fortunately for the party on board the steamer, the Malays had carried off their wounded as they fell, so that there was no trouble with either them or prisoners, who would have been highly inconvenient at such a time, especially as there was no knowing how soon there might be another attack. For though beaten as to their prahus, the Malays almost to a man succeeded in reaching the shore, to join those besieging the fort, and at any time a new attack might be made.

As they came abreast of the prahu that was run ashore and forsaken, Lieutenant Johnson determined to run no risk of its being floated once more, and used, after patching, to annoy; for giving the order to reverse the engine, the steamer was kept abreast, while Bob Roberts and a party of marines and Jacks went ashore and made preparations to burn her.

Ali stepped into the boat with his friend, and advised caution; for he warned Bob that, although severely punished, the rajah was in no wise beaten, and that, as likely as not, a force of men were lying hidden amongst the reeds to protect the injured prahu.

"All right!" said Bob, "I'll be careful." And to show how careful he intended to be, he let the cutter run up amidst the reeds, and jumped out with a dozen men, provided with some fiery spirit, and some spun yarn and matches.

"I think you ought to search the reeds first with a few shots from your marines' rifles," said Ali, who was gazing around very distrustfully; and no wonder, for there was every likelihood of some of the Malays being in ambush.

"No need," said Bob, laughing. "We've given them such a lesson as they won't forget for some time, my lad. Come along."

Ali leaped ashore, and they tried to get on board the prahu, which seemed close in to the bank; but finding this was not the case, they returned to the boat, and pushed off through the rustling reeds to row round to the other side, and there board her by means of a rope.

It was well for the little party that they returned as they did, for in twenty places dark figures were stealing through the thick, long reeds quite unseen, but all converging upon the spot where the cutter ran to the shore.

The return to the boat upset the plans of the ambush, but the Malays who formed the party were not beaten; and finding their first plan hopeless, they immediately adopted another, and began creeping through the reeds, hardly making them rustle as they made now for the prahu.

"Heave up a rope, one of you," said Bob, "unless anybody can climb up."

This was as the bowman held the cutter close up against the prahu's side with his boat-hook.

"If one on 'em keeps the cutter alongside, sir, I can get up, and then make fast a rope," said the bowman.

"All right! up with you," said Bob; and as another man held on by one of the big oars that hung in its place, the boatman hooked on his boat-hook in one of the rattan-twisted ropes, and cleverly climbed up, catching the rope that was thrown up and making it fast, when half a dozen of the sailors, with Bob Roberts and Ali, were soon on the short, bamboo deck.

"It seems almost a pity to burn her," said Bob, who was greatly taken by the workmanship of the craft.

"No, no!" said Ali angrily, as his eyes wandered suspiciously about amidst the reeds; "burn her, burn her! the decks have been stained with blood, and many a poor, innocent creature has suffered outrage at the owner's hands. Rajah Gantang was a cruel, bloodthirsty pirate. Let the river be purified from his boats!"

"But," said Bob, laughing, "we might give it a good washing down, and fumigate it below decks, and afterwards give it a coat of paint. It would be purified enough then, and it might be useful."

"I do not understand you," said Ali seriously; "but let your men be quick; I fear danger."

"What a suspicious chap you are, to be sure, Ali," replied Bob. "I'll be bound to say, if the truth was known, there isn't a nigger within a mile of us. Here, look alive, my lads; it seems a pity to burn such a boat; but orders are orders, and we shall have a gun fired directly, by way of recall. There, that will do; lay the oakum there, and pour the spirits over it. She'll burn like a firework."

The men obeyed in a quiet leisurely manner, quite satisfied of there being no danger if their officer saw none; so the oakum and yarn they had brought were heaped up on the bamboo deck, and another lot thrust into a kind of cabin, plenty of the spirit poured on each, and nothing was needed but the application of a match or two for the work of destruction to begin.

Still Bob seemed loth to fire so well-built a vessel, and he stood pointing out good points in the make of the long light boat, counting the number of sweeps she had carried, examining the shot holes and the like—partly in a bravado spirit, for Ali was all anxiety to get on board the steamer again, scenting danger as he did on every breath of wind, while Bob wanted to show him how matter-of-fact and cool a British officer could be.

"Look!" said Ali suddenly, and he laid his hand upon Bob's shoulder.

"Which way?" said Bob quietly. "I can see nothing."

"You will not see," said Ali in a low passionate voice. "You are so brave, but you are so foolish too. Why risk life when there is danger."

"I don't," said Bob coolly.

"You do; there is great danger now," said Ali. "Gantang's men are creeping through the reeds to spear us."

"Jump down in the cutter then," said Bob, "and you will be all right."

Ali drew himself up angrily.

"A Malay chief never knows fear," he said, as he leaned his hands upon the muzzle of the rifle he still carried, and stood there, proud and defiant, like a bronze statue, he was so motionless and calm.

"I didn't mean to offend you, Ali, old fellow," cried Bob. And as the young Malay saw the open, frank, laughing face before him, and the extended hand, he seized it in his.

"I am not offended," said Ali, "but I'm afraid for you and your men."

"What of?" said Bob.

"That!" said Ali, as a spear whizzed through the reeds and stuck in the bamboo deck.

"Yes, it was close," said Bob coolly. "Who has the matches?"

"Here you are, sir," said one of the men.

"All right," said Bob, taking the box. "Down into the boat, all of you. Go on too, Ali."

"No, I stay with you," said the young chief, just as another spear stuck quivering in the deck.

"Ah! I left it a bit too long," said Bob, striking a match as he dived into the cabin, and the next moment a volume of smoke rolled up.

He then lit another match, and held it to the soaked oakum on the deck, spear after spear being thrown, several of which he escaped as by a miracle. Another moment or two, and the thick smoke formed a veil between the two young men and their enemies, who threw spear after spear, but without effect.

"Won't they be fine and mad?" cried Bob. "Here, give me your rifle, Ali, old fellow, and I'll have a couple of shots at them. No, I won't," he said, handing the rifle back; "I can't shoot in cold blood. Come along, or we shall be roasted ready for our friends there, if they are disposed to be cannibals. My word, how she burns!"

His last words were not uncalled for, as the light wood of which the Malay vessel was composed began to blaze furiously; so fast indeed, that the middy and his friend were driven into making rather an undignified retreat before the great leaping tongues of flame and the rolling volumes of smoke that in a few minutes ran from end to end of the vessel.

"Push off, my lads," cried Bob, as he took his place in the stern-sheets, coughing and sneezing from the effects of the pungent smoke. "Give way!" he cried; "there's a signal flying for our return."

Just then a shot came from the steamer as well, and with the Malays beginning to fire at them from among the reeds, the cutter was rowed rapidly back to the steamer's side, the prahu meanwhile blazing furiously, and promising soon to burn down to the water's edge.

"Come, Mr Roberts," cried the lieutenant impatiently; "you have been a long time."

"Yes, sir," said Bob, smiling at Ali, "there was a good deal of spear-throwing towards the last, and we had to dodge them."

"The enemy is not easily frightened," said the lieutenant, as the propeller once more rapidly revolved; "but we must get back, for I fancy I can hear firing below, and I am afraid they are attacking the fort now for a change."

"What shall you do, sir?" said Bob eagerly.

"It is not the custom, Mr Roberts, for the officer in command to explain his plans to his subordinates; but if you must know, I shall run the steamer as close up to the fort as I can, and there keep her, if the Malays do not prove too strong for us."

Then walking to and fro for a few minutes, he ended by going up to where old Dick, with a bandage round his head, was calmly masticating a lump of tobacco.

"I have never thanked you for your capital idea," said the lieutenant. "That hot water saved us in a terrible pinch."

"Yes, sir," said Dick, grinning, "it saved us; but it warn't my idee at all. 'There's lots of boiling water, Dick,' says Mr Roberts, yonder; 'screw on the hose, and tell the engineer what you want. Then when all's ready, and it seems a good time, lay hold of the branch, and play up among the niggers,' sir; and I did as soon as I could, but my head were in that muzzy state that—"

"There is firing going on," said the lieutenant. "Mr Roberts, clear again for action."

"Action, eh?" said old Dick. "Then I can't do better than say another word to the engineer, for of all the ways to clear the decks this hot water system's about the best." So saying, Dick went to screw the hose on the valve once more, muttering and talking to himself the while, and ever and again slapping one of his legs and bursting into a series of chuckles.

"Lor' a mussy me," he said; "and how I argyed with Mr Roberts there about the niggers not being clean. Why that's what put it into his precious head. I wonder what they looks like to-day, after their washing."

"Took the skin off, I should say, Dick," said Bob Roberts, who had heard the old man's words.

"And sarve 'em right, sir," said the old sailor. "What did they mean to do to us but take us right out of our skins, and end us right off at once? And them as plays at bowls must expect rubbers."

So saying, Dick, who had finished his speech without an audience, seemed quite forgetful of his wound, and went down to the engine-room, where the engineer and firemen saluted him with a broad grin; to which Dick responded with one a little broader, as he stood mopping the perspiration from his face.

"Why, Dick, old man," said the engineer, "after this I think we can show them gunners a trick or two. It would have puzzled them to clear the decks like that. However came you to think of it?"

"Think of it?" said Dick. "I shouldn't never have thought of such a game; it was young Mr Roberts, you know. But did you see 'em run?"

"Run!" said the engineer. "Running was nothing to it; you cleared the deck like a shot."

"Shot!" said Dick scornfully; "I should like to see the shot or shell that would do it half as well. Why, look here, my lads, your shot and your shell kills and murders people, knocks off their legs and wings, and precious often their heads. A shot goes bang in amongst a lot o' folk, and there's an end of it. But here I was with the copper branch in my fisties, and I just sprinkled 'em here and there like a shower and—"

"Give it 'em hot," interposed one of the firemen leaning on his shovel.

"Ay, I just did," said Dick; "not as it was much hotter than it is down here, my lads, but hot I did give it 'em, and there wasn't one who would face it. And that brings me down to why I come here."

"Oh, we know why you come here, Dicky," said another of the firemen, who had just been stoking a furnace, and whose face shone with perspiration. "You said to yourself, you did, there's them poor chaps down there in the engine-room getting half-roasted, and with their throats as dry as brown paper; now, being a good-hearted sort of fellow as I am, I'll just go down below and say to 'em, a nice cooling drink o' lime juice and water with a dash o' rum in it, is what you all wants in a big tin can. Shall I get it for you? That's what you come down here to say."

"Blest if ever I see such a clever chap as you are, Sam Walsh," cried Dick, slapping his leg and laughing. "You can read a fellow just as if he was made up o' large print and big leaves. You've really hit it, but you see a drink like that wants mixing; and don't you see, though you may drink it cold it wants hot water to mix it? and that's what I did come about—more hot water."

"To mix up for us, Dick?" said the engineer, laughing.

"No," said Dick, "I didn't say that, my lad," and a bigger grin came over his face; "what I want is the hot water to mix the grog for the niggers, as it seems they liked the last dose so much, that I'm to get ready some more."

"There's plenty—hot enough for anything, Dick," said the engineer, "and I'll keep up the supply."

"Silence below there!" cried a voice; and the engineer gave his subordinates a nod.

"You'd better get on deck, Dick, old man," he said quietly; and then in response to a signal from above, he seized and altered a couple of handles, listened for a fresh order, and slackened the speed of the engine; while Dick went back on deck, satisfied that there was an abundant supply of hot water ready for the next action, and seeing that the island was once more in sight.

A party of Malays were at the head, but they disappeared amidst the trees as the steamer came steadily down stream, while now as they drew nearer the sounds of smart firing could be heard, telling that an engagement was in progress. Smoke, too, was rising slowly above the feathery palm-trees, but not in such dense volumes as that which could still be seen spreading out like a cloud above the jungle, where the prahu was burning.

A sharp series of orders followed, and every man stood at his post; for boats could be seen going to and from the island, and it was plain enough to the meanest comprehension on deck that if they meant to aid the occupants of the fort they had come none too soon.

Chapter Forty Eight
Pleasant Days at the Fort

Matters seemed to grow worse from the moment that Adam Gray started off on his mission to the steamer, and Captain Smithers' brows seemed to have settled into a constant frown, for it was no light matter to be in command of the little fort, right away from aid, and only with a limited supply of provisions. They might be made to last weeks or months; but the end must come, and he saw no chance of help from outside, unless the steamer went off to the nearest station in search thereof.

Then there was the constant worry upon his brain about the expedition and its fate, for there could be no doubt about Ali's news; the force had been divided by cunning, and with such treacherous enemies he felt but little hope of seeing any of the party again.

Fortunately for him and the sharers of his imprisonment—for it was little else—their minds were too much occupied by the defence of the place to give them time to sit and brood over their troubles. There was always something to do, some weak part to strengthen; and Captain Smithers longed for the help of the lieutenant with the steamer to guard outside of the fort.

There was this to consider too—if Lieutenant Johnson could get the "Startler" off the mud, and round to the other side by Dullah's hut and the landing-place, if they were very hard pressed the fort could be abandoned, and, with the women, they could take refuge on board. Or better still— though he felt reluctant to make such an arrangement—the women could be got on board, and then the fort could be defended to the last extremity.

In the course of those next hours while awaiting Gray's return, the Malays made two or three sharp attacks, all of which were repelled; and then, unable to assist, they waited, and listened to the engagement going on upon the other side of the patch of jungle that clothed a part of the island. The heavy reports of the steamer's guns made the frames of the lightly-built dwellings rattle, and the smoke could be seen rising above the trees; but how the tide of war set it was impossible to tell, and Captain Smithers, as he walked up and down, felt as if he would have given anything for a trusty native spy who would have sought out news of what was going on.

Failing this, and not daring to send out a second party, although Tom Long volunteered to go, there was nothing for it but to wait, especially as their besiegers had evidently been greatly augmented in numbers, and one of the soldiers had but to show himself for a moment to bring upon himself a shower of bullets.

The suspense grew maddening, as the noise of the engagement between the prahus and the "Startler" increased. The yells of the Malays could be plainly heard; then the reports of the heavy guns ceased; there was a little rifle firing, the occasional crack of a revolver; and lastly came the faintly-heard noise of men contending in deadly strife.

This lasted for a while, and the occupants of the fort mentally pictured the scene going on, but they could not comprehend the strange shrieking they heard as of men in terrible pain.

Captain Smithers' heart sank, and he glanced at Tom Long, in whose countenance he read a confirmation of his fears; and on looking farther he saw Mrs Major Sandars, with Rachel Linton and her cousin, watching him attentively.

They read his face too as he turned away, and their dread also seemed confirmed.

That ominous silence of the steamer's guns pointed to the fact that she had been boarded by the Malays in too strong parties to be successfully resisted, and a deep gloom sank upon all within the fort.

There was not a man present who would not willingly have gone to the help of those on board the steamer; but not only were they hemmed-in, but had they made a successful sally they had no means of reaching her.

Nothing could be done then but wait, in the hope that some on board would escape and join them; and to this end a constant watch for fugitives was kept up, a dozen men standing ready at the gate to rush out and bring any stragglers in.

Just when they had descended to the greatest depths of misery, and Tom Long was debating with himself as to whether he ought not to go to Miss Linton and try to comfort her, telling her that so long as his arm could wield a sword she might reckon herself to be perfectly safe, there was a peculiar crashing sound, with a fresh burst of yells and cries.

The ladies shuddered, and longed to go in and be alone, but their excitement was such that they felt obliged to stay out there in the opening, risking many bullets, so as to be face to face with the worst.

Something terrible had happened they all knew, and at last the suspense was so great that in the presence of the ladies Captain Smithers exclaimed,— "Long, you will have to take a dozen men and learn the worst!"

Tom Long glanced at Miss Linton, and for answer tightened his sword belt, and then examined the chambers of his revolver.

"I'm ready, sir," he said, and he set his teeth, for he felt that he should not come back alive. Still he was a soldier, and he accepted his duty without flinching, though it did need an effort to be calm.

Just then, as he was about to ask what men he should choose, all ears being attentive to catch the faintest sound from beyond the trees— *Boom—crash*! went a big gun report and the blow it struck, coming almost simultaneously; and as in his excitement Tom Long sent his cap high in air, there was another echoing report, with a familiar beating and panting sound.

"The steamer's off!" Tom Long cried. "Hurrah!"

Discipline was forgotten for the moment, and every man shouted with delight, his cheery "Hurrah!" the cheers being renewed directly after by the following reports of the steamer's guns; and they knew by the beat of the engines that she was going up stream, firing as she went, evidently in pursuit of a prahu.

They had plenty of evidence directly after that the Malays had been beaten, for hurrying parties kept coming from the far side of the island where the engagement had taken place, and as Captain Smithers scanned these with his glass, he could see that their slight garments were soaking wet, baju and sarong clinging to their limbs, and showing that they had had to swim ashore.

This was all proof of their having had a thorough beating; and now, with the steamer no longer aground, but ready to come to their help, the spirits of all rose at as rapid a rate as they had gone down.

But it was to be no time of rest for them. Captain Smithers, to meet the difficulty of there being no water to be obtained, save by going under fire to the spring, or making a dash for the river, had been giving orders for the sinking of a well in a corner of the fort, when word was passed from sentry to sentry of the advance of the enemy. Then shots were fired, at first scattered, then rapidly; and it was at once evident, that in revenge for their defeat afloat, the crews of some of the prahus had joined those on the island in a general attack.

The earth-works were well-made, but they required more men to successfully defend them, and after keeping the enemy at bay by a well-directed fire for some time, Captain Smithers, seeing signs of an approaching rush, and knowing well that this must result in severe loss upon his own side, quietly began to draw his little force away from the earth-works, till he had half in the barracks at the loopholes, from which they began a steady fire over the heads of those at the earthen wall, who, in their turn retired half at a time, the first half joining those who had gone before.

Then as the Malays began to realise that the force at the earthen wall was very weak, and showed signs of coming on to carry it by storm, the defenders delivered a sharp volley and dropped out of sight, stooping down and running across to the barracks' white walls. On seeing that they had given way, the Malays set up a loud cry of triumph, and dashed forward, spear in hand, to occupy the deserted earth-works. They were met by a sharp fire from the barracks, which staggered them for the moment, but they rushed on, and sheltered themselves in the ditch, throwing a few spears at the hindmost of the retreating party; but without effect, for the little garrison was soon shut in and able for the time to defy their assailants.

It was evident, however, that they were not to be left in peace, for the Malays now swarmed around them, and dozens might have been shot down; but Captain Smithers gave orders that the fire should be reserved till they attacked.

Just as they had finished the barricading of the entrance, a cloud of smoke was seen rising from the side of the residency, and this was followed by flames, leaving no doubt that the pleasant little house had been fired by the Malays; and Captain Smithers frowned as he determined to administer severe punishment to the enemy, if for this act alone.

Every opportunity was given him for the administration of the chastisement, the Malays exposing themselves freely, running out of shelter to fire, and then retreating again. Sometimes a fierce demonstration was made by spear-armed men, who came boldly up as if to attack, but soon fell back unmolested, for Captain Smithers felt that no end was to be obtained by simply shooting down a few of the enemy, and his orders were to reserve fire till a fiercer attack was made.

This was not long in coming, and it was made quite unexpectedly, just as, wearied out by his efforts, Captain Smithers had left Tom Long in command, and, yielding to the prayers of the major's wife, had gone in to the mess-room to partake of some refreshment that had been prepared.

He had hardly eaten a mouthful—after visiting first the wounded men, to find them being tended by Rachel Linton and her cousin—before the rattle of musketry and the yelling of the Malays told him that something serious had occurred.

Catching up his sword, he rushed to where he had left Tom Long, and in a few words he learned that from two points the Malays had suddenly commenced their attack, which was now being carried on in so fierce a manner that unless they received a sufficiently severe check to quell their courage, they would force the defences, and overpower the little garrison by sheer weight of numbers.

Fortunate it was that the defences had been so well strengthened, the men firing from behind barricades roughly constructed of tables, the mess forms, and bedding; but in spite of the heavy fire kept up and the number that fell, the Malays dashed up, striving to clamber over, and thrusting their spears through the openings in a way that kept the men back, and nearly crushed the fire that had sputtered from the various loopholes that had been left.

Affairs were growing very serious, for Captain Smithers, who had been going from place to place, advising, cheering, and helping the men, suddenly had his attention drawn to the fact that a large party of Malays were bringing bundles of wood, branches of trees, and handfuls of resin, which they were piling up against the barricaded door.

This he well knew meant fire, and the question arose how it was to be stopped.

"They must never be allowed to light it, my lads, as our lives and those of the ladies would not be worth five minutes' purchase. Cease firing on this side, and reserve your cartridges for any who come to fire the pile."

The men responded with a grim smile, and stood waiting for the party whose duty it would be to try and burn them out; and in this time of mortal peril, when danger of so great a kind stared them in the face, the men stood patiently awaiting their fate, seeming the while to repose the greatest confidence in their captain, and standing ready to obey his orders to the last.

It was a splendid example of what discipline and confidence could effect. The men felt that if their lives were to be saved it would be through carefully carrying out the wishes of their officers, and hence no murmur was heard, each man's face wearing a grim look of determination, that seemed to be intensified as Sergeant Lund came round laden with cartridges, a packet of which he handed to each in turn.

"Some sergeants," he said, as he finished his task and stood rifle in hand by the group whose duty it was to shoot down the bearers of the dammar-torches that they felt sure would be used, "some sergeants would, I dare say, be shaking hands with all their mates at a time like this, and looking at things as all over; but I don't, my lads, for I've a sort of faith in our luck turning up shiny side outwards; so cheer up, all of you."

"All right, sergeant," was the reply.

"I wouldn't trust too much to luck though, my lads," he continued, "but I'd squint straight along the barrel of my rifle when I fired. You may be very sorry for the Malay chap you shoot at, but I'd shoot him first and be very sorry afterwards."

"Right, sergeant," said Private Sim, who had been fighting very manfully all day; "they needn't come and be a-trying to burn us out unless they like, need they?"

"No, Sim," replied the sergeant; "but they will, and it strikes me that they'll be come before long, too. Isn't that smoke in amongst those bushes there?"

"Smoke it is," said one of the men, excitedly.

"Don't jump about like that, my lad, but keep cool, or you'll be wasting your cartridges," said the sergeant. "Where's the captain? He was here just now."

"Gone round the other side," said Sim. "Here they come, sure enough. Look; there's a dozen men with torches."

"All right, my lads," said the sergeant. "I don't see that it matters about the captain not being here; you know your duty."

"Yes, sergeant, to shoot down those men."

"No, no, my lads; what you've got to do is to put those torches out, and the way to do it is with the bayonet. Stand ready there to slip over the breast-work, all of you, then a sharp run, and meet them as they come, and then back again under cover."

As he spoke the smoke of the dammar-torches could be seen, and some ten or twelve Malays came running across from the earth-works to set fire to the pile.

There was not a man behind the breast-work whose breath did not come thick and fast at the sight of the lights; for brave as they were, they knew that once the building they defended caught fire, the dry, sun-baked wood must flare away like so much paper; and there were women shut in there with them, whom it was their duty to defend.

It was no wonder then that the men tightly grasped their bayonet-armed rifles, and stood waiting for the command, that did not come. For just as it was upon the sergeant's lips a panting noise was heard, and as every eye was directed up the river, the masts of the steamer were seen coming along above the trees, and for the present the little garrison felt that they were saved.

Chapter Forty Nine
How Ali went to spy out the Land

A tremor of excitement seemed to run through the attacking party; men hurried here and there; the bearers of the dammar-torches paused irresolute, and it was evident to the besieged that contrary orders were being given.

It was also evident to them that the danger signal they were flying was plainly understood upon the steamer, for the noise of the engine had not been heard a minute before there was the heavy report of one of the guns, and almost simultaneously the crash of a shell, which burst over the heads of the thronging Malays, about fifty yards in front of the fort.

No one seemed to be injured, but this dire instrument of warfare caused a complete scare amidst the attacking party: men running in all directions, and then seeming to go over the same ground once again, as a second shell burst with its harsh tearing metallic-sounding crack.

Again came the report of a gun, and the shell burst where the Malays were thickest, sending them scurrying like wild rabbits to the nearest cover, while the steamer now glided slowly down, closer and closer in shore, till at last she covered the river-face of the fort like an outwork, and a cheer rose from the little garrison, and was answered from the "Startler" as the forces, so to speak, combined, ready to act together for their mutual defence.

As the steamer was rapidly moored in her new position, men being sent ashore with cables from head and stern to make fast to the great trees a few yards from the bank, a rush at them was made by the Malays, but a few well-directed shots from the marines' rifles were sufficient to keep them at bay till the task was done; and the little garrison now joined hands with the steamer's crew in clearing the space between them.

The first step taken by Captain Smithers was to regain possession of the outworks—the portion he had given up from being so short of defenders.

This was accomplished without bloodshed; for upon the Malays gathering in force to withstand his efforts, they were scattered by a shell from the steamer, which cleared the way at once. This being done, and a meeting effected full of hearty congratulations, both soldiers and sailors set to work, armed with spades, to throw up a trench from the outworks of the fort to the river, the ditch being so arranged that it took in for safety the trees to which the steamer was moored, and this latter now became as it were the river-face of the fort.

Night had fallen long before the work was left, and this rendered it necessary for a retreat to fort and steamer for the hours intervening till daybreak, when, no interruption having occurred, the digging was resumed, every man toiling with his rifle at his side till the task was done.

The next question was whether it would not be safer for all to take possession of the steamer, even though the extra defences had been made.

Lieutenant Johnson argued that this would be the better plan, as then they could at any time effect a retreat down the river, and make for Singapore or Penang.

But Captain Smithers refused to listen to this proposal.

"No," he said, "it was quite open to the ladies to take up their abode on board, and probably they would be more secure there than on shore; but so far," he said, "all was surmise about the expeditionary party. For all they knew, Captain Horton, Major Sandars, and their men, might have met with the best of treatment, and at the end of a few days they might return, to find the station abandoned by those left in charge."

"I only hope they may," said the lieutenant. "For my part, I feel certain that the whole of the people hereabouts are under the influence of the rajah, sultan included. But I will not oppose you, Captain Smithers, until matters come to such an extremity that it seems to me that we are uselessly risking life, then I must insist on an evacuation of the fort."

"I will not oppose you then," said Captain Smithers; "but you see that now it is as if I asked you to resign your ship."

Lieutenant Johnson nodded; and it having been resolved to hold out to the last, hoping the while that the expedition might return, the next proceeding seemed to be that of sending out a trustworthy spy or two into the country and amongst the people.

Both Bob Roberts and Tom Long were present at what the latter had importantly called the council of war, but nothing definite was decided upon; and, soon after, the two friends were sitting beneath the shade of one of the trees, the Malays having withdrawn to a distance, and hostilities being for the present suspended.

"I think," said Tom Long, importantly, "that the ladies are quite right in declining to leave the fort. They are much safer there."

Bob Roberts laughed, gazed in his companion's face, and laughed again heartily; to the very great disgust of Tom Long.

"Yes," he said, gruffly, "I dare say it is very funny, and anybody can laugh like a buffoon about such an arrangement; but how are they going to be safe on board a vessel whose officers cannot keep her from running aground."

"Well that's a facer, certainly," said Bob, rather warmly; "but if you come to that, where would you have been if we hadn't come to your help — burnt out by this time, with your precious fort."

"Bob Roberts," said Tom Long, solemnly, "or rather I suppose I ought to say Mr Roberts — you are about the most quarrelsome fellow I ever met."

"You couldn't meet yourself," said Bob, "or you would run against one ten times as quarrelsome."

"If you want to fall out," said the ensign, "you might do it in a gentlemanly way."

"If you want me to punch your head, Tom Long, just say so," cried Bob, hotly.

"I repeat my words," said Tom Long, with hauteur. "If you wish to quarrel, sir, you might do it in a gentlemanly manner."

"Gentlemanly be hanged!" cried Bob. "There's nothing gentlemanly in quarrelling or fighting."

"And refer the matter to friends," continued the young military officer.

Bob's face was red as that of a turkey-cock the moment before, but at these words the anger seemed to pass away like a cloud from before the sun, and he burst into a hearty fit of laughter.

"Oh!" he said, "that's what you mean is it? Swords, or pistols, and seconds, early in the morning, with a doctor on the ground. Oh, I say, Tom Long, this is too delicious."

"Sir!" exclaimed Tom Long.

"I say it's too delicious. Duelling be hanged; it's fools' work; and I'm not quite fool enough to let a friend make a hole, or try to make a hole, in my precious carcase."

"Sir, none but a coward would speak as you are speaking," cried Tom Long, indignantly.

"Oh, wouldn't he?" said Bob. "Well, then, I suppose I'm a coward, for hang me if we don't get running risks enough from these coffee-coloured fellows, without trying it on among ourselves."

"I thought you more of a gentleman," said Tom Long, contemptuously.

"Oh, you did, did you?" said Bob; "and I'm a coward, am I? Well, look here, my lad, it's too hot now, but if you like to come on board to-night, or to-morrow morning, and take off your jacket like a man, I'll have it out with you in the gun-room, and old Dick to see fair, and you can bring Private Gray or Sergeant Lund."

"What do you mean?" said Tom Long, haughtily; "swords or pistols, sir?"

"Do I mean swords or pistols, sir?" said Bob, imitating the other's pompous way; "no, sir, I don't mean either. I reserve those lethal weapons, sir, for Her Majesty's enemies, sir, as an officer and a gentleman should; and when I fall out with a friend, I punch his head with my fist—like a man."

"Like a man!" said Tom Long, in tones of disgust; "like a schoolboy or a blackguard."

"No, sir," said Bob, still mimicking his companion; "the schoolboy or man who uses his fists is to my mind not half such a blackguard as the *gentleman* who tries to kill a fellow in cold blood, and calls it on account of his honour."

"The old contemptible argument," said Tom Long, sneering. "No one but a coward would take refuge behind such excuses."

"Then I'm a coward!" said Bob, cocking his heels up on a chair, and sticking his hands in his pockets. "All right: I'm a coward; and as we used to say at school, 'give me the coward's blow,' and if you do, Tom Long, you see if I don't punch your head."

Tom Long rose, and came at him menacingly, and Bob laughed in his face. "I say, Long, old man," he said, "what a jolly pair of fools we are to quarrel about nothing at all."

"I never want to quarrel," said Tom Long, stiffly, for the other's mirth took him aback, "but when a fellow behaves like a coward—"

"In the face of the enemy," interposed Bob, "kick him out of the service, military or naval, eh? Look here, Tommy."

"For goodness' sake, sir, don't call me by that objectionably childish name," cried the ensign. "How should you like to be called Bobby?"

"Not much, old boy," said the middy; "but I don't much care. Never mind, shake hands. No, don't. Let's do it mentally. Here's old Ali coming, looking as black as a civilian's hat. Hallo, Ali, old chap, ain't you precious proud of your dear fellow-countrymen?"

"Poor fellows; poor fellows!" said Ali, sadly, as he looked from one to the other.

"Poor fellows!" said Long.

"They're a jolly set of sharks, with stings in their tails, that's what they are," said Bob.

"The poor fellows have been crushed down by cruel governments, and made the slaves of piratical rajahs and cowardly sultans," cried Ali, indignantly. "They are a brave set of fellows, and they are only fighting against you because they are set on by their leaders."

"Then all I can say is," said Bob, "that I should like to have a pop at their leaders. But cheer up, old chap, you needn't look so down-hearted."

"Not look down-hearted," cried Ali, passionately, "how can I look otherwise? Where is my father? Where are our friends? What is my position here? Do you think it gives me pleasure to see the poor brave men who are fighting against you shot down by your guns? It makes me wretched."

"Well, never mind," cried Bob, kindly, as he rose and clapped the young chief on the shoulder. "It will all come right in the end."

"I hope so," said Ali; "but tell me, what have you decided to do?"

"Well, that's announcing the secrets of the council of war," said Bob. "Shall I tell him, Long?"

"Oh, yes, we can trust him," replied the ensign. "We are going to stay and fight it out."

"Of course, of course," said Ali, nodding. "You could not give up. You must not give up."

"But we want to get some news of the expedition party by sending a trustworthy spy," said Bob. "Can you get us a man whom you can trust?"

Ali stood thinking for a few moments, and then shook his head sadly.

"They would all say the risk is too great. They would lose their lives if discovered."

"Then what is to be done?" cried Bob.

Ali stood thinking for a few moments in silence, and then he looked frankly from one to the other.

"I will go myself," he said.

The two young men stared at him.

"You?" they exclaimed in one breath. "Why, just now you said the risk was too great."

"That the men would lose their lives!" cried Bob Roberts.

"If they were discovered!" exclaimed Tom Long.

"Yes," said Ali, quietly, and he smiled back in their astonished faces.

"And yet you would run that risk?" said Bob Roberts.

"Yes: why not?"

"But for us?"

"Is one's life to be devoted to oneself?" said Ali calmly. "I am not as you are. You are Christians. I am a follower of the prophet. We call you dogs and giaours. You look upon us with contempt. But men are but men the whole world over, and it seems to me that one's life cannot be better spent than in trying to do good to one's friends."

"But," said Tom Long, "you would be fighting against your friends, the Malays."

"No," said Ali, mournfully. "I should be fighting for them in doing anything that would free them from the rule of idle sensualists and pirates."

"I tell you what," cried Bob Roberts, enthusiastically, "we'll whop old Hamet and Rajah Gantang out of their skins, and you shall be sultan instead, or your father first and you afterwards."

Ali's eyes flashed as he turned them upon the speaker.

"You could be chief banjo, you know," said Bob.

"Chief—banjo?" said Ali, wonderingly.

"No, no; I mean gong—Tumongong," cried Bob.

"Oh, yes," said Ali, smiling. "But no, no: that is a dream. Let us be serious. One of your people could not go, it would be impossible; but I am a Malay, and if I dress myself as a common man—a slave—I could follow where the hunting-party went, and find out all you want to know."

"No, no," cried Bob, earnestly, "I should not like that."

"Like what, Mr Roberts?" said a voice that made them start; and turning sharply, they saw Captain Smithers standing by them, with Lieutenant Johnson.

"Mr Ali here wants to dress up as a common Malay, sir, and go as a spy to get news of the hunting-party."

"It would be excellent," cried the lieutenant. "Mr Ali, you would confer a lasting favour upon us."

"But have you thought of the risk?" said Captain Smithers.

"I have thought of everything," said the young man, quietly.

They all sat down together under the shade of the great tree where they were, and the matter was talked over, it being decided that from time to time Ali was to send messengers with news of his progress, if he could find any trustworthy enough; and all being arranged, he left them, to make preparations for his departure, shaking hands warmly with all, and then going towards the barracks, but only to return directly.

"As you may suppose," he said, "my success depends upon my not being apparently known to you; so if a strange Malay is seen leaving your lines, don't let him be fired at."

"Of course not: I see," exclaimed Captain Smithers. "But shall we see you again?"

"Not to speak to," replied Ali, smiling; and as soon as he had gone, Captain Smithers walked across the ground to give orders about a strange Malay being allowed to leave.

Lieutenant Johnson returned on board the steamer with Bob Roberts; and Tom Long, after seating himself comfortably in one chair with his legs in another, went off fast asleep.

Half an hour after, when all was very still in the burning heat of the sun, when not a breath of air rippled the river or rustled through the trees; when Englishman and Malay were resting, and the very sentries had hard work to keep from going to sleep at their posts, there was a soft rustling noise in the tree beneath which Tom Long was sleeping; and after this had been repeated several times a lithe Malay softly descended till he was within six or eight feet of the ground, when he slipped and fell, but regained his feet instantly, as Tom Long started into wakefulness and clapped his hand to his sword, upon seeing the strange Malay just before him.

The Malay, however, raised one hand deprecatingly, and smiled a very significant smile as he turned to go.

"Here, stop! surrender! Why—Oh! I say, Ali; that's capital," he said, as the Malay still smiled at him. "You quite took me in."

The Malay smiled and nodded, and walked straight off to where a sentry was watching them both; and the man, seeing the Malay come straight from his officer, made way, saluted, and the dark figure passed from the fortified lines and walked away towards where the enemy lay amongst the trees.

"That's a brave thing to do," muttered Tom Long, and resuming his seat he took another sleep, and was awakened the next time by Captain Smithers laying his hand upon his shoulder.

"Ali has gone," he said.

"Yes, I know," said Tom Long. "He quite took me in. It was a splendid disguise."

"Capital!" said Captain Smithers. "The very sentries were puzzled."

"Yes, of course they would be," replied Tom Long; and the captain walked away.

"The sentries must have been puzzled before he came to me," said Tom Long to himself. "That man yonder, though, seemed to take it as a matter of course. I shall be very glad, though, when all this hiding and dodging is over, and the hunting-party are back, for I am not going to believe that they are in danger after all."

And yet Tom Long did believe it, and was as uneasy as the rest; but it was his way of trying to put a good face upon matters.

Chapter Fifty
How Bob fished for Miss Linton

To the surprise and gratification of the English party, the jungle-station remained unmolested for the next two days, giving them ample time to make such little additions to the defences as the officers thought needful. The coming of the steamer gave the occupants of the fort command of the water and a way of retreat in case of extremities; moreover, they had the chance of sharing the ship's provisions. So that with the knowledge of their power of resistance a feeling of confidence began to exist, especially as it was evident that the Malays had been taught the danger of molesting the little party.

The enemy came and went from the island in large numbers, but kept entirely aloof, making no attempt to communicate; while their strange silence excited suspicion in Captain Smithers' mind that some plot was hatching.

The lieutenant joined him in thinking that there was cause for suspicion, and more stringent watch was kept.

Old Dick regretted keenly that for reasons of economy the furnace fires could not be kept up, for he argued still that plenty of hot water was all that was needed to keep them safe. He had, however, to be content with the ordinary precautions, promising himself the extraordinary as soon as the fires were lit.

The ladies had full occupation in tending the wounded, an occupation which saved them from much thinking; for there were no tidings of the party, and now that so long a time had elapsed it became evident that their worst fears would be realised.

In fact the officers began to debate whether the hour had not arrived when they ought to retreat; but the idea was set aside, and once more they determined to hold the station till help should come, since for the steamer to go in search of help was to condemn the little garrison of the fort to destruction.

And now as the hours slowly crept by, with the heat and inaction growing more and more difficult to bear, every thought was directed to the envoy they had sent out, and they waited anxiously for Ali's return, or for some messenger with tidings at his hands.

Though the Malays refrained from attack so long as the occupants of the station kept within their lines, any attempt at quitting the fort at once drew fire. Consequently the supplies within had to suffice, and middy and ensign thought gloomily of the past, when sampans brought daily an abundance of delicious fruit, when flowers were abundant, and fish in plenty was supplied.

Now it was bread or biscuit, and preserved meat either salt or tinned, and preserved vegetables, and so much soup that Bob Roberts said a man might just as well be living in a workhouse.

That evening he made up his mind to try for some fish, and aided and abetted by Dick, a line was rigged up, and payed out over the steamer's stern, the stream carrying down the baited hook, but only into a place where there was no likelihood of a fish being caught. So another line was attached, and another, and another—long sea-lines each of them, till Bob Roberts sat fishing with the end of a line in his hand and his bait about a quarter of a mile down the stream.

To his great delight he found the plan to answer, for before long he felt a tug, and drew in a good-sized fish. This done, he rebaited, and tried again, sometimes catching, sometimes losing, a couple dropping off the hook just as they were raised up level with the deck.

It was about an hour before sunset that Bob Roberts set Dick to work winding up the lines on the reels to dry, and then, having placed the brilliantly scaled fish in the basket, he obtained leave from the lieutenant, who looked longingly at the catch, and involuntarily made the noise with his lips customary with some people at the sight of anything nice.

"What are you going to do with those, Roberts?" he said.

"Take them to the ladies, sir."

"Ah! yes: of course, the ladies first. We ought to study the ladies. But do you know, Roberts, I'm not a ladies' man, and I feel an intense desire to have one of those fish—broiled."

"Yes, sir, of course; but I'll come back and catch some more."

"Yes, do," said Lieutenant Johnson, gazing longingly at the fish. "There," he cried hastily; "for goodness' sake be off with them, Roberts, or I shall impound the lot and hand them over to the cook. You ought not to put such temptations in a weak man's way."

"All right, sir," said Bob, and he hurried over the side and made for the barracks, where, to his great delight, he met Rachel Linton, looking very pale and ill, coming away from the temporary hospital with her cousin.

"I've brought you some fish, Miss Linton," he said. "I thought they would be welcome just now, as there are no fresh provisions."

"Doubly welcome, Mr Roberts," cried Miss Linton, with her face lighting up. "Oh! Mary, I am glad. Mr Roberts, I can never thank you enough."

Bob felt rather disgusted that the idol he had worshipped should be so fond of the good things of this life.

"I have been longing for fresh fish, and fruit, and flowers, so, Mr Roberts," she continued. "You cannot get me any fruit or flowers, I suppose?"

"I could go and try for some," said Bob, rather glumly, "but you mustn't be surprised if I don't come back."

"Oh, no, no; you must not run any risks," cried Rachel Linton. "That would be madness, but I'd give anything for some fruit now."

"She'd better think about her father," thought Bob, "instead of eating and drinking."

"Those poor wounded fellows do suffer so for want of change; but this fish will be delicious. Poor Parker will eat some, I know. If you can get any fruit for my hospital people, pray do so, Mr Roberts."

"That I will, Miss Linton," he cried joyously.

"And you'll catch me some more fish for the poor fellows?"

"Are you going to give all these to the wounded men, Miss Linton?" he said.

"Yes; of course," she replied.

"Why she's an angel," thought Bob to himself, "and I was giving her the credit of being a regular pig."

"Messenger? For me?" exclaimed Captain Smithers, rising up as a soldier advanced.

"Yes sir; it's a Malay, and he says he has been sent by the young chief, Ali."

Chapter Fifty One
Dealings with the Deep

There was no little excitement at this announcement, and Captain Smithers sent at once for Lieutenant Johnson from the steamer, while a file of soldiers went for the messenger who had asked for admission.

The ladies were too much interested to think of leaving, so Mary Sinclair ran to fetch Mrs Major Sandars, and returned with her to see that a rough-looking Malay had been brought up to the group she had left.

Captain Smithers waited a few moments, to allow of the coming of the lieutenant; and meanwhile they all gazed at the Malay, a wild, half-naked fellow, whose scraps of clothing were torn by contact with thorns, and being soaked with water clung to his copper-coloured skin.

He was scratched and bleeding, and gazed sharply round from one to the other in a strange wild-eyed way, as if feeling that he was not safe.

Just then the lieutenant came hurrying up, and the Malay, evidently supposing him to be the officer he sought, began to unfasten a knot in his sarong, from which he took a short piece of bamboo about the size of a man's finger. One end of this was plugged with a piece of pith, and this he drew out, and then from inside, neatly rolled up and quite dry, a little piece of paper.

"You Cap-tain Smit-ter?" said the Malay.

"No, my man, that is the captain," said the lieutenant, pointing. "Captain Smit-ter. Ali Rajah send," said the man, holding out the paper.

"Did Ali send us this?" said the captain, eagerly.

"Cap-tain Smit-ter, Ali Rajah send," said the man again.

"Where did you leave him?" said the captain.

"Cap-tain Smit-ter, Ali Rajah send," repeated the man, parrot fashion, showing plainly enough that he had been trained to use these words and no more.

Captain Smithers unrolled the scrap of native paper to find written thereon,—

"Found the party. Fighting for life in a stockade. Send help in steamer up right river.—Ali."

"Have you come straight from him?" exclaimed the captain, eagerly.

"Cap-tain Smit-ter, Ali Rajah send," said the man again.

"Where is Wilson?" cried the captain, "or Gray? Ah, you are here, Gray. You have made some progress with the Malay tongue. See what this man knows."

Private Gray came forward, and by degrees, and with no little difficulty, learned from the Malay that the English party were in an old stockade upon a branch of the river, forty miles away, defending themselves against a strong body of the sultan's forces.

"Ask if they are well," said the captain.

"He says there are many ill, and many wounded, and that they have buried many under the palm-trees," said Gray, in a low sad voice, "and that when the young chief, Ali, came upon them, they were at the last extremity from weakness and hunger."

Rachel Linton uttered a low wail, but on Mrs Major Sandars passing an arm round her, she made an effort and mastered her emotion, fixing her eyes on Adam Gray as, in a low, deep voice he continued the narrative after, at Captain Smithers' wish, again questioning the Malay.

"He says that after giving him the message to bear, the young chief, Ali, left him, saying that he was about to try and join the party in the old stockade, and fight with them to the end!"

There was a mournful silence at this, and for a few moments no one spoke. Then Captain Smithers leaned towards Lieutenant Johnson.

"Have you any questions to put?" he said.

"Yes," replied the lieutenant, and he turned round to their interpreter.

"Tell me, Gray, what is your opinion of the messenger?"

"At first, sir, I thought him genuine; but since then, there is something in his manner that makes me doubt the truth of his tale."

"And yet it seems feasible?"

"Yes, sir, it does; and I confess I have little cause for doubting him; but still I do."

Lieutenant Johnson turned to Captain Smithers, and they went aside for a few minutes talking earnestly together, while all present watched eagerly for the next scene in the drama they were passing through.

"Gray," said Captain Smithers then, sharply, "ask the messenger if he knows where the old stockade is."

"He says *yes*, sir, perfectly well."

"Ask him if he will guide the steamer there."

"Yes!" was the reply, "if the English officers would protect him from his people, and not let him be seen."

"Tell him," said Captain Smithers, "that if he is faithful he will be handsomely paid; if he is treacherous, he will be hung to the yard-arm of the steamer, and his body thrown to the crocodiles."

Gray interpreted this to the Malay, who smiled, uncovered the hilt of his kris, drew it, took it by the blade, and knelt down before the officers, placing the point upright on the left shoulder close to his neck, then reaching out with his right hand, he motioned to Captain Smithers to strike the weapon down into his breast.

"He says his life is yours, sir, and bids you kill him if he does not lead you to the stockade."

"One more question," said Lieutenant Johnson. "Ask him if there is water enough up the right river?"

Gray questioned the Malay, who nodded eagerly and then shook his head.

"He says there is plenty of water, for the river is narrow and very deep, all but in one place, about a mile from the stockade, and of that he is not sure, he will not pledge himself to its being sufficiently deep; but all Rajah Gantang's prahus have gone up and down in safety."

"That will do," said the lieutenant.

"Yes," said Captain Smithers, "take him aside, give him some food, and guard him well."

It fell to the lot of Adam Gray to take charge of the Malay who ate voraciously of what was placed before him, and then smiling his satisfaction he prepared himself a piece of betel-nut, and lying down in the shade went off fast asleep, evidently wearied out.

Meanwhile a short consultation was held, during which it was settled that at any risk the steamer must go to the assistance of the beleaguered party, Captain Smithers being on the alert to retire into the barracks when it became necessary.

This place he would have to hold with stubborn determination, knowing that the steamer could not be long away, and that Lieutenant Johnson was going with the knowledge that those he left behind were in need of help.

The fires were lit on the instant, and every effort made to get the steam up, but all was done as quietly as possible, so as not to take the attention of the Malays, and about ten o'clock all was ready for the start, when Adam Gray went and roused up the Malay.

The man rose, shook himself, and then accompanied his guide without a word, climbing the side of the steamer, where everything was ready; the cables were cast loose, and at half-steam the great vessel moved softly up the river by the light of the stars, which just made their way visible.

As far as they could see, the alarm of the departure had not been spread; and the steamer glided away so softly, and with so little noise, that there was the chance of her escaping the notice of the Malays, who might not find out their departure until morning.

This would delay any attack that might be made for many hours; but all the same, Captain Smithers felt it better to at once evacuate the outer works, and two hours after the steamer had glided away, almost invisible to those who saw her go, the outer works were lying unguarded, and the whole of the force safely barricaded in the stronghold, with every sentry on the alert.

Everything had been done in the quietest manner. There was neither noise nor loud order; the men caught the lightest whisper; and there was something weird and strange-looking in the silent figures moving here and there; but nothing like so weird of aspect as about a couple of dozen dark shadows that were creeping over the ground taking advantage of every bush or inequality of the ground to cover their movements till they reached the deserted earth-works and crouched there exultingly.

An hour later the sky was overclouded; and in the darkness the Malays came crowding up by hundreds, evidently ready for an assault, while most ominous of all was the fact that numbers of them bore bundles of light wood, and some lumps of dammar ready to continue the task they had had to give up consequent upon the steamer's return.

Chapter Fifty Two
How the Steamer went up the
Right Arm of the River

A night journey on a river when the stars give but little light and the banks are dense jungle overhanging the water's edge, is one of no little difficulty. Certainly the crew of the steamer had upon their side the fact, that the stream, though swift, was deep, and its bottom mud. There were no rocks and cataracts to encounter in its lower course; and even if they did run aground there was but little risk to the vessel. But all the same the most constant watchfulness was needed, and Lieutenant Johnson himself joined the look-out at the bows, communicating by a chain of his men with the engine-room and man at the wheel.

For some distance after leaving the island they proceeded very slowly, little more than mastering the stream; but as soon as they felt that they were beyond hearing the speed was increased, and for some miles—through which the course of the river was well-known—the "Startler" proceeded at a pretty good rate, so that by morning half the journey was accomplished, and they were abreast of the stockade they had attacked and destroyed.

About a couple of miles past this the course of the right river opened out, one that a navigator strange to the river would have hesitated to take, for it was narrow at the mouth, overgrown with trees, and seemed to form a chain of lakes, that were one blaze of colour with the blossom of the lotus.

On the other hand, what seemed the regular course of the river ran broad and clear, and apparently without obstruction of any kind.

The Malay, who was leaning over the bulwark with his mouth distended with betel, pointed one brown arm towards the narrow branch, and the steamer's engines were slackened and nearly stopped while a boat was lowered, and the crew rowed some little distance along the winding, sluggish stream, sounding every few yards, to find the river extremely deep with muddy bottom; and as it seemed to wind right on precisely the same in character, they returned and reported the result to the lieutenant, who at once gave orders, and the steamer entered the narrow, winding way.

To all appearance they might have been the first visitors to those regions, so haunted was the strangely beautiful scene by wild creatures. Birds in abundance fled at their approach. Now it was a white eagle, then a vividly plumaged kingfisher, or a kind of black, racket-tailed daw with glossy plumage. Parrots of a diminutive size and dazzling green plumage flitted before them; and from time to time the lotus leaves were agitated by a shoal of fish, that alarmed by the wash of the steamer rushed away.

Every now and then, too, Bob Roberts, who was feasting on what passed like a glorious panorama before him, had his adventure with Ali in the shooting-trip brought vividly to mind, for some huge reptile or another shuffled into the slow stream, while others lay sluggishly basking, and ill-disposed to move.

Their progress was slow, for the screw-propeller was more than once fouled by the thick weed through which they ploughed their way. So dense was it that at times it gathered in large cables, stretching from bank to bank, and literally barring further progress, till the steamer was backed and driven at full speed against the obstruction, which divided and swept off in hillocks to starboard and to port.

Then a more open stretch of water would be gained, widening quite into a lake, and framed in glorious tropical verdure; large pools would be quite free from vegetable growth, and so clear that the bright scales of the fish could be seen flashing far below. Then the river seemed to wind its way through dense growths of lily and other water plants, amidst which water-fowl in endless numbers disported themselves, but fled away at the sight of the steamer, panting onward through this wilderness of beauty.

For in spite of the anxiety felt by all, and their eagerness to reach the spot where their friends were in peril, it was impossible to help gazing with wonder and admiration at the loveliness of all around. Where the stream narrowed, the great trees growing to the water's edge formed huge walls of verdure, in parts a hundred—two hundred feet high; and over and amidst these wreathed and twined the beautiful creepers, filling up every gap with leaves of the most delicious, tender green. Then a tree would be passed one mass of white and tinted blossoms, another of scarlet, and again another of rich crimson, while in every damp, sun-flecked opening wondrous orchids could be seen carpeting the earth with their strange forms and glowing colours. Pitcher-plants too, some of huge size, dotted the ground every here and there where the steamer passed close to the shore—so close at times that the ends of the yards brushed the trees; and yet the vessel took no harm, for the deep water ran in places to the banks, and though often half covered with weedy growth, the river was canal-like in its deeper parts, where the sluggish stream steadily flowed along to join its more rapid brother miles below.

For some time now Lieutenant Johnson had been bitterly regretting that he had not insisted upon bringing Private Gray, so as to have an interpreter, for his own knowledge of the Malay tongue was almost *nil*. And yet he was obliged to own that it would have been unjust to rob them at the station of part of their strength, when at any moment they might want it all.

Bob Roberts was the better Malay scholar of the two, but his vocabulary only extended to asking for a durian, Good morning! How are you? and the favourite Malay proverbial saying,—"*Apa boleh booat*"—It was to be, or It couldn't be helped.

They had been progressing now for hours, and the heat was insufferable—a heavy, moist heat, in that narrow way, shut in between two walls of verdure, and yet there seemed to be no signs of their journey being nearly ended. Under the circumstances Bob Roberts was set to try and get some information out of their guide, whom he tried with "Good morning," in the Malay tongue; and then, after a civil answer to his remark, plunged at once into plain English with,—

"How much farther is it?"

The Malay looked hard in his eyes, and Bob repeated the question.

The Malay seemed to divine what he meant, for he raised one bare brown arm and pointed forward along the course of the river.

It was a mute but conclusive reply, telling the middy plainly enough that they had farther to go, and once more the attention of all was taken up by the navigation of the narrow winding channel.

Still there was no fault to be found with Ali's message, for the water was deep, and though the steamer seemed at times to be running right into the bank, there was always room to turn what looked to be an ugly curve, and onward they went through the dense jungle.

On either side the primeval forest seemed to stretch away, and where there were changes of a more park-like character, so rare was the sight of a human being there that the shy pea-fowl, all metallic plumage and glorious eyes, could be seen gazing at the steamer before taking flight. There were deer too seen occasionally, and had this been a pleasure-trip the sportsman would have had ample use for rifle or gun.

But this was no pleasure-trip, for the deck was cleared for action, and the men were at their quarters, ready to send shot or shell hurtling through the jungle whenever there should be a reason for such a step.

Another hour, and another, and still the Malay guide pointed before him, gesticulating a little sometimes as if bidding them hasten onwards.

The speed was increased at such times, though it was risky, for the narrowness of the course, and the size of the steamer, rendered the greatest care necessary to avoid running her bows in among the trees.

Lieutenant Johnson stamped impatiently at last as the sun was descending behind the trees, and still the Malay pointed onwards.

"It is enough to make one think it a wild goose chase!" he exclaimed. "We have made a grievous mistake in not having an interpreter. Roberts, you ought to be able to speak the Malay tongue."

"Yes, sir," said Bob, "I ought!" And then to himself, "So ought you!"

Another hour and they were passing through a denser part than ever; so close were they that the large drooping boughs of some of the trees cracked and rustled and snapped as they passed by to get to what seemed to be quite a lagoon shining clear and silvery, as seen by those on board the steamer through quite a tunnel of overhanging branches.

"We ought to be able to hear firing by this time if it is going on at the stockade," said the lieutenant. "What a place to bring Her Majesty's ship into! If I did not know that those poor fellows were anxiously expecting help, not a fathom further would I take the steamer than into yon open water to-night! Here! fetch that Malay fellow here, and let's see if we cannot get something out of him!"

Bob Roberts went forward to where the Malay stood leaning over the bulwarks gazing at the trees on either side—at least he went to where the Malay did stand gazing at the trees, but now to Bob's astonishment the man was not there!

"Where's the Malay guide?" he said sharply to Dick, who was nearest to him.

"Well, sir, if you call that there chap a guide," said Dick, "I've done."

"I say where's the Malay guide?" said Bob, angrily.

"Haven't seen him, sir," said Dick, touching his cap.

"But he was standing here not ten minutes ago, just before we brushed against those trees!" exclaimed the young officer.

"Well yes, sir, I remember as he was," said old Dick, and several of the sailors were ready to affirm that they saw him not five minutes before.

A look round the deck showed that he was not there, and Bob stood looking puzzled; for the man had evidently looked upon himself almost as a prisoner, and not free to go about; he had consequently stood leaning against the port bulwark all the time, except when he had squatted on the deck to partake of the food supplied to him.

"Couldn't have been knocked overboard by the boughs, could he, sir?" said Dick.

"Impossible!" exclaimed the middy; and he hurried off to report the fact that the Malay was missing.

"Are you sure?" exclaimed the lieutenant sharply.

"Certain, sir! He's nowhere on deck!"

"I thought as much!" cried the lieutenant angrily. "Good heavens, Roberts! that we could have been such idiots! Gray was right!"

"I do not understand you, sir."

"Understand? It's plain enough! That man, Private Gray, said he suspected the fellow, and yet we allowed him to gull us with his plausible story. Here, look sharp there!" he cried, as the steamer stood out now free of the tunnel-like canal through which she had passed, and was now approaching the centre of a tolerably broad lagoon.

The lieutenant gave his command in short, sharp, decisive tones, and a minute later a little anchor fell with a splash into the water, and the steamer swung in the just perceptible stream.

"I dare not attempt the journey back to-night, Roberts," he said. "We should be aground in the thick darkness before we had gone a mile."

"But won't you go forward, sir? We must be near the stockade!" exclaimed Bob.

"If we go on till the river becomes a ditch, we shall find no stockade here, Roberts!" cried the lieutenant. "Why should there be one? There is neither campong nor sampan upon the river, and it is evident that there is no trade. No, Roberts, we have been tricked—cheated, and we must get back at full speed as soon as day begins to break. I have been uncomfortable for hours now, as I felt that our poor friends could never have come through such a forest as this. It is only passable for beasts!"

"But the Malay and his message?"

"The Malay is as great a cheat as the old fruit-seller; and that message was never written by young Ali, unless he, too, is an enemy!"

"My life upon it, he is not," cried Bob.

"Then either he has been killed, or our plans were overheard, or betrayed, or something or another! That fellow—I see it all now it is too late—has quietly led us up here, awaiting his chance, and it came when those big boughs swept the side. He swung himself into one of the trees, and is by this time on his way back to his friends."

"But the jungle is not passable!" said Bob.

"Then he will make a bamboo raft and get down the river. Oh, that we could be such fools!"

Bob Roberts stood in the gathering darkness staring at his superior officer, and trying hard to believe that the Malay might have been swept over by accident; but by degrees he felt his mind veering round to the lieutenant's ideas.

The next minute orders were being given respecting the watch on deck, every light was extinguished, and extra care taken lest they should have been led into a trap and attempts be made to board the steamer during the night. But as the hours glided on, all they heard was the distant roar of some beast of prey, or an occasional splash in the water—sounds that had a strange attraction for Bob Roberts, as, with no thought of going to his cot, he leaned against the bulwark watching the fire-flies amid the trees, and mournfully wondered how they were getting on at the station, and what had become of Ali, shuddering again and again as the lieutenant's ominous words recurred to his mind.

Chapter Fifty Three
Private Sim is very Wide Awake

Lieutenant Johnson had said that in all probability Ali had been killed, this being of course his surmise, for he had no real reason for such an assertion. He was quite right, though, about having been tricked, for one of Rajah Gantang's cleverest spies after hearing from his hiding-place the plans that had been made, assumed the part of Ali in disguise, and passed unchallenged by the sentries to go straight to the rajah and plan with him a way to divide the forces by sending the steamer upon a false scent.

This had been done, with the success that has been seen. But though the little garrison was awakened to a sense of its danger very soon after the steamer had taken its departure, it did not realise the fact that they had all been deceived.

All the requisite precautions had been taken, and saving the guard, the little garrison had lain down to sleep, according to Captain Smithers' instructions, for he had addressed them before they were dismissed.

"There may be no danger," he had said, "but we must be on the alert, so let every man lie down in his clothes, with his arms close at hand. Sergeant Lund, see that the men's pouches are supplied with cartridges. To-morrow, my lads, I hope to see the steamer back, with our rescued friends!"

The men gave a cheer and departed. The guard was relieved, and Captain Smithers stood talking to Tom Long.

"My dear lad," said the former, "there is not the slightest need for any such proceeding. Go and lie down. I shall visit the sentries for the first half of the night, and I will call you about three."

"I don't feel much disposed for sleep," said Tom Long, who looked uneasy.

"You are not well. The heat has overdone you a little. You go and have a good sleep," said the captain. "To-morrow I hope we shall have the doctor back among us to set us right."

"I hope so, too," said Tom Long, gloomily; and going to his quarters he lay down, with his sword and revolver beside him, ready for use.

Adam Gray was off duty, and he, too, had gone to lie down. But he could not sleep, neither did he wish to do anything else but lie there and think about Rachel Linton, and how pale and unhappy she appeared. He longed to speak words of comfort to her, and to say others as well; but he dared not, for his position forbade it. Still he could not help feeling that she did not look unkindly upon him, nor seem to consider him to be one of the ordinary soldiers.

He sighed as he thought of other days, and then lay listening to the humming noise made by the mosquitoes—wondered whether Rachel Linton was asleep or awake—whether, if she was awake, she was thinking of him.

Then he drove away the thoughts with an angry exclamation, and determined to think about her no more. But as he turned his face to the open window, and listened to the faint hum of the night insects, Rachel Linton's face came back, and he was thinking of her again, and this time in connection with Captain Smithers.

He knew the captain loved her, and instinctively hated him—Private Gray. He felt, too, that by some means or another the captain knew of, and hated him for, his presumptuous love; the more so that Rachel Linton did not seem to care in the slightest degree for the captain's advances, but rather avoided him.

Private Gray turned again and again, but he could not lie there any longer for the uneasy feeling that tormented him.

The men in the long room slept easily enough, but he could not, and he told himself that he might just as well get up and go and watch with one of the sentries, for then he would be doing something towards protecting the station.

He rose then softly, and fastening on his belt with the bayonet attached, he went cautiously out into the night air, to see that though the stars twinkled brightly, the night was very dark. All was perfectly still, and as he went cautiously round every man seemed to be on the watch, when suddenly a thought struck him which sent a cold shiver through his breast.

He was standing just beneath the window of the officers' quarters, where he knew that Rachel Linton and her cousin would be sleeping, and the sentry nearest, the man who should be on the keenest watch, was, if he was not mistaken, Private Sim.

He could not make out for certain from where he stood, but he felt almost certain that this was the case, and that Sim was occupying the most important outpost of the little fort.

With his heart beating wildly he crept back to the place where the men lay asleep, and going on tiptoe from one to the other, he satisfied himself by the dim light of the lamp swinging from the roof that Private Sim was not there.

"It was utter madness," he muttered to himself. "Lund should have known," and in his excitement he recalled to mind the night when he had found him asleep.

He remembered, too, what a fearful night that was, and he felt that this might prove to be just as dangerous, as he hurried back, catching up his rifle and pouch as he went, and then going quietly along to where Private Sim was stationed.

It was undoubtedly the weakest spot about the fort, and in place of one untrustworthy man, two of the most trusty should have been stationed there. By some error of judgment, however, this was not done, and Private Sim held the lives of all in the little fort within his hand.

Gray thought that after all he might be misjudging him, and therefore he went on cautiously, listening as he stopped from time to time, and expecting to be challenged; but there was no sound to be heard, and as Gray went closer it seemed to him as if no sentry had been placed there. But as he went nearer there was no error of judgment upon his part. It was as he suspected. Private Sim was seated on the ground, his rifle across his lap, fast asleep, and quite oblivious of the fact that his messmate stood close beside him, panting with rage and disgust.

"You scoundrel!" he cried in a low, passionate voice. "Do you not know that the punishment may be death for sleeping at a time like this?"

As he spoke he struck the sleeper heavily upon the head with the butt of his rifle, and Sim started up and grappled with him, just as a dozen Malays sprang out of the darkness, and made at the defence between them.

The struggle between the two was but brief, for Gray threw Sim off, and brought his bayonet to bear against the Malays, forgetting in his excitement to load and fire, so that it was Sim's rifle that gave the alarm.

For the next few minutes the two men fought side by side, their bayonets keeping the Malays back every time they strove to enter the place, and driving them off successfully till help came, and two or three volleys did the rest.

"How was this? How did it happen that you did not see the enemy approaching sooner, Private Sim?" said Captain Smithers, sternly.

Sim trembled for his life, knowing as he did that over matters of discipline the captain was a stern man, and that he must expect no mercy for his fault if Gray spoke out, and told all he knew; so he exclaimed hastily, and with a malicious look at Gray,—

"How could I, sir, when there are traitors in the camp?"

"Traitors! What do you mean?"

"I mean a traitor, sir! Private Gray there came up behind me, leaped upon me, and held his hand over my mouth to keep me still, while he whistled to the Malays to come in by the opening, there."

"You lying—"

"Silence, Private Gray!" cried Captain Smithers, and all that was evil in his nature came to the surface, as he felt that here was an opportunity for disgracing, if not putting his rival to death; and a strange feeling of savage joy animated him for the moment. "Silence, Private Gray!" he cried. "Speak out, Private Sim. Do you mean to assert that this man served you as you say?"

"Look at me, sir!" cried Sim, showing his disordered uniform. "That was done in the struggle; and I did not fire as soon as I could have wished."

"Show me your rifle, Sim," said the captain.

Sim held out his piece, while, choking with rage and astonishment, Gray stood speechless in their midst.

The piece was examined, and it had just been discharged.

"Show me your piece, Gray," said Captain Smithers.

Gray held it out, and it was quite clean. It was not loaded, and it had not lately been discharged.

"I tried as hard as I could, captain!" whined Sim; "but he came upon me so sudden like, that I was mastered at once."

"What were you doing there, Gray? You were not on duty. Your place was in bed."

"I could not sleep, sir," said Gray. "I doubted this man, and I came to see."

"Why, you jumped right on me, sudden like, out of the darkness!" said Sim.

"Silence, Sim!" said the Captain. "Gray, this charge must be investigated. You are under arrest. Sergeant, put this man in irons!"

"But, Captain—"

"Silence, sir! You can make your defence when you are tried by court-martial."

"I hope, captain," whined Sim, "that it won't be my doing as he's punished. I'd a deal rather help a fellow than get him into trouble."

"You are on duty, sir! Attend to your post!" cried Captain Smithers.

He turned angrily then on Private Gray, who was so cruelly mortified, especially as, glancing upward, he saw the window was open, and Rachel Linton and her cousin there, that he could not or would not speak a word in his defence. He gave Sim a look that made that scoundrel shiver, and then said to himself:

"She will not believe that I am a traitor!"

He glanced involuntarily upwards as this thought occurred to him, and the captain ground his teeth with rage as he saw the glance; but feeling as he did that he had his rival beneath his heel, a glow of triumph ran through him.

The next moment, though, all that was gentlemanly and true came to the surface, and he felt that Private Gray was not the man who could be guilty of such a crime. Sim must be the offending party, and Gray be too proud to speak. He could not iron him, or doubt his honour; he was too true a man; and as Sergeant Lund unwillingly came forward with a file of men, the captain motioned him back.

"This is no time for making prisoners," he said. "Sergeant, change the sentry here. Place two men on guard. Private Sim, go to the guard-room: I may want to question you. Private Gray, this is an awful charge against you, and if you are guilty you will be shot."

There was a faint sound as of some one's breath catching at the window above, but it was heard by Captain Smithers and Private Gray alone as they stood face to face.

"I know it, captain!" said Gray, quietly.

"We are in face of the enemy," continued Captain Smithers. "Take your rifle again, and help to defend the place. You had better die by the spear of a Malay. Go to the guard-room now; and mind, if any words pass between you and Private Sim—"

"Quick, sir, the alarm!" cried Gray, pointing out beneath the stars. "The enemy!"

"Fire, sentry!" cried Captain Smithers; and the report of a rifle rang out on the still night air, for the Malays were advancing in force.

Fresh shots were fired on all sides as the men turned out, and were at their various places in a very few moments, the wisdom of the captain's commands being manifest; and as he saw Private Gray go down on one knee and begin firing, with careful aim, at the advancing enemy,—"He's no traitor," he muttered; "and I never doubted him at heart."

He had no time for further thought, for the attack had become general, and the Malays seemed furious, striving hard to gain an entry, but always encountering one or two bayonets at every point, till, after half an hour's fierce struggle, they drew back, leaving a number of dead and wounded around the place.

The defenders of the little fort drew breath at this, and as the firing ceased, the major's wife, with Rachel Linton and her cousin, came round, first with refreshments for the exhausted men, and, as soon as they were distributed, began to bandage those who were wounded.

It was while they were busy over this task, that in the darkness Rachel Linton came upon a man leaning against the breast-work, gazing attentively out at the position of the enemy.

"Are you wounded?" she asked; and at her words Private Gray started round and faced her.

"Only slightly," he said, "in body—but deeply in spirit."

"Let me bind your wound," said Rachel Linton, hoarsely, and her voice trembled as she spoke.

"Which?" he said bitterly, as they stood alone.

"Let me bind your arm," she said quietly now, as she drew a long breath.

"It is but a scratch," he said carelessly, "a spear thrust."

Without another word Rachel Linton slit open the sleeve of the jacket he wore, and deftly bandaged the double wound, for the thrust had gone right through Gray's arm. Then rising, she stood before him for a moment or two.

"You asked which wound would I bind up, Adam Gray," she said sadly. "I have bound up one. If my words will help to bind up the other, let me tell you that I do not believe the foul charge made against you."

The rifle fell against Gray's wounded arm as he caught the speaker's hand in his, and raised it to his lips.

"You have done more," he said; "you have healed it."

For the next few moments he stood there as if holding the hand in his, though Rachel Linton had hurried away. Then he started, for he became aware that Tom Long had seen what had taken place, and was now standing leaning on his sword. But he did not speak, he only turned away, leaving Gray watching, and thinking hopefully now of the charge he had to meet.

"Smithers is a gentleman," he said to himself; "they cannot shoot me for what I have not done."

Then he began to wonder how the steamer had sped, and how soon they would bring back their friends. This was the more important, as he felt sure that a few such determined efforts on the Malay's part, and the little garrison must succumb.

"He is a brave young fellow, that Ali," he thought, "and has managed well."

Then he stood gazing out over the dark ground in front, where here and there he could make out the dimly seen form of some unfortunate combatant, who had not been carried off by his friends.

It was darker now than ever, and he was silently watching for danger, when a faint rustling noise caught his ear, and he brought his piece down to the present, for undoubtedly one of the bodies lying on the dark earth was in motion, and crawling slowly towards where he stood.

Chapter Fifty Four
The End of Ali's Mission

Adam Gray's finger was on the trigger of his piece, but he did not fire, though he carefully covered the figure before him, and watched attentively to make sure that it was no hallucination.

He had marked that figure before; one that lay face downwards, apparently just as the man had fallen from a shot. And now the dimly seen arms had changed positions—there was no doubt of that—and the figure was crawling forward.

What did it mean? Either it was a poor wounded wretch, striving hard to get relief and help, or else it was a trick on the part of a treacherous Malay, who was trying to put in force a North American Indian's tactics, and creeping forward to stab a sentry.

"And so gain an entrance into the fort," thought Adam Gray. "Well, my poor wretch, you will not do it, unless both my rifle ball and bayonet should miss."

Just then the figure stopped, and lay quite motionless; and again Gray hesitated, feeling sure that he must have been deceived, as he gazed now at the figure where it lay, some twenty yards away.

There it was, perfectly motionless, and in that darkness Gray felt that he really could not be sure about it. After all, the figure might be lying where it had first lain. It was impossible to say.

His doubts were dispelled the next moment, for the figure was once more in motion, and stopped short as the lock of the sentry's rifle clicked.

"Don't shoot!" said a voice in English; "I am a friend."

"If you move again, I fire!" said Gray in a low, stern voice. "Who are you?"

"Is that Private Gray?" said the voice.

"Mr Ali, is that you?" cried Gray, leaning towards him.

"Yes, it is I," said the figure, crawling rapidly towards him.

"What are you doing with the enemy?"

"Trying to make my way to you. They will not see now. Give me your hand, and I will climb up."

Gray leaned out over the breast-work, gave his hand to the young man, and, with a little exercise of his muscular strength, half-drew, half-aided him to climb into the stronghold—just as Captain Smithers and Tom Long leaped upon them, seizing each his man, and holding his sword to his throat.

"You doubly-dyed scoundrel!" cried Captain Smithers. "Caught him in the act! Call the guard there!"

"Don't you know me, Long?" said a voice that made Tom lower his sword point.

"Ali!" cried Captain Smithers; "you here?"

"Yes, I am back," said the young man sadly.

"Gray, my good fellow," cried Captain Smithers, "fate seems to have ordained that I should doubt you."

"Fate is sometimes very cruel to us all, sir," said Gray, coldly, as the captain set him free, and turned to Ali.

"You found them, then?"

"No," said Ali, sadly.

"But the stockade?"

"What stockade?"

"Where you found them. The steamer went off early in the night."

"The steamer went off? Where?"

"Don't waste time, man, in puzzles," cried the captain, excitedly, as he felt that something was wrong. "You sent a messenger?"

"I sent no messenger," said Ali, excitedly.

"Yes, yes; the man with the writing in a bamboo?"

"I sent no man," said Ali, sadly. "You have been cheated—over-reached by your enemies."

"But did you not find them?"

"No, I was hemmed-in at every turn; and at last, in despair I have crawled back here, hardly saving my life, your sentries are so keen."

"This is dreadful," said Captain Smithers. "How we have been deluded!"

He took a few steps to and fro, and then paused before Ali, gazing at him searchingly.

"Sir," he said, "we are each of different nations, and your people are at war with mine. Why should I trust you? why should I believe in your words? How do I know that I am not talking to one who believes it to be a virtue to slay people of my creed?"

Ali looked at him wonderingly for a few moments before he spoke, slowly,—

"Because you know that I am honest," he said; "and if I am not, you have your resource there. Kill me."

Captain Smithers resumed his agitated walk to and fro.

"This is dreadful!" he said, excitedly. "Those poor fellows have been inveigled away like the hunting-party, and perhaps by this time there is a second massacre."

"I think you exaggerate," said Ali, quietly. "The hunting-party have been led away by a ruse, and the steamer sent upon an errand by a clever trick. But Captain Horton and Major Sandars are not men to give up the lives of their following without a bitter struggle. And as for Lieutenant Johnson—"

"And Mr Roberts," interposed Tom Long.

"Yes, with Mr Roberts," said Ali, "he is too strong in guns and men to be easily overcome, unless by—"

"Treachery? Yes," said the captain. "And that is what I dread."

"To such an extent," said Ali, with a quiet smile, "that you doubt your friends."

"For the moment only," said Captain Smithers, holding out his hand, which the other frankly grasped. "You must remember—my position, sir."

"I do," said Ali. "Now give me a rifle and revolver; we may be attacked at any moment."

"We?" said Tom Long holding out his hand.

"Yes," said Ali, smiling; "and if we get safely through this trouble you will have to try and make me more of an Englishman than I am."

Even while he was speaking the Malays renewed their attack with the greatest pertinacity, it being evident that their object was to capture the fort before the steamer could render help. They seemed to be roused to a pitch of mad fury by the resistance they encountered and their losses, attacking with such determination that it needed no words on Captain Smithers' part to warn his little garrison that they must fight to the death.

With a civilised enemy it would have been quite reasonable to have surrendered long ago, but with such a foe as Rajah Gantang, a pirate of the worst Malay type, such an act as surrender would have meant giving all up to a horrible death.

Never was daylight more welcome than when it appeared to the defenders of that little stronghold, who, gaunt, haggard, and faint with exertion, saw the sky suddenly turn to orange and gold; and then the sun rose over the widespread jungle, sending the wreathing night-mists floating amidst the feathery palms, and seeming to dissolve into thin air.

The first order given by Captain Smithers was to have a signal of distress run up to the top of the flagstaff; the next to try and strengthen the defences, which were sorely dilapidated. Some of the barricading planks and forms were torn down, others riddled with bullets.

Through the rough straw mattresses spears were sticking in a dozen directions, and what had looked hopeless again and again during the night seemed doubly so by day.

But Captain Smithers was not made of the stuff to give up. He had those under his charge whom he was ready to render his life to save; and the spirit that animated his breast seemed to infuse itself in the spirits of the others. He was half mad with jealousy; and angered almost beyond bearing at the thought that Rachel Linton should favour, as he was sure now that she did, a private soldier in preference to him. But he cast away all narrow selfishness, for he was obliged to confess that Gray was no common man, but evidently a gentleman by education if not by birth.

Casting aside, then, all unworthy thoughts, he roused Tom Long from a short sleep that he had made him take. He said a few encouraging words to the men, and then went to join the ladies, who had anticipated his wishes, and were ready with plenty of refreshments for the jaded defenders of the fort.

It is wonderful what efficacy there is in a cup of hot coffee and a big biscuit. Men who, ten minutes before, had stood rifle in hand, dejected and utterly worn-out, lost their haggard looks and seemed to pull themselves together after partaking of the cup of comfort that the ladies brought round.

Rifles were wiped out, belts tightened; and with brightening eyes the men seemed ready to give a good account of the enemy when they closed in for their next attack.

"I have bad news for you, Captain Smithers," said Rachel Linton to him, quietly, as she took the cup she had given him from his hands.

"I don't think you can give me worse news than I already know," he said, sadly.

"Yes, but I can," she said, with her brows knitting with pain for his suffering. "The heat of the day will soon be upon us, and we have no more water."

These words roused the captain to a less selfish view of things, and he stood for a moment or two thinking. It was indeed a tantalising position, for, glittering and sparkling in the sun, there before them flowed the bright river, no drop of whose waters could be reached on account of the thronging enemy.

"I will see to it at once," he said, quietly; and as Miss Linton left him, Tom Long came up.

"We must have a well dug at once," he said. "Take charge here, Long, while I pick out a place."

Ensign Long assumed the command, but now without any of his old consequential airs. Adversity was taming him down, and to his surprise he found himself talking in a very different tone to his men, who yielded a readier obedience than of old.

Captain Smithers was not long in selecting a place for the well, and in a very few minutes a squad of men were at work, some digging, others bearing off the earth in baskets to pile up in front of weak places and add to their strength.

It was a hard call upon the men, that digging; but even while they worked the demand for water arose, and they slaved at their task, knowing the tortures that waited them should they not succeed.

Every man worked in turn, except those badly wounded, though even some of those carried away the baskets of earth.

Among others, Private Gray was ready to aid in this way, after vainly trying to handle a spade, a task rendered impossible by his wound. He was hard at work over his work, carrying basketful after basketful with one hand, when Captain Smithers came up, saw how he was striving, and stood looking on for a few moments.

"We shall have to put off your court-martial yet, Gray," he said grimly. "Give me that basket. Sit down awhile."

Gray was ready to resist, but his officer's words were law, and sitting down to rest, and wipe the streaming perspiration from his face, he watched his captain slave away at the toil with the others, for in those perilous times show and uniforms were forgotten.

It proved to be a harder task than had been anticipated. Captain Smithers had expected to find the subsoil of the island all soft alluvial earth, in which, from the neighbourhood of the river, there would be an abundance of water. It had never occurred to him that if the island had been of soft earth it would long before have been washed away. It was found to be rock at a short distance down, composed of a soft limestone, through which they had to chip their well.

A dozen times over alarms of attack—some real, some false—were given, when spade, pick, and basket had to be laid on one side, and rifles seized. The attack repelled, the fight for water was renewed; and to the intense delight of all, about ten feet down the pure life-giving element came gushing in a clear current from the rock.

Meanwhile Ali's eyes, which were more experienced in the ways of the enemy than those of his companions, read plainly enough that far from being damped by their ill-success they were preparing for a more general assault, and he confided his opinions to Tom Long.

"I can't see any difference," said Tom Long, after a careful inspection through his glass. "They looked just like that every time they came on, and—ah! there are some more of them, though."

"More," echoed Ali. "They are doubled in number. Look, too, at the way in which they are making bundles of reeds and canes."

"Well, let them," said Tom Long; "our rifle bullets will go through those fast enough. If I were Smithers, I'd give them a good searching fire now, and let them know that our rifles make fine practice at a thousand yards' distance. Those fellows are not six hundred."

"Better wait till every shot is more likely to tell," replied Ali. "The bullets would of course go through those bundles of cane; but do you not see what they mean?"

"No," said Tom Long, quietly, "unless they mean to burn us out."

"That is what they do mean," replied Ali. "And look! Quick! give the alarm! They are coming on at once!"

"Let them," said Tom Long, phlegmatically. "They won't alarm us. Nice people your fellow-countrymen, Ali!"

"Fellow-countrymen!" said the young Malay, scornfully. "My fellow-countrymen are gentlemen! These are the scourings of the country, with half the scoundrels from Borneo, Java, and Sumatra—men who have lived all their lives upon piracy and murder."

"Well, whatever they are," said Tom Long, coolly, "they are coming on, so I may as well let the lads know. All right, though; every one is on the alert, and I daresay we can give a good account of them before they get back. Are you sure that these are all a bad lot?"

"Sure?" cried Ali. "They are the scum of the east."

"Then we'll skim them a little more," said Tom Long. "Hi! sergeant, let me have a rifle and some cartridges; I think I should like to pot a few cut-throat pirates myself."

Sergeant Lund handed him the required rifle, Captain Smithers coming up at the moment, and as he swept the surroundings of the little fort with his glass his countenance changed a little, for grave as had been their position before, he felt now that unless help quickly came it was absolutely hopeless.

Chapter Fifty Five
How the Hunting-Party fared

There was a thick mist hanging over the forest when the bugle rang out the *reveille*, and, some eagerly, some thinking rest the better thing, all the hunting-party began to gather outside their tents, where the best apologies for tubs and baths were provided for the officers.

No sooner, however, did the Malays see this than they laughingly led the way to a little river, evidently a tributary of the Parang, and setting the example plunged into its deep, clear, cool waters, showing themselves to be adepts at swimming, and laughing to scorn the idea of there being any crocodiles there.

The water was deliciously cool, and one and all the officers gladly availed themselves of the jungle bath, emerging fresh, and their nerves toned up ready for any work that was to fall to their lot that day.

By the time they returned to the camp an *al fresco* breakfast was ready, half English, half Malay. There were tea and coffee, potted meats and sardines, and side by side with them, delicious Malay curries, made with fresh cocoa-nut, sambals of the most piquant nature, and fresh fish and blachang—that favourite preparation of putrid shrimps. Fruits were in abundance—plantains of various kinds, mangosteens, lychees, and durians smelling strong enough to drive away a dozen Tom Longs, had they been there. In short, the sultan had given orders that his cooks should do their best; similar instructions had been given by Captain Horton and Major Sandars; and the result was a breakfast fit for a prince—who could put up with a picnic and a camp-stool, beneath an umbrageous tree.

"Whatever you gentlemen do," said Doctor Bolter, "pray restrain your appetites. You see," he said, taking his seat cross-legged, like the Malays, in front of a dish of blachang, and its neighbour a delicious chicken curry, "you will to-day be exposed a good deal to the heat of the sun; you will exert yourselves, no doubt; and therefore it is advisable that you should be very moderate in what you eat and drink. Thanks, yes, major, I will take a glass of claret before my coffee. What a thing it is that we can get no milk."

So saying, the doctor set to work, "feeding ferociously," so Captain Horton said, with a laugh, and partaking of everything that took his fancy, finishing off with a cigarette.

The sultan smiled his satisfaction as he sat at the head of the table, eating little himself, but giving instructions from time to time to his slaves that they should hand fruit and other delicacies to the guests that were near him.

The various officers followed the doctor's example, telling one another that they could not be far wrong if they imitated their medical guide. The only one who did not seem to enjoy his meal was Mr Linton, who felt worried, he hardly knew why, about their position.

Now that he was away from the residency, an undefined sense of trouble had come upon him, and he could not help feeling how helpless they must be if the Malays turned against them. Certainly they were all well-armed, and could make a brave fight, perhaps win their way back; but if they did, he felt sure that something would have gone wrong at the island.

The preparations for the fresh start chased away his forebodings, and the packing having been rapidly performed, soldier, sailor, and Malay were soon in motion, the long train winding its way through the dense jungle, with the rattan panniers and howdahs of the elephants brushing the lush verdure on either side.

The morning was deliciously cool, and as they went on and on through the forest shades, where at every turn something bright and beautiful met their gaze, the whole party were in the highest spirits; and the discipline only being kept tight as to the order in which they marched, the men laughed and talked, sang and smoked, and seemed to be thoroughly enjoying themselves.

And certainly it would have moved the spirit of the most cankered denizen of a city to see the beauty of the parasites that clustered and hung from tree to tree. The orchids were of the most brilliant colours; and now and then they passed a lake or pool in the depths of the jungle which would be covered in places with the flower of the lotus, while in every sunny opening the great clusters of nepenthes—the pitcher plant—brightened the scene.

These latter delighted the Jacks amazingly, and not being allowed to break their ranks, they sent the Malays near them to pick anything that took their fancy. These "monkey cups," as they called them, were constantly picked ostensibly for the purpose of supplying the sailors with a drink, for each contained more or less water; but it was never drunk, for in each there were generally the remains of some unfortunate flies, who had gone down into the treacherous vegetable cavern, and being unable to clamber out had miserably perished.

During the heat of the day there was a halt once more, the Malays staring at the sailors and soldiers sitting about under the trees for a quiet smoke and watching the elephants, which, being relieved of their pads and howdahs, walked straight into a great pool near to which they were halted, and then cooled themselves by drawing their trunks full of water and squirting it all over their sides.

"I'm blest," said one of the Jacks, "if they ain't the rummest beggars I ever see. Just look at that one, Bill. Lor' if he ain't just like a bit o' annymated hingy rubber."

"Ah?" said his mate, "you might fit a pair o' blacksmith's bellows on to the muzzle o' that trunk of his, and then blow him out into a balloon."

"When are we going to begin to hunt tigers?" said another. "Oh, we ain't going to hunt them at all, only keep 'em from coming by us, and driving 'em up to where the orficers are."

"I say," said another sailor, "this here's all very well, but suppose some time or another, when these Malay chaps have got us out into the middle of these woods, they turn upon us, and whip out their krises—what then?"

"What then?" said a soldier, who heard him; "why then we should have to go through the bayonet exercise in real earnest; but it won't come to that."

Two more days were spent in the journey, and then, upon his guests beginning to manifest some impatience, the sultan announced that they were now on the borders of the tiger country; and that afternoon there were preparations for a beat when a couple of tigers were seen, but they managed to escape.

The sultan smilingly told his guests that at the end of another march the game would be more plentiful; and once more there was a steady tramp along one of the narrow jungle-paths, into a country wilder than ever—for they were away from the rivers now, and no traces of cultivation had been seen.

There was no dissatisfaction, though, for if the officers shot no tigers they found plenty of jungle-fowl and snipe, upon which they tried their powers with the gun, and made goodly bags of delicious little birds to add to the daily bill of fare.

Another day, and still another, in which the expedition penetrated farther and farther into the forest wild. The officers were delighted, and Doctor Bolter in raptures. He had obtained specimens of the atlas moth, a large flap-winged insect, as large across as a moderate dish; he had shot sun-birds, azure kingfishers, gapers, chatterers, parroquets; and his last achievement had been to kill a boa-constrictor twenty-four feet long.

It was no dangerous monster, but a great sluggish brute, that had hissed at him viciously and then tried to escape. But the doctor had for attendant a very plucky little Malay, appointed by the sultan, and this man was delighted with his task, following the doctor anywhere. Upon this occasion he had come upon the serpent lying coiled up, evidently sleeping off a repast of a heavy kind.

The boy shouted to the doctor, who was trying to stalk a lizard in an open place; and this roused the serpent, which began to uncoil, one fold gliding over the other, while its head was raised and its curious eyes sparkled in the sun.

The boy waited his opportunity, and then darting in cleverly avoided the reptile's teeth, and caught it by the tail, dragging the creature out nearly straight as he called to his master to fire.

The serpent was apparently puzzled by this proceeding, and threw itself round a tree, hissing furiously as it menaced its assailant. Then sending a wave along the free part of its body to the tail, the Malay was driven flying on to his back amidst the canes.

The retreat of the reptile was cut off, though, for this interruption gave the doctor time to come up with his little double fowling-piece, from which a quick shot sent the menacing, quivering head down upon the earth; and then going up, a second shot placed the writhing monster *hors de combat*.

There was no little mirth in the camp as, faint and perspiring profusely, the doctor and his Malay boy came in, slowly dragging the long quivering body of the serpent, which the former at once set to work to skin before it should become offensive. Then the skin was laid raw side upwards, and dressed over with arsenical soap, a dose of which the Malay boy nearly succeeded in swallowing, being attracted by its pleasant aromatic odour.

"Laugh away," said the doctor, "but I mean to have that skin set up and sent to the British Museum, presented by Doctor Bolter," he said importantly.

"Well," said Captain Horton, "for my part I would rather encounter a fierce Malay than one of these writhing creatures. Take care of yourself, doctor, or you'll be constricted."

"Yes," said Major Sandars, entering into the joke, "I'll give orders that every swollen serpent is to be bayonetted and opened if the doctor is missing."

"Laugh away," said the doctor; "I don't mind."

"That's right," said Captain Horton; "but for goodness' sake, man, wash your hands well before you come to dinner."

"All right," said the doctor; and that evening, after dinner, he took the Malay boy into his confidence.

"Look here," he said, "I want to shoot an Argus pheasant. There must be some about here."

"Argus pheasant?" said the Malay boy, staring, and then shaking his head.

"Yes, I heard one last night."

Still the boy shook his head. He had never heard of such a bird.

"Oh, yes, you know what I mean," said the doctor; "they keep in the shelter of the jungle, and are very rarely shot; but I must have one."

The boy shook his head.

"Don't I tell you I heard one last night, after we had camped down? It calls out *Coo-ai*."

"No, no! no, no!" cried the boy; "*Coo-ow, Coo-ow*."

"Yes, that's it," cried the doctor. "You know the bird."

"Yes, know the big spot bird; all eyes," said the boy. "Sees all over himself; like a peacock. Hunter no shoot him, see too much far."

"But I must shoot one," said the doctor.

"Yes, you shoot one," said the boy. "I take you to-night." The doctor rubbed his hands and was delighted; and after the dinner, when the officers and chiefs were sitting smoking and sipping their coffee by the light of the stars, he rose and took his gun, for the Malay boy was waiting.

"Off again, doctor?" cried the major.

"Yes," said the little man, importantly. "I am going, sir, to add to my collection a specimen of the celebrated Argus pheasant—*Phasianus Giganteus*."

"No, no, doctor; no Latin names after dinner," cried several voices.

"As you please, gentlemen," he said.

"The sultan says, shall he send a score of his men to protect you?" cried Captain Horton.

"For goodness' sake no!" cried the doctor in dismay. "My dear sir, this bird is only to be shot by approaching it most cautiously at night, or by laying patiently near its haunts."

"Laying what, doctor—eggs?" said a young officer.

"No, sir; a stick about the back of impertinent puppies," cried the doctor, angrily. "I said lying—lying in wait near the bird's haunts."

"Oh, I beg your pardon," said the young officer; and the doctor went off in dudgeon.

"I say, Thompson," said the major, "don't you be poorly, whatever you do, until the doctor has got over it, or he'll give you such a dose."

"I'll take care, sir," said the young man; and they went on chatting about other things.

Chapter Fifty Six
Doctor Bolter's Bird

Meanwhile the doctor followed his Malay boy—as he was called, though he was really a man—through a narrow path right away from the camp and into the jungle.

The doctor was ruffled exceedingly at his slip of grammar, and looked very much annoyed; but the thought of being able to secure a specimen of the much-prized Argus pheasant chased away the other trouble, and he walked on closely behind his guide.

"How far have we to go, my lad?" he said.

"Walk two hours," said the Malay, "then sit down and listen. No speak a word till *Coo-ow* come. Then make gun speak and kill him!"

"To be sure!" said the doctor, nodding his head; and then almost in silence he followed his guide, often feeling disposed to try and shoot one or other of the nocturnal birds that flitted silently by, or one of the great fruit bats that, longer in their spread of wings than rooks, flew in flocks on their way to devastate some orchard far away.

Quite two hours had elapsed, during which the Malay, apparently quite at home, led his scientific companion right away through the gloom of the wilderness.

At last he enjoined silence, saying that they were now approaching the haunts of the wondrous bird; and consequently the doctor crept on behind him without so much as crushing a twig.

They had reached an opening in the forest by the side of what was evidently a mountain of considerable height, and the doctor smiled as he recalled the fact that the Argus pheasant was reputed to haunt such places; when to his intense delight there soddenly rang out from the distance on the silent night air a peculiar cry that resembled the name given to the bird—*Coo-ow*. For the moment it seemed to the doctor as if some Australian savage was uttering his well-known *Coo-ay*, or as if this was the Malays' form of the cry. But he knew well enough what it was, and following his guide with the greatest caution they crept on towards the place from which the sound had seemed to come.

It was weird work in that wild solitude far on towards midnight, but the doctor was too keen a naturalist to think of anything but the specimen of which he was in search. He knew that the native hunters, out night after night, could not shoot more than one of these birds in a year, and it would be quite a triumph if he could add such a magnificent thing to his collection.

Coo-ow—rang out the strange cry, and it seemed quite near. Then again Coo-ow, and this time it appeared to be a long way off.

This was tantalising, but he concluded directly after that the second cry might be that of another bird answering the first.

They were now in amongst a number of low bushes, which gave them cover, while it made the surrounding country less black than when they were in the jungle path. There they could only grope their way with outstretched hands; here they could have gone on at a respectable foot pace without danger of running against some impediment in the path.

The doctor cocked both barrels of his gun, after opening the breech and making sure that the cartridges were in their place, and, in momentary expectation of setting a shot, he kept close behind the Malay.

Coo-ow! came the cry again, this time a little to the left; and the Malay stretched out a hand behind him to grasp that of the doctor as he went cautiously on.

Coo-ow! again, but a little farther off, and with his nerves throbbing with excitement, the doctor kept up the chase, now seeming close to the bird, then being left behind, but never once getting within shot.

It was very provoking, but the guide was in earnest, and the doctor would have gone through ten times the trouble to achieve his end.

And so they stole on through the thick brushwood, with the bird repeating its cry so near from time to time as to make them feel that they must get a shot directly; but still the hope was deferred.

A lighter patch in front showed that the forest was a little more open, and the Malay loosed the doctor's hand for a moment to clamber over a block of stone—when there was a rushing noise, what seemed to be a heavy blow, a hoarse cry, and then silence, broken directly after by a low deep growling just in front of where Doctor Bolter stood—petrified and unable to move.

He was too much taken aback by the suddenness of the incident to comprehend for a time what had taken place; but directly after, with his hands wet with excitement, and his heart seeming to stand still, he realised that some great animal had been stalking them, as they had been stalking the Argus pheasant, and, waiting for its opportunity, had sprung upon and seized the Malay.

There was the low snarling growl not two yards from where he stood, just the noise upon a larger scale that a cat would make when crouching down over the rat that it had seized; and the doctor felt that there could be only one creature in the jungle that would seize its prey in such a manner—the tiger.

In spite of his bravery and the strength of nerve that had often made him face death without a tremor, Dr Bolter felt a cold shiver pass through him as he realised how near he was to a terrible end. The tiger might have seized him instead of the Malay—in fact, might spring upon him at any moment; and as he felt this, he brought the barrels of his gun to bear on the dark spot where the tiger lay crouching upon its victim, and with his fingers on both triggers stood ready to fire at the first movement of the beast.

That first movement, he knew, might be to spring upon him and strike him down; and nature bade him flee at once for his life—bade him drop his gun, run to the first tree, and climb into its branches—escape as a timid beast, a monkey, might have done.

Education, on the contrary, bade him stay—told him that it would be the act of a coward and a cur to run off and leave the poor fellow lying there to his fate, the horrible fate of being torn and half devoured by the tiger—bade him be a man, and do something, even at the risk of his own life, to save the Malay who had been stricken down in his service; and as these thoughts came to Doctor Bolter his eyes dilated in the darkness, and he strove to make out the positions in which tiger and man were lying.

It was some time before he could make this out, and then it seemed to him that the tiger had struck the Malay down upon his face, and was lying upon him, with his teeth fixed in his shoulder.

Just then the unfortunate man uttered a loud cry, when the tiger gave an angry snarl, and Doctor Bolter was able to assure himself of their relative positions. In fact there was the side of the tiger's head not six feet from him, and dare he fire it was almost impossible to miss.

But the gun was loaded with small shot, and even at so close a range he might injure the unfortunate Malay, if he were not beyond the point when a fresh blow would do him harm.

Doctor Bolter stood unable to move. He did not feel very much alarmed now, the danger was too near, but he could not for the moment act.

At last, though, his nerves seemed to become more set, and setting his teeth he held his piece ready, and with one motion advanced his left foot and went down on his right knee, at the same time raising his gun to his shoulder.

It was done in a moment—the tiger raising its head from the victim with a savage roar; when with the mouth of the piece not eighteen inches from the creature's head, Doctor Bolter drew the triggers, almost together.

There was a brilliant flash in the darkness, which showed him the glistening teeth of the savage beast and its glaring eyes—a double report—and with a furious roar the monster sprang forward, crashing into some bushes, and then all was still.

Quick as lightning the doctor threw open the breech of his piece, and inserted this time a couple of ball-cartridges, closed the gun, and stood ready for the monster's attack, knowing though that it must be sorely wounded, for he had aimed straight at its eye, and the small shot would, at that distance, have the effect of a bullet.

A minute—two minutes, that seemed like hours, did the doctor stand there, expecting to hear some movement on the tiger's part, either for attack or retreat; but it did not stir, and he dared not fire again at random.

Just then there was a low groan, and a faint movement at his feet.

The doctor's piece swung round involuntarily, but directly after he recalled that it must be the Malay, and with dry throat and lips he spoke to him.

"Are you much hurt?"

There was a few moments' pause, and then the Malay spoke.

"My shoulder is gnawed; I can't use my arm."

"Can you crawl behind me?" said the doctor, hoarsely.

For reply the Malay rose to his feet, and staggering slightly, he made his way behind where the doctor stood.

"I dare not move," said Doctor Bolter. "The beast may spring upon us again."

"No," said the Malay, whose voice sounded stronger; "he is dead. Have you a light?"

The doctor held his gun with one hand and pulled out his match-box with the other, when, in spite of his wounds, the Malay knelt down, drew a piece of dammar from the fold of his sarong, stuck it in a cleft stick, and then striking a match he fired the dry grass and lit the dammar, which made an excellent torch.

With this advanced he took a couple of strides forward, and holding the light down, there lay the tiger on its side, the white under fur showing plainly, the doctor seeing that the creature's neck and legs were stretched out, and that it was indeed dead.

"Thank heaven!" he muttered, fervently: and standing his gun against a tree he set to work piling up dead wood and dry canes to make a fire, when by its light and that of the dammar-torch the doctor proceeded to roughly dress the Malay's wounds.

The tiger had seized him by the muscles of his left shoulder and clawed the upper part of his arm — terrible wounds enough, but not likely to prove fatal; and when the doctor had done all he could to make the poor fellow comfortable, the Malay lay down, gazing up at him as he trickled a little brandy from his flask between the poor fellow's lips.

"You are good," he said at last. "You saved my life. Now I shall save yours."

"Save mine?" said the doctor. "Well, I hope we shall have no more tigers to face."

"No," said the man, "not from tigers, but from men. You did not eat blachang to-night?"

"No," said the doctor. "Why?"

"Sultan Hamet had *toobah* put in it to-night: same as to make fish sleep."

"What? I don't understand you!" cried the doctor excitedly.

"Sultan Hamet means to have all the English krissed to-night while they sleep," said the Malay; "but you have saved my life: shall save yours."

Chapter Fifty Seven
How Doctor Bolter got in a Mess

Doctor Bolter felt as if the place was swimming round him, and the fire-light seemed to dance as he heard these words. Then, as he recovered himself somewhat, he gazed full in the Malay's eyes, to see that the man was looking up at him in the calmest and most unruffled way.

"Are you mad?" exclaimed the doctor.

"No," said the Malay. "I say what is right. Sultan Hamet joins with Rajah Gantang to kill off all the English—the sultan here; the rajah there, with his prahus."

"It is impossible!" cried the doctor. "You are deceiving me."

"No, no, I tell the truth," said the man; "but you shall not be hurt. Let them kris me first. You shall live."

"Let us get back," cried the doctor, seizing his gun; and the tiger with the beautiful skin, which he had meant to have for a specimen, was forgotten.

"No, no," said the man, "you must stay in the jungle. The tigers are better than Hamet."

"Can you walk?" said the doctor, quietly.

The man got up for answer.

"Can you find your way back?" said the doctor.

"Yes," said the other, with a scornful look. "I could find the way with my eyes blinded."

"Then start at once. Here, take some more of this."

He gave the injured man another draught from his flask, for the poor fellow seemed terribly faint.

The few drops of brandy gave him new life, and he displayed it by throwing himself on his knees before Doctor Bolter, and clasping one of his legs with his uninjured arm.

"Don't go back, master," he cried piteously. "You have been so good to me that I could not bear to see you krissed. Stay away, and I will keep you safely. My life is yours, for you saved it; and I am your slave."

"My good fellow," said the doctor, sadly, as he laid his hand upon the Malay's shoulder, "you do not understand Englishmen."

"Yes, yes, I do," cried the Malay. "I like—I love Englishmen, I was servant to the young chief Ali before the sultan had him krissed."

"Young Ali krissed?" cried the doctor.

"Yes, he was too much friends with the Englishmen, and made the sultan jealous."

"And the wretch had that brave, noble young fellow killed?"

"Yes," said the Malay, sadly. "His father, the Tumongong, prayed upon his knees that the brave boy's life might be spared, and offered to send him out of the country. But the sultan laughed, and said that the young chief would come back again with a swarm of English soldiers, and seize the jewels, and put him to death, and make himself sultan. Then the Tumongong swore an oath that Ali should never come back, and went down on his face before Sultan Hamet; but the sultan drew his kris and pricked him with it in the shoulder, and told him that he should die if he named his son again."

"The villain! That brave, noble young fellow, too!" said the doctor, excitedly.

"Yes; he was so brave and handsome," cried the Malay. "I loved him, but I was obliged to hide it all, for if I had spoken one word they would have krissed me, and thrown me into the river. So I had to be silent; but when they wanted some one to go with you I offered, and they said 'Yes' because I could speak English, and the sultan gave me my orders."

"And what were they?" said the doctor, sharply.

"To wait till to-night, and then lead you out of the jungle if you did not want to go, and stab you with my kris."

"And you did not do it?"

The Malay smiled, and drew his kris in its sheath from out of the folds of his sarong, handing it to the doctor.

"I am not a murderer," he said.

"But suppose the sultan had asked you why you did not kill me," said the doctor, "what then?"

"I should have told him a lie. He is a liar, and full of deceit. We do not think it wrong to deal with such a man in the coins he gives. I should have said you kept me back with your gun."

"Take your kris, my lad," said the doctor, quietly. "I trust you. Now lead me back to the camp."

"No, no," cried the Malay. "I dare not. I cannot take you back to death."

"I—must—go," said the doctor, sternly; and the Malay made a deprecating gesture, indicative of his obedience.

"My people may have proved too strong for Sultan Hamet and his treacherous gang."

"Yes—yes—they may," cried the Malay, eagerly.

"They may have given him such a lesson as he will never forget."

"I hope they will make him forget for ever," said the Malay in a sombre tone. "He is not fit to live. My kris is thirsty to drink his blood."

"Forward, then!" cried the doctor, "and tell me when you feel sick. Find water if you can, first thing. Does your wound pain you?"

"It feels as if the tiger kept biting me," was the reply; "but I do not mind. Shall we go back?"

"Yes; and at once," cried the doctor, and following his companion, they rapidly retraced their steps through the dark jungle, the guide, as if by instinct, making his way onward without a moment's hesitation, seeming to take short cuts whenever the forest was sufficiently open to let them pass.

As he stumbled on over the creeper-covered ground, the doctor had many a narrow escape from falling, and he could not help envying the ease with which his guide passed the various obstacles around them. The chief thought that occupied the doctor's mind, though, was that which related to the drugging of the party's food that evening.

The Malay had mentioned what drug was to be used, namely *toobah*, a vegetable production—in fact the root of a plant which the doctor knew that the Malays used to throw in the pools of the rivers and streams, with the effect that the fish were helplessly intoxicated, and swam or floated on the surface of the water. This plant he had several times tried to obtain and examine, while he made experiments upon its power; but so far he had been unsuccessful. Would it have the same effect upon the human organisation that it had upon a fish? That was the question he had to solve in his mind; but no matter how he turned the subject over, he could extract not the smallest grain of comfort.

The only hope he could derive from his thoughts was that the English discipline, with its regular setting of sentries and watchfulness, might be sufficient to defeat the enemy's machinations, and a sufficiency of the officers and men be unaffected by the poison to make a brave stand until the rest had recovered.

That might happen; and slightly roused in spirit by this hope, he kept steadily on. One thing was fixed in his own mind, and that was that it was his duty to get back to his party, either to fight with them, to help the wounded, or to share their fate.

"Not that I want to die," muttered the doctor. "There's that collection of butterflies unpinned; no one but me could set up all those birds, or understand the numbering; and then there's that boa-constrictor wants dressing over; and worse than all, I've killed my first tiger, and have not saved its skin."

"Humph!" he exclaimed directly after, "it seems as if I am to have a hard job to save my own skin."

Just then the Malay reeled, and caught at a tree they were passing, when the doctor had only just time to catch him and save him from a heavy fall.

Laying his gun aside, he eased the poor fellow down upon the tangled grass, trickling a few more drops from his flask between his lips, and then giving the flask a bit of a shake to hear how much there was left.

"Better now," said the Malay, trying to rise. "The trees run round."

"Yes, of course they do to you," said the doctor. "Lie still for a while, my good fellow. Is there any water near here?"

"Little way on," said the Malay, pointing. "Listen!"

The doctor bent his head, and plainly enough heard a low gurgling noise. Following the direction in which the sound seemed to be, he came upon a little stream, and filled, by holding on with one hand to a little palm and hanging down as low as he could, the tin canteen slung from his shoulder. From this he drank first with avidity, then refilling it he prepared to start back.

"And I always preach to the fellows about not drinking unfiltered water," he muttered. "I wonder how many wild water beasts I've swallowed down. Well, it can't be helped; and it was very refreshing. Let me see! Bah! How can I when it's as dark as pitch! Which way did I come?"

He stood thinking for a few moments, and then started off, cautiously trying to retrace his steps; but before he had gone twenty yards he felt sure that he was wrong, and turning back tried another way. Here again at the end of a minute he felt that he was not going right, and with an ejaculation of impatience he made his way back to where the stream rippled and gurgled along amidst the reeds, canes, and beneath the overhanging branches.

It was not the spot where he had filled the canteen, but he knew that he must be near it; and he started again, but only to have to get back once more to the stream, where there was a rush, a scuffling noise and a loud splashing, that made him start back with a shudder running up his spine, for he knew by the sound that it must be a crocodile.

Worst of all he was unarmed, having left his gun beside the fainting Malay.

All he could do was to back as quietly as he could into the jungle, with canes and interlacing growths hindering him at every step; thorns tore and clung to his clothes, and he felt that if any creature gave chase to him it must overtake him directly. His only chance of safety then was in inaction; and fretting with annoyance he crouched there, listening to the shudder-engendering crawling noise made by evidently several loathsome reptiles about the bank of the stream.

After a while this ceased, and he made another attempt to get back to the Malay, going on and on through the darkness, and from time to time shouting to him. He knew that he must be crossing and recrossing his track, and blamed himself angrily for not being more careful. His shouts produced no response, and the matches he lit failed to give him the aid he had hoped; and at last, utterly exhausted, he sank down amidst the dense undergrowth to wait for daylight, with the result that nature would bear no more, and in spite of the help he knew his companion needed, the danger of his companions, and the perils by which he was surrounded from wild beasts, his head sank lower and lower upon his breast, and he slept.

Not willingly, for he kept starting back into wakefulness, and walked to and fro; but all in vain, sleep gradually mastered him; and he sank lower and lower, falling into a deep slumber, and, as he afterwards said, when talking about the adventure, "If I had been in front of a cannon, and knew that it was to be fired, I could only have said—Just wait till I am fast asleep, and then do what you please."

The sun was up when he started into full wakefulness, and his clothes were drenched with dew.

"If I don't have a taste of jungle fever after this, it's strange to me," he said, hastily swallowing a little white powder from a tiny bottle. "A stitch in time saves nine, and blessed is the salt quinine."

"Humph! that's rhyme," he grunted. "Only to think that I should go to sleep. Ahoy-oy!" he shouted.

There was no reply, and his heart smote him as he felt that he had neglected the poor Malay. Then he felt that he was lost in the jungle; but that did not trouble him much, for he was sure that if he followed the little stream he should find that it entered a larger, and that the larger would run into one larger still, probably into the Parang, whose course he could follow down. But that would be only as a last resource.

Chapter Fifty Eight
The Dose of Toobah

Doctor Bolter's was a painful position, and he could not help feeling how utterly weak man is in the midst of nature's solitudes. He could have stood meditating for long enough, but he had to find his companion; and after shouting for some time and getting no answer, he listened for the rippling noise of the stream, and heard it sounding very faintly far-off on his right.

Making for it as a starting-place, he found the tracks he had made, the grass being trampled down in all directions. What was more, he found his trail crossed over and over again, and even followed by that of crocodiles, whose toes were marked in the mud wherever it was laid bare.

Twice over he startled one of the reptiles, which fled before him with a rush into the stream, which was little better than an overgrown ditch, and the doctor hastily backed away.

He soon found that all endeavours to hit upon his way back by the trail were useless, and once more he began to shout.

To his great delight his cry was answered, and on making for the sound he heard directly after the rustling of bushes being thrust aside, and soon after stood face to face with the Malay.

"I have been sleeping," said the latter, smiling. "My arm is better now."

"If our English fellows could stand injuries like these!" muttered the doctor, who looked with astonishment at the light way in which the Malay treated the terrible injury he had received.

"Do you feel as if you could lead the way back?" he said, after halting and rebinding the Malay's wound.

"Oh, yes," the Malay said cheerfully; and he at once set off.

"But my gun?" cried the doctor. "I have left it behind."

The man led him back to the place with the greatest ease, and after wiping the wet and rust from lock and barrel, they set off through the dripping undergrowth, and had been walking about half an hour, the doctor's excitement growing each minute as they drew nearer the camp, when his guide suddenly stopped and laid his hand upon the other's arm.

"Listen!" he said; and as he spoke there was the distant sound of a shot, then another, and other.

"Thank heaven!" cried the doctor, "they are making a fight for it. Get on quickly."

They went on along an old overgrown track, with the sound of the firing growing each minute nearer; and the doctor's heart beat joyfully as he made out that a pretty brisk engagement was going on.

Soon, however, the firing began to drop off, to be renewed from time to time in a straggling manner; and to his great joy the doctor found that those who fired were coming along the track he was upon.

"Yes," said the Malay, who seemed to read his countenance; "but they may be enemies."

Yielding to the latter's solicitations, they hid themselves amidst the dense undergrowth a few yards from the track, and waited patiently.

It was not for long. Soon after they had taken their stand they could hear voices; and directly after the doctor hurried out as he saw an advance guard of the men of his regiment under a lieutenant.

The men gave a hearty *Hurrah!* as they saw him, and the lieutenant caught him by the hand.

"Glad to see you, doctor; we thought you killed."

"Yes; and I did you," cried the doctor. "How are you all?"

"They'll tell you behind," said the lieutenant. "Forward, my lads."

The guard moved on, and the doctor came upon the little force, firing going on again in the rear.

He met Major Sandars directly, and their greeting was warm in the extreme.

"The scoundrels tried to poison us," said the major.

"Yes, yes, I know," cried the doctor; "but is any one hurt?"

"A few scratches there in the dhoolies," said the major.

"No one killed?"

"Not a soul, thank heaven," cried the major. "But we shall have our work cut out. Ah, here's Horton. All right in the rear?"

"Yes," was the reply; "we are keeping them back. Ah, doctor, I am glad to see you again. You know what's happened?"

"Partly," said the doctor; "but tell me."

They were moving forward as he spoke, and he learned now that the little force was working to hit the river higher up in its course, and from thence try to communicate with the island and the steamer.

"You had not been gone above a couple of hours before, as we were sitting smoking and chatting, and thinking of turning in, first one and then another began to complain of pain and drowsiness.

"The major there was the first to take alarm, thinking it was cholera; but it was Mr Linton who saved us. He no sooner realised what was the matter than he slipped out of the tent, and without waiting for orders made his way to the sergeant's guard, and got the fellow on duty to collect all the men he could to come up to the tent. How many do you think he got?"

"Twenty—thirty—how should I know?" said the doctor impatiently. "Go on."

"Four," said the captain. "All the others were down and half delirious. Fortunately my Jacks had escaped, and thirty of them seized their rifles, and followed Mr Linton at the double to the hut.

"They were just in time. That scoundrel Hamet had given an order and withdrawn from the tent; at one end of which about a hundred of his cut-throats had gathered, kris in hand, and were only waiting for us to get a little more helpless before coming upon us to put us out of our misery.

"Bless your heart, doctor! it would have done you good to see the Jacks clear that tent at the point of the bayonet! And then, while half of them kept the enemy at bay, the other half brought in the sick men, and laid 'em side by side till they were all under canvas.

"It was horrible, I can tell you," continued the captain. "We were all in great pain, but the dull sleepy sensation was the worst, and it seemed no use to fight against it. We all, to a man, thought that we were dying, and so did the sailors, who had not touched the horrible stuff. And yet we could hear every word as plainly as if our power of hearing had been increased, though we could not speak.

"'Give them water,' I heard the sergeant say.

"'No, no,' said my boatswain; 'you get the rum keg in, my lad, and give 'em a strong dose apiece o' that.'

"The Jacks fetched it in under fire, and they gave us a tremendous dose apiece, and I believe it saved our lives!"

"I'm sure it did," said the doctor. "It set up a rapid action of the heart, and that carried off the poison."

"I dare say it did," said the captain, "but it gave me a beautiful headache. However, the sergeant and the boatswain lost no time, but took matters in their own hands, cut the ropes, and let the tent go by the board, for fear the enemy should set it on fire, and then made the best breast-work they could all round us, a little party charging out every now and then and bringing in boxes, cases, tubs, everything they could lay hold of, to strengthen our position. One time they fetched in half-a-dozen spades, another time the axes; and little by little they formed such a defence, that tipped as it was by our fellows' bayonets, the Malays dare not try to force.

"We soon found, though," he continued, "that they were furious with disappointment, for spears began to fly till our lads searched the nearest cover with some bullets, when the enemy retired a little farther, and then the boys got in the spears and made an abattis with them.

"In spite of the danger and the sudden surprise, our fellows enjoyed it, for they had the pleasure of driving the scoundrels out of their own camp, and they had to put up with the shelter of the trees all night. They made four savage attacks upon us, though, and the first time, from too much ground having been covered by the breast-work, the enemy nearly carried all before them, and it came to bayonetting and the spears getting home; but our brave lads drove them back, and then a few volleys sent them in to cover.

"The next time they attacked, the major and a dozen of the soldiers were ready to help a little. They were too ill to do much, but they held their pieces and made a show of bayonets, and the major managed to take the command.

"The next time we all of us managed to make a show of fighting; while a couple of hours after, when the enemy made their last and most savage attack, they got such a warm reception that they let us have the rest of the night in peace."

"And this morning, then, you began to retreat!"

"Yes," the major said, "there was nothing else for it."

"But why not have retreated by the way we came?" said the doctor.

"Because, my dear fellow, the whole country's up, and this was the only way open. If we had gone by the track our fellows would have been speared one by one, for the jungle is too dense to skirmish through. But here's Linton; he will tell you better than I can."

As the retreat continued, the rear-guard being always closely engaged with the Malays, who pressed upon them incessantly, Mr Linton came up, begrimed with powder, and shook hands.

"This is a horrible affair, doctor!" he said sadly.

"Don't say horrible," said the other, cheerfully. "We shall fight our way through to the river."

"I hope so," said Mr Linton. "But we have scarcely any provisions. Not more, certainly, than a day or two's rations. That is bad enough; but you do not understand my anxiety. We have let ourselves be drawn into a trap, and the whole country rises against us."

"Let it rise," said the doctor, sturdily; "we'll knock it down again."

"But the residency, man—the steamer!"

"Phew!" whistled the doctor. "I had forgotten them."

"I had not," said Mr Linton, sadly, "and I fear the worst."

"Keep up your spirits, man. There are those on the island, and aboard that steamer, who will keep every Malay in the country at bay."

"If they are not overcome by treachery, as we nearly were."

"We must hope then," said the doctor; "hope that those in charge will be more on the alert. I say, though, Linton, did you give these people credit for such a trick?"

"Yes; for I have had more experience of them than you; and I blame myself most bitterly for not being more cautious."

"Regrets are vain," said the doctor. "Let's do all we can to make up for our lapse—if lapse it has been."

"We will," said the resident. "Would to heaven, though, that I could feel more at ease about those we have left behind. If we only had a guide on whom we could depend, matters would not be so bad."

"I have one for you," said the doctor, joyfully.

"Who? Where is he?" exclaimed Mr Linton.

"Here, close at hand," he said.

And hurrying on to where he had left the Malay guide in charge of a couple of soldiers, he found that he had arrived only just in time; for feeling was very strong just then against every one wearing a dark skin, and the men were looking askance at one whom they believed likely to betray them at any moment.

"A Malay!" said Mr Linton, doubtfully.

"Yes, and a trusty one," said the doctor, decisively. "I will answer for his fidelity."

"That is rather bold, doctor," said the major, who just then came up; "but these are times when we must not be too particular. Can he understand us?"

"I was the young chief Ali's servant, and I speak English," said the Malay, quietly.

"That is no recommendation," said Captain Horton, sharply. "That young chief deserted us, like the rest."

"No," said the doctor; "he was assassinated for taking our part; and this man nearly shared his fate."

This decided matters in favour of the Malay being retained as guide; but there was still a difficulty, and that was, would the poor fellow, injured as he was, be able to undertake the duty?

He said he could, however; and as soon as he understood what was wanted, he went to the front, and the retreat was continued.

Chapter Fifty Nine
Like Brothers in Distress

It was a strange country to struggle through, for roads hardly had any existence. The rivers were the highways, and upon the banks the villages or campongs of the Malays were invariably placed. There were a few narrow tracks, such as the one the retreating party hurried along, but all else was dense jungle, the untrodden home of wild beasts. So dense was it that there was fortunately nothing to fear from attack on either side. It must come from the front, or else from the rear. Neither friend nor foe could penetrate many yards through the wall of verdure that shut them in to right and left. To have tried to flank them without literally breaking a way through the canes and interlacing plants was impossible.

On being asked how long it would take to march to the river and strike it high up, the Malay replied, three days of hard walking; and the hearts of his hearers sank as they thought of their position, with scarcely any provender, no covering against the night dews or heavy rains, and only the earth for their resting-place, while a virulent enemy was always on their track, striving hard to cut off all they could.

There was no other course open, however, but to face it, for it would have been madness to have tried to fight their way through the hostile country; and every one bent manfully to the task.

As they struggled on through the steamy bush the rear-guard was changed again and again, a fresh party of defenders taking up the task of keeping the pursuers at bay, and to each man in turn was the warning given that no shot must be fired unless it could be made to tell; consequently the fire was less fierce, but, as the Malays found to their cost, more fatal.

The end of the third day was approaching, and the progress of the party had grown slower and slower, for their guide's strength had failed. The poor fellow had fought on bravely in spite of his wounds, insisting that he was well enough to walk, when all the time he was suffering intense agony; and this was not to be without its result.

During the day the Malays had attacked far more fiercely than usual, and though always repulsed, it had not been without loss. Several men had fallen, while others were wounded, increasing terribly the difficulties of the case, for the injured men had to be carried by those who found that their task of fighting their way through the jungle in the midst of the dense heat was already as much as they could bear.

Still no one murmured. The pleasure-trip had turned out to be one of terrible misery, but each man, soldier or sailor, had a cheery word for his neighbour; and whenever an unfortunate received a spear or bullet wound, the doctor was on the spot directly, tending him; while a couple of his comrades deftly cut a few canes and bound them together, making a light litter, upon which the wounded man was placed, and carried on the shoulders of four men.

The wounded made a terrible demand upon the sound; and now, to add to their trouble, men began to fall out of the ranks stricken down by disease.

It was no more than the doctor anticipated; but it was terrible work.

Captain Horton was one of the first—after fighting bravely in the rear—to go to the doctor and complain of his head.

"I can't get on, doctor," he said. "The giddiness is dreadful, and the pain worse. Give me something to ease it all."

The doctor said he would, and prescribed what he could from the little case he had with him, but he knew what was coming. Captain Horton had taken the jungle fever, and in an hour he was strapped down upon a litter, raving with delirium.

Then another, and another, went down, the officers falling one after another, till Major Sandars was left alone with the doctor, who had to divide his time between attending to his many patients and handling a rifle to help in their defence.

The consequence was that on the third night, instead of being near the river, they were halted in the dense jungle, with their outposts on the alert, and the rest throwing themselves beside the sick and wounded, too much exhausted even to care for food.

Major Sandars and the doctor stood talking together beneath the shade of a silk-cotton tree, whose leaves seemed to keep off a portion of the heavy falling dew, and the former was waiting for an answer from his companion, who, however, did not speak.

"Come, say something, doctor," exclaimed the major; "what do you think of affairs?"

"What can I say?" replied the doctor, sadly; "we can go no farther."

"But we must," exclaimed the major, impatiently. "The river must be reached, and a message sent down to the steamer."

"There is only one way," replied Doctor Bolter.

"How is that?"

"Leave the sick and wounded behind, and push on. The poor fellows can carry them no farther."

"Then we'll stop where we are," said the major, sharply, "for I won't leave a man behind."

"Of course you will not. I knew you would say so. Then all I can recommend is that we stay as we are for a few days, and try and recruit."

"With bad water, and hardly any provisions," said the major. "Ah, Bolter, this is a terribly bad business."

"Yes," said the doctor, holding out his hand, which was eagerly grasped, "it is a terrible business. But you know what the foreigners say of us, Sandars?"

"No: what do you mean?"

"That the English never know when they are beaten. We don't know when we are beaten, and our lads are like us. God bless them, poor fellows, for they are as patient as can be!"

"What do you advise, then?" said the major. "It is your duty to advise."

"I did advise," said the doctor, laughing. "I proposed lopping off the bad limb of our little party, so as to leave the rest free to hobble on."

"And suppose I had consented to it," said the major; "made the sick and wounded as comfortable as we could, and pushed on with the rest, what would you do?"

"Do?" said Doctor Bolter; "I don't understand you."

"I mean, of course you would have to come with us; for the Malays would butcher the poor fellows as soon as they came up."

"Come with you, major? Are you mad? Why, who would tend the poor boys, and see to their bandages? No, my dear Sandars. Your place is with the sound, mine is with the unsound. Go on with your lot—poor fellows—and see if you can reach the river. You might perhaps send help in time to save us. If you didn't, why, I should have made them comfortable to the end, and done my duty."

"My dear doctor," said Major Sandars, holding out his hand.

"My dear major," said the doctor. "Good-bye, then; and God bless you!"

"What!" cried the major. "And did you think I was going?"

"Of course!"

"More shame for you, then, for thinking me such a cur. Leave you and these poor fellows here in the midst of the jungle, to be murdered by those cowardly pirates? Not I. Why, the men would mutiny if I proposed such a thing. No; we'll wait a few hours, and then get on a few miles and rest again, the best way we can."

"But you will only get the poor fellows killed if you stay," said the doctor.

"Well, hadn't we all better be killed like men doing our duty, than go off and live like cowards and curs?"

"Of course you had," said the doctor, speaking huskily. "But I felt that it was my duty to leave you free."

"Doctor," said the major, laying his hand upon the other's shoulder, "there's nothing like trouble for making a man know what a deal of good there is in human nature. You're a good fellow, doctor. Hang it, man, you've made me feel as soft as a girl!"

He turned away his face, that staunch, brave soldier, for a few moments, and then the weakness was past, and he turned sharply round to the doctor.

"Now," he said, "you shall see what stuff our soldiers and sailors are made of. Come here."

He led the doctor back to the rear, where the guard, sun-blackened, haggard fellows, with their clothes hanging in rags from the thorns, were on the watch, and this being out of earshot of the sick and wounded, who were all ranged side by side beneath a couple of shady spreading trees, he gave the order for the men to fall in, when, with the precision that they would have shown upon a parade ground, the soldiers fell in, making one line; the sailors another in the rear.

"Face inwards!" cried the major, and he turned first to the sailors. "My lads," he said, "your officers being all down, the duty of commanding you has fallen upon me, and I thank you for the ready way in which you have obeyed my orders. You have been as willing and as trusty as my own boys here, and that is saying a great deal."

There was a little shuffling of feet at this, and the men looked uncomfortable.

"I am sorry to say," continued the major, "that matters have come to such a grievous pass with us, that I have to make a statement, to which I want to hear your reply. I have no occasion to speak to you, for I know that you will to a man obey my orders to the last; but I want to hear what you will say."

There was a pause here, and then the major went on,—

"Matters have come to this, my lads, that I see you can stagger on no longer with the loads you have to bear. In fact, two more poor fellows are down, and it will take every fighting man to carry the others. So I have been talking the matter over with the doctor, and it has come to this, that our only chance is to leave the sick and wounded, and push on, make for the river, in the hope of getting help, and coming back to save them. What do you say?"

"Lord love you, sir," cried one of the sailors, "why, afore to-night them niggers would have sarved every one of our poor mates like the doctor, there, sarves the black beadles and butterflies—stuck a pin or a kris through 'em."

It was a grim subject to jest upon, and it was a serious thing; but there was a roar of laughter from the men, and the doctor chuckled till he had to hold his sides, and then wipe his eyes.

"I hope not so bad as that," said the major, when he had called *Attention!* "It is, however, I fear our only hope. Will some man among you speak?"

There was a shuffling and a whispering at this, and every man nudged his neighbour to begin, but no one spoke till the sergeant felt that it was his duty, and going along the front of both ranks he had a few words with the soldiers and the jacks. After this he retook his place and saluted.

"Men seem to be all of one opinion, sir," he said gruffly.

"And what is that opinion?" inquired the major.

"They say, sir, as I say, that they wouldn't like their mates to desert them in a time of trouble like this."

"That's right, sergeant," shouted a sailor.

"Yes, that's a true word," shouted another.

"Attention, there!" cried the major, sharply. "Go on, sergeant."

"And if so be as our officer don't order us different, we'll all stick to one another, sick and sound, to the end."

"Hear, hear; hurray!" cried the men, as with one voice.

"Do I understand, my lads, that you will stand by the sick and wounded to the last?"

"Yes, sir, all on us!" shouted the men in chorus.

"Yes, sir," cried the joking sailor, "and we'll all carry one another till there's only one left as can carry; and he'll have a jolly hard time of it, that's all."

The stern discipline was for a moment forgotten, and a hearty roar of laughter followed this sally.

"Attention!" cried the major after a few moments, and he spoke as if he was deeply moved. "It is only what I expected from my brave lads; and I may tell you now that this is what Doctor Bolter and I had determined to do—stand together to the last."

"Only we won't have any last, my lads," cried the doctor.

"I hope not," said the major. "We'll go on more slowly and take longer rests, for I must have no more of you men down with sickness. Let us hope that we may win our way safely to the ship and the island yet. I would send out a little party to try and fetch help, but I fear they are beset at the residency already, and I do not think a detachment could succeed. I propose then that we all hold together and do our best."

"That we will, sir," cried the men, and a voice proposed three cheers for the major.

These were hardly given before he held up his hand, and in a few words thanked them, while the doctor was called away.

"And now, my lads, we will go forward once more, and do the best we can. If we can only get a mile a day it is something, and every man will lend a hand. We will march at once. Yes, doctor? More bad news?"

"Yes," said Doctor Bolter, bluntly; "our guide has broken down."

"Broken down?"

"Yes, he is quite delirious."

"And," muttered the major, "we are worse than helpless without a guide."

Chapter Sixty
Signals of Distress

The night passed on board the steamer without any alarm, and at daybreak steam was up, and with the men at their quarters and every gun loaded, they set off on their return journey.

As the lieutenant said, it was no use to murmur about their misfortune; all they could do was to try and make the best of matters by getting back as soon as possible.

He could gladly have gone on at full speed, but caution forbad it. There were mudbanks and turns innumerable; and even going slowly, the length of the vessel was so great that again and again they were nearly aground upon some shoal, or brushed the overhanging trees with their bows.

Of one thing the lieutenant felt certain—that they had not been led into this narrow river without some plans being made for keeping them there. Therefore every man was on the alert for an ambush, or something that should stop their further progress towards the mouth of the sluggish stream.

It was terribly slow work, and Lieutenant Johnson stamped with impatience as he saw how poorly they progressed, speaking snappishly to Bob Roberts when the latter ventured upon some observation.

This went on three or four times, when, feeling hurt by a sharp remark on the lieutenant's part, Bob exclaimed,—

"You needn't be so hard upon me, captain; it was not my fault."

Lieutenant Johnson turned upon him angrily, and was about to say something severe, but Bob's injured look disarmed him, and he held out his hand.

"I'm hipped, Roberts," he said, and hardly know what I say. "Steady, there; steady!"

This to the man at the wheel as they were rounding a point; but the order had a contrary effect to what was intended; it flurried and unsteadied the sailor, who took a pull too much at the spokes, and before anything could be done to check the steamer's speed, her sharp bows had cut deeply into the muddy bank of the river, and she was aground.

"Was anything ever so unlucky?" cried the lieutenant; and then he gave order after order. Guns were swung round so as to sweep the bows should the Malays try to board them from the shore; the engines were reversed; the men tramped from side to side of the deck; everything possible was done: but the steamer remained fixed in the mud without a possibility apparently of getting her off.

The jungle was of the densest all around, and the men approached the bows with caution, for the head of the steamer was right in amidst dense foliage, and it was quite probable that any number of the enemy might be concealed and ready to hurl spears at the slightest chance.

Neither seeing nor hearing signs of the enemy, the lieutenant at last ordered Roberts to try and land and see if the Malays were near. "It's a risky job, Roberts," he said kindly, "but you must take it. I cannot leave the steamer."

"Oh, I'll take it," said Bob, coolly, and examining his revolver, he drew his sword, and telling the men to follow, ran forward, scrambled over the bows, and leaped ashore, the men imitating his example, for the bank was only some six or eight feet below the bulwarks.

But though they were landed there was little more to be done, unless they had been provided with billhooks to clear the way. The undergrowth was nearly as dense as a hedge, and after trying in half-a-dozen different ways, and only penetrating some twenty or thirty yards, they were obliged to give up, drenched with perspiration, their flesh full of thorns.

"I've got something biting my legs horribly," cried Bob, turning up his trousers, and then giving a shudder of disgust, for half-a-dozen leeches were busy at work making a meal upon him, and several of the sailors were in the same predicament.

"There, my lads, we may as well get on board," said Bob, grimly, "I don't like shedding my blood in the service of my country after this fashion. We can do nothing here, and it would puzzle a cat—let alone a Malay—to get through."

So they returned on board, satisfied that there was no fear of an attack from that quarter, and the rest of the day was devoted to trying to get the steamer out of her unpleasant predicament.

Night fell with the men utterly wearied out, and, in despair, Lieutenant Johnson was taking himself to task for his bad management, as he termed it, when Bob Roberts suddenly seized him by the arm.

"What is it, Roberts?"

"A shot off yonder in the jungle," he exclaimed.

"I did not hear it," was the reply; and they stood listening; but there was nothing but the hum of insects and the distant splash of some reptile in the muddy river.

"If we could have only heard some news of those poor fellows, I would not have cared," said the lieutenant after a pause. "Perhaps at this time they are anxiously hoping that help may come, and wondering why we have not sent in search of them; while we, with men and guns, are lying here helpless as a log. Oh, Roberts, it's enough to make a man jump overboard and—"

"There it is again," cried Bob.

"What?"

"A shot!" he cried excitedly. "I'm sure I heard a rifle-shot."

"Any of you men hear a shot?" said the lieutenant to the watch.

"No, sir; no, sir."

"I heard nothing, Roberts," said the lieutenant. "You are excited with exertion. Go below and have a glass of sherry, my lad, and put in a dose of quinine. I can't afford to have you down with fever."

"No, thanky," said Bob; "I could manage the glass of wine, but I'm not going to spoil it with the quinine, I'm— There now, what's that? If that isn't a rifle-shot I'm no man."

"Then it isn't a rifle-shot," said the lieutenant, grimly. "I heard nothing."

"Beg pardon, sir, I think it was a shot."

"There's another!" cried Bob, excitedly. "It's our fellows somewhere."

There were a couple of distant shots, faintly heard now by all.

"You're right, Roberts," said the lieutenant, hastily; "but it is not obliged to be our fellows."

"They couldn't have followed up from the island, sir," cried Bob; "so it must be."

"Unless it is a party of Malays shooting."

"Then they are shooting our men," cried Bob. "They wouldn't be hunting when it's getting dark."

"There's another shot," said the lieutenant, now growing as excited as his companion. "What shall we do?"

"Fire a big gun," said Bob.

"That would be letting our enemies know where we are," said the lieutenant.

"Well," said Bob, sturdily, "let 'em know. It will show 'em that we are not afraid of them."

"You are right, Roberts," said lieutenant Johnson, quickly. "Unshot the bow gun there."

The gun was opened; the shot cartridge drawn out, a blank one substituted; and directly after, the black darkness that had seemed to settle down over them was cut by a vivid flash, and the utter silence that was brooding over the river was broken by the deep-mouthed roar of the great breech-loading cannon.

The report seemed to roll off into the distance and echo amongst the mountains; and then, as it died away, they all listened with strained senses for some reply.

It came, just as they expected—three rifle-shots in succession. Then a pause, and three more rifle-shots.

There was a pause then, and the silence seemed awful, for the report of the great gun had driven every living thing near at hand to its lair.

"Three marines," said the lieutenant, sharply, "fire as I give the order. One—two—three!"

The three shots rang out at stated intervals, and the men reloaded and fired as before.

Then they waited again, and the signal was answered in a peculiar way that left no doubt whatever in the minds of those on board, and a murmur of satisfaction ran through the little crew.

And now, for the first time, Lieutenant Johnson began to wonder whether he had doubted the Malay guide without cause. He might have been swept overboard after all, and the hunting-party be really hemmed-in at some stockade.

A few moments' consideration, however, showed that this could not be the case, for they had journeyed back many miles before the steamer ran aground; and though the river winded a great deal, it was impossible that the stockade could have been higher up. The firing certainly came from quite another direction, away from the river; and shots that were evidently not signals were now heard again—one or two, then three or four together, as if men were skirmishing, and then came several volleys.

There was a fight going on, that was evident; and as the two officers realised this, they felt half-maddened at their helplessness.

They wanted to go to the aid of those who were fighting, but it would have been utter madness to have attempted to land with a detachment in the dark and try to hack a way through the jungle. They might have fired signals and had them responded to, but it would have been a helpless, bewildering piece of folly; and with pulses beating rapidly with excitement, and every nerve on the stretch, they felt themselves bound to a state of inaction, still they felt that they could fire signals to guide those who might, perhaps, get nearer, or, if shut in some place, fight the better for knowing that help was so near.

They did all they could, sending up a rocket from time to time, and twice, at intervals of about an hour, firing a big gun, each signal eliciting a reply from the distance; and then, at intervals of ten minutes, a rifle was fired, while, when six, seven, and eight bells were sounded, the same number of rifle-shots were heard.

It was a night of general watching on board the steamer, no man seeking shelter, though about seven bells the rain began to pour down with all the violence of a storm in the tropics, accompanied by thunder and lightning of the heaviest and most vivid description.

For about four hours this kept on, guns being fired in the intervals, when the thunder ceased for a few moments; but no answering shots had been heard for some time.

One thing was very evident—the party engaged were entrenched somewhere, and defending themselves, for their answering shots had been no nearer; in fact, all felt that travelling through the dense jungle was impossible until daylight set in.

The night was about half gone when the storm ceased as suddenly as it had come on; the clouds were dispersed, and the moon shone out clearly, showing them that the sluggish river was sluggish no longer, but running fast, and threatening to fill up to the top of its high banks, the water coming down evidently from the mountains.

This revived the hopes of all on board, and not without reason, for the steamer was gradually shifting her position; and hardly had a boat been lowered, and a hawser made fast to one of the big trees ashore, before she lifted more and more; and in a few moments more, to the delight of all, they felt the branches sweeping the rigging, and the steamer moving free and clear.

The men, forgetting discipline, and the need perhaps for silence, gave an involuntary cheer; which ceased on the instant as, from somewhere lower down the stream, there came a faint, "Ship ahoy!"

"Ahoy!" was answered.

And after a brief colloquy a boat was lowered down, with half-a-dozen marines as well as the crew, Bob Roberts taking command, and cautiously steering her towards where the man who hailed seemed to be.

The boat was allowed to descend the stream stern foremost, the men dipping their oars occasionally to keep her head right, and to prevent her being swept down too swiftly.

The next minute, at the word, they gave away, and the cutter was run in beneath the branches to where one of the crew stood in the moonlight, with a soldier by his side.

"Why, it's Parker!" cried Bob, catching the man's hand.

"Parker it is, Mr Roberts, sir," said the man faintly. "I thought we should never have done it, what with the storm and the thick cane. We've about cut our way here."

"And the captain and Major Sandars?" cried Bob.

"'Bout a mile away, sir, through the jungle, wanting help badly."

"Can we get there to-night?" cried Bob. "But jump in my lads, and we'll hear what the lieutenant says. Come: why don't you jump in?"

"I'm bet out, sir, and my mate too," said the sailor. "We're a bit wounded, sir. We volunteered to come for help when we first heerd the dear old 'Startler' speak out, but it's been a long job. Will you help us aboard, mates?"

Half-a-dozen willing hands soon had the two poor, drenched, wounded, and exhausted men on board the cutter, and five minutes after they were on the deck being questioned by the lieutenant.

"I told the captain, sir, as I'd ask you to fire two guns if we got here safe. He's down with fever, sir, and it would cheer him up if he heard the old gal say—begging your pardon—as she was close at hand."

The word was given, and a couple of heavy roars from the "old gal," as the sailor affectionately called his ship, bore the news to the captain; and then, in answer to the lieutenant, both of the messengers declared that it would be impossible to get to the helpless party that night.

"I wouldn't say so, sir, if I didn't feel," said Parker, "that the lads would only go losing theirselves in the wet jungle, and do no good. If you'd start at daybreak, sir, and take plenty of rum and biscuits, as well as powder and shot, you might get them aboard."

Then by slow degrees those on board learned from the worn-out messengers the whole of their experience, and how that since Major Sandars had appealed to the men, and they had sworn to stick together to the last, they had only made journeys of about a mile in length through the dense jungle. The guide was still delirious, and half the men down with sickness or wounds. Food they had had of the most meagre description, and that principally the birds they had shot. Their ammunition was fast failing, and the time seemed to have come that evening to lie down and die, so weak were they, and so pertinacious were the attacks of the enemy — when a thrill of joy ran through every breast as they heard the signal shots, and knew that there was help at hand.

Chapter Sixty One
How Bob Roberts turned the Tables

Never was daylight looked for with greater anxiety than that night on board the steamer.

With the first flush she was allowed to float lower down, till abreast of the spot where the two men were taken on board, and then every available hand was landed, under Bob Roberts' command, to try, by firing signals and listening for the reply, to reach the place where the worn-out party were making their last stand.

The two poor fellows who had come on board were in too pitiable a plight to move, and, even if they had gone, they could not have guided the relief party, who, only twenty strong, leaped ashore, eager to reach their friends, and inflict some punishment on the Malays, while the others retreated towards the ship.

Every man was laden heavily with food and ammunition, Lieutenant Johnson's difficulty being to keep the brave fellows from taking too much, and hindering their fighting powers, as, with a hearty cheer, they plunged in amidst the interlacing canes.

The task was hard, but less so than they expected—resolving itself as it did into hacking the canes and forcing their way through; for before they had gone far they could hear firing before them, and it was kept up so vigorously that there was no occasion to fire a single signal.

Hour after hour did they toil on, till the firing suddenly ceased, and they were for a moment at fault; but Bob Roberts and Old Dick, who were leading, suddenly heard voices close at hand, where the forest growth was thinner; and hacking and chopping away, they had nearly reached the spot when the firing suddenly began again furiously for a few moments, and then once more stopped.

The next minute the way was clear, and Bob Roberts, with his twenty blue-jackets and marines, went in at the double to an opening in the jungle where the remains of the hunting-party were making a desperate stand against a strong body of Malay; who, spear against bayonet, were pressing them home.

The middy took it all in at a glance, and saw that in another minute the weak helpless wielders of rifle and bayonet would be borne down, and they, and the sick and wounded lying in the long grass, massacred to a man.

Major Sandars said afterwards that the oldest colonel in the service could not have done better; for, with his sun-browned face lighting up with excitement, and waving his sword, Bob Roberts shouted his orders to the men, sprang forward, giving point at a great bronze-skinned Malay who had borne the major down and was about to spear him, while with a hearty British cheer the marines and blue-jackets dashed up, poured in a staggering volley amongst the thronging enemy, and followed it up with a bayonet charge along the beaten-down jungle alley, till, dropping spear and kris, the Malays fled for their lives.

Others were hurrying up to be present at the massacre; for the news had spread that the English had fired their last cartridge and were weak with starvation; but as they met their flying comrades the panic spread. The reinforcements were magnified a hundred times; and it wanted but Bob Roberts' quick sharp halt, form in line two deep, and the firing in of a couple of volleys, to send all to the right-about, a few of the hindmost getting a prick of the bayonet before they got away.

Pursuit would have been in vain, so Bob left a picket of five men under Old Dick to keep the narrow path, bidding them fell a tree or two so that their branches might lie towards and hinder an attack from the enemy, before hurrying back with fourteen men to the little jungle camp.

He tried hard, but he could not keep back his tears as the gaunt bleeding remains of a fine body of men gathered round him to grasp his hands and bless him; while, when one strange-looking little naked object came up and seized him by the shoulders, he felt almost ready to laugh.

It was hard to believe it was Dr Bolter standing there, in a pair of ragged trousers reduced in length to knee breeches, and nothing else.

"Bob, my dear boy," he said, "I can't tell you how glad I am; but give me some rum, biscuits, anything you have, for my poor lads are perishing for want of food."

The men's wallets were being emptied, and food and ammunition were rapidly distributed, for not a scrap of provision nor a single cartridge was left with the major's party.

"Why, you are laughing at me, you dog," cried the doctor, as he came back for more provisions; "but just you have forty patients, Bob Roberts, many of them wounded, and not a bandage to use, Bob, my lad! My handkerchiefs, neck and pocket, went first; then my Norfolk jacket, and then my shirt. Poor lads! poor brave lads!" he said piteously; "I'd have taken off my skin if it would have done them good."

"Ah, doctor," said Bob, in a voice full of remorse, "I'm only a boy yet, and a very thoughtless one. Pray forgive me. I meant no harm."

"God bless you, my lad; I know that," cried the doctor, warmly. "You've saved us all. Boy, indeed? Well, so you are, Bob; but as long as England has plenty of such boys as you, we need not trouble ourselves about the men—they'll all come in time."

It was a pitiful task, but every one worked with a will; and now that they were refreshed with food, reanimated by the presence of twenty fresh men, supplied with ammunition, and, above all, supported by the knowledge that not a mile away, through the newly-cut path, there lay a haven of rest in the shape of the steamer—men who had been fit to lie down and die, stood up, flushed, excited, and ready to help bear the sick and wounded towards the river; while, to make matters better, the Malays had had such a thrashing in this last engagement that they made no fresh attack. The consequence was that half-a-dozen weak men under Major Sandars made a show in the rear, and all the strong devoted themselves to helping to carry the invalids to the steamer.

More help was afforded too from the steamer itself as soon as Lieutenant Johnson found that there was no fear of attack, and in the end all were got safely on board; and long before night Dr Bolter, clothed and comfortable, had all his sick men in berths and hammocks, well tended, already looking better, and he himself walking up and down the deck chuckling and rubbing his hands.

The losses had been severe, but far less than might have been expected, owing to the devotion of the men, who had struggled on till they could get no farther, and would have perished one and all but for the timely succour brought by the middy, and indirectly by the emissary of Rajah Gantang, who little thought when he took the steamer, by his clever ruse, up the solitary river, that he was leading them where it would be the salvation of the hunting-party who were doomed to death.

Not a moment had been lost, and as soon as all were on board, the steamer recommenced her downward course towards the residency, where all felt that help must be urgently needed by the little party who had its defence.

Chapter Sixty Two
Captain Smithers proves a True Officer, and Private Gray a Gentleman

In truth help was urgently needed at the little fort; but had its defenders been compelled to wait for that which the steamer would afford, every one would have been either butchered or taken off into a terrible captivity.

Captain Smithers when he looked round had seen the enemy coming on in such strength; and with a demonstration so full of clever plan, backed up by determination, that he could not help feeling that the critical moment had come, and that they must either surrender or meet death like men.

If he surrendered, the probabilities were that they would all be massacred, save the women; and as he thought of them he raised his eyes, and found those of Private Gray fixed upon him, as if reading his very soul.

"You know what I was thinking, Gray," he said, resentfully.

"Yes, sir," said Gray, sharply; "you were debating within yourself whether you should strike the Union Jack in token of surrender."

"I was," said Captain Smithers, angry with himself at being as it were obliged to speak as he did to this simple private of his regiment. "And you advise it?"

"Advise it, sir? For heaven's sake—for the sake of the ladies whom we have to defend, let us fight till the last gasp, and then send a few shots into the magazine. Better death than the mercy of a set of cut-throat pirates."

Captain Smithers was silent for a few moments, and then he said quietly,—

"I should not have surrendered, Gray. You are quite right." He hesitated for a moment or two, and then said hoarsely,—

"Gray, we hate each other."

"This is no time for hatred, sir," said Gray, sternly.

"No," said Captain Smithers, "it is not. In half an hour we shall be, in all human probability, dead men. Rank will be no more. Gray, I never in my heart doubted your honesty. You are a brave man. Now for duty."

"Yes, sir," said Gray, in a deeply moved voice—"for duty."

Crash!

There was a sharp ragged volley from the enemy at that moment as a body of them advanced, and a shriek of agony from close by, followed by a fall.

"Some poor fellow down," said the Captain, hoarsely. "Who is it, Sergeant Lund?" he said, taking a dozen strides in the direction of the cry.

"Private Sim, sir. Shot through the heart—dead!"

The captain turned away, and the next minute the fight on all sides was general, the enemy winning their way nearer and nearer, and a couple of prahus sending a shower of ragged bullets from their brass lelahs over the attacking party's heads.

"Stand firm, my lads; stand firm. Your bayonets, boys!" cried Captain Smithers, as with a desperate rush the Malays dashed forward now to carry the place by assault, and in sufficient numbers to sweep all before them— when *boom! boom! boom! boom!* came the reports of heavy guns, and the fire from the prahus ceased.

"Hurrah! my lads; steady!" cried Tom Long, waving his sword. "The steamer! the steamer!"

"No," cried Captain Smithers, "it is from below. It is a heavily-armed prahu."

"No," cried Tom Long; "a steamer! a steamer!"

He was right, for a little-gunboat was rapidly ascending the river, and one of the prahus began to settle down in front of the fort, while the other used her sweeps to get away.

Another minute, and just when they had won an entrance, beating back the defenders of the barricaded gateways, a panic seized upon the Malays, for shell after shell was dropping and bursting in their midst; and before Captain Smithers and his brave little party could realise the fact, the enemy was in full retreat.

A quarter of an hour later, and the gunboat was moored abreast of the fort, and congratulations were being exchanged.

He had said nothing, not daring to hope for success; but Ali had, as soon as he could, sent a fisherman in his boat to try and convey word of the danger to the Dindings. The message had been faithfully borne, and the little gunboat sent to help to keep the enemy at bay, till the steamer could come from Penang with a detachment of infantry on board.

The heavy guns were too much for the Malays; and just as it had been decided that the gunboat should ascend the river in quest of the "Startler," the latter came slowly down the river with her rescued freight.

In a couple more days the Penang steamer had arrived with a battalion of foot, under Colonel Hanson; and the next thing heard was that the Sultan Hamet, with Rajah Gantang, had fled up the country, the minor chiefs sending in their submission to the British and suing for peace.

Doctor Bolter became almost the greatest man at the station after this, and he went about laughing as he kept—to use his own words—"setting men up," speaking of them as if they were natural history specimens. First he had to be thanked by Rachel Linton for saving her father's life; then he found Captain Horton blessing him for his recovery; and one way and another he had a very proud time of it, though, to his great regret, he had no chance of pursuing his favourite hobby.

The Malay who acted as his guide was recovering fast from the tiger's clawing, and had attached himself to the doctor as servant when matters settled down; and it was affecting to see the poor fellow's delight upon encountering Ali alive and well.

Matters were soon arranged, and a busy party were at work rebuilding the residency, a number of Chinese joiners being enlisted for the task.

Meanwhile the fort and barracks had to be the general dwelling; and Bob Roberts and Tom Long were looked upon as heroes.

It so happened, that one day Colonel Hanson entered the mess-room, where Captain Horton, Major Sandars, Captain Smithers, and the other officers, were grouped about. Mr Linton and the ladies were present; and on one side stood a group of soldiers, foremost among whom were Sergeant Lund and Private Gray.

Major Sandars advanced to meet the governor's messenger, and he was about to make some remark, when Colonel Hanson turned round, caught sight of Private Gray, and started with astonishment.

The next moment he had gone forward to where Gray stood, looking very stern and troubled, and caught him by the hands, dragging him forward, and evidently forgetting all the stiff etiquette of the army.

"Why, my dear old Frank," he cried, shaking his hands, and seeming as if he could hug him, "this is a surprise! this is a meeting! Why, where have you been? Soldiering too, and wearing the scarlet! My dear old Frank," he cried again, with his voice shaking with emotion, "I feel as weak as a child; upon my word I do."

"Colonel Hanson," said Gray, quietly, but evidently very much moved, as he saw that they were the centre of every gaze, "this is indeed a strange meeting. I little thought it was you. But you forget; we belong to different circles now."

"Forget? Different circles? Do we indeed?" cried Colonel Hanson, whose face was flushed with excitement. "I forget nothing. Come here," he cried, and dragging Gray's arm through his, he faced round to where the astonished officers and the resident were standing.

"Major Sandars, Mr Linton, gentlemen, this is my very dear old friend, Francis Murray. We were schoolfellows together at Eton, and—and—and—I can't tell you now all the good brave things he has done for me. For years he has been missing; that wretched Overend and Gurney smash broke him, and he disappeared. And, Frank, you foolish fellow, I have been searching for you high and low to tell you that that cantankerous old lady, your aunt, was dead, and had changed her mind at the last moment, quarrelled with that lot who had got hold of her, sent for her solicitor, and left Greylands and every farthing she had to you. Thank goodness I have found you at last. Now sign your application to buy out at once. I will forward it home, and take upon myself to consider it accepted, pending the official discharge."

While this was going on, Captain Smithers, whose heart felt like lead, had gazed from one to the other. Now his eyes were fixed with bitter jealousy upon Private Gray, and now upon Rachel Linton, though she saw him not, but, pale and flushed by turns, she was gazing at Gray.

He was a true gentleman at heart, and in spite of his misery and disappointment, that which he had just heard gave him some satisfaction. It had been one of his bitterest griefs—one with a poisoned sting—that feeling which always haunted him, that Rachel Linton should prefer a private soldier to him, an officer and a gentleman. For that she did love Gray he had long felt certain. Gray, or Murray, then, was a gentleman, who, like many other gentlemen, had enlisted, and served as a very brave soldier. Yes, he was, Captain Smithers owned to himself, a very brave soldier, though he had felt that he hated him; while now—now—

"I'll fight it down," said Captain Smithers to himself.

"Heaven helping me, I'll be a gentleman as well as an officer. He has won, and I have lost. I ought to like him for her sake, and I will."

It was a brave effort, and it required all his strength—but he did it. He looked first at Rachel Linton, and then at the sweet sympathising face of her cousin, and went up close to them.

"Rachel," he said, holding out his hand and speaking in a low voice only heard by her and Miss Sinclair, "I give up. Let me be a dear friend, if I can be nothing more."

Miss Linton held out her hand frankly and cordially, and he held it a moment in his. Then dropping it, he walked straight across to where Colonel Hanson was standing with Murray in the midst of a group, and holding out his hand, he said,—

"Mr Murray, I am your debtor for my life. Henceforth let us, too, be very dear friends."

The two young men clasped hands in a firm strong grip, each reading the other's thoughts, and they instinctively knew that henceforth all enmity between them was at end. It was all Frank Murray could do to stand firm, for he knew how great an effort this must have cost his rival, and he mentally vowed to repay him all.

"Well," said Major Sandars, laughing, "this is a surprise indeed. Gentlemen all, Private Gray was so good and true a man in the private's mess, that I for one am quite sure he will be a welcome addition to ours."

"Mr Murray will grant that I have always looked upon him with respect," said Mr Linton, cordially. "I owe him too deep a debt," he said, holding out his hand, "not to feel intensely gratified at this change in his position."

The other officers warmly shook hands, Tom Long amongst the number; while, when it came to Bob Roberts' turn, he said with his eyes sparkling,—

"I say, Mr Murray, I am glad, 'pon my word." Bob Roberts and Tom Long strolled out together on to the parade ground, crossing it to get under the trees where a group of soldiers and Jacks were standing.

"I say, Tom Long, this is a rum game, isn't it?" said Bob.

"I call it beastly," said Tom. "Well, there's one consolation, young fellow, your nose is out of joint in a certain quarter."

"No," said Bob, "it's yours. I've long enough given up my pretentions. Miss Linton and I are the best of friends; but I'm sorry for you."

"Bother!" said Tom Long. "I wish I hadn't been such a fool. Why, whatever are they talking about?"

"I always knew he was a gentleman," said Sergeant Lund, authoritatively. "The way he could write out a despatch was something wonderful, that it was. Ha! I'm sorry he's gone!"

"Tell you what," said old Dick, "its about my turn now. What would some of you say if I was to turn out to be a mysterious orphan, and be a skipper or an admiral?"

"That's quite right, my lads," said Bob Roberts, sharply. "Old Dick is a mysterious orphan, and if you open his shirt you'll find he's marked with a blue mermaid."

"That's a true word," said old Dick, grinning. "But, Master Roberts, sir, don't you think you might pass your word for us to say a half dollar down there at the canteen? What's just took place has been hard on our emotions, sir, and the consequence is as we are all werry dry."

"I think you're more likely to turn out a fish, Dick—a shark, than anything else," said Bob. "But I don't mind. Will you be half, Tom?"

Tom Long nodded; and the men went off laughing to the canteen, to drink the health of Frank Murray, late Private Gray, and ended by saying, through their mouthpiece, Dick, that,—

"This here is a werry strange world."

Chapter Sixty Three
The Last of it

There is not much more to say about the various people who formed the little world at the jungle-station.

Despatches were sent home, in which Major Sandars and Captain Horton dwelt most strongly upon the bravery of the young officers serving respectively beneath them. Captain Horton said so much respecting Bob Roberts, that poor Bob said he felt as red as a tomato; while Tom Long, instead of becoming what old Dick called more "stuck-upper" on reading of his bravery, seemed humbled and more frank and natural. Certainly he became better liked; and at a dinner that was given after the country had settled, and Colonel Hanson and his force were about to return, that officer in a speech said that from what he had heard, Mr Midshipman Roberts and Mr Ensign Long would become ornaments of the services to which they belonged.

And so they did, and the truest of friends, when they did not quarrel, though really their squabbles only cemented their friendship the stronger.

They both visited Mr and Mrs Frank Murray at their pretty bungalow at Parang, where Rachel was settled down so long as her father retained his post at the residency; but their most enjoyable visits were, as years went by, to their friend the sultan, who was fast improving the country, and encouraging his people to become more commercial, in place of the arrant pirates they had been. For in a very short time in the settlement of the country under British protection, the rank of sultan had been offered to the Tumongong, who refused it in favour of his son Ali, and this was ratified by the Governor of the Straits—Sultan Hamet dying a victim to excess, and the piratical Rajah Gantang of his wounds.

Which was, so said old Dick in confidence to the two young officers, "a blessing to everybody consarned, for that there Rajah Gantang was about the wussest nigger as ever suffered from the want of soap."

The last the writer heard of Dick was, that he was the oldest boatswain in the service, and that he was on board that rapid gunboat the "Peregrine," commanded by Lieutenant Robert Roberts, RN.

It need only be added that Captain Smithers got over his disappointment, and two years later married Mary Sinclair, who makes him an excellent wife. So that none of those concerned had cause to regret the trip up the Malay river in HMS "Startler."